ANATOMY OF A MAGICIAN

the ADVENTURES of BOURAGNER FELPZ

VOLUME II
Anatomy of a Magician

GOLDEEN OGAWA

with Illustrations by the Author

HELIOPAUSE

The Adventures of Bouragner Felpz, Volume II: Anatomy of a Magician

Copyright © 2013–2016 by Goldeen Ogawa
Illustrations copyright © 2017 by Goldeen Ogawa
Cover illustration and design copyright © 2017 by Goldeen Ogawa

"The Magician Returns" was originally published in *Apsis Fiction 1.1: Mesohelion 2013.*
"A Horse in the Night" and "The Ghost of Castle Hill" were originally published in *Apsis Fiction 1.2: Perihelion 2014.*
"Griffin's Blood" and "The Three Fates of Talias Minn" were originally published in *Apsis Fiction 2.1: Aphelion 2014.*
"The Stone Man" and "The Withered Hand" were originally published in *Apsis Fiction 2.2: Perihelion 2015.*
"The Moonfoot Problem" and "The Case of Countess Baronia" were originally published in *Apsis Fiction 3.1: Aphelion 2015.*
"The Goblin's Fiddle" and "The Silver Chimera" were originally published in *Apsis Fiction 4.1: Perihelion 2016.*
"The Hidden Road" was originally published in *Apsis Fiction 4.2: Aphelion 2016.*

FICTION/Fantasy, Historical
FICTION/Fantasy, General

First Edition 2017

ISBN: 978-1-945781-07-0

DEDICATION

As the first volume was dedicated to three men, this, the second, is dedicated to one woman: to Rachel Goldeen, who in our adventures together was as supportive, helpful, encouraging and enabling as Corianne ever was to Felpz, and without whom they never would have happened. Thank you so much.

—GOLDEEN OGAWA

NOTE FOR THE READER

The stories that follow are set in a world rather like our own, in a time not far off from our late nineteenth century. However, there are two crucial differences. First, that magic is quite real in this world, and as a result there are a myriad of other, smaller differences that will become apparent as the reader progresses. Second, it has its own calendar, and while I have changed the names of the months and days of the week to correspond with our own, I have left the numbering of the years alone. This could cause some confusion, since their calendar is somewhat older than our commonly used Gregorian calendar and thus can give the impression that this story takes place in the future. But this is only because their calendar (called by its creators the *Cordian calendar*) has had a head start of about four hundred years.

For readers who are comfortable navigating their way through fantasy worlds, this one should be fairly straightforward. For novice travelers, know this: the world you are entering is completely separate from our own, with its own unique history, geography, religions and politics. However, enough parallels may be drawn between it and ours that, without any more explaining on my part, you should be able to get along just fine.

CONTENTS

INTRODUCTION

By Dr Milain Clifford Birch, dracologist and daughter of Corianne Birch

As a small child I had little knowledge of my mother's life before her marriage. If she spoke of it, which was rare, it was with detachment, as though she were speaking of someone else entirely. I recall her telling me about the Purple Magician, as she called him, but my father never liked hearing about the man, and would become upset if he heard my mother speaking of him. So the stories surrounding the Purple Magician became the stuff of late-night bedtime fables. These were some of the happiest times in my childhood, which was fraught with turbulence as a rift slowly grew into a thundering chasm between my parents.

Imagine my surprise when, after having grown up and out of my childhood and home, this wild character reappeared, proving himself more real than I'd ever dared hope. And though the following stories adequately demonstrate his magical prowess, for me the best miracle of all was the revelation that my mother's young life and adventures were far from forgotten. I am also delighted that she has continued going on adventures, because I believe this is the best way to stave off the ravages of age. Do not be deceived by her retreat to the idyllic pastures of Stanton Leaning. She is as active and energetic at sixty as she was at fifty and at forty-five, and if my mailbox is anything to go by, she does not lack material with which to work.

I was a little flabbergasted when she asked me to write the introduction to this second collection of adventures, since I directly participated in only one and, really, considered such a preamble unnecessary. But here we are, so I might as well tell you this: you are in for a cracker of a ride, and your only regret at the end will be that there are not twelve more adventures hidden at the back of this book. But rest assured, I know my mother has at least two or three untold adventures up her sleeves, and it is my personal mission to get them out of her.

MILAIN CLIFFORD BIRCH
Glendraig, Aldonica, 2314

Milain Clifford Birch is the daughter and only child of Corianne Birch and Willem Harper. Born in Redling in 2288, she studied magio-zoology at the Redling University of Magic, before pursuing her doctorate in dracology at the Draconian Institute of Crogard. She lives with her husband and children in Glendraig, Aldonica, where she works to facilitate cooperative relations between the humans and dragons of northern Aldonica.

one

THE MAGICIAN RETURNS

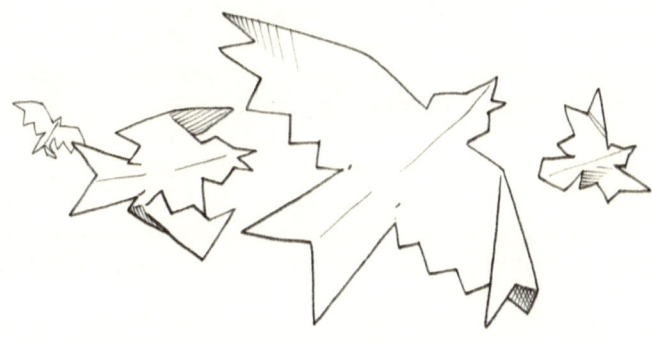

Prologue: Being the Reminiscences of Corianne Harper Birch
2287—2306

IN THE YEARS AFTER THE DISAPPEARANCE of my guardian, Mr Bouragner Felpz, my life followed a trajectory common to many women of my generation. At the age of twenty I acquired a husband, and shortly thereafter a child, who gave me such warmth and happiness that I was able to ignore my husband's growing collection of faults for nearly a decade. When these did begin to intrude upon my horizons I busied myself with erecting veils to cover them over; faith in my original infatuation and assurance in the complete rightness of our union allowing me to turn a blind eye to matters which any sensible woman would recognize as harbingers of marital doom. But I would have stayed, despite the misery attendant on a neglected and exploited wife, had my husband not had the decency to run off with a younger, prettier, and even more foolish woman.

The darkness in my heart at the time seemed to preclude my ever finding happiness again, and the rational arguments to the contrary posed by my beloved daughter (who has been and still is the very pinnacle of intelligent reasoning) fell on deaf ears. Yet I weathered the emotional storm, and when it finally passed I took a look at my situation and was surprised to find it had been improved by my husband's desertion rather than otherwise. So when the divorce papers appeared on my doorstep I signed them with a light and happy heart, and set about putting together a life that was better suited to my desires.

The first and most immediate concern were the affairs of my daughter, then only fifteen, who was even at that early age showing the precocious talent which would eventually take her over the mountains and far away on the backs of dragons. At the time, however, it was only a distracting and sometimes destructive preoccupation with the behaviors of magical lizards. These she would bring home of an afternoon and let loose in her room, which had become something of an indoor terrarium. It was impossible to keep a cleaning lady, so I was obliged to take on all the responsibility of housekeeping. This was just as well, for our finances were in dire straits following the divorce, and I could not have hired help even if I thought it would do any good. I could have gone through and tipped my daughter's collection out onto the streets and sent her off to boarding school, except I had taken a harsh dislike to those institutions in my youth and had made up my mind long ago that no child of mine would ever suffer such a place.

I found employment as a typist, and my dear daughter—ever so responsible—set up a sort of consulting veterinarian practice for persons with exotic pets. She was not possessed of great learning, my daughter, but she did have a fiercely curious and intelligent streak which allowed her to root out problems more learned physicians could not fathom. Her talents did not long go unnoticed, and after she cured a sapphire salamander belonging to a certain Viscount she was offered a junior position in the Royal Academy of Magi-Zoology.

If it seems I speak overly much of the exploits of my daughter let it not be blamed solely on maternal pride, but also a way of explaining how I came, in my fortieth year, to be living alone in a dreary flat in west Redling, stubbornly clinging to a life of minimal comfort. It was not, this time, out of neglect; indeed it should have pleased my daughter better had I taken up residence in her quarters provided by the Academy. But I had spent the better part of my life living under a roof provided by someone else, and to be making my own living—albeit a humble one— gave me an amount of gratification a more lavish abode could not.

Nor was I neglected by old friends: in those first dark days after my husband left I was given the relief of visiting my old acquaintance Hydegan, who had recently retired from his career as a necromancer, married the woman Armata, and moved his family (which consisted of the happy couple and a manticore named Sorn) south to Sherndale, where he occupied his time raising bees and (he assured me) nothing else. They made a strange couple; Hydegan had grown grey and weathered in the intervening years, though no less energetic, but Armata had not changed at all. In fact her unchangingness was so complete she put me in mind more of a porcelain doll than a living person. But it was not the first time I had encountered someone with unconventional aging qualities, so I did not enquire.

What could not be ignored between us was an absence. Felpz's absence had been felt keenly by the magical community, and even I, insulated as I was by my family and my own domestic problems, couldn't help but notice an increase in strange occurrences. Not so much in matters of crime: Hydegan's profession had flourished in his own time, and now necromancers were employed as a matter of course to attain direct and incontrovertible statements from persons who had, historically, been universally famed for not speaking. No, it was the little things: people gone missing, *roads* gone missing, weird and grotesque events that, if not direct crimes, certainly shook nerves and lost fortunes.

"There are too many checks and balances for the world to fall completely out of whack without him," Hydegan mused sadly one night, when conversation had bent to our departed friend. "But he was a big one; the world will be hard put to replace him."

As far as I could tell, the world seemed happy to forget Felpz ever existed. On one cold, rainy day in winter, not long after my daughter's turn of good fortune had left me alone for the first time since my childhood, I happened by chance past a familiar street. With a start I realized it was the lane on which Felpz's house sat, and before I could stop myself I started down it, if only to see my old home once more. I had not been back to visit it, or our old landlady Mrs Bryce, since before my wedding. Now I felt a pang of guilt as I walked along, counting houses. Felpz's house had been peculiar in having the number 0000, out of order from the other residences, and I had developed a system for finding it when I lived there of counting the houses on the west side of the street. It was the fourth house from Kings Street and the seventh house from Bridgeton Way, and I had been on that same road, heading for the Underground station that sat at the top of it. Now I counted: One, two, three, four, five, six . . . seven.

I stopped and stared at a fat brick house that had been painted pink.

Confused I turned around, wondering if, under the clouds and in the rain, I had gotten my orientation mixed. But across the street was a bicycle repair shop—closed—with a To Let sign in the upper window.

Besides, now that I looked around, I knew for certain that this was indeed the place: the bend of the street, the angle of the trees; they were all familiar. But the house was not. To make doubly sure I counted the houses down to Kings Street.

There were only two.

I came back up and stopped, staring at the mortar seam that separated the third house from Kings Street and the sixth house from Bridgeton Way. That was where Felpz's house had been. That was where it should have been still. But it was not. Not that the house had been bought and repainted. It was simply *not there*. It had gone; gone like its master into some far, distant place that I could never reach. I wrapped my shawl tighter about my shoulders, turned my head into the rain, and began to make my way slowly home.

To say that my life at that time had become a drab brown thing that flowed slowly from one day to the next would paint it more bleak than it was in reality, but it describes well how I felt at the time.

My work as a typist allowed me to keep myself in active living, but it was not fulfilling work, and I would often have attacks of mental rebellion in which I would type out stories instead of whatever paper my client had set me. It was in these attacks that the first incarnations of the stories collected in *A Study of Magic* were pried out of my mind. They were near the surface anyway, having been preserved as bedtime stories for my daughter when she was younger. With my daughter grown, and I farther from my youth that ever, I suppose I feared I would forget my early adventures, and I did not want to be remembered only as a meek mother and wife. What surprised me was that even after I had written down all the adventures I could remember—even the littlest ones that I shall not dignify with publication—I began to make up stories as a way to alleviate my boredom. It seemed I would never be content with a safe and steady life, and if I could not have adventures of my own, I would jolly well make them up. Turning this newfound proclivity into gainful employment was was, however, out of the question, and so I was forced to admit to myself that I would remain—and probably expire as—a pitiable, if respectable, working matron.

Part One: Unexpected Friends
Fall and Winter, 2307

IT WAS A DARK TEMPESTUOUS AUTUMN and all of Redling was ablaze with the first news of Bouragner Felpz in over twenty years—unfortunately, the news was that he had been murdered. I followed the case in the papers with mounting feelings of cold dread: I had been certain, convinced beyond a doubt, that my old guardian was an immortal. And though I had long since despaired of ever seeing him again in my lifetime, it was some small comfort to think of him as being simply elsewhere, hopefully enjoying a pleasant vacation from the trying events of the mundane world.

Now, however, a prince had come forward claiming to have killed the magician. He called himself the Violet Prince, and his claims would have been dismissed as madness had he not the very convincing argument of being a fairy.

Fairies, as all adults know, are capricious, powerful, dangerous beings, not at all like the wildflower sprites which have been ascribed their name in recent years by certain foolish children's authors. Having had some direct experience with a fairy myself, I could not easily discount the prince's claim, nor could I share my daughter's happy incredulity; for she only knew of Felpz through my stories, which had been carefully tailored to portray Felpz in the most flattering light possible. She had never seen Felpz as I had: exhausted, worried, and vulnerable.

The facts of the case were well documented at the time, but I shall recount them here for the edification of those who have forgotten, and for future readers who may not have been present during the original events.

It was in the early fall, just as most trees were beginning to think of shedding their summer coats, when a group of them in Ringcaster Park turned bright purple instead of the usual oranges and yellows — and stayed that way. I went down to visit them myself during the second week of the phenomenon and saw that the leaves were indeed a strong shade of violet. It is true that some trees bear leaves of a reddish-purple tint, but these trees looked as though their leaves had been replaced by the petals of violets or pansies.

Here was an oak, with its wide, wobbly leaves: purple. And here was my namesake, the birch, with its teardrop leaves: purple. No other part of the trees were changed.

I found the overall effect to be deeply disturbing, as I had strong association of the color with my lost guardian, and any reminder drew up a cold, twisting ache in my heart, like remembering a lost loved one.

Not everyone was so moved by the change, and soon magicians from the University had come down to take notes and samples. They thought it was a practical joke. Then one of the students made the mistake of cutting a branch to take back for study. According to the report in the paper the poor student was suddenly enveloped in a whirlwind of purple leaves, which tore first at his clothes, and then at his skin. He dropped the branch in his surprise, and the evil wind vanished. Then a man walked out of a nearby tree and began to harangue the university delegation.

He was a tall man with long fair hair, an aristocratic nose and dark eyebrows that turned up at the end like a bird's wingtip, and he wore a sumptuous robe that shimmered with every shade of purple. He also wore a star upon a chain around his neck, and it was by this sign that the magicians knew him to be a powerful fairy: for it was not a decorative star as you or I would imagine it, but a real star the fairy had plucked out of the sky and trapped in a lump of crystal. It blazed so that the magicians found it difficult to look upon the fairy, and they were forced to shield their eyes or turn their heads away.

The fairy chastised them for cutting one of his fingers without permission (he seemed to think of the purple-leafed trees as extensions of his own person), and was threatening to cut off a finger from the offending student in retaliation when one of the magicians, who was also a student of Fae Studies, mollified the fairy by throwing herself at his feet and begging his forgiveness. Her companions probably thought this a shameful thing to do, but it appeased the fairy, and instead of cutting off any fingers he satisfied himself with striking the offending student with the branch, so hard the poor man fell down, and stalked away back into the tree.

Now that it was known a fairy was responsible for the changed leaves the King's own royal magicians were called in to deal with it. These were on the whole a fine and learned set of men—and one woman— but all their knowledge of fairies came from reading accounts of other magicians who had, with more or less success, dealt with them in the past. They were keenly aware that they missed the expertise of one who had personal experience, and in an unusual show of humility one of them wrote in a treatise published in the papers that: " . . . now more than ever we feel the loss of Bouragner Felpz, the magician who was himself associated with the color purple and was so instrumental during the great flood two decades ago, and who had more experience in the dealings of Faerie than any other mage since antiquity."

It was a handsome acknowledgement, but it backfired terribly when the fairy himself heard of it. He came storming out of his trees and de- manded an audience with the royal magicians, where he declared for all the country to hear that he had killed the magician Bouragner Felpz and taken his color.

Amid the storm of controversy and dismay that coursed through the city following this, a small part of my mind wondered at this preoccu- pation with the color purple. It had been one of my guardian's most recognizable characteristics, but I thought it merely a personal fancy of his. It never occurred to me that one could own a color, as one does a chair or a pen, as this fairy seemed to understand it. To my surprise the royal magicians took it in stride, going so far as to issue decrees to the ef- fect that "anyone owning garments of any hue or shade of purple would do well to keep them out of sight of the Violet Prince, or hand them over for safekeeping to R.A.M . . . "

They were, however, validated in their concern when, on the morn- ing after the first snow the fairy cast a spell that compelled anyone who wore an article of purple clothing to come and join him in a macabre cel- ebratory ball, which was held in the clearing with the violet-leafed trees. A number of ladies and a few men were forced from their lives and made to march through the snow to the park, where they were compelled to dance, day and night, for three days. Whatever magic the fairy used to bring them kept them vitalized for the duration of the dance, but when their master abruptly lost interest they collapsed where they stood, and several of the ladies contracted life-threatening illnesses. One of the gen- tlemen made the mistake of confronting the Violet Prince, and the fairy in his rage split him in two like a woodcutter splits a log.

At the time the most color in my wardrobe was a faded blue dress my husband had purchased for me in the sunnier days of our marriage, so I was not worried that I would find myself a target of fairy's magic. I was however distraught over the fate of the poor dancers, and over the prince's claims on the life of my former guardian. I was particularly needled by his insistence that he owned the color purple, as I had no idea how such a thing could be possible. So one day in December I left my typewriter early and made my way down to the Library at St Argents, which at the time housed (and still does houses) the country's most extensive collection of books of magical lore.

It was a walk I knew well from my daughter's early days, when she would spend hours down at St Argents, digging up tomes on obscure species or attending lectures by visiting professors from the university. Many a time did I have to make the walk down Regnant Street and across Chutnam Court to fetch her back for dinner of an evening.

Now, in the wan winter light with the trees all bare and dark against the overcast sky, I felt more keenly the passing of years, and the certainty that everything, everywhere, eventually dies. So caught up was I in my melancholic divertissement that I quite failed to notice the tradesman who was just backing out of his shop with a cart of shoes, and into him I ran, sending his wares scattering over the sidewalk.

The man was singularly displeased, as he had every right to be, but refused any offer of help I gave, and shooed me away with a shake of his brown gnarled hand. I only caught a glimpse of shaggy dark hair escaping from under a cloth cap, and below that a pockmarked face, sharp and jagged like a chipped axe blade. Not wanting to remain in the company of such a rough looking fellow I hastily took my leave and briskly walked the final distance to the library steps. There I sat, catching my breath for some moments as a crowd of university students, recently let out from their afternoon lecture, swarmed up the steps around me. Their clamor of cheerful voices and happy young faces soothed my nerves, and I followed in their wake.

Many writers have described the majesty of the Library at St Argents, but in this narrative I can only allow time for a brief allusion to its vaulted entrance lined with statues of scholars and learned magicians, the stone griffin with ruby eyes guarding the wing devoted to the sciences, and the sapphire-eyed horse opposite, rearing above the doorway to the extra-natural section, and the crumbling stained glass window depicting the crowning of Arell the Great. On that day the December afternoon light cast the figures in pale, ghostly hues, and the dark seams in the window reminded me of the bare branches of the trees outside.

I started with the books on old Fae law, of which the library had few, but they were all available. To my dismay the university students were also occupying this branch of the library, and more than once a young fellow was so impertinent as to come over and take books off the collection on my table without asking. Nevertheless I had more material than I could easily manage: Fae law was an intricate, arbitrary thing, but the only reference I could find to color was in the Ruling of Titanna, in which the Fae queen had divided up sections of Faerie according to the colors of the rainbow and given them away to various Fae nobility. The book referenced one *Chromium Magica* as the definitive text on the subject, but I did not have it in my pile. I moved on and found a promising entry in the *Omnibus Encyclopedia of Magical Acts* on Uses of Color in Magic, but upon closer inspection it only covered the intrinsic magical capabilities said to be inherent in each color. From it I did learn that red countered enchantment, and that magic itself had a color, which the *Omnibus* helpfully described as " . . . somewhere between neon yellow and dark white, visible only to dragons and some cats." It also referenced *Chromium Magica* for further information.

I went back to the shelves, carefully guided by the index card in my hand that said the library did indeed have a copy of *Chromium Magica,* but its place on the shelf was empty. It must have been taken down by one of the students. Reluctantly I gathered up a few of my books as offerings and approached the nearest table of students. They were surprisingly polite: no, they did not have *Chromium Magica* on their table. But did you know, Avars had just left with a stack of books. Maybe he had taken it?

So I went to the librarian, who was a thin grey man in a pale grey suit. Yes, their copy of *Chromium Magica* had just been checked out. By whom? Well, he really couldn't say. When would they have it back? Well, the person was a student at St Argents, so it might not be returned for three weeks.

I returned home in a frustrated and irritable mood. Instead of finishing the day's work, I typed off a letter to my daughter to vent my feelings.

The next morning brought with it a thick roll of winter fog; it coated the street and slowed traffic to a crawl. I bundled up in all my woolens and put the kettle on, determined that this day would not be wasted on frivolous distractions.

There was a knock on the door. Leaving the pot to steep I descended the cracked and creaking stairs, for the first floor tenant was a deaf old man whose knees quite prevented him from receiving visitors.

The door opened onto a bank of white fog, and for a moment I wondered if I had been the victim of a practical joke. But then out of the fog, appearing like a ghost in a play, was the tradesman I had tripped over the previous afternoon. I recognized his chipped hatchet face, though he had removed his cloth cap and was holding it to his chest. Now I could see his dark hair was greasy and unkempt, and there were two lines of jagged scars, one each extending up from the corners of his mouth. It made the smile he gave me look uneven.

"What do you want?" I asked cautiously, drawing back into the house, ready to slam the door in an instant.

"Beg pardon, Ma'am," he said, ducking his head respectfully. He had a thick southern slant of an accent which made his ma'am's sound like *mom,* and it put me distinctly off. But I noticed on closer inspection that he seemed neither threatening nor angry, and I relaxed my hold on the door somewhat.

"Know it 'snot right manners, followin' a lady home like," he said. "Devil take my soul and put it on a spit may he, but it felt right *wrong*, you know, lettin' an old curve go in such a brusque manner. Would never have spoken that way to ye, only I dint recognize you right off. But I never forget a brave bird, and you were the bravest I ever knew. So I thought on it, and when I saw ye come plowing back last ev'ning I decided what's the harm in seeing she got safely home? If she in't who I thinks she is she can hardly blame me for makin' sure no one bothers her, an' if she *is*, well, I can call proper like the next morning, and not give her a scare. I hope you don't mind, ma'am. It has been an *awful* long time."

I stared at the man on my doorstep as he spoke this rather lengthy introduction. As he did I felt pangs of recognition; something about his mannerisms, the tilt of his head, all seemed familiar to me. I squinted down at him through the fog.

"Excuse me, sir," I said. "Do I *know* you?"

The man grinned. It was the scar on his left cheek, I saw, which had healed crookedly, that prevented that side of his mouth from smiling properly. But I could see his teeth were very white and square, and this confused me for some reason. It seemed incongruous that such a face should have good teeth.

"Ain't got no vicar 'nymore," he said. "Gave off needling ten years back. Honest tradesman now, guild member an' all. *An'* got new teeth. Traded a pearl sphinx eye I got off a sailor in a game of steeps to a witch in East Angles. Best thing I ever did."

An image came into my head, of a scrawny boy of indeterminate age, who smiled raggedly even then, before he had scars on his cheeks.

"My goodness," I said, my voice a mere whisper. "*Milky?* Is that *you?*"

"Goin' by Edder Thorne these days," said the man on my doorstep. "But I'll always be Milky for *you*, Miss Cor." He frowned. "Or will it be Mrs Harper now?"

"My *dear* Milky," I cried, throwing the door open and grabbing him by the arm. "Miss Cor will do fine. Come in, come *in* and tell me everything!"

A few minutes later we were settled in my dingy kitchen, and I had dusted off my best china and gotten out a bit of stale cake for the occasion. Milky sat at the little table, watching me bemusedly as I bustled around finding fault with just about everything.

"You've done rather well for yourself, Miss Cor," he said kindly.

"Don't mock me," I said, shaking a finger at him, but weakly. I could see he was bone thin under his well worn clothes, and those scars on his face spoke of dark times indeed. To him, I imagined, my little kitchen must seem safe and luxurious.

He must have seen me looking, for he laughed and brushed his cheek with a finger. "Got these in Gisgey," he said wryly. "Picked the wrong alley. Bad night." He shrugged. "But I walked away. More'n you could say for t'other dolls."

He had gone to work, he told me, briefly for Hydegan after I was married. He left after only a few months; "Got tired of dead things talking to me. 'Snot right, Miss Cor. Let the dead be dead and the livin' be alive. Naw, I left. Went back to needling for a while. Got caught. Did time. Finally read the letter Felpz left me. That helped. Went north after they let me out. Got these," he tapped the side of his face. "And these," he tapped his white teeth. "Went level after that. Started as an assistant to this antiques dealer in Ro'ford; I could keep the young needles off his wares on market day. Helps to know their tricks. Eventually I got guilded, began doing restorative work. Turns out nimble hands are good for lots of things. I'm not as comfortable as you, but I never been hungry in the last three years."

"I don't believe that," I said, eyeing his slight frame. "But don't worry, you show yourself promptly at my door of an evening, I'll see you have a good supper at least."

Milky laughed. "Miss Cor, I am a grown man now, I can find my own cheer."

"And *I*," I replied, "am a grown mother. Don't waste your energy fighting me."

Milky sat back in his chair. He seemed surprised. "You have a family then?" he asked.

I showed him the latest picture my daughter had sent back: she was sitting on a wood bench, a wyvern resting its wounded foot in her lap. Milky raised his eyebrows.

"And you?" I asked. "Is there a Mrs Milky?"

The question seemed to displease him. He handed me the picture back, shaking his head. "No family," he said shortly. "Never had, never will."

"Never say never," said I brightly, trying to restore the good humor that had so suddenly left the room, but Milky only looked at me sadly. I decided that, along with his Gisgey Grin, he must also carry invisible scars left by loss of love, and had in the intervening years probably experienced more than just physical hardship and pain. And if he did not yet feel ready to expound upon the subject, I hardly wanted to press the matter, knowing from experience how sensitive emotional wounds could be. I cut him another slice of cake and changed the subject.

While he ate I gave him a brief recap of the past two decades of my life, which served to restore the good humor in the room. Eventually, after we had demolished the cake and were waiting for the second pot of tea, our conversation turned to the inevitable topic: the Violet Prince and his extraordinary claims.

"He can't 'ave killed 'im, 'e just *can't* 'ave," Milky said, striking the table with the palm of his hand.

"I'm glad you at least retain some optimism," I said. "All the authorities seem to take his claim at face value. They say his ownership of the color purple is proof. How does one *own a color* anyway?"

"Deep magical stuff," Milky said. "Beyond me. But I don't believe him anyway. Abharus doesn't, and he's been researching this for a month now."

I had, while Milky spoke, been in the process of pouring tea. When he mentioned *Abharus* I jumped so that I nearly spilt hot water all down my apron.

"Did you just say *Abharus?*" I demanded, turning round.

"Yes," Milky said, his eyes wide with innocent surprise. "He's been in Redling for the better part of a year now, trying to find out where Felpz went. Dint you know? He's been doing research at St Argents lately. I thought you must have gone down to meet him at the library yesterday."

I put Milky's cup of tea down on the table so hard it splashed. "That *rascal*," I cried. "I have not seen a single silver hair of his in *twenty years*." I stood up, breathing heavily. First Milky appeared on my doorstep, now news that my old friend Abharus was in my very city. Indeed, had probably been in the same room as I just the day before. My heart raced.

Milky regarded me cautiously, wiping at the spilled tea with the cuff of his sleeve. "He told me he would be doing research at the Argent Camera until ten o'clock," he said modestly. "If we leave shortly we should be able to catch him."

This news appealed to me greatly, but it was to be a wasted errand: in vain did we make the journey through the cloudy morning down to St Argents, for the Library was quite deserted. Walking back through the fog Milky was most apologetic, though I assured him it was no fault of his own.

"You know what a slippery doll 'e can be," he said, pulling up his collar against the cold. "I reckon he was there today, jes dint want to be seen. I can only find 'im wen he *wants* me to, the little bugger ... " Milky trailed off, his diatribe against our friend interrupted by a commotion up Regnant Street.

A crowd had materialized out of the fog, comprised of all manner of persons; I saw a charwoman, her mop still in her hand, and a young solicitor standing shoulder to shoulder, both craning their necks to see above the crowd. As we drew closer I caught a glimpse of what held their attention: a golden glow emerged from the fog, and with it came drafts of warm air and the smell of wildflowers. It was quite the most enchanting sight, and it made my gut twist in agitation. I slowed my step, and almost at the same time Milky took me by the arm and dragged me down the nearest alley.

"Milky, what—"

"It's the fairy," he hissed, pressing himself up against the stones of the nearest house.

No sooner had he said it than I became aware of the sound of drums approaching. Craning my neck around Milky's shoulder I caught a glimpse of dancing children in the street, and following behind them at a steady walk was the fairy. I knew it could only be him by his flowing blond hair and his brilliant purple suit, but there was also a fineness about the bones of his face and hands that looked wholly inhuman.

Behind the fairy were two little fox-faced people, who were throwing paper birds into the air. These swerved and darted about, littering the sidewalk. One managed to flit into our alley and land at my feet.

"Don't touch it," Milky hissed, but he needn't have warned me. The charwoman and the solicitor had both grabbed birds of their own and were now meekly following the fairy down the street. They joined an already substantial crowd, each of whom clasped a little paper bird in their hands.

Together we hid in the alley, watching the strange procession go by, until our necks ached from keeping our heads turned to look and the last of the stragglers scrambled past. As the crowd cleared, I saw we had not been the only observers of the fairy's latest escapade: across the street, leaning against the railings of Regnant Park, in a veritable snowdrift of white paper birds, was a small figure in a battered brown coat. Despite the cold his trousers were turned up and his feet were bare, and from under his cap escaped a single shock of brilliant silver hair.

I felt my heart leap and catch in my throat. Across the street the figure plucked one of the paper birds from the pile at his feet and examined it. He did not seem to notice us.

Pushing Milky aside I charged across the road. It would have been a poor thing if a carriage had been coming, but in the wake of the fairy's procession the road was quite deserted. I walked right up to the boy, who was so engrossed in the study of his paper bird that he did not seem to notice me. I folded my arms and raised an eyebrow at him, but still he paid me no attention.

"Better met late than never, eh *Abharus?*" I said, startling him so that he nearly dropped his bird.

The person who appeared to be an eleven-year-old boy blinked up at me with huge, soulful brown eyes. He frowned.

"Most people don't notice me unless I want them to," he said slowly. "Do I know you?"

"You slippery doll," Milky said, coming up on the other side of him. "I'd never guessed that was you. How'd you spot him, Miss Cor?"

Abharus barely spared Milky a second glance, but stared at me, his eyes widening. "Golly, Corianne, is that *you?*"

My frustration evaporated and I beamed down at him. I didn't care that he saw a worn out matron instead of the bright young girl he had known last; didn't care that the passing decades had wrought no change in him.

I opened my arms wide. "The one and the same," I said. "Now what have you here?" I reached for the bird he held, but he pulled it away.

"Better not touch it yet, I'm still unravelling its enchantment," he said.

"You seem quite unaffected," I pointed out.

"The enchantment was meant for humans," Abharus said.

Milky and I exchanged glances, then looked at him expectantly.

Abharus sighed, as if being forced to admit something he was not at all proud of. "I am only *half* human," he said, and went back to studying the paper bird.

"Wot's yer other half, then?" asked Milky. "Fairy?"

"Something like that," Abharus said, not looking up. He pocketed the bird and set off down the street in the direction of St Argents. By unspoken agreement, Milky and I followed close on his heels. After we had been walking for a few minutes in silence Milky burst out:

"Alright Quicksilver, what's got your tail so hard? I've never known you so slippery."

"Not here," Abharus said quietly, and pointed.

We were just passing the end of Regnant Park, and there on the corner was an evergreen. Only it was not green: its branches were covered in purple foliage that stood out like a flame on that grey day.

"Enemy territory," he explained. "Wait until we are inside."

We followed, more subdued now, past the library the and through one of the student gates that led onto the campus of Danovial College. Milky looked around apprehensively, as if expecting to be ordered off by a warden, but the scattered figures on the field ignored us. Once a professor, her nose deep in a book, detoured onto the grass to go around us without even looking up.

"Can't they see us?" I asked.

"*Most people,*" Abharus said, "don't notice me unless I want them to. Come through here . . . " he led us through the postern door of a red brick dormitory, up a flight of dirty stairs, and finally into a tiny cramped room half filled with books. He shut the door, and made a curious sign over the lock with his left hand.

"We can talk now," he said.

"Well thank goodness for that," I said, wedging myself into a corner so Milky would not gore me with his elbows. "Abharus, what is going on here?"

"I am *trying,*" Abharus said, as if very put upon, "to bring back Bouragner Felpz."

"Here now," Milky said, nearly knocking over a pile of books in his haste to turn around. "I thought you was jus' tryin' to find out where he went?"

"Yes, well—" Abharus took the paper bird out of his pocket and laid it on a little desk, the only space in the room not covered in books. "Things have gotten serious."

"The Violet Prince," I said. "What is his game anyway? And is it so important that he's got the color purple? Did Felpz even *own the color purple?*"

"I don't pretend to rightly understand it," Abharus said, running his finger along a line of books. Picking one he pulled it out and opened it. "It's weird magic. *Old* magic. Here, this explains it better than I ever could," and he handed me the book.

To my surprise I found I was holding a copy of the *Chromium Magica*. I raised an eyebrow at him. "Going by Avars nowadays, are you?"

"How did you know that?" Abharus said.

I gave him a significant look, and went back to the tome in my hands. Seeing Milky trying to crane his neck around to get a glimpse I read the entry out loud.

"*Concerning Color Demons,*" I read. "*A collection of ancient primordial demons. They manifested in the living realm as colors, one for each color in the spectrum of light. As this included colors beyond those visible to humans, it is not known exactly how many there originally were. According to Favarian, the Elven historian, the Greater Elves slew three of these demons, thus rendering the colors red, yellow and blue harmless against them. There are a few accounts of fairies doing similar things, and legends abound of human magicians occasionally fighting the color demons, with more or less success. It is said that if a magician (or fairy or Elf) defeated a color demon they would then be entitled to that color for the rest of their career. It is generally considered that they would enjoy certain powers over that color, and in some cases even receive magical aid from it. However, no documented case exists on record, and the entire matter remains suspect. Many magicians over the course of history have labeled themselves as one color or another, but these are considered to be cases of pure vanity . . .*"

I put the book down and blinked at Abharus. He smiled sheepishly at me.

"It sounds a bit fanciful, I know, but it supports what Felpz himself told me."

"And what, pray tell, did Felpz tell *you?*" I asked, a little nettled.

"This was before your time," Abharus said, wincing at my tone. "I asked him why he always wore purple. He said it was his color. So I asked him what that meant. He told me he'd won it in a duel."

"Oh. Do you mean to say he fought one of these color demons?"

"I don't think so," Abharus said. "From the way he explained it, the color kind of attaches itself to whoever owns it, and can be passed from one person to another."

"So it's possible," Milky said in a hoarse voice. "It's possible this fairy poof actually *did* snuff him?"

Abharus sat down on the only clear space on his desk and kicked his legs. "I think I would know," he said seriously. "I would *know* if something like that happened to Felpz. Which is why I've been trying to bring him *back.*"

I looked around his cramped and crowded room at all the books. "Any luck?" I asked.

Abharus shook his head. "I've tried everything short of directly summoning him, and not gotten a thing."

"Wot 'bout summoning the bugger then?" Milky asked.

Abharus looked at his knees. "That could be . . . dangerous."

I sniffed. "This whole situation looks rather dangerous to me," I said. "We have a wild fairy prancing around central Redling commandeering the color purple and bullying the populace. No one is doing anything about it—everyone is frightened of him, I think—"

"And with good reason," Abharus interjected in an undertone.

"—so why not summon Felpz? I think it's high time."

Abharus sighed, picking at a splinter in the table. "If I'm to do that, I'm going to need help."

"'Swot we're here for," Milky said resolutely, and I could have embraced him.

"You don't mind running a rather significant risk?" Abharus asked.

Milky and I looked at one another. I could tell we were both thinking back to earlier "significant risks" we had run together in the past, for the sake of Bouragner Felpz. But it must have been a surprise for Abharus when we both burst out laughing.

It was agreed they would visit me that evening for supper, and Abharus would bring the necessary books of magic and explain the instructions to us. If everything seemed in order, we would attempt the summoning at midnight.

We all had good appetites that evening. For Milky's part I think that a good appetite exists in the very bones of his person, but Abharus and I ate more than our usual share. The meal quickly turned lively as we shared stories of that one inscrutable magician who was putting us to so much trouble this evening. Abharus had just begun an account of his very first meeting with Felpz when the most extraordinary thing of that extraordinary week occurred.

It all happened very quickly at the time, but I shall tell it in order in the hope that you shall not be confused.

A wind howled down the street and slammed into my window. I jumped up to close the shutters, for fear the glass would shatter, but Milky caught me and pulled me back. He had seen what I had not: that all the books of magic that Abharus had brought had leapt into the air like so many birds, and were flying at the window. A candle, which rested on the mantlepiece, blazed to life, casting the room in a bright light. Like that, the window was no longer a window, but a mirror: in its dark glass (for night had fallen) was reflected the three astonished faces of myself and my companions, and the black flapping shapes of the books.

What happened next is difficult to describe, even after long consultation with my fellow witnesses. What we all agree on is that the printed words from all the books flew from their pages and into the window-mirror, where they created a tunnel beyond the glass. Our reflections vanished, replaced by this tunnel made of light and words.

This I barely had time to grasp. Once I had done so the next thing I was aware of was another light at the far end of the tunnel, growing closer. At first I thought it moved slowly, but then all of a sudden it was right up on the other side of the glass. I thought I could see the dark shape of a person behind it, before the light solidified into a tiny glowing yellow ball, and the person behind it tumbled out of my window and into my parlor.

In that instant I caught a glimpse of flailing legs in tattered pale trousers and a dark coat. Then all the lights went out, and we were plunged into black chaos.

Milky shouted, Abharus shouted. I gasped as a cold hand grabbed my ankle. I fumbled around on the floor, trying to get a grip on our mysterious intruder. I felt a pair of bony shoulders under a thin wool coat, then a sinewy neck, and above that a head.

Then Abharus had the sense to summon a light, and the room bloomed into view once again. I looked down and found I was cradling the man's head in my lap. He was gazing up at me out of tired eyes, with a face that appeared to have suffered infinite strain, so it was a moment or two before I recognized him.

"Excuse me, madam," Bouragner Felpz said in a hoarse whisper. "Could I trouble you for a glass of water? I am *parched*."

Part Two: The Trial of the Violet Prince
December, 2307

MILKY WAS THE FIRST TO RECOVER. He took the decanter from the table and filled a glass with it. I helped Felpz into a sitting position so he could drink it. To my horror he felt like a skeleton under my hands, and his hair was in a truly terrifying state: all greasy and sticky it was, with one side long and rank, falling in a tangled heap at his shoulder, and the other side cut short enough that it stuck straight up into the air.

When he reached for the glass I saw he carried a cane in his hand. He frowned and shook it away into thin air. Then he took the glass and drank deeply.

The water seemed to revive him. He handed the glass back to Milky, and looked around him with a little of the old sharpness that I remembered.

"I appear to have got the wrong house. I do apologize," he said, struggling to get up. "Sorry to intrude. I'll be off now."

"Mr *Felpz*," Abharus said, striding into view, his hands on his hips. "*You* are in no condition to go *anywhere*."

Felpz paused. He looked at Abharus, his eyes narrowed in concentration.

"Abharus," he said at last, relief evident in his voice. "Well this is very fortunate. I do believe I would be a goner by now without the intervention of unexpected friends."

"More fortunate than you realize," Abharus said. "Who do think saved you from cracking you head open when you tumbled in here?"

Abruptly Felpz looked around. He saw me. There was a moment of complete and utter confusion, and then recognition dawned on him, clearing his face as it broke into a smile.

"My dear Corianne," he said.

"Hello, Felpz," I said tightly, afraid that, should I say more, I would begin to weep.

Looking around him now Felpz quickly spotted Milky, and frowned, glancing from him to me. "But my dear Corianne," he said. "This is not your fool."

Milky burst out laughing. "I should 'ope not, Mr Felpz, sir. I'll wager I'm not the brightest candle in the basket, but I was never anyone's fool. It's Milky, sir; all grow'd up and tossed through the mill, but still me all the same."

Felpz was smiling too, now, and I believe he would have laughed only he had not the energy. "I must say this is a welcome surprise," said he. "I'd never have imagined the three of you living under one roof."

"Oh no, it's not like that," I said, and we all began to explain to him the circumstances that had brought us together, with Abharus chipping in a few nervous words about the fairy. But we had hardly got started before Felpz held up an imperious hand and halted our narrative.

"As fascinating, and even urgent, as these matters are," he said. "I really must insist on a nap of some sort before I do anything else. Is there a sofa, perchance? Or at least a comfortable chair I might borrow?"

I scoffed, and led him to my own bedroom. There the three of us put him to bed, seeing he had a glass of water handy, and plenty of blankets. Abharus leaned over by his ear even as his head hit the pillow, and whispered furiously:

"But sir, it's really very important; there's a *fairy*, and he's claiming *your* color. I think he's also just enchanted half of Redling, I don't—"

Felpz raised a long warning finger to silence him. Without even opening his eyes he said; "There is nothing so urgent as my getting some sleep, Abharus. Fairies are immortal, you know, he can wait another day."

Abharus looked ready to argue, but Milky and I bundled him out of the room before he could speak another word, and I gently closed the door behind us.

We eventually persuaded Abharus to sleep on the sofa, and Milky insisted I sleep in the only other bed, in my daughter's old room. However, once there I found it quite impossible to get to sleep after the excitement of the day, so I got up and pulled Milky out of my best armchair and sent him to bed. I sat in his place, watching as the fire fell low in the grate, and outside the wind slowly died away.

I must have slept eventually, for suddenly I found there was a terrible crick in my neck, and my hands were freezing. I stoked the fire and went and made myself a pot of tea. I went back to sleep waiting for it to steep, and then next thing I knew light was streaming in the window, and I could distantly hear the chimes of Bluehall ringing nine o' clock.

Felpz had not yet emerged by noon, and after some deliberation I was dispatched to check up on him. Knocking at the door of my own bedroom I found it open, and bearing a tray of breakfast and tea as a peace offering, I went inside.

Felpz was not abed. He was sitting at my dressing table, having obviously conjured himself a bowl of hot water, performing his toilet.

I have never known a man as meticulous in his presentation as Bouragner Felpz—one of the reasons I was so shocked at his appearance the night before. Now he seemed much more himself, and looked it too.

The ragged trousers and purple blazer he had been wearing were thrown over the foot of my bed, and he was dressed in a sharp white shirt, silk cravat and lavender dressing gown. He had undone the tangles in his lopsided head of hair, and was inspecting the whole affair, critically, in the looking glass.

"I am tempted to take it off altogether," he said as I entered, not turning around. He pushed it this way and that with a comb, and sighed. "But I expect the visual aspect would not be very pleasing. Better to put it back the way it was, don't you think?"

"I am sure you know best," I said amiably. I was so happy to have him back, my old guardian could turn his hair pink for all I cared. Besides, I was also distracted by his clothes: I knew for certain my dressing gown was not lavender, and I couldn't fathom where he got the shirt and trousers. I caught Felpz's apologetic look in the mirror, and sniffed.

"Have you been doing magic?" I asked him.

Felpz shrugged, pushing at his hair with his hands. "Only as much as I was obliged to," he said mildly. "The dressing gown is yours, so is the shirt and tie—I borrowed that ratty old lace thing and pushed it into a more appropriate shape. The trousers are an old apron—all, I assure you, temporary measures until I again have access to my own wardrobe."

"Did you do the color yourself, or does that happen automatically?" I asked, tugging at the sleeve of the dressing gown.

In the mirror, Felpz gave me a sharp look, and continued his gaze as he pulled at his hair. "It tends to do it by itself," he said. "Though I can influence the shade, if I want to."

He turned around in his chair to look directly at me for the first time that morning, and I noticed his hair was now back to its original modest cut, parted neatly on one side and brushed smoothly back over his scalp. It was a luxuriant dark brown, without a thread of grey in it, and the face that looked at me from under it had lost all trace of the worry and wear that had been so evident the night before.

"How much do you know?" Felpz asked.

I explained to him about the Violet Prince, my own research, and Abharus's conclusions. When I had barely gotten to the end he burst out laughing, slapping his knee and putting his other hand up to catch his forehead.

"Felpz," I reprimanded gently. "This is a serious matter."

"Oh, serious, very, yes," Felpz gasped between snorts. "Fairies can be quite vindictive creatures; who knows what he has planned for his captured retinue. Oh, it may be only that he wishes to spirit them away to his gloomy domain for all eternity, but you never know when someone like him could get in the mood for a mass sacrifice. Ahem. Yes, very serious. But not something to be faced on an empty stomach, and I see a plate of breakfast there on the side table. Do you sit there, dear Corianne, and tell me what has been going on in your life during my absence, while I sate my appetite. I deduce it has been some years, but I'm afraid I can gather no more than that."

I would have much rather it been I who was asking the questions—I had so many!—but I could not deny my guardian this courtesy, and in truth we spent a most enjoyable half hour while I filled him in on the current state of the world. And it can be said to his credit that, when he learned of my husband's faults, he was nothing but sympathetic. Eventually we were joined by Milky and Abharus, and the conversation turned from reminiscences of the past to plans for the immediate future.

The setting was Ringcaster Park on a sunny winter afternoon. Snow had fallen in the night, gently cloaking the grounds in white, and throwing into stark contrast the brilliant purple leaves of the trees. There was a crowd in the central square, and though at first this appeared to be a random confusion of persons, if an observer were to look closely they would find that the crowd divided into two distinct categories: about half were enchanted, the other half looked on in horror.

Of the onlookers all that could be said in general was that they were people of the city: tradesmen, charwomen, a few members of the clergy, and a significant contingent of ladies and gentlemen. And there were Milky, Abharus and myself. We were all backed up against the edges of the square, staring dumfounded at the scene which was taking place within.

From his trawl through the city the Violet Prince had selected the prettiest girls and women, dressed them in gorgeous ball gowns, and put them to dance. This would not have been so bad, except the day was wicked cold and the poor ladies, though their dresses were very beautiful, were not at all protected by them from the temperature.

Yet as uncomfortable as they must have been, their suffering was nothing compared to what had befallen the men: these had been warped and crippled by magic, and were forced to act as servants in the odd scene the fairy was enacting. Some carried bottles of wine, others plates of delicacies. A few had been set up and made to play instruments on a little dais at the edge of the clearing, but their music was halting and sad.

Through the crowd of dancers the Violet Prince moved gracefully, his long coattails trailing out behind him, the star on his breast twinkling and flashing. He picked his partners seemingly at random, danced a few measures with them, and then left them for another. Most of the ladies seemed rather relieved when they were no longer the focus of his fierce attention, but some appeared inexplicably smitten by him, and would trail after him wistfully. One of these, a tall, otherwise strong-looking woman with dark hair in a shimmering sunset gown, was even more persistent than the others. Indeed, it looked as though she were quite desperate to speak with the prince, and was at his elbow every time he turned from one partner to another.

I pointed this poor woman out to Milky, who shook his head sadly. Abharus took no notice; he was glancing around, searching for where Felpz would appear. Our friend had said to look for him in unexpected places, but had not told us any more than that.

"Go down to the park, and see what is to be seen," he had told us after breakfast. "I shall join you directly."

We had been here now over half an hour, and no sight nor sound of him was to be found.

Out in the square, among the dancers, the desperate lady had cornered the Violet Prince by hanging onto his elbow and speaking earnestly into his ear. At first he laughed, trying to shake her off, but when it became clear she was firmly attached to his arm he bent his head to listen.

Whatever the lady said, it upset the fairy greatly. His handsome face twisted into a horrible grimace, and with a wave of his hand he brought the dancing and music (such as it was) to an end.

"*What?*" his sharp, aristocratic voice cut through the suddenly silent crowd. "He is *here?*"

The lady shook her head, said something in which I caught the words " ... soon ... " and " ... angry ... "

The Violet Prince looked sharply around square, at the mass of frozen dancers (they had all frozen in the positions they had been in when he stopped the dancing), and at the crowd of astonished onlookers. His almond eyes narrowed dangerously.

"*There!*" cried the lady in the sunset dress, pointing into a spinney of purple aspen trees.

The fairy's reaction was extraordinary. Whirling around as if he had been stung he cast a bolt of magic at the ground in front of the trees. It arced from the star on his breast up into the sky and then down like a piece of lightning. Where it hit, the ground exploded from the force, bending the trees backwards and scattering clods of earth and snow everywhere, leaving a blackened, smoking crater.

The Violet Prince stared intently at it, as though he expected Bouragner Felpz to rise up along with the smoke. So concentrated was he that he did not notice the color bleeding out of his own costume and into the lady's dress. His fine coat went from violet, to ash rose, to a dirty grey; meanwhile the lady's gown flushed with dark purple, like pouring ink into a glass of water. She grew perhaps a little taller then, and her gown twisted and wrenched itself into the shape of a long coat and trousers. Her shoulders grew a little wider, her hips a little narrower, and her hair shrunk down against her head.

When at last the fairy turned around he found that it was no lady that held his arm, but Bouragner Felpz himself.

For one instant the fairy stared, utterly astonished. Then he cast magic at Felpz. He had to cast it with one hand because Felpz still held his other firmly, and as the bolt of magic fell upon them I saw Felpz raise his free hand. The magic crackled on his arm, seeming to catch and hold there. Then with a shove of his other arm he channeled it straight into the fairy.

For a moment they were held perfectly still inside a nebula of searing magic, then it collapsed into the fairy, concentrating on his chest, where the star rested.

There was a clap like thunder, and a gust of wind nearly blew my cap away. The fairy was blown right off his feet, landing heavily on the cold stones of the square. He seemed dazed, and looked somehow smaller than before; his star was gone.

Bouragner Felpz loomed above him, tall and dark and very, very purple. He spread his arms wide, as if inviting the fairy to stand.

"You have put the people of Redling to a great deal of inconvenience through your lies and trickery," he said, loudly so that all the square could hear. "Taking advantage of my absence you falsely claimed my color as your own. Well, here I am. Do you care to win it properly?"

The fairy staggered to his feet, looking very pale and grey against the stones and the snow. He looked at Felpz, his eyes rimmed with red and staring hatefully. He looked at the crowd of former dancers, who now cowered away from him, huddling together and shivering. Then he turned and ran, jerkily, out of the square and into the spinney of aspens. Their branches were naked now, and their fire-colored leaves lay in a heap on the ground around them. The fairy ducked between their pale trunks, and was gone.

A cheer went up from the crowd, dancers and onlookers alike, and I admit Milky and myself contributed to the uproar. For his part, Abharus began quietly going around to the people the fairy had enchanted, putting them back into the right shape, or sensible clothes as the case required.

In the hubbub I found myself separated from Milky, and jostled over to the little dais. Being unable to see through the thronging crowd I climbed up onto it, hoping to catch a glimpse of my friends, only to find Felpz already there. He was sitting quite comfortably, his legs hanging over the edge, while he lectured a group of magicians who stood below.

" . . . entirely unacceptable," he was saying. "Give a fairy an inch, he takes seven leagues. Be grateful he was a comparatively unambitious fellow, or he might have easily waltzed into Waldrin Palace and enchanted your queen away. What? It's King Coreinath now? Well, whatever monarch is on the throne. I apologize, I have been absent for some years. That is another thing: know your history, ladies and gentleman; whatever a fairy might *claim* don't take it unquestioningly as fact, and understand that no matter the circumstances of my disappearance, I *always come back.*"

The circle of magicians on the ground—some of whom I now recognized as Royal Magicians—nodded and accepted Felpz's admonishments in chagrined humility. One of them came forward, her hat humbly in her hands, and asked whether this meant Mr Felpz would be available for consultations once again. To this Felpz held up a hand. "Two weeks," he said. "I need two weeks. I have not exactly been on holiday these past twenty years, and coming home to find a fairy causing trouble with my color was not restful either. No, you shall have to do on your own for two more weeks. Good day, and good luck." Putting on his hat Felpz rose and, seeing me waiting, courteously extended his elbow.

"Home, Corianne?" he suggested hopefully, and I heartily agreed.

Milky caught up with us on the edge of the park, and Abharus not long after that. We walked leisurely up the street, and I noticed with delight that Felpz was working traveling magic, shortening our journey by bending the road beneath our feet. In no time at all we were on Kings Street, and then we were turning onto that familiar road with its brick-faced houses and trailing ivy. This time I carefully counted the houses: one, two, three (that was the house that had been painted pink) . . . and then there was a house that had not been there before. Or, to speak more accurately; there was a house that had come back. It made sense, now I thought about it, that a magician's house might not behave like a normal house, and might take itself away if the magician did not need it.

Felpz let us in, and for the first time in twenty years I entered my old home. There was the checkered black and white tile; the enormous potted plant in the corner; and on the stair sat another familiar figure: a smoky black shadow roughly the size and shape of a dog, which stared at us out of limpid pale eyes.

"Una!" I cried in joy, and ran over to the creature, extending my hands for her to nuzzle at.

"I see you have kept the house in order," Felpz said happily, coming up behind me. Una made a cheerful *whuffing* sound, and led the way up the stairs.

So it was that in the next ten minutes I found myself comfortably settled in Felpz's sitting room, Abharus and Milky on either side, and Felpz
lounging on the sofa, his dark coat exchanged for his old lavender dressing gown—his own, he assured me, and not an enchanted nightshirt.

"To be honest I am glad he did not take me up on the challenge,"
Felpz said. "The fairy, I mean. I am not fully recovered from my ordeal,
and it would have been . . . difficult. But it is always a terrible shock when
you find your own magic turned against you, and I was confident getting
hit with a bolt of it would be enough to discourage him." He smiled
lazily at us, reaching into his pocket and pulling out a little wooden flute.

"Still a bit of a risk, though," Abharus said soberly. He seemed to be
nerving himself up to ask a question. "Is is true, then? Did you really
defeat one of these color demons?"

Felpz looked up in surprise. "Goodness no, why would I do that?"
he said. "They are harmless fellows, for the most part. No, to be perfectly honest I won the color purple in a duel, from a *fairy* who had slain
the purple color demon. It was not my intention to win a color; the duel
was her idea. But win it I did, and so I am stuck with it until someone
can win it back from me. No one has been able to do so yet, and I doubt
anyone ever will; I have grown rather attached to it you see."

"Ah," said Abharus, and leaned back in his chair. He still gazed at
Felpz intently, and I knew there was something else on his mind. Indeed,
I fancied it was the same thing we were all wondering, and as Milky appeared too deferential to ask Felpz himself, I gave voice to our collective
question.

"There is still one last thing, Felpz, that I am not quite clear about,"
I said.

"And what is that, Corianne?"

"Where exactly have you *been,* all these years?"

Bouragner Felpz froze, his flute halfway to his lips. He got a distant expression on his face, as though he were looking past the walls and
earthly confines of the room, into a dark and faraway place he did not
much like.

"Trapped," he said at last, and his words were clipped and short. "I
was trapped, and did not rightly see a way out. I had . . . hm . . . help . . .
from unexpected friends," he smiled, drawing back into the present, his
eyes losing their distant sheen. "Milky, would you like your old job
back?" he asked.

"Why, yessir, I'd like that very much, sir," Milky said, sitting up
straight and smiling his crooked smile.

"And you, Abharus?"

Abharus fidgeted in his seat. "I expect to be staying in Redling for
some time. There isn't anywhere else I need to be."

"That is good," Felpz sighed. He raised the flute to his lips, took a
breath, and put it back down again. "My blushes, I nearly forgot. Corianne, as you are still with us, what are your plans?"

I laughed. "You will be able to find me at 16B Carpenter's Lane, as you would know perfectly well if you had bothered to look this afternoon."

"I did have other things on my mind," Felpz said, shaking a finger at me. "But now that I know, should any problem of particular interest run across my path, I shall be sure to involve you in my search for its solution."

So saying he set the flute to his lips, and began at last to play.

two

A HORSE IN THE NIGHT

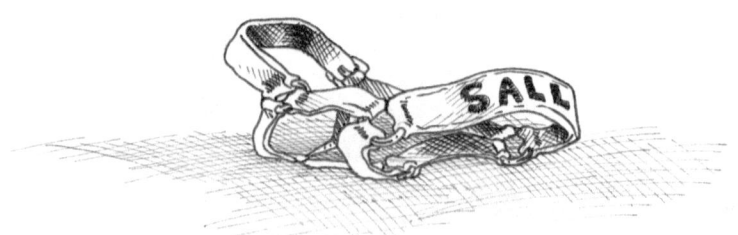

IT WAS IN THE LATTER HALF OF 2311 that I found myself, against all expectations, once more inhabiting the quarters of my friend and former guardian, Mr Bouragner Felpz. He had prevailed upon me to do so on the grounds that important business required him to go abroad, and that he was loath to leave his flat unoccupied in the interim. I was immediately suspicious: Felpz had been absent for the better part of the last two decades not only from his flat, but as far as I could tell, from the entire world. Why did he now desire a caretaker?

"But my dear Corianne, this will be *different*," he insisted one morning over tea in my shabby little kitchen. "This commission may take as little as two weeks, or it may take two months—but whatever the duration I shall be in regular contact through the usual channels; Royal Post, telegrams and all that. It's not as if I'm off to ride the Greater Realm or any such nonsense; I am only going to Elgany. And Una does become so despondent when she is in that place alone. If not for me, do it for Mrs Bryce."

Mrs Bryce was our old housekeeper, whom Felpz had located by some miracle and re-engaged in his service. Now well into her seventh decade she was snowy-haired and wrinkled, but just as stalwart as ever. I had no doubts she could handle an empty apartment for any length of time. What actually convinced me to take the offer was not anything Felpz said, but pure self-interest: I had discovered that I enjoyed nothing so much in the world as sitting in a cozy chair and writing stories, but the necessities attendant upon a woman living alone quite prevented me from doing so most of the time. So the idea of a holiday at Felpz's flat, where supposedly I could sit and write all the day long, was a rather attractive one.

I made the necessary arrangements with my employer to take a fortnight's holiday, and the next weekend I moved back into my childhood lodgings. The following two weeks were immensely pleasurable and productive, for being back amongst all of Felpz's old things I was able at last to make real headway on the stories that have previously been published in *A Study of Magic*. Then the two weeks were up and I had to return to work, but Felpz had not yet returned to Kyreland. The case in Elgany had inflated to momentous proportions, and the notes I got from Felpz were brief and enigmatic, but they made it clear he would not be returning until the month was over. To make up for it he sent me a generous allowance every two weeks, and this allowed me to live modestly but comfortably.

In the end the whole debacle would eat up three months of the year, during which time I was obliged to let the lease on my own flat lapse and move over my possessions and integrate them with Felpz's own. Felpz himself returned near the winter solstice to find his apartments even more cluttered than usual and myself in the middle of it all, busily writing away.

I had seen little of my friend in the three years since his dramatic reappearance, so great had been the demands on his time by persons of more importance than I. To my certain knowledge, in addition to the Elgan case, he had also been employed by two of the royal houses of Svenia and had been called all the way to Milany on a matter he would only describe as "dark, Corianne, very dark. Not worth your attention." All these he conducted with an incredible amount of energy and enthusiasm, and even now after a long journey he appeared as vibrant and cheerful as I ever did see him. He fairly waltzed into the sitting room thrusting a long package at me.

"My, what is this?" I asked, turning it over. It was heavy and cylindrical.

"Elgan sausage," Felpz proclaimed, beaming at me. "I thought you would like it. Warm up that drab little home of yours. Although, by the look of things"—he glanced around the room—"you have done a pretty good job of moving yourself in here."

I took a breath to begin explaining my predicament to him, but at that moment there was a pounding on the front door, followed shortly by a pounding on the stairs, and into the already crowded room burst a haggard young man, his tie blown over his shoulder and his coat buttoned up crooked.

Seeing that some new calamity must require my friend's attention, I withdrew deferentially into the background while the young man picked his way through the mess, talking in breathless gulps.

"Thank the Lady you're here, sir—only man who can help—Miss Hilldebrand is very poor and the doctors don't give her another week. But I *know* it is not a common illness, it can't *be*—" he stopped and grasped at Felpz's hand across a crate containing my best china.

"If you think so I cannot deny it," Felpz said mildly. "But I am a poor hand at physical ailments, better you should consult a—"

"I tell you it is *not* a physical ailment," the young man said. "It is those dashed horses!"

"I think," Felpz said, stepping over the crate and taking the man by the arm, "that you should come sit down—there must be a chair available somewhere, oh move that empty birdcage would you, Corianne?—have something to drink, and tell me calmly, in order, and in detail why you are here."

Finding myself by the door, I discreetly put my head through it and called down to the bemused Mrs Bryce, "Tea, if you please, and maybe something stronger. Looks to be another one of his flustered cases."

But once the young man was seated and had taken of Felpz's flask of brandy he calmed down beautifully. His name was Jorgen Wassermein, he told us, and immediately Felpz's head went up.

"Excellent, an Elgan name," he said. "I have just come from a country replete with Jorgens."

"Oh, then you know how to pronounce it. Good," said our young man. "It is always so confusing to people who see it spelt first, as the J is like our Y and the W is really a V and . . . " he trailed off as Mrs Bryce entered and laid the tea imperiously before him. "Thank you," he said, meekly. "You would think my family, having been in Kyreland for three generations, would have picked up some of the local names, but there you go. Look, now I am babbling. Forgive me."

"As long as you babble of your current problems, I see no difficulty," Felpz said lazily, leaning back in his chair. "Please begin."

Young Wassermein drained his tea in one gulp, and took a deep breath.

"I shall begin at the beginning—oh, but where is the beginning?" he said. "I think the engagement would be a good place to start; that is where it all began for me, you see. I am engaged to Miro—er, to Miss Hilldebrand, and we are to be married next spring . . . if she survives the winter. Which the doctors say she won't. Which I won't believe! Wait, I am to begin at the engagement, where was I?"

The story that eventually emerged, which for the sake of the reader I shall lay down here in my own words rather than Jorgen Wassermein's, was this:

He had become engaged some months ago to a young lady of considerable charms named Mirona Hilldebrand, whose family raised horses on the steppes of Torland. At first all was sweetness and delight, but then some calamity befell her family and she was obliged to return home. Young Wassermein and the lady continued to exchange letters during this time, and from these he gathered that the crisis had something to do with the family's horses, but she would not elaborate further. In the fall he made the journey north for what was to have been a short visit, only to find Miss Hilldebrand a pale, worn-out ghost of the girl he had met earlier in the year. Amending his plans to accommodate a much longer stay, Wassermein intended on remaining until she recovered. However her condition continued to deteriorate, despite the attentions from all the best doctors in that area, and now her life was despaired of.

Bouragner Felpz shook his head sadly at this somber tale. "Much as I would like, I fear I cannot help you in this case: a wasting illness that baffles even the doctors ... "

"Oh, but I have not told you all!" cried Wassermein, jerking in his chair as if he meant to jump right out of it. "I have not told you about the *horses.*"

Felpz looked at him, placidly expectant. Wassermein tugged at his collar, and coughed.

"At first I thought I was imagining things, but I've talked with Gladys—er, that's the parlormaid—and she has noticed the same thing. It may seem poor confirmation, the evidence of a servant, but the subject seems taboo among the rest of the family. It is like this, Mr Felpz: nearly every night since I have been there, I have been woken by the sound of horses galloping around the house."

Felpz put his head on one side and regarded our guest, curiously.

"I know what you may say: is it not ordinary to hear hoofbeats at a stable? But these are thundering hoofbeats, like a herd of a hundred or more, and they seem to pass within inches of the house; while I know they only have half a dozen out to pasture, and these are certainly not let loose in the stable yard."

"Have you ever seen this mysterious herd?" Felpz asked.

"That is just the thing, Mr Felpz. I have *not,*" Wassermein said, an odd triumphant gleam in his eye. "You can be sure Gladys and I have waited up for them on many nights, but though the sound came through clear enough—indeed it felt as though they were right on top of us!—we never saw so much as hoof or tail of them."

Felpz's eyes seemed to brighten and focus at this information, and he rubbed his long hands together in agitation. "And you think this phenomenon has something to do with Miss Hilldebrand's illness?"

"Sir, I know it in my heart. For she is always worse after the hoofbeats sound particularly loud, and demands to be taken to see the horses in the pasture. She has become quite obsessed with them, I'm afraid."

"Has anyone acquiesced to her requests?" Felpz asked.

"Oh, good lord no, she is in no state to leave her bedchamber."

"Ah ... " Felpz seemed disappointed. "A pity. It might have resolved matters." Then his eyes focused on Wassermein again, and now there was something hard in them, more like a cat that has spotted its prey.

"Mr Wassermein," he said, firmly and without apology. "If you indeed desire this mystery to be resolved, I would be more than happy to investigate. Ah, no, do not think of financial compensation, let me finish: and I really mean let me finish, for you may find the outcome not at all to your liking."

Wassermein, who had half risen from his chair, sat down again. "Do you think, if you do so, Miss Hilldebrand will live?"

"I do think so," Felpz said.

"And, can you solve this mystery?"

"My dear boy, I already have."

"Then tell me!"

"No, forgive me; the solution is not so simple as merely telling. I shall have to come up and see the girl myself. The girl and, preferably, the horses as well."

Jorgen Wassermein sank back into his chair, looking deflated. "Then how much longer must I wait?" he wailed.

"Only a little longer," Felpz said, soothingly. "I have just returned from one long journey. I need some time to rearrange my things before I embark upon another, and Corianne here always takes overly long to pack."

And with that young Wassermein had to satisfy himself. But as I showed him the door Felpz, who had darted off into another room, put his head in again.

"Just one last question, Mr Wassermein," said he. "The weather, these past few months?"

"Unusually dry," said Wassermein in clipped tones. "Passing clouds, but no rain."

"Thank you," Felpz said earnestly, and ducked out again.

Sometimes I cannot fathom my friend. I know this caused me great distress in my younger days, but I have since learned to take it in stride. Whatever plan or conception he had brewing in that head of his, I knew he would reveal all the relevant details at the time he deemed most suitable. So I did not question this rather mercurial desire of his that I should accompany him, reasoning that his motives would be plain enough in the end. That night I packed what little I felt I would need—a spare frock, nightdress, a good coat, and my toothbrush, my notebook and pen— and the next morning, when he had desired we should leave, I pinned on my hat without bothering to check it in the mirror, and was waiting patiently in the hall when I heard his voice crying out upstairs asking if I was ready yet.

I coughed loudly, and his head appeared a moment later over the banister.

"How did you manage that?" he demanded, looking astonished at my readiness.

"Nineteen years of being a mother," I told him. "It forces one to become organized."

"Well, since you are so well organized, perhaps you could organize us a cab to Bodsworth?" he called down and darted away again. I couldn't help but smile.

He was full of the same nervous energy for the entire journey, and by the time we boarded our second train (Miss Hilldebrand lived in a sufficiently remote place that our trip required two transfers), my patience was sorely depleted.

"Felpz, do tell me what vexes you so," I asked of my friend. "Do you doubt your ability to save this girl?"

"Save her?" He seemed surprised at my question. "Oh, I believe I can save her all right. Saving her for this Wassermein fellow, that I do not know."

"You certainly speak as though you have a full understanding of the case," I said, hoping this would goad him into explaining it to me.

"Yes, well, I did recognize certain telltale signs," he said dismissively.

"Such as?"

He pinned me with a sharp look, and I could tell he was not best pleased to be questioned so. "You remember what Wassermein said when describing his night vigil to see these mysterious horses?"

"He didn't see them. He could only hear them."

"'The sound came through clear enough,'" Felpz quoted. "'Indeed it felt as though they were *right on top of us.*' Does that not suggest anything to you?"

"I fear it does not," I admitted.

Felpz turned his face to the window and stared out at the bleak winter scene. "It is a nightmare, make no mistake," he said, as if to himself.

Reason's Hall, the Hilldebrand family stable, lay some miles from Kyrwich, on the edge—just as Wassermein had said—of the Halsteppes. Wassermein himself drove us from the station, in a cart pulled by a giant dapple-grey mare. Felpz immediately inquired if this was one of the Hilldebrand animals, to which Wassermein replied in the affirmative. Felpz then had to go about to the horse's head and peer at her eyes around the blinkers. Not finding whatever it was he sought, he patted the beast firmly on the neck and climbed up next to Wassermein.

"A fine animal," he said innocently, by way of explanation.

"They tell me she is over twenty," Wassermein said, a little confused.

"Do they go in for long lives, these Hilldebrand horses?"

"I couldn't say for certain; it wasn't the horses that I came to see," Wassermein said, coldly.

It was late afternoon by the time we arrived, and the sun was low in that big, bleak northern sky. Reason's Hall was the only homely fixture in an expanse of bare, brownish hills. It made up for its inhospitable surroundings by being a most charming building. Two branches of stables on either side of the main house made a crescent about a busy courtyard, for the business of the stable continued despite the tragedy within. The house itself was built of fine, dark wood, with steepled gables and a motif of running horses bordering the doors and windows.

Throwing the reins to a stablehand Wassermein bounded up the steps to the front door—then paused, finding himself alone—for Felpz remained standing in the courtyard, watching the traffic of equines as they were led to and from their stables.

"About how many horses are kept here?" he asked.

Wassermein was at a loss, but the stablehand, who had not got far with our horse and cart, turned and said, "Twelve in the stable at the moment, sir, and . . . oh . . . six more out to pasture."

"Would it be possible to see the six that are out to pasture?"

The lad grinned. "You're in luck, sir, as we feed 'em down in the troughs of a winter evening. Be there around sunset and you'll see them all right." The lad pointed out of the crescent of buildings, to where the hills dipped into a seam. Only then would Felpz be persuaded to come inside.

We had barely divested ourselves of our hats and coats when from up a flight of stairs a booming voice rang down on us:

"I don't know *what* Mr Wassermein was thinking when he invited that man into our house, but I won't stand to have his sort around, Merlock! It will be the end of our dear Mirona!"

And from above us, descending like a giant bird of prey, came a large woman of advanced years wrapped in a gaudy red silk robe, one giant blue-veined hand clutching the banister as she labored down the stairs. She froze at the sight of us, the silk drapes of her robe quivering about her.

I have never been inclined to call a woman ugly, as I find that to be hypocritical, more so as my own appearance rapidly approaches that of a withered apple, but this woman was so remarkably unattractive that it is really the only word for it. Perhaps once she had been as fair as any girl, but time and age had taken their toll on her face, and this unavoidable progression had been compounded by heavy application of powdered makeup. To make matters worse, she had such a scowl plastered across her countenance as to put the fiercest troll to shame.

Felpz, who had stood unfazed at far worse sights, merely bowed politely and smiled, as if the woman's remarks had been complimentary.

"Mrs Hilldebrand, I presume?" he inquired pleasantly.

The woman stood up straight, thrusting out her quivering chest, and glared down at him out of black-rimmed eyes. "My name, sir, is Courtier. Unlike *some* weak-willed women I chose to keep my god-given name when I married."

"Ah yes, of course," Felpz said understandingly. "My friend Birch here is the same. And Mirona is your . . . ?"

"*Miss* Hilldebrand," said this disagreeable woman, "is my niece. And none of your business, so you may take yourself away again." She flicked a hand imperiously.

A most extraordinary feeling washed over me then, something akin to a cold wind that brought with it a feeling of nausea and dizziness. It passed so swiftly I almost thought I had merely taken an odd turn, but I saw Felpz sway on his feet, as if he too were buffeted by some invisible force. Then he shook himself and squared his shoulders, gazing at the woman Courtier with undisguised irritation.

"Now Madam," he said in a very different tone. "If you have any idea who I am you must realize such tactics will not deter me. Stop that at once," he said sharply, as Courtier raised a hand in protest. "And release Mr Hilldebrand, I wish to speak to him."

From behind the bulk of Courtier stumbled a small, dark man, looking rather sunken in his coat, like someone who has lost significant weight over a short time. He blinked at Felpz, adjusting thick, round glasses over his eyes.

"It's very kind of you to come so far," he said in a small, timid voice. "But she has seen all the best doctors already. Are you some sort of specialist?"

"Mr Felpz is a *magician*," Wassermein said triumphantly, before Felpz could respond for himself. He looked a little annoyed at this, which was understandable considering Courtier's reaction.

The woman scoffed and took hold of Mr Hilldebrand's arm, whispering audibly into his ear; "Send that pretentious man away, brother-in-law, magicians are never any use when it comes to practical illnesses."

It was my turn to gasp, this time at the sheer rudeness of the woman. But Felpz smiled a small, secretive smile, and spoke over whatever poor Mr Hilldebrand was about to say: "Now sir, my friend Birch and I have traveled a long way today; at the very least allow us a tour of your fine stables, and then maybe you could recommend an inn where we may stay the night?"

There was no inn for miles around, and Felpz knew that perfectly well. Wassermein, whose face had gone redder and redder as Felpz spoke, suddenly smiled as he realized Courtier would have to invite us to stay the night.

Courtier nearly didn't. It was Mr Hilldebrand who showed the enterprise of graciously extending his hospitality to us. This made his sister-in-law glare at him, but she labored away upstairs again in a shuddering of red robe without saying a word.

"Now," Bouragner Felpz said, cutting through Mr Hilldebrand's jabbering apologies. "I should very much like to be shown your stables, before it is too dark."

This was arranged at once. Wassermein excused himself, explaining a little coldly that he had no interest in horses, and went upstairs, presumably to do battle with the woman Courtier. Mr Hilldebrand, who seemed a sadly distracted man, transferred us into the hands of his head trainer. A small, fiercely competent woman named Branch, she led us briskly on a tour of the stables. These were the two arms of the crescent, both long, low buildings. Inside they were bright from the many lamps hung between the stalls and warm from all the horses, snorting and nickering at us from behind the bars. Each stall door had a little bronze plaque affixed to the front, and on this was engraved the horse's name. *Charisma*, I read on one as we passed. *Tango,* on another; *Hoverwell,* and so on. Felpz went up to each one and peered questioningly in, once or twice he went so far as to stick his hand into the stall for the horse to sniff. Branch protested at first, but when she saw this had no effect on his actions, she gave up.

At the end of the eastern barn was an empty stall whose door stood open, and by the look of it had not seen a horse for some time. I could see the little square of pale wood where the plaque ought to have been, and the area smelled of new straw.

Felpz walked right into this last stall and stood very still, his back to us and his arms partly outstretched, for several minutes. Seeing Branch about to interrupt him I laid a hand gently on her arm and shook my head.

Whatever it was Felpz was searching for, he did not find it in that stall. He came out with a his face bunched into a dark frown, and indicated the missing plaque.

"Whose was this?" he asked.

Branch's face fell. She shook her head.

"Miss Hilldebrand's pony. The one she used to ride as a wee lass. But it died. Very sad. Founder." The woman's mouth drew into a hard, thin line. Felpz made a silent "Ah," shape with his mouth, and shook his head.

"When?" he asked as we left the barn.

Branch blinked at the question, and had to think for a moment. "About two months ago now," she said.

Felpz nodded then, as if this was what he expected to hear.

"The *calamity* Mr Wassermein spoke of?" I murmured as we made our way down to the pasture, where already the entire herd of horses had gathered by the troughs for their evening meal.

Felpz did not speak, but shot me a bright, intense look that told me I was right.

The troughs made a long line beside the fence, so the stablehand charged with feeding the horses could wheel the hay along, tossing it over at regular intervals. Felpz, Branch, and I paced behind her, slowly, since Felpz insisted on repeating his activity from the barn; every horse we came to he would stop and lean over the fence until the animal looked up at him. And though the herd was comprised of two bays, a black, and three chestnuts of varying degrees of redness, I could not distinguish anything unusual about any of them. But Felpz came away bright and chuckling and rubbing his hands. He thanked Branch so profusely for her tour, and complimented her stock so highly, that the woman was quite pink by the time we left for supper.

This was probably the most awkward meal I had ever experienced, with Wassermein and Courtier shooting each other evil looks across the table, and poor Mr Hilldebrand caught in the middle. I kept my head down except when simple politeness dictated I make conversation, at which point I tried to keep strictly to mundane topics. Felpz stared airily over Courtier's head the whole time, in a way which would in the past have made me hot with embarrassment, but now I found rather amusing.

After we had been released from the meal Felpz murmured something about sending a message, and vanished.

"Posting a *letter?*" Wassermein cried. "At this hour?"

"You must remember, Felpz is a magician," I said demurely, sipping my coffee. "When he says he is going to send a message, he probably doesn't mean posting a letter."

I watched the family sharply as I said this, and though Wassermein and Mr Hilldebrand only gave me polite blank looks, the woman Courtier's face flashed with fear for a moment. I made a mental note of this, and determined to visit Felpz before I went to bed and tell him of it.

When I got to his room, however, the thought was put clean out of my head by what I found there. A strange blue light shone through from under the door, and I hesitated before knocking, reluctant to interrupt his magic. But his voice sounded perfectly cheerful and relaxed when he called "Come in!"

The light, I saw, was emanating from a small blue fire burning in midair in the center of his room. It was quite cool, and made a low, fizzing hum.

"Two, if you please," Felpz was saying to the fire. "If at all possible. I have a friend who will not want to be left out of this. Can you ride, Corianne?"

"I took lessons as a child," I said cautiously. "I daresay I could, provided we did nothing strenuous."

The fire dipped and dimmed for a moment, and I got the strangest impression it was looking at me.

"Well, do your best then," Felpz said to the fire, and he dismissed it with a wave of his hand. The room faded into total darkness before Felpz conjured a warm yellow light which affixed itself to the ceiling. He looked more excited and pleased than I had seen him in a long time.

"Better get along to your own room," he said. "All your warmest clothes, and make sure it's something you can ride in—*astride*, mind you, we'll have none of this side-saddle nonsense. Then meet me down by the troughs in two hours."

It was late by now—past nine—and as it appeared Felpz planned to hold another one of his all-night escapades, I reasoned I should spend the two hours resting, but the excitement of the prospective adventure quite prevented me. At half past eleven I dressed myself in the clothes I felt most suitable for a midnight ride, and went down through the dark house, tip-toeing past the parlor where a candle burned and Wassermein held his own vigil.

The night air was frigid but blessedly still. Even so I turned up my collar and made certain my coat was fully buttoned before I ventured further. The crescent moon hung in the western sky in a halo of cloud, which in turn shone with a pale silvery light. In this way the night was much brighter than one would expect, and after waiting a few moments for my eyes to adjust I was able to see well enough to make my way across the yard with little trouble.

Felpz was waiting, a tall dark pillar against the pale ground, and beckoned me to join him. He was wearing a long coat that flapped around his legs, and a scarf that nearly covered his nose, but above it his eyes were bright and excited. He held a finger up, a gesture for silence, so I went and stood at his side and did not speak.

It is always difficult to figure the duration of time one waits when there is no timepiece handy, and nothing to do by which to measure its passing. So I will guess and say it was half an hour later that we saw movement at the side of the house.

Felpz calmly slipped his hand into mine, and I knew without being told that we were both now invisible. I had learned to recognize the tingle of magic over the years, though I still had no idea how he did it.

Movement again, this time in the black shadow of the barn, and a young woman appeared, hurrying across the open ground towards us. Despite my reasonable assumption that we were invisible, I couldn't help the feeling that she would notice us any moment, and not be pleased to find herself discovered.

But the woman ran on, faster now, almost desperately, until she reached the fence not a few yards from where we stood. She was wearing a strange, pale-grey costume with trousers and high boots. A cloak of silvery white trailed elegantly behind her as she vaulted the fence and pelted away across the pasture.

When she had disappeared over a hillock I chanced a low whisper: "Who was *that?*"

"Mirona Hilldebrand, I should think," Felpz said in his normal voice.

"She did not appear ill to me," I said.

"I did not believe for a moment she was. Eyes to the sky now, Corianne."

I looked up, just in time to catch a glimpse of a large dark object traversing the clouds below the moon, before it was lost against the shifting grey.

"The rest of the herd will be coming soon. Any questions, Corianne, ask them now."

I swallowed my initial inclination to gape and gasp, 'What is *going on?*' as I knew such broad questions never elicited satisfactory answers from Felpz. Better to ask for specifics and then piece together the big picture myself.

"Why were you so interested in the horses this afternoon?" I asked instead.

"Do you know what a *night mare* is?" Felpz returned, and by the careful way he spoke the words I knew he meant something other than bad dreams.

"I'm afraid I don't," I admitted.

Felpz sighed. "Well, that is all right. Put it like this, Corianne, if you were to take all the magic inherent in a given horse, intensify it a hundred fold, and put it back into the shape of a horse, you would have a night mare."

Seeing my nervous glance over his shoulder to the pasture beyond, he smiled encouragingly and went on: "Oh yes, horses are *very* magical creatures. It is a strange, wild sort of magic, quite different from ours. Night mares are practically made of the stuff. They do not fully exist in our domain, you see: they run in that grey space between worlds that is the haunt of fairies and other spirits."

"The stairwells," I said, remembering how he had once described our world to me: as a tall house with many stories, each floor being a different level of reality.

"Or the floorboards," Felpz said. "That metaphor does break down at a certain point. Remind me to give you a lesson in related world theory when we get home."

"But what does this have to do with the horses here?" I asked.

"Night mares can interbreed with common horses," Felpz explained. "You would find strains of *equus ferus noctis* in just about any exceptional horse you care to name. Several of the Hilldebrand horses struck me as particularly magical, which only confirmed my original theory that Miss Hilldebrand has been engaged for the past few months in *night riding*."

"So what we just saw . . . must have been Miss Hilldebrand on one of those horses!" I exclaimed, pleased with myself for coming to this conclusion on my own.

"Precisely," Felpz said.

"But . . . why on earth is she doing it? And why would she try to hide it?"

"That was what I wished to ask her," Felpz said, smiling ruefully. "But if I could hazard a guess, I imagine she is trying to become a Nightrider." Then, to my questioning glance, he added: "They are that elusive group of people who have managed to make riding night mares their way of life. Fascinating people, but it's very difficult to join if you are not born to it."

"So what do you intend to do now?"

"I intend to *talk* to her, in a place where that woman Courtier cannot interfere."

I opened my mouth to ask him another question, but my words were replaced by the distant sound of hoofbeats. They grew closer, growing into a huge thundering roar that seemed to surround us. It sounded as if the horses must be all around us, yet the yard was as deserted as ever. Finally I came to realize that the stampede was *overhead*, but looking up I saw only the high cloud cover, with perhaps a few distant shadows flickering past the moon.

Eventually the sound died away, and we were left alone in the night once more.

Or almost alone.

"Oh *good*, here comes our transportation," said Felpz. "Right on time as well."

A dark figure had appeared in the pale strip of ground beyond the shadow of the house and the stables. Though human-shaped, it appeared somewhat draconic because of its towering, horned helmet. It was flanked on either side by a large dark horse, and together this trio was walking towards us over the pale ground.

It struck me then as a sinister sight, but Felpz went to greet this imposing character with a glad cry, beckoning me to follow.

"Hallo Bouragner," said this strange person, speaking with a foreign accent I did not recognize, like many accents all jumbled together, and the voice so deep and husky I could not tell for a moment whether it was a man or woman. Then the clouds shifted and moonlight washed across the figure, revealing a face I would not soon forget.

Round and brown-skinned, streaked with the black hair that escaped from under the horned helm, it could have been a sweet, girlish face, except for the horrendous black tattoos that swarmed over its eyes, outlining them in inky black and curving outward in hooks and curls. This vision grinned at us with improbably white teeth, and touched the brim of her helmet—for it was a woman—as a salute to me before striding forward and embracing Felpz.

I heard Felpz give out a quiet *"Oof,"* as this character's arms closed around him, and though he reciprocated (rather gingerly), he also contrived to extricate himself as soon as possible.

"Friend," he said, holding onto the woman's shoulders so as to keep her at arm's length. "Allow me to introduce my companion, Corianne Birch." He gestured, and our new friend turned to face me. She did not leap upon and embrace me, to my relief, but merely extended one gloved hand. When I took it I was surprised to find it, though powerful, rather smaller than my own. She smiled at me from under that horned helm, and the starlight glinted in her dark eyes.

"Tell me, Corianne," she said, with her strange jumbled accent and deep husky voice. "Do you ride?"

"Not since I was a child," I admitted.

A shadow flitted across her face, but then she shrugged to herself. "Perhaps that is for the best," said she; "remember then, what it was like to ride as a child, and you may do well."

She led to me to the larger of the two dark horses, and placed a hand upon its shaggy neck. "Theonar will carry you," she said. "She is my own mare and will not let you fall. Come, be introduced."

Hesitantly I took her outstretched hand and allowed myself to be drawn close to the beast. Theonar was easily as tall as any thoroughbred, but of a heavier conformation that made her seem much larger. She bent down her great head to me, and blew damp, warm air into my face. Still holding my hand, our friend guided it up, so that Theonar could sniff it, and I felt the tickle of whiskers.

With a snort so sudden it made me jump Theonar ducked her head, then turned sideways and took two strides, so that I was now even with her saddle.

"Give me your knee," said our friend, so commandingly that I obeyed without thinking, and the next moment found myself propelled up the side of the horse. My groping hands found a saddle, and I threw my free leg over it. There I sat, my thick skirts bunched uncomfortably and my legs dangling uselessly on either side, for the stirrups were too long. Our friend made herself busy about my knees adjusting the leathers, and soon I felt my toes being fitted into the irons.

"Remember to keep your heels down, so you do not lose them," she said.

I could hardly expect to do so much. The saddle was different than the one I had learned to ride in, being the kind that you sat in astride, with an odd sort of cup at the back that prevented one from sliding off behind, but hardly anything in front; thus I feared I might go tumbling off over the horse's withers and over her long neck. I was also having difficulty finding the reins in my steed's mass of black mane.

"Theonar will not suffer a bridle," said the woman from around my knee. "But if it makes you feel more comfortable . . . " She detached from the saddle a long piece of smooth rope, which she threw over the horse's neck and then affixed each loose end to the halter I had taken for the animal's bridle. Putting these rudimentary reins into my hands she looked up at me seriously. "But remember it is not your place to steer. Just hold on."

At this I glanced nervously at Felpz, and found he had mounted the other horse and was sitting bent over, with one hand resting on the animal's neck. Looking up he smiled at me, an odd wild light behind his eyes.

"Now we shall see if we cannot find Mirona Hilldebrand," he said, and gave his horse a decisive pat on the neck.

The next moment we were off. At first it was horrible, and quite terrifying: I had forgotten how dreadfully high up one was on a horse's back, and how they jerked and swayed. We shot forward at a full gallop, leaving the stable behind in a whirl of dust, and I was glad I had grabbed a handful of mane instead of the useless reins.

Peering through the whistling night air that blasted in my face, I saw that we were heading directly for the pasture fence; a sturdy stone wall covered in vines. I held on tighter, preparing for the jump.

What happened next was one of the most wondrous sensations I have ever experienced outside of dreams. The horses leapt; I felt the lunging stride, the sudden snap as we left the ground, and then a moment of weightlessness.

That moment stretched on and on and on. We hung in the air, as if suspended in time at the zenith of our leap. It was only as I felt the wind tug on my hair and garments, and looking down I saw my mount's shoulders and legs moving in the motions of a gallop, and below that—surprisingly far below that—the ground wheeling away beneath us, that I came to realize the truth:

We were *flying*. Weightless and swift as the shadows that chased across the pale moors, we hurtled up into the night sky, the horses galloping up the air as if they swam through some sky-like ocean.

I felt no fear of falling, for I was as weightless as my magical steed. Indeed my chief concern was holding onto her thick black mane, for in my featherlight state I kept feeling as though I would be blown clean off her back.

Together we wheeled up through the sky and into the bank of clouds. Arms of fog so thick they battered at me streamed past, and the sudden chill made my eyes water. Then, as quickly as we had entered, we shot out of the clouds and into the world above, where we galloped over a frothing silvery sea, and the sky, deep and dark and pricked with countless diamond-bright stars arced above us. The curving horn of the moon shone beside us, bigger and closer than it appeared from the ground. I guessed we must be very high, yet I could breathe as easily as ever.

Galloping weightless over the grey clouds, it seemed to me that the stars in the sky were not points of light affixed to a dark firmament, but distant storms of fire burning in an endless black ocean.

As if responding to my inner thoughts, my horse altered her course, angling away from the false surface of the clouds, and out toward the stars. For a moment the starry ocean was no longer our sky, but an array of distant lands waiting to be explored.

"Eyes ahead, Corianne," Felpz called somewhere below me. Looking around I discovered that we had drifted quite far from him, and instinctively I jerked on my rudimentary reins to bring Theonar's head back around. The horse swished her tail angrily, but she descended back to the clouds, and soon we were running alongside Felpz once more.

"Felpz!" I cried, my voice high from excitement and nerves. "This is *the* most astounding thing!"

Across the misty glow of the silver fog I caught the glance Felpz sent me, and knew from his expression he was enjoying himself as thoroughly as I.

We *flew* — weightless, swift as shadows, on our dark, silent horses. The cold clear air cut across my face, making my eyes stream with tears, but my heart was light as a moonbeam and a bubbling joy boiled up in my breast that once or twice leapt out of my mouth in the form of involuntary laughter. I could not bring myself to feel embarrassed, for any feelings of shame and discomfort had been left on the ground below.

Cutting across the sea of clouds we passed towering mountains made of white, billowing fog. Here and there the clouds thinned, and I caught glimpses of a dark land far, far below. That it was no land I knew — certainly no part of Kyreland — did not trouble me. I looked down on wild mountains dotted by gleaming caps of snow and covered in dark, pointed trees, and I laughed for their beauty and their wonder.

How long we flew I do not know. On the one hand it felt like an eternity of sky and clouds and delightful weightlessness, but on the other it might have only been ten minutes. I suspect that time was not behaving in its usual, steady fashion, so I have given up trying to make any kind of guess. I do remember that after some duration we were suddenly overtaken by a teeming mass of dark running bodies. Wild manes and tails flew like flags around us; hooves beat against the air, and I was surrounded by the smell of horse, with a sharp undercurrent that reminded me of thunderstorms. Theonar's head went up, and I found myself clutching at the vertical edge of her neck, but she did not buck or dance about, for which I was grateful.

The herd parted around us, overtook us, and surrounded us. The horses were of all shapes and colors, though in the silvery moonlight they appeared tinged with grey. It was then I noticed that some of the horses carried riders: dark figures in flowing capes with horned helmets like that of Felpz's friend. They drew no weapons, indeed I could not tell if they carried any, but brought their galloping horses closer so that one of them could hail Felpz.

Contrary to their frightening appearance, this greeting sounded distinctly glad, as if the rider were hailing an old friend. Felpz answered in a language that I thought was Svenian, and the rider seemed to understand. It made a swinging sort of gesture with its arm, and as one the whole herd, with us at its center, changed course. We banked around until the moon was at our back, and ran on into a dark stretch of night.

After a time the herd opened again, and I found a new rider admitted to our circle. This one wore a light grey cloak, and she rode a horse so chestnut it appeared red even in the pale moonlight. It took me a moment, but I soon realized she must be none other than Mirona Hildebrand.

She was not best pleased to see us. When Felpz brought his horse alongside hers she made to pull away, but Felpz reached across and took her by the arm. I saw him speak to her, but his words were lost in the wind. Whatever he said did not soothe her, but she reluctantly reined in her horse, and together we came to a halt on a promontory of cloud overlooking the wild black mountains. The other riders flowed around and past us, and soon were lost in the dark horizon.

Then, to my astonishment, Felpz dismounted. He slid off his horse and walked across the clouds to Mirona Hilldebrand. Uncertain whether this was an effect of the night horse's magic, or some doing of his own, I remained firmly upon Theonar's back. As such I feared I would not hear what was said, for Felpz spoke in quiet tones, but my horse seemed to read the eagerness in my seat, and walked over to stand beside them.

The young woman was whispering indignantly: "You've no right to interrupt my Run. This was my last, now I shall have to do *another* before they will accept me."

"My dear, you have not listened to a single word I have said," Felpz said gently. "You simply cannot *do* it like this. Your father is distraught, your fiancé . . . "

At the mention of our friend Wassermein, Mirona Hilldebrand scoffed and waved her hand dismissively.

"I am no longer bound by such earthly desires," she said loftily, and my heart sank for the poor man.

"Yes, but *he is*," Felpz insisted.

Mirona Hilldebrand's eyes flashed. She was quite astonishing to look at in the ordinary way: high cheekbones and elegant arching brows. In the moonlight, with her pale hair blown into a halo around her head and her eyes glaring out of dark hollows, she looked like an angered Seraph descended from Heaven.

"Men," she hissed. "You are all the same. You will never understand. Up here I am free, truly free, for the first time in my life. You cannot force me to return."

"They will come looking for you," Felpz said, letting her implied insult slide off him. If he had felt a fraction of the joy I had during our wild ride, he knew well what drew Mirona Hilldebrand to the sky.

"They will think I have died," Hilldebrand said with triumph. "Aunt Geneva has seen to that."

"But do you not see how unfair that is to them?" Felpz pleaded. "If you do not tell them the truth, then I must."

The figure of Mirona Hilldebrand stiffened visibly. She seemed to have gone still with rage and indignation.

"You mean to undo all my hard work? To compromise my only chance at true freedom and happiness? See!" She turned to me, gesturing at Felpz with one arm. "See how men only support the desires of their own kind?"

I said nothing. I did not like to say to this fiery woman that I rather agreed with Felpz, but I also doubted Wassermein would let her go, were he to learn the truth.

"My dear Miss Hilldebrand," Felpz said, and his tone was no longer deferential and placating. He looked up at her with a steady gaze, and his voice took on a quiet intensity that riveted us both. "If I had desired to stop your riding, you would not be here tonight. I beg, do not let that bitter old woman color your judgement. Surely you must see that the right and honest thing is to make a clean breast of the matter. Then you may return to the sky with a clear conscience."

"If I go back to ground," Hilldebrand said, bending low and hissing the words into Felpz's face. "They will never let me go again."

"I promise I will not allow that," Felpz returned, meeting her gaze.

There was a tense silence. Turning my eyes from the tableau, I saw that one of the night riders had returned, and sat watching us from across a frothy sea of white cloud tops. Their horse was small, almost a pony, with a mane so bushy it fell down over its face.

Hilldebrand seemed to sense them. Her head jerked around.

The rider raised a hand, as if blessing us, and then rode away into the night.

All the fight seemed to go out of the young woman. She slumped in her saddle. Turning back to Felpz she said, "Then I will trust your word, much grief may it bring me."

Felpz smiled up at her, quite kindly I thought, considering the tone she had taken with him. "You will not be disappointed," he said.

As soon as he stepped away, Mirona Hilldebrand spurred her horse on, and she was soon a small dark shape, moving swiftly across the clouds. Felpz sighed and remounted, turning his own horse around.

"Come, Corianne," he said tiredly. "Let us return to earth and see what sleep can be had before the dawn. I fear tomorrow will be a particularly trying day."

When I woke late the next morning, to the sound of the maid frantically calling me for breakfast, I thought for a moment that I had dreamed it all. I had a vague memory of that fantastic flight, of descending through the clouds and skimming low over dark lands. Of landing in the stable yard, where Felpz's friend in the horned helmet took away our horses, and of creeping back up through the house to our rooms.

Then I attempted to sit up, and my protesting muscles informed me loud and clear that yes, it had all been real. That brought home the memory of Mirona Hilldebrand, and I hurried to dress and make my way out into the house in the hope of finding Felpz before Wassermein found him.

I failed. Felpz was already at breakfast, with Wassermein on one side and Mr Hilldebrand on the other. Courtier was not at the table; dear Mirona was poorly today, and needed constant attention. I couldn't help glancing at Felpz when I heard the news, but he serenely spooned sugar into his tea and remarked, "Illnesses often get worse before they break."

"I hope you are right," said Mr Hilldebrand. "But it so reminds me of the illness that carried off her poor mother, I fear this may be the end."

"When was this?" Felpz asked, staring vaguely at his cup.

"Oh, twelve years ago this solstice," the old man said sadly.

"You never told me!" Wassermein cried, thumping his knife and fork down on the table. His eyes were red-rimmed, and he looked to have gotten rather less rest than we had.

"I didn't want to worry you, lad," said Mr Hilldebrand.

Wassermein turned to Felpz, pleading, but my friend was still staring ahead in a vague, distant way.

"Mr Hilldebrand," he said at length. "I would like to impose upon you for one more day. I have a keen interest in birdwatching, you see, and the steppes here pose an attractive challenge. Corianne, you can make yourself comfortable in the library for one day, can't you? I expect there are some very soft chairs there, which you should enjoy."

The chairs in the library were soft, but I found the confines of the house to be stifling, even oppressive, after the wild freedom of last night. After an hour I could stand it no more. As it was a bright, fair day, I took up my notebook and pen and hobbled out to the stable yard, where I was able to locate a hard bench with a wonderful view of the open, rolling pasture, and there I sat, laying down the first draft of what was to become this story.

The day passed quickly, as winter days do, and it was already dark by the time we gathered indoors for dinner. Felpz arrived late, his nose red from the cold, and looked expectantly around the room, seeming disappointed in what he found there. But he had no sooner taken his seat than Geneva Courtier arrived, looking flustered and very red in the face herself. He looked up, his eyes gleaming, but the woman ignored him, taking her seat and angrily gesturing at the maid to bring her meal.

Felpz waited until the agitated woman had her silverware in hand, then spoke in a cordial, calm voice.

"How was Miss Hilldebrand today?"

Geneva Courtier dropped her fork with a clatter. She glared at Felpz across the table, and I very nearly saw sparks fly from her eyes.

Felpz smiled placidly, resting his elbow on the table and idly tapping the side of his face with one finger. "Did she . . . ask for me, by any chance?"

The woman stood up so fast she knocked her chair over behind her. Pointing a trembling finger at my friend she cried, "You are the Devil incarnate, man!"

Felpz actually laughed; he seemed flattered. "Hardly," said he, but I imagine only I heard him, for Courtier was shouting again.

"I want him *out* of my house, Merlock!"

Poor Mr Hilldebrand looked bewildered and torn, but Wassermein was fairly shaking with rage.

"This is *not your* house, Madam Courtier," he said through gritted teeth.

Something shimmered in the air between Felpz and Courtier then. Something vague, on the edge of sight; I do not believe the other men noticed it at all, and I'm certain only I saw Felpz make a sharp, cutting motion with his hand.

Mr Hilldebrand seemed to fill out, the lines of his clothes disappearing as he straightened up.

"You know, I think I would like to visit my dear Mirona," he said, with more authority than I would have credited him with a minute ago. "It occurs to me I have not seen her in *months.*"

"Neither have I!" cried Wassermein, as if he only just realized this.

"Then we shall," Felpz said, neatly laying his napkin over his plate and standing up. He led the men out of the room, Courtier glaring after them. Not wishing to be on the receiving end of such a look, I stood politely aside and motioned her to go ahead of me.

Thus I was the last to enter Mirona Hilldebrand's chambers, and I found them already in an uproar.

The young woman, far from being sick in bed, was standing beside it, very tall and straight with her shoulders squared. She wore the same grey costume that we had seen on her the previous night, and her eyes were set in cold determination.

Courtier was shouting. In a wailing sob that grated on my nerves, she cried; "How *could* you Mirona? After all that I have *done? How* could you *betray me?*"

A pained expression crossed Miss Hilldebrand's face, and she raised a hand as if to shield herself from the glare of her aunt.

Silently, Felpz crossed the room and went to stand beside her. Clasping his hands modestly behind his back he leaned over and spoke quietly in the woman's ear; "Would you like to explain matters, or shall I?"

Miss Hilldebrand shook her head without hesitation, and Felpz, with a shrug, held up one of his own hands, palm out, as one does when asking for silence.

He must have done more than that, for silence fell like a curtain, and Courtier, midsentence, was cut off with a gulping sound.

"Dearest Father," Miss Hilldebrand began, twining her hands nervously in her cloak. "Darling Jorgen. I fear I have misled you both terribly. You must understand I did so only because I thought it would be the best course of action; the only one that would allow me the freedom that I desire. However, Mr Felpz says it is better to be honest, and since he has promised to intervene on my behalf should you try to stop me from doing what I wish, I see no reason to withhold the truth from you."

There was a settling in the room, as if now it was attention to Miss Hilldebrand's words rather than Felpz's magic that held them silent, but I noticed that he did not lower his hand, and Courtier continued to glare at them both.

"The truth is," Miss Hilldebrand said, taking a deep breath. "The truth is that I have not been sick at all. That was Aunt Geneva's idea. Aunt Geneva," — here her hard eyes turned to the older woman — "is very good at making people believe what she wants them to." She smoothed down her cloak, and looked at the floor.

"The truth is that I have been night riding. I have been ever since I was a child. Do you remember the evening when I was seven, and I rode Sally out over the steppes and did not return until dawn? That was my first flight. It was a full moon that night, and as it rose, huge and milky white over the distant mountains, a flight of dark horses ran out of the sky, skimming over the earth. Sally took off after them, but far from being thrown off, I found myself possessed of an unearthly weightlessness, and together we flew up into the sky and joined the herd.

"I have been night riding ever since. Though it was only in the past few months that I earned my cloak and became a Nightrider. Do not blame yourself for your ignorance, father, for the only one I confided in was Aunt Geneva. And to you, Jorgen, I owe an apology. For it is tradition for Nightrider initiates to spend time on earth, among their own people, before they make the final decision. I had thought, when you asked me to marry you, that perhaps I would remain grounded. But when news came that Sally had died, I knew I must return to the sky."

Her eyes, shining now, turned to her father, and she said, very carefully and seriously; "Night mares do not die. They are all *up there*, running in the night. You see now I had to go. I went to Aunt Geneva, and she told me not to worry, she would fix everything, leave it to her. I did not know she would put about that I was deathly ill, and when I found out it was too late to change things. I believed that if you knew the truth you would stop me. I still believe you will try, but I tell you I am going to be a Nightrider, and you cannot stop me. Sally was not the only horse in whose veins flowed the blood of night mares. I am taking Cavaly, and I will go."

She finished, raising her chin defiantly, and crossed her arms.

For the first time since this astonishing deposition began I turned my gaze from Miss Hilldebrand, and found it drawn to her father. Far from being enraged, he was staring at her with a look of heartbreak, and there were tears running freely down his face. I felt for him more deeply than I can possibly describe, and I still regret that I did nothing at the time to comfort him.

It would have been near impossible in any case, as Wassermein was shaking with frustration, and as soon as Miss Hilldebrand stopped — that is, as soon as Felpz lowered his hand — he burst out:

"Mirona, this is really quite ridiculous. We are *engaged*. This little obsession of yours will pass. You must be ill — have brain fever, something of that sort — because this is *madness!*"

Miss Hilldebrand flinched away from him as he advanced toward her. This surprised Wassermein, who stopped and held out his hand beseechingly. For answer, the young woman removed a little velvet pouch from a pocket in her costume, and dropped it into his outstretched hand.

"There is the ring you gave me," she said, her voice cold and firm. "I do not bear you any ill will, Jorgen, and I hope you find another woman who is more deserving of you to put it on."

She made to leave the room, but Wassermein stood solidly in her way, his hand clenching convulsively around the little velvet bag.

"Mr Wassermein," Felpz said softly. "I did warn you, the resolution may not be to your liking."

Wassermein glared at Felpz so that I thought his eyes would burst from his head. Then Mr Hilldebrand came around and gently drew him aside by one arm.

"Come, my son, this matter seems to have been mishandled by all involved, let us not make it any worse." He looked at his daughter, his eyes still full of tears, but he managed to say without his voice even wavering; "Go to your mother, Mirona. She must be waiting."

For one moment, Mirona Hilldebrand's face was open, stunned. Then she threw herself onto her father, kissed him on the cheek, and ran out the door.

Wassermein tried to dart after her, but Mr Hilldebrand still held him by the arm.

"Let us go down and see her off, shall we?" said the older man, and marched the younger, at a stilted walk, out of the room.

Felpz and I made to follow them, but we were stopped in the door by Geneva Courtier. The woman was looking almost chastened, but her chin still jutted in an impudent manner.

"I fear I misjudged you terribly," she said, quite handsomely, I thought, but Felpz looked down at her and did not seem impressed.

"My dear lady," he said, his usually smooth voice like gravel. "It occurs to me that you could have circumvented this entire altercation if you had only employed your powers properly."

Courtier looked understandably hurt, and then a little of the old belligerence came back into her face.

"As a woman I could not," she said. "They would not have respected my authority."

"You are a *magician*," Felpz said, rounding on her. "That is all the authority you need. You must be a talented one indeed, if you managed to deceive the doctors who attended not only your niece, but your sister as well. Think, woman," he continued, softening. "If I had behaved as you seem to believe all men must, where would we be now?"

Geneva Courtier stared at him blankly, and if she had anything to say in response, she said it to our retreating backs.

Out in the stable yard the night was clear, with the harsh winter stars glittering in the depths of the dark sky. The moonlight cast the scene in a pale, colorless light, starkly illuminating the two grey-cloaked figures who stood, casting long dark shadows across the ground. Beside each one was a horse, saddled and bridled, their long necks arched and their ears at erect attention to the small group of people gathered on the house steps. As we joined them I found they were Mr Hilldebrand, Wassermein, and the trainer, Branch.

The poor woman's face was as white as the moon, and she was whispering frantically to the two men; "She rode down out of the *sky* man, and then Cavaly jumped the pasture fence and went to stand by her. Then your *daughter* came out. They've been waiting there for ten minutes. What is this about, Mr Hilldebrand? Because I'll swear across my heart that woman is your late wife!"

Mr Hilldebrand did not answer. He stared across the pale moonlit ground as the two women mounted their horses and together swung their heads around to face the night.

One—the one I fancied was Miss Hilldebrand's mother—stopped and looked back. I could not make out her face under her grey hood, but she raised a hand to us in farewell, before the horses surged into motion.

My heart thrilled at the sight, remembering well the feeling of the ride, as the two horses with their grey-cloaked riders leapt into the air and swam upwards to the sky. In the distance, from high above, I heard the thundering of many hooves, and chanced to wonder what caused the sound—since I knew all they were running on was air.

For a moment the moon was darkened, eclipsed by flying grey capes, and then the riders were gone, swallowed up by the starry sea of the night sky.

Mr Hilldebrand collapsed on the steps, sobbing, and this time I knelt beside him. I had no words for him, so I put a hand on his shoulder, hoping that such a simple gesture could help drive away the feelings of loneliness and abandonment I could but imagine were coursing through him.

"Oh, do not pity me," he said, fishing around in his coat pocket for a handkerchief. I gave him mine. "I had long ago given up on the Lady in Heaven, you know," he said, a little shamefully. "I had resigned myself that I would never see my dear wife again, neither in this life or whatever comes after—if anything indeed does. To know that they will ride forever among the stars—that is a better heaven than anything providence could promise."

As he dried his eyes, I turned and looked up at Felpz to see what he thought of this novel opinion, but my friend was staring wistfully up at the sky, a small, sad smile on his face.

Wassermein, who had run forward a few steps when the horses took off, stomped back into the house and slammed the door behind him. Felpz sighed, dragged his eyes down from the sky, and followed him.

Whatever words passed between the two men did not restore Wassermein's good humor. The next morning he was inclined to be gruff and spoke in short bursts, as if leashing some internal rage. Having once been young and in love myself, I had some sympathy for his predicament. Though I felt there was little I, an old matron, could say to assuage his feelings. What good would it do to tell him that the pain would pass? That the heart can heal from even the deepest cuts? A recently injured heart does not wish to hear such things.

It was Branch who drove us into town, and we left the house to the two men, Geneva Courtier having taken herself away while the winter morning was still dim. In the cart Felpz was inclined to be wistful and dreamy, and it wasn't until we were comfortably settled on the first of our three trains home that my curiosity drove me to break his reverie.

"You knew it was night mares from the very beginning, didn't you?" I said, trying to keep the accusing tone out of my voice, and not entirely succeeding.

Felpz smiled and shrugged, having the grace to look a little sheepish. "What good would it have done had I explained things to him from the first?" he asked. "A man like that does not like to think there is anything so important to his betrothed as himself."

"It is just the way young people in love feel," I pointed out.

Felpz spread out his hands and shrugged. "I would not know," he said simply.

Rather than pry into my friend's romantic history I let that subject drop, and asked another question:

"Will they really ride forever?"

Felpz shrugged. "Nothing lasts forever—not the real, infinite forever. But the Nightriders will ride as long as there is a night to ride in. And the night, Corianne, comes as close as anything to lasting forever."

"And the hoofbeats we heard? How do you hear hoofbeats on thin air?"

"Ah, that is an interesting phenomenon," Felpz said, leaning forward. "It has to do with magic, and the fact that air is really not all that thin. It is the sound, Corianne, of the night mares' magic pounding on the earthly air. You can't hear it when you are above, but from below it can sound very much like thunder."

There was another question that had been skittering around the corners of my mind. I had not asked it yet because every time I closed in to think about it it slid away like a piece of eggshell dropped in a bowl of yolk. This was a feeling I knew well from my younger days; when Felpz did not want me to notice something he made it difficult for me to think about it, and just knowing that allowed me to trap the thought between both fingers, as it were, and pull it out.

"Felpz," I said. "Just who was that person who lent us the horses?"

"Ah," said my friend, leaning back in his seat.

"Was she a Nightrider also?" I prompted.

"Hmm, no, not exactly," Felpz allowed. "She is generally referred to as the Wild Rider. You'll find her thoroughly described in that handy volume of *The Myths and Legends of Ancient Ria* I have somewhere in my study. I'll be happy to lend it to you when we get home. That re-minds me," he said, gladly jumping to a different topic. "By your loyalty to me as my faithful house-guard you seem to have fallen into some-thing of a predicament vis-a-vis the lease on your old lodgings, which has expired, and—last I checked—a small Idrian family has taken over. I propose, to make things easier all around, and as all your worldly pos-sessions are already there, that you resume inhabiting your old room in my flat."

He crossed his legs, clasping his hands around his knee, and looked at me expectantly.

I laughed. There seemed nothing else I could do.

"Very well," said I. "But I'm not a girl anymore, Felpz. I want my own study."

"That can easily be arranged," he said at once, a smile creeping over his face.

And so, as we rattled on through the winter countryside, our conver-sation turned from the problems of Wassermein and Hilldebrand, to the much more pleasant problems attendant on arranging my belongings in Felpz's little flat.

Author's Note

The strange woman who lends Felpz and Corianne their horses is Fenn Telfrei, the Wild Rider of Ria, who appears in many myths and legends from that area. In that mythology she is depicted as a fierce, warlike woman who rides from island to island (Ria being made up of a chain of five islands) with her band of similarly fierce women on their magical flying horses, causing mayhem and mischief, and occasionally—when there is no one else around to do it—righting wrongs. She is famous for her spiked helm, Harid face tattoos, and her great bay mare, Theonar. The horse she lends to Felpz is prob-ably Stagahein, the Storm Mare, who has her own set of legends. What Felpz did to earn the goodwill of such a traditionally prickly character is unknown, though considering his wide-ranging adven-tures, it must not come as a surprise that he has friends in the most remarkable places.

three

The GHOST *of* CASTLE HILL

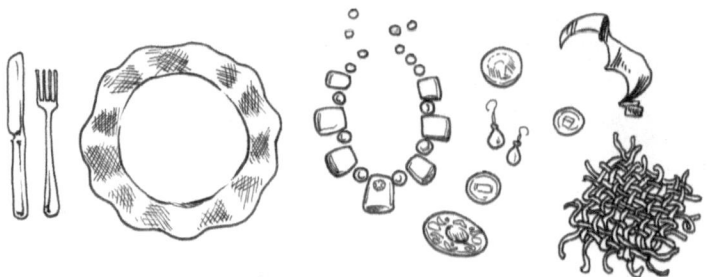

Note on the Language and Alphabet of Cairdra

This story contains many Cairdric words and names. Because the alphabet of Cairdra is a confusing one I have chosen to use the traditional Kyrish spellings for all the names, as these are pronounced phonetically. In cases of the language being spoken, or to help illustrate the differences between Kyrish and Cairdric, I have preserved the Cairdric spelling. To help my readers puzzle out the correct pronunciation for these words, I have attached a pronunciation guide to the Cairdric alphabet at the end of this story, as well as translations for all the Cairdric words contained herein.

—G.O.

WHEN I COLLECTED THE MAIL one spring evening in 2312 I noticed a letter that seemed rather the worse for wear. It was postmarked a week before, and water had washed out much of the address. Only my friend's name was legible, and this explained why it had been successfully delivered at all; for every postman in the city knew where to find the famous magician, Mr Bouragner Felpz.

Had they come inside the house between King's Street and Bridgeton Way that evening, however, they would have been sadly disappointed in him. When I returned with the mail I found him in the sitting room as I had left him: staring despondently out the window into the lively spring sunset.

There was something about the springtime, with its turning of weather and the brightening of the air, that brought with it a disturbance in the ambient magics to which my friend was so finely attuned. Such was his sensitivity that this disruption could send him into the most tiring fits of apathy and ill temper, made worse by the physical ailments that often accompanied them.

That evening was a typical example of such. He lay sprawled on the sofa surrounded by an ever-increasing mess of soiled handkerchiefs, which he would conjure out of the air whenever he felt a sneeze or coughing fit coming upon him. A pitiful sight in his faded lavender dressing gown, with his normally neat head of dark hair all ruffled and standing on end, and his eyes red-rimmed, he would have elicited sympathy from anyone. Except myself. I had been confronted with this fixture in my home for the better part of the last week and knew full well that his problems mostly stemmed from boredom and that his symptoms could be easily relieved by a little excitement. So it was with little tact that I left his letters on the pile of kerchiefs nearest and went briskly back to my writing desk.

I heard, but paid no heed to, the sounds of pathetic coughing and the crinkle of papers as he opened the letters and read their contents. I was loath to admit my interest in the water-stained envelope, and forcibly kept my back to him. Silence, blissful silence, descended as he read his mail.

"Have you ever been to Bruin Cair Frell, Corianne?" he asked after some minutes. His voice sounded stronger, free of coughs or hitches and more like its usual deep and resonant self. I chanced a glance around.

Bouragner Felpz was looking at me alertly from under a wing of raised dark eyebrow, the one brown eye visible twinkling in the gaslight. He was holding the damaged letter carefully in both hands.

"I can't say I have. That is in Cairdra, is it not?" I replied, smiling at the surprise on his face. "My daughter studied briefly in Trefellin. At one point she sent me some rather fancifully illustrated brochures in an attempt to induce me to visit," I explained.

"Well," said Felpz generously, as if the girl could not be blamed for this, "it is a somewhat fanciful place. Cair Frell is deep in the mountains among green-sided valleys and frothing white rivers, and do you know what it means? Cair Frell? Castle Hill. Hardly definitive in a country replete with both. But beautiful country; their sheep produce the softest wool, and they make a good mead—at least they did three hundred years ago." He folded the letter and looked straight at me, all trace of distemper gone from his face. Silently I thanked the sender of that bedraggled letter.

"Would you like to go there?" he asked, radiating good will.

I narrowed my eyes and looked again at the letter, a little shrewdly. Long experience of my friend's moods told me this had not been brought on by a social invitation. No, there was some calamity, some magical mystery, that called to his sense of investigation and adventure—only that could have caused such a radical improvement in him.

"Tell me what is in that letter first," I said.

"Oh pooh," said Felpz, vaulting himself off the sofa and shedding kerchiefs everywhere. "There will be time enough on the journey tomorrow; the Cairdrians never really got the hang of trains, and I suspect we will be on the road all day."

I sighed and went to pack my travel case.

The capricious spring weather, which had been holding sunnily for the past week, saw fit to send us a rainstorm as we pulled out of Redling. Fat drops of water splattered on the windows, and the landscape was streaked with grey and silver as we pulled out of the city. But it was a gentle storm, and the patter of water on the roof provided a pleasant backdrop to our conversation.

"Now, Felpz," I said, folding my hands in my lap, "I have you sufficiently trapped. So what is it which calls you forth on this errand?"

Felpz accepted my gentle barb with good humor, and readily handed over the battered envelope, along with a small book with *Legends of Cyrdry* stamped in peeling gold letters on the front.

"Be so good as to read it aloud to me," he said, lacing his fingers behind his head and leaning back, his eyes closed. "You always manage to clarify things so wonderfully. Then you may turn to page thirty-eight of that book; it contains an entry there which you may find relevant to the matter at hand."

Obligingly I removed the letter and smoothed it out on my knee before holding it up to the light, beginning to pick my way through the scratchy writing.

This is what I read:

Magician,

You will not know me, and we have never met, but I know well of you. I provided sanctuary to your friend Abharus in his time of need, and you may ask him to vouch for me. In fact I ask that you do, for I wish you to have no doubt in your mind that what I tell you is the truth, and that we have very real need of you in Brvyn Cayr Mhryl. ["That is Bruin Cair Frell spelled in the traditional Cairdrian manner, but it is pronounced the same." Felpz interjected when I stumbled over the spelling.]

am no great hand at letters, but since it was I who first saw the ghost, I feel it best that I lay down what happened in my own words, and strive to give you as much detail as I possibly can.

Know first that I am Raddyc dyl Morgvn ["That is pronounced Rathic del Morgun, or near enough," Felpz provided helpfully] and though I wandered wide in the world as a young man, lately I found myself longing for the white-capped mountains and steep green valleys of my native lands, and returned to Trymhylyn ["Trefellin, dear Corianne. Do you remember nothing of the Cairdric alphabet?"] to find that the land missed me as much as I had missed it. I took up residence below Cayr Mhryl and there established myself as an herbman, using the knowledge gained during my travels to help my native people. And though I flatter myself that there is no one in the country who knows plants and their properties as well as I, and though this knowledge extends to those with magical attributes, my interests have always lain in the practical—I have little knowledge of the vagaries of this world's mystical side.

My story begins some months ago, on a full moon night that was so bright I woke mistaking it for day. Finding the night so brilliant and beautiful, and my mind and body awake, I took a walk upon the paths that cross the Brvyn. As I reached the summit of the hill I glanced back and thought I saw a light upon the path below. Yet when I looked again all was in darkness.

Returning to my walk I crossed the summit, where there are still ruins of the old castle that once stood atop the hill. The path threads its way between pieces of wall and piles of treacherous stones, which were coal black in the moonlight. Rounding a large piece of ruin I came upon a sight I will not soon forget: laid out before me on the path was a pale figure—no larger than a child—which glowed in the moonlight with a soft golden radiance.

I shook my head at such a vision, and when I looked again the apparition was gone—only a puddle of dark mud lay upon the path.

Now somewhat disconcerted I made my way back home as swiftly as I dared. I went back up the hill the very next day, but could find no trace of the apparition.

The next week passed in peace, and I had begun to believe that I had dreamt the whole strange experience, when one night I was woken by a mad howling outside my door.

My neighbor down the vale keeps sheepdogs to protect his flock, and I recognized their baying. Unable to sleep from the noise I peered out my window, and saw there on the side of the hill a light that flitted about and glinted gold. I watched for many hours, and as time passed I came to believe I saw the pale legs of a child running naked upon the night grass, clothed only in a glittering golden cape. It was then that I remembered the legend of Brvyn Cayr Mhryl, and the ghost that is said to dwell there.

So much I understood come the morning, but after that there was no sign of the ghost for many weeks. Yet in recent days it has appeared again, always at night, and always upon the Brvyn Cayr Mhryl. Many of the younger folk from Trymhylyn have been out to see it, and they (who do not keep our native tongue as well as I would like) have begun to call it the Ghost of Castle Hill, and go up to tease it for sport.

All of which, though alarming, would not be enough for me to write to you. Except that now one of these foolish youths—a student, I understand, from Dunchurch—has gone missing, and I fear that this ghost is no harmless spirit. In any case, Brvyn Cayr Mhryl is haunted, and I feel the solution is entirely out of my grasp.

I would be unspeakably indebted if you would come and show this your most sharp and urgent attention.

Sincerely yours,

Raddyc dyl Morgvn
Herbman, Brvyn Cayr Mhryl
Cyrdry
4 of March, 2312

"But this was written almost three weeks ago!" I exclaimed when I had finished.

Felpz shrugged. "Time passed cannot be regained. The best we can do is go there as swiftly as possible. Are you familiar with the tale of the Bruin Cair Frell ghost?"

I had to admit that I was not. Felpz tapped the little book he had handed me along with the letter. "Page thirty-eight," he repeated. "It will clarify his story somewhat."

Dutifully I turned to the prescribed page. As it is a short legend, and bears directly on this present story, I will reproduce it here.

From Legends of Cyrdry, *Chapter 8.*

THE GOLDEN CLOAK

Long ago in a green valley on a hill there was a castle. On a dark and stormy night a ragged peasant girl came to the door and asked admittance from the rain. The guards were quick to sneer at such a poor thing, but the girl offered them the hair off her head. Pulling back her hood the guards were astonished to see that her hair was of the finest shining gold, and they quickly agreed. They let her inside and sat her down by the fire, where they sheared off her gold hair at the roots. While the guards were gloating over their gold, the girl got up and walked down and down, down to the bottom of the lowest cellar, where she lay down and died. They found her in the morning, as cold as the stones she lay on.

The lord and lady of the castle were saddened by this, and had the poor girl buried in a lead coffin in the castle chapel. Her hair, which was threads of the finest gold, they had woven into a magnificent cloak that the lady wore on special occasions.

But ever after, it was said, the castle was haunted by the ghost of the girl, who drifted from room to room, wailing in a low, beseeching voice. The lord and lady found they did not like to live there anymore, and eventually they left, taking their retainers and servants and guards with them. And the lady laid the gold cloak, woven of the girl's hair, upon her body, and sealed the coffin shut.

Now the castle is a ruin, but the hill remains. And if you go walking there at night, you may meet a pale ghost clothed only in a cape of shimmering gold. If you do, best give her any gold you have upon you; she will repay you with safe passage through the night.

Thoughtfully I closed the book and handed both it and the letter back. "You think it is the same ghost?" I asked.

Felpz hummed to himself as he slipped the items back into his pocket. He smiled at me, but said nothing.

We changed trains in Grenling, and thence began our journey into Cairdra. Now we rode in a somewhat rundown carriage that bumped and clattered over rough points and climbed slowly into the green and blue hills. These were of a steeper, rockier variety than the downs of Dales or the Halsteppes, more vibrant and packed close with glossy-leafed trees on their north sides. These sparkled in the sun from the rain, as the clouds retreated to crouch low upon the mountains.

We reached Trefellin in the afternoon, and it was a wonderful relief after the stuffy air of the train to step forth into the bright sunlight and breathe in the crisp, rain-sweetened air. Such was my delight at the change of scenery that when we discovered that the only train to Cair Frell had left an hour previous my spirits were not dampened in the slightest.

"Never mind," I said as we came away from the ticket counter—having had to content ourselves with purchasing tickets for the following day. "Milain could never speak highly enough of the Goodihoo Teahouse, I'm sure they will know of a suitable place to put us up for the night. And"—I ruffled through my daughter's letters, which I had pasted into a book for convenience's sake—"I wonder if the Thrag Evith Emporium is still in business. Milain says they have the best selection of native bronzeware."

Bouragner Felpz looked at me, a trifled bemused.

"And what am I to do, dearest Corianne, while you are plying yourself with tea and perusing knick-knacks?" he asked, making a valiant attempt at consternation.

"Why my darling Felpz," I said, affecting surprise. "I thought you would be all over sticking that long nose of yours into the business of Trefellin. After all, this is where Rathic's disappearing students are from. Perhaps you may be able to root out some knowledge that will aid you in solving this mystery. Oh, but stay with me," I added, grasping his elbow to make sure, "at least until we have secured lodgings for tonight, and know where you may find me come evening." So speaking I led him out of the station in the direction of High Street.

Despite my daughter's excellent directions and the use of a penny map obtained from a street vendor, Goodihoo Teahouse proved elusive, until Felpz pointed out the sign of an owl perched on the letters "GVDEHV" and suggested that might be my selfsame "Goodihoo" in Cairdric. We entered, and were greeted by a charming man of middle years. They remembered my daughter, and were happy to recommend the Te Gwyn—an inn which was conveniently located around the corner. Felpz and I agreed that we should meet there in the common room at seven, and leaving me to see our bags installed he took off in a flutter of purple coattails.

For my part I spent a delightful afternoon in the upper room of Goodihoo's lounge, watching the procession along the street from the vantage point of a bow window, and writing industriously. When evening came I retired to the inn, and unpacked a book to read while I waited for Felpz.

Seven o'clock came and went with no sign of him, and I supped alone. That is, I took my evening meal without the company of my friend; for it proved I was not the only traveler to turn to Te Gwyn for hospitality that night. Seated at the table directly behind me were two young, vociferous women in drooping black dresses that clacked as they moved from all the beads sewn onto them. As I dove bravely into the extremely Cairdric supper the kitchen had supplied, I couldn't help but overhear their talk, for they spoke in that particular kind of whisper that is meant to say *we are speaking confidentially to one another* but is nevertheless audible to everyone in the vicinity.

I attempted to ignore them for as long as I could, but lacking any other distractions I eventually gave in to shameless eavesdropping.

"He puts too much store in his precious *magician*," one was saying when I began paying attention. "But how long has it been? Two weeks? Three? A month? And not a word back. The man is either far too busy to pay attention to a country bush wizard like our Rathic, or he doesn't exist at all."

"I heard he was *killed*," said the other, with surprising relish. "Knocked out in a duel with a *fairy*."

The first girl made a derisive noise.

It was with some amazement that I realized they were referring to my friend. I had half a mind to turn around and tell them what for, but rationalized that I would learn more—and therefore be of better assistance to Felpz—if I kept quiet and marked what was said.

There was the scrape of cutlery on porcelain as one of the women tore viciously at her food. "There's no trusting these city mages either way," she said. "Got no sense of country history."

The other girl made noises of agreement. "Look at the Dunchurch student—it's a wonder *he's* not dead."

"As good as, though," murmured the first woman. "What a *foolish* boy—did his mother never tell him not to chase after ghosts? Run, yes, but in the *other direction*."

Her companion actually *tittered* at that, and I couldn't help turning around to get a look at these two insufferable girls.

They were not, it must be said, actual girls. They were, I guessed, older than I had been at the time of my marriage, but with their short, modern haircuts they appeared younger. Though one was light and rosy and the other dark and olive-skinned, they nevertheless gave off the impression of being related. Not sisters, then, but likely cousins.

I had been sitting back to back with the dark one, and in turning I caught the eye of the rosy-cheeked girl. We locked gazes for but a moment, yet I must have let some of my displeasure show in my face, for she quickly looked away, and after that they finished their meal in silence.

Felpz did not appear that night either, and I regret to say I fretted over this more than I ought. I dreamed that a tall man entered our rooms and stood uncertainly by the door. I asked, in the vague way of dreams, whether he was Felpz. He said he was not, and in my dream I saw that this was so, for this man was sandy-haired, and though tall he had none of the assured bearing and carriage of my friend. I told him sharply to go away, which he did, and I fell back into dreamless slumber.

The two women were already at breakfast when I came down the following morning—refreshed from my rest and determined to *enjoy* my day, Felpz or no. No sooner had my meal arrived, however, than Felpz sat down across from me in a whirl of purple coat.

"Tell me you won't be finishing that, Corianne," he said. "For I think I could eat a breakfast and a half today."

My joy and relief at seeing him was eclipsed only by my delight in the girls' reaction to his appearance. For this time I had made sure to sit where I could keep them in view, and at my friend's words both their heads snapped round and they stared with blatant incredulity.

This so amused me that I cheerfully gave Felpz my breakfast, and went to order another for myself.

"Don't even try to tell me what you have been up to," I said, watching Felpz tuck into his meal. "It can wait for the train ride to Cair Frell." This was in part only decent, considering how hungry he obviously was, but I was also loath to give my erstwhile dinner companions any kind of explanation.

"I hope your day was satisfactory," Felpz said once we were installed on the train to Cair Frell. He had the grace to look apologetic, which charmed me.

"Sufficiently so," I replied, and recounted the conversation I had overheard the evening prior.

My friend threw back his head and laughed heartily at the girls' description of him, but he frowned and knotted his hands under his chin when I mentioned the Dunchurch student.

"Not dead but as good as . . . " he repeated thoughtfully. "That is troubling."

"He must have been found, at least," I said. "If they are able to say that with any certainty."

"Partly found," Felpz murmured, turning to stare moodily out the window.

I asked him what he meant by that, but he would not reply, and to my queries as to how he had passed his day he would only smile and shrug.

"Preliminary actions," he said eventually, and lapsed into silence for the remainder of our journey.

The train shuddered over the tracks, and the old, dingy windows rattled in their frames. As we climbed out of the vale of Trefellin I saw the hills rise into sloping green mountains, some of them so high that their tops were singed purple-brown, or lost in the low-hanging white clouds. A thin, spitting mist descended from them in the late morning, streaking against the windows and obscuring the view further.

We stopped several times but never passed through any towns; all I could see were snug homesteads, nestled in green valleys or perched on rain-swept headlands. This reminded me of the old lore regarding Cairdra: that when the Kyres swept up from the southeast, unifying the disparate kingdoms into the country's present state, the Cairdrian culture survived largely intact by virtue of the fact that, upon sight of Arell's advancing army, they disappeared into the hills and could not be found for many years. Seeing the isolated fashion in which so many modern Cairdrians chose to live, it was clear to me that the independent spirit which had defined their people for so many ages was still living strong.

Felpz finally roused himself, and we exited at a station that was to my eyes no different than the ones we had already passed: a line of wooden buildings with a small stable attached to one end, and a single house a little ways uphill.

The porter performed a comical double-take at the sight of Felpz, and actually tripped over the toes of his boots as he scrambled across the wet platform towards us.

"Bless my heart sir," he said, in a barely decipherable Cairdric brogue. "I must apologize, but it's you, sir, it's really *you.*"

"I should hope I am myself," Felpz said amicably, allowing the flustered man to shake his hand.

"Only, we'd all but given up hope of hearing from you—and, ha! *Here you are.*" He laughed, his wrinkled prune of a mouth stretching into a smile as warm and bright as a newborn babe's. "Rathic will be beside himself. Why, look at me! *I'm* beside myself. That I can tell my grandchildren I've shaken Bouragner d'Felpass *by the hand*—I'd never!"

I saw a perfect stillness descend on my friend at the sound of his old, full name. He went like a statue, the only movement being the mist that swirled around him and glinted as it settled on his hat and coat; his face frozen into an expression of mixed shock, amazement, and a glimmer of what might have been joy.

"You remember me?" he said, and it was only due to my intimate knowledge of the man that I caught the lift and strain in his voice, the only sign of how truly agitated he was.

The porter, bless him, was oblivious to the revelation he had bestowed upon my friend. "Of course we *remember,*" he said, all smiles. "We *preserve* our stories, here in Cair Frell. I tell you, there's not a lad nor lass worth their feet that wouldn't know you at sight. But look at me I'm coming all to pieces. Come along, ma'am, I'll take those bags. I'll put you in the coach with Hunith—she brought it down on account of those university ladies what were too fine for Ghedvale's cart, but I couldn't bear it if we didn't give the *promhor devyn* our best. Step right this way, sir, just this way."

So speaking we were led off the platform, and glancing behind I just glimpsed the two women from the inn descending from the train. A part of me was seized with the desire to see their reactions when the porter returned, but I pushed the unwholesome feeling away.

Hunith turned out to be a young, lissome girl, made bulky by the many layers of coats she wore to protect herself from the weather. The coach was old and smelled of mold, but it was warm and dry within, and I soon became glad of it—indeed I felt quite sorry for poor Hunith, who sat out in the open. Yet the girl was resolutely bright, and when I voiced my concern she only laughed.

"You've not been here for a winter, mother," she called back through the stinging rain. "This is what we call a *mild* day." She glanced back at us, smiling fit to burst, perhaps to demonstrate just how impervious she was to the precipitation, but I saw how her eyes lingered on Felpz, grown wide with wonder, before she whipped her head round again to concentrate on steering the bushy-maned pony over the road that climbed the shoulder of the hill.

"You made quite an impression the last time you were here," I remarked to Felpz with a sly grin.

"That was in my younger days," Felpz replied, a wry twist to his mouth. "I am not sure whether to be pleased or disturbed that they remember."

I opened my mouth in a silent "ah," for I knew well that when Felpz referred to his "younger days" he meant a time centuries past, and I probed no further. Experience had taught me that my friend was loath to delve into the deep well of his unnaturally long life, and I deemed it best not to pry where he was reluctant to go.

The road wound on, twining such that we reached the summit of the ridge without ever seeming to strain uphill. There a green valley, cloven by a frothing white river, opened out below us. Though the wind blew a grey, misty rain across it, all the trees had put out their spring foliage and the bright new growth seemed to stretch and unfurl into the welcome moisture. I saw roofs nestled in the folds of the hills as they sloped down to the watercourse, but no central collection that would indicate a town.

Hunith pulled the coach to a halt, and pointed with one well-wrapped arm to a promontory of rock and earth that jutted incongruously from a smooth green slope.

"There you can see Castle Hill," she called back to us. "What we call the *Brvyn Cayr Mhryl*. Rathic keeps the house on the far side. I should have you at his doorstep by dinnertime."

It was a long ride down into the valley of Cair Frell, for the road wound back and forth along the side of the inner slope as much as it had the outer. However, this proved to render the journey much more comfortable, and afforded us good views of Castle Hill from many directions.

I have called it incongruous. I say this because all the land around it was gently sloping green, mottled with patches of forest. A soft land, whose bones lay deep beneath a protective layer of earth. Castle Hill jutted from the side of one of these sloping arms, where the earth had fallen away, and in its place rose a tumble of brown rock, glossy dark in the rain. Green things grew in the cracks between the stones, and at its summit I could just make out the frail remnants of a human castle: a part of a turret or a piece of wall. There was so little left I could not imagine what it would have looked like when whole, but even without that mental image I could see it would have commanded a dominant presence in this valley. Whoever had built it, and later lived in it, must have held great power over the land.

Lost in thought, I did not realize that I had spoken these musings aloud until Felpz replied.

"The foundations are Crowan," he said. "Beyond that, not enough remains to be able to say with any certainty who lived there."

"But *you* know," I said, giving him a shrewd glance.

Felpz raised his brows, all innocence. "I hope this does not come as a crushing disillusion," he said with a sheepish laugh, "but I do not know all things. The Castle of Cair Frell was raised by a Crowan garrison, but it fell into ruin sometime in the Dark Ages; those problematic centuries that lie between the two Wizard Wars. Even in my youth we knew little enough of what went on then, save convoluted folktales such as the one you read yesterday. I had to go to great lengths to discover anything more material, and when that opportunity presented itself, I confess I had larger matters on my mind and did not bother to inquire after the inhabitants of a small Cairdric castle."

"I do know," he said after some minutes of brooding silence. "I do know who lived in the hill beneath. Or at least *what*. Oh yes," he said, seeing my surprised expression. "That is no ordinary hill. It is right there in the name, in fact: *Bruin*. Oh, there are no concrete records, but I have seen others of its kind. *Cair* is a castle of the kind humans build; the sort that sits atop the ground. *Bruin* is a castle made by the fae folk; a castle beneath the earth. Yes, there are two castles of Castle Hill," he said with a laugh. "And one of them is still very much intact, if no less deserted."

Armed with this knowledge I looked again at Castle Hill, and indeed the jumble of rocks made much more sense now, if one believed they had been brought there and shaped by fairies. A hill on the outside, a palace within, which would open to admit only those whom the fae lord deemed worthy—but now long abandoned. The humans that they had preyed upon for so long had come and built their own castle atop the one built by the fae. And even after that human castle had fallen into ruin, now humanity's modest homes and farms gathered close, and they walked upon the fairy hill not knowing what lay beneath their feet.

Then I cast a glance at Hunith, who had said nothing but drove with one ear cocked toward us and no doubt overheard at least some of our words, and wondered if perhaps they knew very well indeed.

We crossed the river at a stout stone bridge that joined two halves of what passed for the center of Cair Frell. Hunith explained this was the domain of Munegir, who had the largest holding in the valley and opened his house to the people of the town as a place for public meetings and council. Hunith worked a portion of his land, and it had been from his stable that the pony and coach had been acquired. Common courtesy dictated we stay with him, or at least stop and pay our respects, but Felpz was growing impatient by then, and insisted we press on to Rathic's house.

Such was the reverence the people of Cair Frell held for my friend that Hunith did not protest at all, and we drove past the hall and across the bridge with hardly a break in our speed.

A darkness was closing in on the grey mist, but the rain had abated as we began our final ascent up to the base of Castle Hill. This passed with uncommon swiftness, and it seemed in no time we were making our way round the curve of the hill itself, the rocks and ruins hidden in the mist above us, and there, twinkling from within a little grove of old, thick-trunked oaks, were the yellow lights of Rathic's house.

Hunith, who I guessed knew these roads from childhood, must have noticed this trick of my friend's, but she seemed quite unperturbed at her abbreviated journey, lighting down to hitch the pony to the post and then coming around to unload our bags, even as the door to the little house burst open and Rathic came stumbling out.

He was an old, grey-haired man. Short, but broad shouldered, and he walked with a sturdy, rolling gait. I had hardly clambered down from the coach before he was clasping Felpz's hand, pouring out effusive praise and gratitude, and then giving me the same treatment.

"It's not as if I haven't seen a strange thing or two in my time," he was saying as he led us inside. "But this one takes my hat and sits on it. I simply don't know what to do—"

He might have gone on, but was interrupted by a muffled thudding sound from the coach, and we turned to find poor Hunith had collapsed under the weight of Felpz's trunk.

Felpz fairly levitated to her side, lifting the offending piece of luggage off her.

"Never mind me, sir," Hunith said, her pride as a hardy Cairdrian country girl at stake. She struggled to her feet and managed to wrestle the handle out of Felpz's grasp. "Took me by surprise is all. I've had to carry sheep what were worse than this, yes, and for longer." With a heroic effort she managed to lift the case a few inches off the ground, and hurried it away inside before any of us could stop her.

Rathic's house was a comfortable, low-beamed place, smelling strongly of the herbs he collected. Pots and jars decorated any available flat surface, and a large cauldron sat over the fire in the hearth. Bunches of herbs and dried flowers hung from the rafters, in perilous close proximity to the lanterns hanging from same. These had been lit, as the darkness had closed in prematurely because of the mist and now clung close to the small-paned windows.

Rathic generously shared his dinner between us, and took out a fresh loaf to give to Hunith to keep her company on her journey home. Once we had seen her depart he turned to Felpz with a grim expression.

"I did not like to say anything with the girl present; the locals have been precious calm all these weeks, and I don't want to upset them."

"You believe this apparition to be . . . malevolent?" Felpz asked, taking a seat at the low parlor table and crossing his legs.

"Let me first give you a better explanation of past events," Rathic insisted. "Go on and eat your dinner while I talk, for you must be tired after your journey."

I ate. Felpz seemed too fascinated by Rathic's story to touch his food, but sat leaning back in the home-carved wooden chair, his hands neatly folded in his lap, his eyes fixed brightly on our host.

"You know enough of the history of this place," Rathic began. "And I trust your companion does as well. It's not uncommon knowledge. Well, let me tell you, the news of *the* ghost of Cair Frell seen again in modern times, it quite took fire over in Trefellin, and from there spread outwards into Kyreland. We had a group of students up the next week. All young, brash men. Not the sort to pay any heed to old folktales. They went up to the hill and held vigils there seven nights in a row, and on the seventh they came down one short. Harlan Corder was—er, is— his name. It was his disappearance that caused me to write to you."

"But now we hear he has reappeared," Felpz prompted.

"After a fashion, yes," said Rathic with a heavy sigh. "They have his body down at Munegir's hall. His colleagues wanted to take him to the hospital in Trefellin, but his condition began to deteriorate the farther he got from Cair Frell. He's unconscious, you see. A *coma*, the doctor called it. He lies there still as stone, hardly breathing, his heart beating so slow and weak that you could miss it. The local lads who found him took him for dead at first."

"I will have to see him," Felpz declared. "But first, tell me all that has happened since you wrote, and the *exact* circumstances of Mr Corder's disappearance . . . and reappearance."

"As for Mr Corder that is simple enough," said Rathic. "He was missed from his vigil on the seventh night—I understand the lads held it in the dark, and when dawn came he had inexplicably vanished. No sight, no sound had disturbed them in the night. He was simply . . .

spirited away. He was discovered a week later, lying in a dell below Cair Frell. It was a funny thing, though. The boys that found him said he was lying curled on his side, as though he had lain down to sleep and never woken. Also there were leaves and twigs caught in his clothing, as though he had been forging through the bushes—as he would have had to to reach his resting place."

"Likely, then, that he walked there himself?" I offered.

"Walked," conceded Felpz. "Or was led."

We all paused to consider the implications of this.

"Well," said Rathic briskly. "Since then we've had no end of trouble. Tourists and students and ghost hunters from all over. We make them stay in Trefellin, though. We're a quiet holding, Cair Frell, and between us I don't think the ghost likes them."

"You have seen it since?"

"Sometimes," said Rathic. "She's not shy about showing herself—except to curious students—but I can't stay up all hours. Hunith sees her most, I think, for she goes on night rounds. She says the ghost rarely comes down from the hill, but that she is always running and leaping about, looking in crannies and corners, searching for something. She makes faces at you if she catches you watching."

"Does this ghost always appear the same?"

"All the reports are consistent: a young girl, head shorn, wearing only a white shift and a cloak of gleaming gold."

Felpz leaned forward at this, and I could tell he was truly interested. "This cloak . . . can you describe it?"

"I can do better, *devyn*," said Rathic, his chest swelling with pleasure. Taking down a hand-bound book he opened it and removed a rough-edged piece of paper. "For I did see her once since writing to you, and quite close at that. I came upon her all of a sudden, standing in the path up to the Frell. I got a good look at the cloak, and have drawn a likeness here."

Felpz took the paper, glanced at it, and nodded—as if it contained exactly what he expected to see. "You will like this Corianne," he said, passing it to me. "Perhaps you can add it to the file you are no doubt keeping on this case."

I quickly cleaned my hands on the tablecloth, but seeing Rathic's expression I added hastily: "I would want only to make a copy." Taking the drawing carefully I could see why Rathic would be pained to part with the original: it was a beautiful picture rendered in a skilled, delicate hand. It showed a short cloak with a high, curving collar, made of a heavy and detailed weave that formed itself into swirls and knots around the edges. Shield-like plates were joined across the shoulders in an angular pattern, and dark circles suggested the places where stones might have been placed. I fear the copy I did eventually make and which I include here does not do Rathic's original justice, but it will give the reader a good idea of what the garment looked like.

"You are familiar with the legend of the Ghost of Castle Hill?" Rathic asked anxiously.

"We refreshed our memory of it on the way here," Felpz assured him. "But I think there is more going on now than what was told then."

Seeing that I had finished eating he stood up abruptly. "I have a mind to visit Mr Corder's body," he announced, but his eyes darted in the direction of the hill, which loomed large and invisible beyond Rathic's parlor window, and I could tell he had more in mind for the night.

"I would be a poor host to let you go alone," Rathic said, levering himself to his feet.

I excused myself this time. After two days of travel and Rathic's excellent dinner I felt tired and lethargic, and not at all in the mood to go cavorting across Cairdrian hills at night—as I knew Felpz intended to do.

Felpz was made to wait while Rathic showed me to his guest room and saw I had everything I wanted, but then at last they were off into the night, and I could relax and set about the pleasurable task of catching up on my journal and making my copy of Rathic's drawing.

I must have fallen asleep in my chair, for I was woken by the sudden feeling that I was being watched. Blinking my eyes open I saw this was indeed the case: a man stood in the open doorway, pale in the dim light of my low-burning candle.

My initial alarm and consternation were quenched as I looked again, and saw that his face was drawn tight in panic and he was visibly shaking. Such a sorry creature it was impossible to fear, and I found myself bounding out of my chair, the weariness gone from my bones.

"Forgive me," I cried. "I did not hear you enter. Rathic's not at home, I'm afraid, but please sit down. You look like you've had a bad turn—let me warm you some bread and brew a pot . . . "

I trailed off, for at my words the man had begun to gape, then gasp, and finally turned on his heel and fled the room.

A man in that condition, and only in his shirtsleeves, should not be allowed out at night! This was the only thought in my head as I took off after him, taking up my shawl from the peg by the door, and following him out into the dark.

I could see him still as a tall, pale streak on the dim road, and that sight brought back to me my dream of the previous night.

"Wait!" I called after him, wrapping my shawl tight as I pursued him.

The man stopped—so abruptly that I nearly hurtled into his back. As it was I grabbed his arm firmly—both to steady myself and to prevent him flying off again. He turned to me, his face pale as a sheet and that mad panic still dancing behind his eyes.

"Who *are* you?" I demanded.

He stared at me, his mouth agape. In a strangled whisper, he said: "I'm Harlan Corder."

I stared at him, thunderstruck. He was certainly the man from my dream, but he was also just as certainly real and solid.

"Well, have no fear of me, boy," I assured him, trying to soothe his nerves. "I've come with my friend, the magician. We are here to help."

Harlan Corder was a plain man in his early twenties with an untidy crop of straw-colored hair and large amber eyes. These were pinned on me now with an expression . . . well . . . as if he had seen a ghost.

"Who are *you?*" he gasped, and before I could answer he went tumbling on in a ragged, breathy voice: "How is it you can see me? *Touch* me? Is this some new trick of hers?"

The questions broke over me like waves on a shore, and I let myself be pushed and pulled by them. The poor man must have woken up and run off, thinking himself still a ghost. Astonishing that he had made it all the way to Rathic's house unseen.

"My name is Corianne Birch," I said, relaxing my grip on his arm somewhat, but laying a soothing hand on his back. "I saw your apparition in a dream last night, and now I see you here. I can touch you because you are a man like any other—and as for tricks, I don't know of any. Who is this woman you speak of?"

Harlan Corder did not answer, but I saw him glance furtively upwards, behind Rathic's house. The Castle Hill, I realized, still loomed behind us, and I took his meaning.

"Is she angry with you?" I asked urgently; for if the ghost was volatile I did not want to meet it alone and without Felpz's protection.

"Not with me," gasped Harlan Corder. "But yes, she is very angry."

"I see," I said, trying to sound calm while my mind worked furiously. It would do no good to remain out here and catch a chill with a tormented spirit on the loose—though it seemed the mist had lifted, and it was actually a mild spring night. Better to get Corder indoors, warmed and calmed, and wait for Felpz to return.

But when would that be? Felpz had gone to see Corder's body at Munegir's hall. What would he do when he discovered it missing? He might take off and begin searching the roads for it—never guessing that I had him safe and sound at Rathic's house. Knowing Felpz, there was no guarantee that I would see him again this night—or even tomorrow morning.

How long had I slept? Long enough for Felpz and Rathic to have reached the hall—especially with Felpz's way of speeding up journeys. There would be people there. Witnesses Felpz would want to question. There was a chance, if we hurried, that he might still be there when we arrived. At any rate, there would be *other people* who would help me take care of Corder and who knew this land intimately and could be sent out in search of Felpz should he be absent.

It had not seemed like such a long way from the bridge to Rathic's house, though I realized this was due to Felpz's interference. But I remembered seeing the path of the road from across the valley, and knew we only need follow it to be taken down to Munegir's hall.

All this passed through my mind in an instant, and Corder was still gazing at me with mixed wonder and fear when I set off down the road—propelling him in front of me.

"Come along," I said when he resisted. "My friend went down to Munegir's hall—if we hurry we may catch him, or perhaps meet him on his way back. You did not pass two men on your way here? One short and grey-haired, the other tall, dark, and clothed in purple?"

Corder looked bewildered. Who knew what rambling route he had taken on his trek, I reasoned. Upon closer inspection he did look as though he had been forging through the undergrowth: there were grass stains on his knees and leaves caught on his coat.

"Never mind," I said cheerfully, taking his hand as he fell in beside me. "Felpz will sort everything out, you'll see."

It proved to be a long walk in the dark, but we went briskly, and the night air was so fresh and sweet I never felt tired or sore-footed. The moon, a waning crescent, was high in the sky over the shoulder of a green mountain, and by its weak light we were better able to see the road before us.

At last we came around a bend and there, nestled in the crook of the valley, were the many lights of Munegir's hall, bright against the dark landscape. I could hear the rushing of the river and caught glimpses of it as flecks of white in the black corridor of its bed.

We came down the road in sweeping bends, crossed the river at the stone bridge, and hurried into the courtyard of the hall.

Here I half expected to see a stablehand at least, but it was deserted. However, torches burning by the doors and a low hum of voices within suggested that the homestead was still awake and active.

I marched up to the wide front door—Corder having slipped timidly behind me—and banged the knocker sharply.

There was a momentary lull in the murmur of voices, and a few moments later the door was heaved open by a young lad of no more than ten. At the time I thought he must be blinded by the torches and we standing too far back in the dark; for he glanced outside and spoke no word, showed no sign of having seen us, and seemed puzzled. I had just opened my mouth to speak when the door was dragged shut again in our faces.

I blinked, quite astonished at this rudeness. I reached out and knocked again.

When this produced no response whatsoever, I shrugged and tried opening the door myself. It was heavy and old, but I put my shoulder to it and was able to shove it open wide enough for us to enter.

The little hall beyond was deserted—the boy clearly having felt he'd done his duty, not having heard my second knock—but there was light streaming in from a nearby door, and beyond that the swell of many voices talking at once. I caught a few shrill words from a familiar female voice—one of those insufferable girls from Trefellin!—and below that the calm, soothing rumble of Felpz.

At the sound my heart went limp with relief. He was *still* here. I could discharge Corder into his capable hands, and find someone to make me a cup of tea.

I pulled Corder—who had gone inexplicably stiff—toward the doorway.

We emerged onto a crowded scene: the doorway opened onto a long hall, half filled with a great table, with lamps hung from the ceiling. Chairs that should have been set up along the table had been pushed back against the wall by the storm of people gathered around it. These were mostly strangers to me, though I glimpsed Hunith near the back, and Rathic standing at one end. There too were the girls from the inn, dressed very fine in more clacking black dresses, standing opposite Rathic. The rest were obviously locals, mostly men and a few women in plain clothes of grey, green and brown. These all looked over fifty, save the boy I had glimpsed earlier. This one was in the process of threading his way to the head of the table, pushing himself between bodies.

It took me a few moments to spot Felpz, for he was sitting down with his face lowered to examine something on the table. He only looked up when the boy arrived and began talking to the man sitting next to him, who stood up abruptly.

This was a tall man, weather-beaten like the rest of the locals, but odd in that he had a head of flaming red hair with a beard to match. Though his clothes were no more fine than the rest, something of his bearing asserted authority, and I guessed he must be Munegir.

"Felpz!" I called across the room, pushing my way through the throng of people, who did not seem to see or hear me.

Felpz did, bless him, and shot to his feet. Everyone stared at him, then turned to gaze at where he looked.

"Thank heavens you're still here," I said, pulling the resisting Corder behind me up the newly-formed aisle. "I've found your missing man, awake if not exactly well. Would you believe, he wandered into Rathic's house?"

I meant to chuckle a little, to show that I was not at all bothered, but the laugh died in my throat, replaced by a lump as cold as ice.

The movement of the crowd had afforded me a clear look at the table, and now at last I saw what was lying on it.

It was Harlan Corder.

I suddenly noticed a number of other things as well: how the people in the hall—save Felpz—were not so much looking at Corder and I, but at the place they saw Felpz was looking. How the boy at the door had not seen us, and how only Felpz seemed able to hear my words.

I took a firmer grip on Corder—the Corder who had walked with me to Munegir's hall—and said with what I felt was commendable calm:

"Dear Felpz, do you mind explaining what is going on?"

Felpz stepped clean up onto the table, across the body that lay there, and jumped down the other side, sending the crowd scattering out of his way. He paused as he drew near, hesitant as if we were horses and he feared he would spook us.

"Corianne," he said, a little tightly. "What are you doing here?"

"Bringing you your missing man, I thought," I said, indicating Corder, who was trying to hide behind me. "Only you seem not to have lost him at all."

"Not a ghost," said Felpz, as if speaking to himself. "Not a spirit . . . a . . . *projection*? Corianne, take my hand."

I took his outstretched hand without a second thought. There was a sharp fizz, and something jolted through me. All at once the people in the hall gasped and drew back. A few of them pointed.

This served to convince me that Corder and I had indeed been invisible up until that moment.

"Felpz . . . " I said, trying to keep the waver out of my voice.

"Nothing to worry about," said Felpz briskly. "Tell me, how did you manage the door?"

"The door?" I repeated, dumbly.

"Yes, yes, the *door*. You've gone incorporeal, or hadn't you noticed? How did you manage the front door?"

"I . . . " I looked around, puzzled. "I knocked," I said, my eyes landing on the boy by Munegir's side. "That boy came and opened the door, but he didn't let us in—"

"I dint *see* you, mother!" cried the boy, who was white as a sheet.

"—so I took the handle and . . . well . . . I pushed. It was heavy, but I am not so aged and frail as all that," I added reprovingly.

Felpz leaned back and regarded me with something close to respect in his eyes. I felt my spine straighten in response. But then he turned to Corder and asked:

"Now what have *you* been doing all these weeks?"

Harlan Corder, still holding my hand very tightly, came around to my side. His eyes kept darting about the hall, lingering in shadowy corners.

"She can't reach you here," Felpz assured him. "To be honest, I do not think she meant you any harm at all."

"You can say that when you've seen her," said Corder, the words bursting out of him like water through a breached dam. Then, having spoken, he kept going, the speech pouring out of him.

"I've been right here mostly," he admitted. "I didn't like to go far from . . . " he waved at the body on the table. "Only last week, right, those two ladies came awful close to discovering her bones. And I thought, well, maybe I could get through to them? So I followed them back to Trefellin, but never did they speak to me. Then, last night it was, this lady here shows up. It's hard being far away from my body, see? And—well—she made it feel easier. So I hung around. And I think she saw me—she spoke to me anyway, which was more than anyone had done before. So I followed her back here. Not sure what I intended to do, but when I went to speak to her she sat up and left her body behind, like I'd done. Lady forgive me but I was so shocked I ran away. Only she chased after, like, and she can touch things and move things, and now you can see us and . . . and . . . "

The apparition of Harlan Corder swallowed. His chest heaved, though now I realized I did not hear any air moving in or out. With a sinking sensation I realized why I had felt so light and energetic since waking: one would, I suppose, feel that way without a body to haul around.

"It is all well," Felpz was saying to Corder, soothingly. "The worst is behind you, and we will soon set all to rights. Corianne," he went on, breaking my gloomy thoughts. "Have *you* seen the ghost yet?"

"Not to my knowledge, no," I replied. "But I've only been this way a few hours.

Felpz shrugged. "It may work to our advantage in the end. Corder, is it? I don't suppose you have any knowledge of prehistoric Cairdra?"

"It was my major," Corder admitted.

"Ha!" cried Felpz, and clapped his hands—inadvertently letting go of mine.

There was another collective gasp, and I surmised Corder and I had disappeared. I sighed to myself and refused Felpz's hand when he offered it again. It would be easier, I thought, not to keep on shocking people with disappearances and reappearances.

"Have it your own way," he said. "Only it'll be unpleasant if anyone walks into you; you're much more solid than Corder."

His words made everyone in the hall freeze, including myself. In the relative quiet we all heard the pounding on the front door, and a muffled voice beyond.

The boy at Munegir's side, who looked like he was going to be sick, made a feeble motion to leave. Munegir clapped a hand on his shoulder and shook his head, thereby raising my opinion of the man. He himself left the table—steering well clear of the place he had last seen Corder and I—and disappeared into the entry hall.

We heard the door open. There was an exchange of voices, and then Munegir reappeared, carrying a small wooden box that must have been quite heavy from the way his arms were straining.

"Blast me, this is a night for strange sights," the man said. "Here's a delivery for *you, devyn,* and as strange a messenger as I ever did see. A dark lad, and for a moment, I thought he were covered in feathers."

"Likely because he was," Felpz remarked absently, taking the box and cracking it open.

As one, we all leaned forward to get a glimpse inside, but Felpz shut it again sharply. He looked up at us, his brown eyes bright and gleaming, and smiled.

"There will be stranger sights to see this night, if you follow me," Felpz said to Munegir. He cast his gaze wide over the waiting crowd. "All of you, in fact, are welcome to join us—if you don't mind staying up all night and perhaps getting rather wet. The more witnesses, I fancy, the better. Also, we are going to be in need of shovels, one per person should do it, saving Corianne and Mr Corder. Yes, shovels," he said, turning round on the spot so his purple coattails flew out. He looked around the room and seemed satisfied. "Shovels, and I have something to pick up at Rathic's cottage—but that is on our way—with luck, we shall have this whole matter settled and our discorporated friends re-embodied in time for breakfast. Come along."

He marched out of the hall. As one the entire crowd followed him.

The walk back up the hill went much faster with Felpz leading the way—after all the shovels in Munegir's stable had been collected and doled out. The ladies in black dresses were reluctant at first, but when they saw Felpz's disapproving expression they deigned to take a small hand-spade apiece.

"They are archeologists," Corder explained to me. "From Grenling."

Corder still looked ghostly pale, especially in the flickering lamplight, but he was more talkative and energetic now.

"Then they should be well accustomed to dirt," I said, setting my hands on my hips.

Corder actually smiled at that. "Good heavens no," he cried. "They are scholars, not explorers. I was surprised to see them out here. Misses Kildre and Brackenmoor," he pointed first at the dark one and then the rosy one.

We walked in a disorganized procession behind Felpz. The natives gave him respectful distance, and not even the vivacious Misses Kildre and Brackenmoor dared walk at his side. This left a safe empty area directly in his wake, into which I led Corder. In this manner we crossed the bridge and ascended once again the side of Castle Hill.

In what felt like no time at all we came in view of Rathic's house. I heard amazed gasping coming from the archeologists, but the locals took it with their usual impassive fortitude.

I waited outside while Felpz went in to collect whatever he needed. Seeing Corder's body had been shock enough; I had no wish to see my own.

Eventually he came out again, now carrying one of his own trunks as well as the wooden box. He brushed away all offers of help, and set off up the hill.

It was a pity, I thought, that the first time I climbed Castle Hill it was in the dark, and I was—how did Felpz put it?—*discorporated*. On the other hand I did not feel physical fatigue, nor aches in my feet, nor the apparent chill of the night—everyone else had been obliged to bundle up in coats and scarves.

I also discovered that I could see rather better beyond the glare of the lanterns; in the weak moonlight I could make out the shape of the hill above us, riddled with sheep paths and shrubby trees, and crowned with the remnants of the ancient castle.

The road narrowed to a mere footpath above Rathic's house, and we were obliged to walk in single file behind Felpz. I had to take Corder's hand again, for he would keep drifting off the path as if he forgot it was there. When I saw him walk clean through a drooping tree branch I understood why, and held on all the tighter.

The starry sky, blue and purple to my ghost eyes, opened before us as we neared the summit. Felpz had gone at such a pace that only Rathic had been able to keep up—everyone else was stuck plodding behind Misses Kildre and Brackenmoor—and the two men stood alone before the little humps of grass-covered earth and rock that had once marked the front gate of the castle. Felpz put down his burden with evident relief and turned to Rathic.

"You know where her bones are," he said in a soft voice that nevertheless carried well to my ethereal ears. It was not a question.

Rathic nodded and his wide shoulders drooped.

"We don't like to make it generally known," he said. "On account of what happened the last time someone found them."

"*What* happened?" I asked, tugging on Felpz's sleeve.

Felpz looked around at me, but Rathic just seemed confused. I sighed inwardly.

"Why don't you ask your friend to explain," he said with a slight smile. Then with an effort he took up the luggage and box again, and motioned with his shoulder for Rathic to lead the way.

"What *are* they talking about?" I asked Corder, and squeezed his arm for good measure.

He looked around at me, surprised.

"Did you not know?" he said. "Long ago — must be over a hundred years now — some farmers came up the hill to get stone for their houses or fences or some such. They accidentally uncovered her tomb, and in it they found *the* golden cloak — the one from the legends. But either they didn't know it or they didn't think much of it. They left the bones alone, but they took the cloak and divided it up between themselves as plunder. No one knows what happened to the pieces."

As I followed Felpz's straight purple back through the mess of tufty grass and tumbled heaps of moss-covered stone I pondered this. According to the story, it was the girl's hair itself that was gold. But whoever heard of someone whose head grew metal hair? It was ridiculous; I had assumed it was just a turn of phrase. Now I looked again at the way Felpz strained to carry his burdens, and I wondered.

Rathic led us, sure-footed and with purpose, to the center of the hill where a good bit of masonry still remained in the form of a rough square. Within there was a patch of empty earth, covered in new spring grass, and it was here Rathic stopped.

"We reckon this used to be the cellar, or the way to it. There are still some of the old stone slabs under the grass — the ones that were too heavy to move."

Felpz set his load down with evident relief, then stood for some moments resting his chin in his hand, a finger tapping at his lips, apparently deep in thought. His gaze bored into that little square of grass, and eventually he nodded to himself.

"We had better do it the conventional way," he said at length, and looked around.

There was a grumbling of voices drawing near, and lanterns flashed from between the ruins. The rest of the party from Munegir's hall had caught up with us, and Felpz smiled in satisfaction. As soon as they arrived he set them to work with their spades and shovels, digging down into that square of grass.

The center of the ruins quickly became crowded, and Corder and I climbed up onto a handy crag to stay out of their way. It was covered with thick moss which must have been cold and damp, but I felt only its soft springy form beneath me. Come to that, I didn't feel the chill of the air that was evidently strong enough to cause people's breath to rise in steam before them.

I had almost decided that being discorporated was really not such a bad thing, when I saw something beyond the ring of lamplight that, had there been blood in my veins, would have made it run cold.

At first I thought it was a mere flicker of yellow light reflected off the night dew upon a bush, but it grew and solidified into a recognizable shape. Then it winked out of sight.

I only glimpsed it for a moment, but I knew what I had seen: a short, pale girl wrapped in a glinting golden cape.

I caught the flickering again, this time in the shadow behind a pillar, close to where Felpz stood surveying the work. I saw a pale hand reaching around the rock, and the face wore such an expression of hatred and fury that I was almost struck dumb with horror.

I made an inarticulate sound of alarm.

Everyone carried on as if they hadn't heard, but Felpz's head shot up to look at me. I pointed to where I had seen the ghost, but by the time he turned his head she was gone.

Corder was on his feet. "You can see her? *Did you see her?*" he demanded.

"I think so," I said. "She looked angry."

Corder's apparition tugged at his hair in distress. "We should not be disturbing her tomb!" he cried. "This is where she came to us the night she took me—she does not like people to be here!"

Before I could do anything he leapt down from our perch and dashed in among the crowd, batting his hands ineffectually at their arms and faces.

It was shocking to see him move through the other people, though they seemed unharmed by it. Some of them gave slight shivers but otherwise did not notice.

I had just turned to Felpz, who had seen Corder and was moving to intercept him, when I felt a small, cold hand close upon my ankle.

It was a wonder I did not scream. But the hand felt so small and fragile—a child's hand—and it was cold and shaking slightly. It felt real and solid in a way that the rest of the world increasingly did not.

When I looked down I was not at all shocked to find the ghost clutching at my leg.

I was aware first of two great, pale blue eyes gazing at me out of a gaunt face the color of the moon. Her shorn head was smeared with dirt, and there was a dark patch behind one ear that looked suspiciously like blood. The cape rested heavy on her shoulders, and the arm of the hand that held my limb was bone thin and trembling slightly.

Perhaps it will surprise my readers, but to own the truth I was not greatly frightened by her. Rather, all my latent motherly instincts were aroused, and I bent down toward her, one hand partly outstretched.

"Here now, child, what is it you want?"

The girl—I could no longer think of her as a ghost—shook her head violently, and I saw she had strange, elongated ears, with tufts of fur on their tips. At present they were pinned back against her head, like those of a frightened animal.

She spoke, her voice high and weak, in something that sounded like Cairdric but was probably much older. I didn't understand a word of it.

"I'm so sorry," I said. "I can't understand you. Please, come, talk to my friend. I'm sure he will understand." I pointed at Felpz, who had managed to reach Corder and was holding him by the arm.

The girl hissed, revealing crooked, blackened teeth, and pulled back—removing her hand. Already her pale feet, where they protruded from under the cape, had begun to go transparent.

"No, no," I cried, reaching out to her. "He is a friend, *friend*—" I wracked my brain for what few Cairdric words I knew. "*Cymhael*," I tried desperately. "*Cymhaelew,*" I pointed to myself, then at Felpz.

The girl hesitated. She frowned, as though the word were familiar to her. Then she shook her head.

"*Drvydh,*" she whispered, soft but distinct. "*Drvydh drvg.*"

"Droo-ith?" I repeated. "*Druid?* No, no, he is not a druid—*dym drvydh*—he is a magician!" What had the porter called him? "*Devyn promhor, cymbhael.*" I said, despairingly now, as her face faded into the dark wet leaves of the bush behind her. I swore.

Those unfortunate words dropped into a ringing silence. I turned and saw that Felpz was staring at me. He held Corder at arm's length, while he held the other hand raised, palm out, as if asking for silence. I knew that gesture of old—Felpz was not asking for silence, he was holding everyone around him still and speechless. Rightly enough, the crowd around the grave was unnaturally quiet as they watched him.

"She was here?" he asked.

"Didn't you see her?" I returned.

Felpz shook his head. "It matters little now," he said with a shrug. "But I am glad to know that she is close. Step over here, Corianne, this will interest you."

I came down from my seat and went over to where a large dark hole had been opened in the earth. At the bottom, still half buried, was a collection of pale broken things that, with a little imagination, might have been bones.

"It appears," said Felpz, coming to stand at the head of the grave and laying out a sheet over the disrupted earth, "that there has been something of a misunderstanding here." He knelt on the cloth and placed his suitcase and the box beside him. Then, as he continued to speak, he opened first one and then the other, and began to lay their contents out before him.

"The legend that you know, as with many legends of its time, is incorrect in a few key points," he said, pulling something heavy and golden out of his suitcase. "There was indeed a fairy *bruin* here in prehistoric times. And there *was* a human castle built on top of it during the Dark Ages. And there *was* a girl with golden hair."

More pieces of gold joined the first in front of Felpz's purple knees. A few were twisted, disfigured things, but there was also a good number of medallions, coins, and jewelry.

"But she did not give it freely in exchange for hospitality. It was *taken* from her by force. Likewise she did not lie down and die—but was struck dead by greedy human hands. Struck dead for the hair on her head."

No wonder his load had weighed on him so, I thought to myself, seeing more and more golden artifacts produced first from his suitcase, and then the wooden box.

"Who was she? That I do not know," Felpz went on, and now he needed to exert no effect to keep his audience rapt and silent. They stood and stared, transfixed. "The fairies of this land had long since passed into their own realm by that time. It is likely, I think, that she was a forgotten changeling. A fairy raised as a human. Perhaps, even, she was a crossling—the hybrid offspring of a fae and a human. Something lost, left behind, returning to the only home she knew."

The final offering of the wooden box was a dinner service, each utensil forged of exquisite buttery gold. Felpz sat back from his display, looking almost like some foreign street merchant setting out his wares for sale. He looked around his assembled audience, then to me where I stood directly across from him. Finally his eyes settled on a place a little below and to the left of my shoulder. Even without looking I knew that the ghost was present once more. His eyes grew bright and glittered in the lantern light, as though reflecting the gold before him.

"And she found it, but changed beyond recognition, taken over by the same race that had driven her people away. And they did not respect the sanctity of guests, but drew her in with honeyed words and then struck her down for the fortune she carried on her head. As if that was not bad enough, her grave was later desecrated, and the treasure that was rightfully hers was stolen once more. The golden cloak from the legends *was* real, though the rural farmers who dug it up knew not what they held. If they had, they might not have behaved so disrespectfully."

His face turned slowly across Munegir and his fellows, Rathic, Corder, and the two archeologists, but his eyes never left the presence behind me.

"They cut the cloak," he said. "Split it between them. Those pieces in turn were split, and split again and again. Used to settle debts, buy land, stock, or melted down and reforged." He flicked a hand at an intricately carved brooch.

"When I first heard of the activity on *Cair Frell*, my mind immediately went to the cloak, and to the ambiguous nature of the legend. It has taken me many resources and a good deal of my own energy to gather all those scattered pieces together again, and though it is not within my power to right an ancient wrong, I *can* show due respect to the dead. I can restore their dignity."

Bouragner Felpz got slowly to his feet. It was one of those times when he seemed to expand, rising upwards impossibly tall and lean. His coat fell around him in dark purple folds, and for a moment it looked like some other, longer, more intricate garment.

Then it was just Felpz in his evening jacket, raising his arms above the arrayed treasure.

There was utter silence on the hill. It seemed the wind itself held its breath.

The change began as a faint glow over the assembled pieces. Then it rose and took on a more tangible feel, like heavy mist on the shore. Finally it spread out until it was a pale purple nimbus, shot through with streaks of orange and gold, that surrounded the cloth and the pieces of gold, staining Felpz's shoes with light.

Then, slowly, the pieces of gold began to melt. The dinner service went soft and glowed white-hot, began to flow together, and eventually re-formed as another piece of the original cape. I recognized it from the ethereal version I had seen just moments ago.

The brooch did the same thing, its little ball of blobby gold rolling slowly across the cloth until it joined a larger nugget, which in turned joined another, which finally spread out to form the collar.

All the pieces were glowing now, and the crowd had to avert their eyes it was so bright. My immaterial ones, however, were quite unaffected, and I was able to watch in awe as the pieces of gold, looking more like shards of sun, fused together into a recognizable shape.

As the real gold cape came together at Felpz's feet, I felt a familiar cold hand slip into mine. I glanced away for a moment and sure enough, there was the ghost. She was glowing too, though softer; a reflection of the golden light.

"*Cymhael?*" she whispered, her eyes very wide.

"*Cymhaelew,*" I said, squeezing her hand.

Together we watched the cape—for it was recognizably the cape now—as it cooled to a glossy, creamy golden color. It was indeed very beautiful; part woven thread, part beaten metal, with intricate designs of knots, and strings of indentations like beads hammered into its surface.

The purple nimbus around it dimmed, and the rest of the crowd chanced to uncover their eyes to take a look. But it did not disappear entirely, and Felpz did not lower his hands. He had his eyes tight shut, and there was a tense arch to his back that suggested he was straining furiously at some inner struggle.

All at once a wind rushed down upon the hill, and the nimbus around the cloak brightened to pure white. The wind passed clean through the ghost and I, but it swept off hats and tugged at the scarves and jackets of everyone else. It whipped up the tails of Felpz's coat, and now it really did look as if it were no coat at all, but a long and flowing robe. It flapped about, snapping in the white light of the nimbus, and upon the ground the cloak began to change again.

It writhed, like countless tiny worms thrown upon the ground. It jerked and jack-knifed, and finally the hem unraveled, casting free the threads of the cloak.

The gold cape of the ghost of Castle Hill disappeared into a million fine strands of hair, the intricate designs lost in waves of gleaming tresses, and the beaten plates melting and splitting, reforming into gently curling locks.

It lay in soft waves, a head of perfectly golden hair, across the cloth. The light about it slowly dimmed, until it was illuminated only by the plain lanterns—at least the ones that had not been put out by the wind. The wind itself gave one final puff, and then everything went still.

Felpz's arms dropped to his sides as if letting go of a heavy burden. Then his shoulders drooped, and he actually swayed on his feet. He steadied himself with some effort, and straightened the lapels of his coat, which had gone back to its old self.

Casting his eyes modestly aside, he reached out a trembling hand, offering it to the ghost. He spoke some words in her ancient tongue, and then looked up at us hopefully. I did not need to understand the language to take his meaning.

"Come on," I said to the little ghost, and tugged her hand. "*Cymhaelew.*"

She came entranced as I led her around the grave and into the dancing reflected light from the bed of gold hair.

There was a collective gasp from the crowd around us, and I guessed we had become visible to all. I paid them no heed: my full attention focused on Felpz, the ghost at my side, and the glimmering artifact that lay between us.

When we stood at the lip of the grave, its dark mouth yawning beside us, I hesitated. The ghost clung to my side, half hidden in my skirts.

Felpz smiled a secretive smile, and carefully lifted the sheaf of golden hair. He flung it out, letting it fall into the pit next to us, and as it left his fingertips the entire thing burst into flame. Blue-white fire ran its length, licking up and down every strand, and I saw the fine threads melt before my eyes, run to a golden rain that fell heavily and steamed in the wet earth. From out of the fire Felpz drew something bright and golden, but clearly insubstantial, and as the burning, melting bundle tumbled into the pit I saw it was the ghost of the golden hair.

Felpz made a hard, shoving motion with his hands, and the whole thing flew through the air straight at us. The little girl gave a cry of wonder and leapt forward to meet it.

I had the sense to draw away at the last moment and saw the girl surrounded by a confused whorl of gold light. It whipped about her, lashing the earth beneath her feet, and when it dissipated she no longer wore the ghostly version of the gold cape, but appeared to me a small girl in a plain white shift, with a head of rich golden hair that tumbled in thick locks down to her feet.

She hung in midair above her open grave, gazing from me to Felpz with a look of amazement and delight, and her eyes sparkled like twin suns.

She gave a little cry in the immortal language of a joyous child, and shot upwards into the night sky, waves of gold light streaming behind her.

"Brace yourself, Corianne!" I heard Felpz cry, the moment before there was a great burst of light, like a firework, so bright that for a moment it lit the hilltop as if it were day. In that moment I saw everyone: Felpz beside the grave, Rathic some paces behind him. Munegir, Kildre and Brackenmoor, and the rest of the contingent from the hall, clustered among the moss-covered pillars and pieces of wall. And Harlan Corder, where he crouched against a tree, one arm up to shield his face.

The next moment I awoke with a start in Rathic's guest bedroom, my neck in a horrible crick.

This time I had the good sense to stay put. I made myself a cup of tea in Rathic's kitchen and went to bed—though I was too excited to sleep.

In this way I missed the last escapade of Harlan Corder, who, being thrown suddenly back into his body as I was, awoke in Munegir's deserted hall and panicked. Not realizing he was corporeal once more, he ran out into the dark morning, trying to find his way cross-country to the hill.

Felpz explained to me as we sat having tea in Rathic's parlor the next day that it had taken the whole party the rest of the night to find him, since he, Felpz, was too tired to help.

"Bullying time into flowing backwards, and to the extent as it applied to that cloak—" he shuddered, closing his eyes.

Corder was found at last, however, and taken into the custody of Misses Kildre and Brackenmoor, who proved to be surprisingly competent nurses, and I am happy to say I hear he made a full recovery from his ordeal, though he quite lost his appetite for adventure.

"What will happen to the grave now?" I asked. "We had a good crowd of witnesses last night; word shall surely spread."

"Oh, I'm sure it will," Felpz said with a grin. "But any graverobbers will have to get past Kildre and Brackenmoor: they have claimed it as an archeological excavation. In fact, they wanted to take the whole lot—bones, melted gold hair—back to Grenling for more research."

"And what did you say?"

"Why, I gave them my blessing, Corianne. I told them I thought it should not be a problem, provided the bones and the hair were kept together. Besides, if the ghost took issue with it, I felt confident she would *let them know.*"

I gave my friend an arch look.

"They have decided to perform their research on site, and the locals are designating it a national heritage monument. I suggested an obelisk be placed over the grave, once the archeologists are finished with it. There is nothing quite like a good obelisk with the right runes on it, I find, to deter graverobbers."

He sipped his tea and gazed out the window, where the morning mist had evaporated into a bright golden afternoon.

"And the ghost?" I prompted.

"What she does now remains to be seen." Felpz shrugged. "Hunith says the wildflowers are just coming out down in the valley. She has offered to bring the coach around and take us on a tour. Would you like that?"

I laughed at the sudden change of subject, but agreed wholeheartedly.

However, it should interest my readers to know that they *did* raise an obelisk over the grave of the girl with the golden hair. Felpz himself carved the runes onto its face, and I understand that it has indeed proven effective at keeping away vandals and thieves.

Rathic tells me that the ghost has been seen dancing around its base on fine nights, or sometimes perched at its top. She no longer wears the cape, he says, but her hair is very long and bright.

Appendices to "The Ghost of Castle Hill"

APPENDIX I: THE CAIRDRIC ALPHABET

The Cairdric alphabet is a phonetic one, but the pronunciation for some of the letters is quite different from ours. (Not unlike the Welsh alphabet!) The Cairdric alphabet has no I, J, or Z, and a G is always hard. When writing foreign words which require a J sound, native Cairdrians will use G as a substitute.

A	"Ah" as in F*a*ther
Æ	"Ae" as in D*ay*
E	"Ee" as in Tr*ee*
I	"Ai" as in R*igh*t
Y	"Ih" or "Eh" or "Uh" as in F*i*t or Fr*e*t or *U*p, depending on the word
O	"Oh" as in *Oa*k.
V	"Oo" as in Y*ou*
W	"Ow" as in Cr*ow*d
C	"Kuh" as in *C*at
CH	"Chuh" as in *Ch*at
S	"Suh" as in *S*nake
SS	"Shuh" as in *Sh*ade
B	"Buh" as in *B*oy
H	"Huh" as in *H*owl
D	"Duh" as in *D*uck
DH	"Th" as in Brea*th*
DD	"Th" as in *Th*em
L	"Luh" as in *L*ove
LL	"Fluh" as in *Fl*ame
F	"Vuh" as in *V*ast
G	"Guh" as in *G*ate
M	"Muh" as in *M*other
MH	"Fuh" as in *F*ather
N	"Nuh" as in *N*ever
R	"Ruh" as in *R*iver
P	"Puh" as in *P*uddle
X	"Ess" as in Prince*ss*
U	"Wuh" as in *W*ater
UH	"Whuh" as in *Wh*at an inscrutable alphabet this is.

Brvyn   Cairdric spelling of "bruin." A kind of cave or underground palace; a fairy castle. Pronounced like "brew-in."

Cayr   Cairdric spelling of "cair." A kind of castle. Pronounced like "care."

Cymhael   (Plural: *Cymhaelew*) Cairdric for "friend, friends." Pronounced like "kih-fail" and "kih-fay-lee-ow" respectively.

Cyrdry   Cairdric spelling of "Cairdra." Pronounced the same.

Del   See *Dyl*.

Devyn   Cairdric for "wizard," usually a powerful one, or one held in high esteem. Pronounced like "dew-in."

Drvydh   Cairdric spelling of "druid." Pronounced like "drew-ith."

Drvg   Cairdric for "bad" or "malevolent." Pronounced like "droog."

Dyl   Cairdric particle used in naming. Means "child of." Pronounced like "del."

Dym   Cairdric for "not," "none;" a rejection. Pronounced like "dim."

Evith   Kyrish spelling of the Cairdric word *Yfydh*. Means "pearl."

Ghedvale   Kyrish spelling of the Cairdric name *Gydfæl*. Means "learned prince."

Gvdehv   Cairdric for "goodihoo" — an owl's call. Pronounced like "goo-dee-hoo."

Hunith   Kyrish spelling of the Cairdric name *Hvnydh*. Means "heron."

Mhryl   Cairdric spelling of "frell." A hill, especially a tall, isolated one. Compare to "tor."

Morgun   See *Morgvn*.

Morgvn   Cairdric spelling of "Morgun" a derivative of "Morgan." Pronounced like "mor-goon."

Munegir   Kyrish spelling of the Cairdric name *Mvnyger*. The name of a legendary sword in Cairdric mythology. Pronounced like "myoon-eh-gear."

Raddyc   Cairdric spelling of "Rathic." Pronounced like "Ra-thik," means "he who guards."

Rathic   See *Raddyc*.

Thrag   Kyrish spelling of the Cairdric word *Ddræg*. Means "dragon."

Trefellin   See *Trymhylyn*.

Trymhylyn   Cairdric spelling of "Trefellin." A small city in southwest Cairdra. Pronounced like "Tra-fell-in."

four

GRIFFIN'S BLOOD

SOME OF MY READERS have been disappointed at how little I have spoken of my daughter in these semi-autobiographical tales. They have expressed a certain amount of curiosity about the young woman who, as I mentioned before, "has gone far on the backs of dragons."

I do not find this surprising at all. The fact is, however, that although my daughter leads an exceptionally interesting life, it is very much her life, and I believe that when the time is right she will tell her own story in her own words. So I have taken care not to become sidetracked with her affairs, as these stories deal in the doings of my friend, the magician Bouragner Felpz, and not those of my daughter, the dracologist.

Once, however, their two paths did cross. The result was so extraordinary that reports of it have already been published in several newspapers and scientific journals. My version I present here, not only as an example of my friend's remarkable powers—but also to shed some light on the doings of that incurably adventurous woman, Milain Harper Birch.

It happened in the long days of that glorious summer of 2315. The past two years had been exceptionally busy ones for me, for as some of my older readers may remember, 2313 was the year in which I began to publish the accounts of my adventures as a young girl with Mr Bouragner Felpz. Though the first installment was met with no great fanfare, I was surprised and heartened to receive many letters requesting more stories about my friend, and the fulfillment of these requests served to fill my days to the brim. Furthermore, that year I was quite overwhelmed with collecting those stories into the volume which would later become *The Adventures of Bouragner Felpz: A Study of Magic.*

So I had not been on any adventures of a magical nature in some months, and those of the past year had all been small, quiet affairs—amusing enough to regale friends with over dinner, but hardly worth the trouble of writing down—when I received an urgent letter from my daughter.

Letters from Milain were not so unusual; we corresponded regularly and frequently, and many of these stories of Felpz began as letters to her. Similarly, I have been carefully filing all her letters to me against the day she inevitably decides to write her own memoirs. No, it was not the letter that surprised me, but the manner in which it was delivered.

I was sitting up in bed one morning, so absorbed in my writing that I ignored the call to breakfast. From the sitting room I heard a sharp tapping on the window, but dismissed it as one of the ravens that frequently delivered messages to Felpz. This assessment was confirmed a moment later when I heard Felpz greet the creature and let it in. I heard the flapping of wings and a muffled crash as it landed among the breakfast things. Then there were steps in the hall, a rap on my bedroom door, and Felpz put his head in.

"Ah, Corianne," he said. "Do you mind setting aside your quill for one moment? Only there is a wyvern in the other room who, if you do nothing, will eat your breakfast."

"Me?" I cried, jolted abruptly out of my world of ink and words. "Wyverns are your province, Felpz. Tell him to go away yourself."

"You would not love me if I did so," Felpz said. "He brings a message from your daughter."

Disbelief washed over me. I set aside my notebook and hurried into my dressing gown and across the hall. The door opened onto the bright, cluttered room, and I entered to find the breakfast table even more crowded than usual with the small wyvern perched in the middle of it.

For those of you who have not seen a wyvern, a small distinction must be made: they are not, as my daughter has told me many times, dragons. Though they appear reptilian, and have similar leathery wings and long, toothy snouts, they lack the third set of appendages that form a dragon's forelegs, and they cannot breathe fire—though adults can hiss jets of steam. They do not grow as large as dragons—the largest documented specimen being only twenty feet long—and cannot use magic to assist their flight.

This particular wyvern was either a juvenile or one of the smaller species. He—and I trusted Felpz's word on this—was the size of an albatross, with the addition of a stubby tail. He had a smattering of red feathers around his head and across his shoulders, and his scaly skin was a deep mahogany hue. His wings were currently folded tightly along his sides, with the fingers that protruded at the wyvern equivalent of a wrist held questioningly over my plate of biscuits.

He looked up guiltily as we entered, and I remembered more of my daughter's lectures on wyverns: though they did not have the vast, inhuman wisdom of dragons, they were of an intelligence and temperament similar to a human child. With this in mind I cleared my throat politely and wished him good morning.

"Good morning," said the wyvern. He had a high, chirping voice, but his words were clear and precise. "Message for you from Birch girl. Urgent. Am to wait for your reply. Came long way this morning. Hungry." He looked longingly at the tray of sweets.

"You may have one biscuit," I said, coming to sit at the table. "I do not think my daughter would thank me if I sent you back with an upset stomach. What do you normally eat?"

The wyvern turned around on the table, flaring his wings for balance. Their webbing was a brilliant orange, and as they opened and closed it looked like a flash of fire.

"Biscuits?" he said hopefully, extending one of his legs to which had been secured a roll of paper.

I looked helplessly at Felpz as I removed the document.

Felpz cleared his throat deferentially. "I am sure we can provide you some roast chicken, which will no doubt agree with you better."

"You may have two biscuits while you wait." I relented at the wyvern's drooping crest, and unrolled my daughter's letter.

While the wyvern helped himself I read with interest the following message:

Draco Abbey, Crogard
21st June 2315, 3:30 AM

Dear Mother,

I hope Radcliffe has found you safe and swift. I would have written in the ordinary way, but something has come up and I need your advice as soon as possible.

Two weeks ago the dragons began acting very strangely. They will not talk to me, which is troubling. More troubling still, earlier this evening one of them killed a sheep and carried it away. This is the second poaching in as many months—the first was a fortnight ago—and it has undone all the progress I have made with the local farmers, who are understandably upset. It is further troubling because these are lesser fire dragons, and they only hunt when their young are hatching—which they have no eggs to hatch this season.

I have been up half the night flying around on Tero, who at least still helps me, trying to discover if there is a nest. Around midnight we were nearly knocked out of the sky by a greater elder dragon gliding up from the south. This is serious: we have not had elder dragons here in over five hundred years. None of us have any experience with elder dragons, and I am at a loss for what to do.

My colleagues on the farm are full of ideas, but they strike me as foolish and dangerous. Dr Vayar, the director, is considering writing to a preeminent draconic scholar from Aldonica. However, I know that neither of them has had direct contact with elder dragons—merely studied them extensively through the writings of medieval experts. But these stories and anecdotes from history are contradictory at best, and allegorical most of the time. What we need is someone who has known these dragons, and knows how to speak to them.

However, there is no one of my generation or the five previous who have even seen an elder dragon, much less spoken to one.

Which is why I'm writing to you, mother. I believe you do know someone who has direct experience with these dragons: your friend Mr Felpz. If you could convince him to come up and advise us I would be immensely grateful.

I have attached a description of the dragon in question, in case Mr Felpz might recognize it.

Wishing for a swift reply,

Your loving Milain

As I read this remarkable document I could feel my eyebrows slowly climbing up my forehead, and by the time I finished they must have been close to my hairline.

"I trust all is well with your progeny?" Felpz asked from across the table.

I looked up to find him watching me intently, his dark eyes sparkling. On the table the wyvern—Radcliffe—had polished off the biscuits and was eyeing my breakfast hopefully.

"Well with her, I believe so," I said. "Her world, perhaps not. Here." I thrust the letter and the attached slip into Felpz's eager hands, and began upon my breakfast before Radcliffe could steal it.

While I ate, I watched Felpz's expression of mild surprise and curiosity slowly harden into sharp concentration. When he got to the attached description he was so enthralled as to read it aloud, interspersed with his own thoughts.

"Greater elder dragon—this means nothing to me—reptilian, short bodied—that would make it a northern drake—wingspan of . . . three hundred feet or more? Well. That certainly narrows it down. Could be Armandoros . . . or Therangaar . . . but they have been far out of this world. I would have felt it if they had returned, I am sure. Mordicade? No, that is a fanciful notion. Let me see . . . she gives no mention of its colour, or the style of its spinal ridge. Understandable, given the circumstances. No, I'm afraid I cannot identify it from this. And it may be a dragon unknown to me—I have known dragons, my dear, I have not known them all . . .

"Well, I suppose we must arrange a trip to Crogard at the nearest possible moment to see if we can't resolve the matter."

He spoke lightly, but I could tell from the tenseness about his form and the gleam in his eye that this was an unusual and serious situation. I knew also from my daughter's tutelage that dragons came in three kinds—mostly. The lesser or common variety, which still inhabit the high rocky areas of this country; the greater dragons, which have mostly moved into the inhospitable heights of the Dragonridge Mountains; and the elder dragons, which as far as I could tell consisted of a few named individuals of the sort found in stories and legends—none of whom had been seen in Kyreland for many hundreds of years. What she could have meant by a greater elder dragon, I could only guess.

"Still hungry," Radcliffe chirped. "Chicken?"

"Have a care with how you eat," Felpz chided. "Lest you lose your ability to fly. Now take this note, my good drake," he said, scribbling something on a slip of paper and handing it to the wyvern, "and take it back to your mistress."

Radcliffe took the note in one spiny claw, eyeing Felpz cagily.

"She's not my mistress," he said. "She is the Birch girl." And with a clatter and a snap of leathery wings he was at the windowsill, and a moment later he was gone.

"What do you make of it, Felpz?" I asked, getting up to close the window.

Felpz shrugged. "I make nothing of it as yet," he said. "A dragon will do as a dragon does and to question it is folly. Still, there can only be four or five dragons of the size your daughter describes, and I should like to meet this one—whether or not the situation requires my attention. You will come, of course?"

"I should not dream of missing this opportunity," I exclaimed. "Besides, it has been years since I visited Crogard."

Felpz clapped his hands. "Excellent," said he. "Now I have one more letter to write, and then we may be off."

He was as good as his word. It was a sign of just how enthusiastic my friend was that all our luggage appeared at the door already packed—quite literally by magic. I took this as a sign in general that the journey would receive similar assistance, and indeed the interminable train ride passed much more quickly than I remembered.

The last time I visited my daughter had been in the fall of '12, when she had only recently become installed at the Draconian Institute at Crogard. Then the mountains had been bleak and forbidding, the air cold, and the weather a miserable combination of spitting rain and stinging snow. The dragons had made themselves scarce in their caves, and apart from showing me around the venerable buildings of the Institute, there was not much we could do.

Now it was summer, and the mountains rising from the southwestern lowlands were high and green and refreshingly cool looking. Here and there among their pine-covered sides I could see the occasional cliff or peak of brilliant gold stone—a reminder that Crogard was, under its cloak of Kyrish soil and vegetation, a part of the great Dragonridge Mountains: that mighty range that stretched the length of our entire continent. Hewn into sharp spires by the fire of ancient dragons, they are an everlasting reminder that, though those dragons are now a rare sight in our world, they were once the indisputable rulers of it, and their legacy will last beyond the scope of humanity. Indeed, it abides in the very bones of this earth.

We alighted in Rivenstone, the small town that had gathered around the College of Rarities—that most isolated and idiosyncratic branch of Redling's University of Magic—from which it was only a short journey by coach to Draco Abbey, as the locals had affectionately dubbed the Draconian Institute. As we waited for our bags to be unloaded, I caught Felpz looking intently around the station, as if expecting to see a familiar face. This puzzled me, as despite our long friendship he had never set eyes upon my daughter—whom I was expecting to meet us.

But Milain was nowhere to be seen, and it was a different figure from my past who eventually presented himself by the door to Main Street: A small, silver-haired boy in a disheveled brown suit and pale bare feet, who saluted us as we drew near.

"Abharus!" I cried, swooping down and embracing him. "This is a most welcome surprise!" I knew that, though he still appeared to be a child of no more than twelve, he was in fact over ten years my senior. Nevertheless I could not resist the habits I had developed when my daughter was young, and he bore my attentions with admirable fortitude.

"Hardly worth making a fuss," he chided me, patting my arm. "Didn't Mr Felpz tell you he called me?"

"What? Why, no!" I looked about distractedly. Abharus's choice of words was curious, but I did not think they were inaccurate. Abharus traveled in and out of our world, and for all I knew Felpz had summoned him from some distant adventure. "Where have you been?" I asked. "How did you get here before us?"

Abharus coughed modestly, and nodded towards the coach waiting outside. This coach was nothing unusual—it looked like any sober black cab—but the horse than pulled it was . . . difficult to look at. It had a shimmery, ethereal quality to it that made the eye want to slide away. I got the impression of hooves and a wild, feathery mane and tail, and a pillowing turbulence above its withers that might have been a disturbance of air, or might have been restless wings. Its colour was even harder to describe, like a patch of sunset on a cloudy day sitting in the street.

"Ah, Abharus," said Felpz, sliding up beside us with a porter in tow. "And you've brought Yuragorn, excellent. This way, Jecab."

"Yuragorn?" I asked while our luggage was being stowed.

Abharus looked up at me through his silvery bangs, and smiled angelically. "Yuragorn is good to have around when you're dealing with dragons," he said.

We climbed into the coach, and I saw that although Abharus sat in the driver's seat he held no reins, gave no command. Yet as soon as we had settled in, the coach moved smoothly off, and we began to pass swiftly through the town, heading steeply up Main Street towards the abbey.

Felpz leaned forward and proceeded to spend the remainder of the journey deep in quiet conversation with Abharus. I sat back and let them converse without even trying to eavesdrop; I had learned long ago that my friend would explain all when all would be clear, and I would not get a morsel of information before then.

Draco Abbey had once been the cornerstone of a large convent that lay just beyond the town at the top of a low hill. Since the nuns had moved out and the dracologists had moved in nothing had changed about the exterior—save a few modifications that made it easier for small dragons and wyverns to land on the roof. The gardens that extended down the far side of the hill had been converted into hatcheries, nests, and a long strip of scorched grass where the larger dragons could land comfortably, but approaching from the town, the only visual clue was the bordering wall; this had been built of natural flint which had slowly chipped away, leaving sharp glassy spikes at the top, and the intact bricks, glossy blue-blacks and deep browns, gave the impression of scales. Milain had told me that when the scientists moved in they thought the wall looked so fitting they left it as they had found it.

Today there were a number of people gathered around the gate, angry farmers and craftsmen by the look of them. They were shouting heatedly at two burly young men who stood on either side of the gate looking bored and long-suffering. As we drew nearer I saw why they seemed so relaxed despite the throng around them: they were guarded by the presence of a dragon that sat in the middle of the gate.

It was curled tightly in on itself, its wide, webbed wings furled against its back, and the giant head resting serenely on feet with talons the length of my forearm. It was, I thought, a very beautiful dragon, deep chocolate brown with flecks of orange and crimson, like frozen flames, speckling its scales. Its spinal ridge flared red with gold tips, and the great eye that opened at our approach was improbably pure and blue.

At this movement from the dragon the crowd drew back abruptly, and we slipped through. The two youths at the gate did not seem to notice our strange excuse for a horse, but I was certain the dragon did: its crest went up like a fire being stoked, and it backed away from the gate almost respectfully.

Milain had told me it was best to be polite but direct with dragons; that they could sense fear in humans, but respected those with the self-control not to show it. So though my heart was pounding at the sight and my limbs shook a little, I boldly poked my head out of the carriage and said:

"Good-day, we are here to see Milain Birch. Could you please tell us where to find her?"

The dragon blinked at me, its eyes like two huge pools of sapphire flickering in firelight. Then it spoke.

To one who has never heard a dragon speak, it is important to understand that they do not speak as we do; their mouths and lips and tongues are the wrong shape for human language. Some dragons, with a lot of practice, have learned Kyrish and other languages, but these are rare. Mostly, dragons speak with intent. The sounds that come out are predominantly growls and hisses, which form themselves into words somewhere between the dragon's lips and a person's ears. Like many things about dragons, it is a magic not well understood, and not all dragons do it. (Whether because they cannot, or more likely, choose not to, was one of the things my daughter was studying.)

This dragon was fairly good at it, and its words came across clear and precise.

"Birch girl is not here," it said. "I wait for Mother Birch and Purple One. I lead; you follow." With that it flowed to its feet and began walking down a side road that led along the edge of the abbey. We had to wait for several moments, as the dragon was a long and slender one and had a lot of tail.

We followed the dragon around to the back, where there were stables for such livestock that the Institute required. The dragon stopped outside and sat down on its haunches, curling its tail around its legs like a cat—except because the dragon's tail was so long it made several complete circuits.

"Leave your cart here," it said.

We disembarked, and a young stable boy came running to take our luggage. As Abharus helped him load it onto a handcart I tried again to get a look at our horse, but found it quite impossible.

As the boy wheeled the cart away the dragon raised its spiny head, nostrils flared, and then glided to its feet.

"Follow," it said, and began leading us out of the stables and through the gardens behind the abbey.

We followed the dragon—and the strange, horselike creature, having detached itself from the coach, followed us—through an orchard of hardy-looking apple trees, past a high hedge smelling strongly of herbs, and finally out onto a wide field, spotted with clumps of grass, but so covered with scars and gouges and charred black earth that it could hardly have been called a lawn. From where we stood it sloped down in a gentle curve to a cleft where a small river divided us from the towering heights of the Crogard mountains.

There was activity on this field. People running about and two dragons—even larger than our guide—crouching, as small figures climbed down off their backs. One of these was a slender person whose rusty-blond hair was valiantly trying to escape from her helmet in the gusting wind blowing up from the river. She dropped lightly to the ground, impatiently unsnapping the helmet and tugging it free. Then my daughter walked up the hill to greet us.

Milain Birch is taller than her mother by almost a head—nearly as tall as her father. Her hair was pale flaxen when she was a girl, but now it has darkened to a light reddish-blond. Her skin is similarly reddish from all her time out of doors, and her eyes are very small and bright and blue. She favors leather and heavy cotton clothes in tones of tan and brown, and categorically refuses to wear skirts. That afternoon she was dressed in a leather tunic fastened around the waist by a thick belt from which hung many pockets and pouches. She wore sensible trousers tucked into knee-high leather boots, and was just in the process of pulling off her thick leather flight gloves when she reached us.

"Thank you, Spheron," she said to the dragon next to us. Then she reached out and embraced me. "Mother!" she cried. "I am so happy you came at once. Radcliffe said you would. And these must be your fr-friends—" It was to her credit that she stumbled only a little in her speech as she beheld Abharus and Felpz standing beside me. For she had been hearing stories of the Purple Magician and the immortal boy with the silver hair all her life, and having them appear so suddenly in her own world must have been a shock.

But a woman who works with dragons soon learns to conquer her base emotions. Managing somehow to make it look natural, she bent almost double and offered her hand to Abharus.

"Milain Birch," she said.

"How do you do?" Abharus said gravely, shaking the proffered hand.

Milain rose and looked at Felpz. I cannot guess what went through their minds, but I know mine was all in turmoil seeing these two equally important—and until now mutually exclusive—halves of my life put together for the first time.

"Mother has told me all the stories," Milain said by way of greeting Felpz. "Even the ones she didn't put in her books. She told them to me first."

Felpz smiled. He raised a hand and tapped a long finger against his lower lip—a habit I noticed he performed when something interested him greatly.

"Miss Birch," he said, cocking his head forward like a bird of prey that has spotted a target. "I'm sorry, I must ask—what have you got in your pockets?"

Milain started in surprise, then smiled to herself. "I should have expected as much, coming from you. Well, we've made some progress since I wrote to Mother, and this is the result." She reached into a pouch on her belt and removed a small glass bottle, half full of a dark brown liquid.

Felpz leaned forward until his nose was almost touching the glass. He sniffed.

"Explain," said Abharus.

"In order of events," Felpz added, taking the bottle from her. "Preferably. Leave no detail out."

My daughter smiled a little bemusedly. "As you wish," said she. "Walk with me, won't you? Tero wants to meet you."

"I caught a few hours of sleep after I wrote you that letter," she continued as we made our way slowly down the hill to where one dragon—a deep blue one—still waited. "Then we went out on a dawn patrol. There has been no sign of the elder dragon since it arrived, but the eyries are in an uproar; all the drakes, even the wyverns, felt it arrive."

"This elder dragon," Felpz said, enunciating the qualifying word with elaborate care. "Can you be more precise as to its appearance?"

"It was large," said Milain flatly. "The night was dark. I only got an impression of its size and shape. You'll have to ask Tero; she got a better look at it than I did."

Felpz seemed to accept this. "Go on." he said.

"Thank you. Well, I couldn't see how a dragon that large could have disappeared without a trace—even in mountains such as these. So I've had every rider out searching, and around noon today Marigold found . . . well, he called it a murder scene, but to be honest I'm not certain if it was murder. Something was killed there, though. That bottle is filled with some of the blood we found."

"Yes, and interesting blood it is," Felpz remarked.

"It is not dragon's blood," Milain announced, as if this somewhat diminished its interest as far as she was concerned. "But there was a lot at the scene; I am satisfied it is not human. There was no body," she explained. "Though it looked as if something had been dragged away. There were dragon footprints there too, which concerns me."

"Dragons do kill, sometimes," Felpz remarked gently, as one introducing an unpleasant truth to a child.

"Yes, but all our dragons are adults," Milain said, the problem at hand distracting her. "They feed almost entirely on ambient energy discharge. Wind and sunlight, the waterfalls of the river. Trains, they love the energy of trains. I wish more people understood that—how they eat the energy of a thing, not the thing itself. Some of them have gone as far west as Hexindale, following the southern railway line. It's caused some worry. And then of course Crogard is rich in ore—they have no need to hoard treasure."

Felpz considered this, and shrugged. "Have there been any new developments since?"

"None at all," said Milain. "I'd only just returned from visiting the site when I heard you had already arrived. Here we are. Tero, this is the magician."

Tero was a magnificent dragon, if I consider myself any judge. Even bigger than Spheron, tall and sleek and blue-black, she had a crest of spines that shimmered in the sunlight, and this was raised to its full height as she watched us approach.

Felpz stepped forward, and the dragon bent her head so they were almost nose to nose. Man and dragon stood motionless for some minutes, until Abharus lost patience and cleared his throat.

Felpz looked around at us, as though we had woken him from a doze.

"Well, it is certainly no dragon I know of," he said, straightening his lapels. "Though that isn't saying much. This blood, though, does trouble me." He held up the little bottle and frowned at it.

"You know whose it is?" my daughter asked.

"No, but I think I know what it is. Corianne, can you tell me what you had for breakfast two weeks ago?"

I gaped at him. "How can I possibly be expected to remember that? And what relevance does it have to our case?"

Felpz smiled a little twinkling smile at me, and handed me the bottle.

"Try answering now. What did you have for breakfast two weeks ago?"

"Two slices of toast with strawberry preserves, a cup of tea, a biscuit and a small bowl of porridge," I said promptly. Then I gasped and clapped a hand over my lips. The words had formed in my throat and got out of my mouth before I realized they were there. "Felpz, what is this?" I cried.

Abharus snatched the bottle from me, and holding it tightly said with dead certainty:

"It's griffin's blood, Corianne."

"A griffin? In Kyreland? But how did you—"

My daughter nudged me gently with an elbow. "Griffins are emblems of truth. They say it's impossible to lie when in the presence of one."

"A somewhat inaccurate description," Felpz said, plucking the bottle from Abharus's unresisting hands. "The truth—and be sure I speak it here—is that griffins possess the element of truth. This manifests itself by compelling honesty in people who are nearby. Holding a piece of a griffin—such as its blood or bone—magnifies the effects tenfold. It will summon the truth out of you, even if you have forgotten it or are unsure."

My daughter, who had been listening to this shrewdly, nodded once. "Well then, Mr Felpz, what has become of the griffin whose blood this is?" she asked.

Felpz frowned. "I'm afraid that I do not know, and so this blood helps us little in that regard. However, if Tero will be so good as to show me the way, I would like to take a look at the place where you found this sample."

"Oh, but Tero isn't—" Milain began, intending no doubt to begin a long explanation of how dragons are not horses and do not carry people on their backs unless they know and respect them, but Tero was already fanning her wings and extending one long, spiny foreleg towards Felpz.

Instead of mounting the beast, Felpz stepped gently onto Tero's claw and took a firm hold of the spike protruding from her elbow. He made us a stiff bow.

We watched in astonishment as the dragon's huge wings spread wide, the long fingers embedded in the webbing like dark branches, with the membrane between glowing from the sun shining through. For a moment we were enveloped in a deep blue shadow, and then with an almighty clap Tero leapt into the air.

We were buffeted by a sharp stinging wind, and I felt a tingle along my skin from the blast of pure magic the dragon used to fling herself into the sky. I ducked and turned my head away from the turbulence, and when I looked again Felpz was only a tiny figure clinging to the leg of the soaring beast as she veered off across the low peaks.

Milain was staring after them with the look of one who has just witnessed a railway accident.

"Tero allows no one to ride her—no one but me." Then she shook herself. "No, I should not be so surprised, should I? Where has Spheron got to?"

"If you plan on chasing after him," I said sternly, "make allowances for at least one more passenger; I am coming with you."

"Yes—you are?" My daughter looked around distractedly.

"I'll find my own way," Abharus said, and quietly disappeared. I am convinced only I saw him go; Milain was too preoccupied pouring instructions on Spheron to notice.

Spheron, it appeared, was not so obliging as Tero. He agreed to carry us, but not on his back: Milain had to run back to the stables and fetch out what she called "the basket."

This was a contraption I was already familiar with. On my previous visit Milain had coaxed me into taking a short dragon flight in the basket, an experience I spent the following days trying hard to forget. The basket was a stiff sack made of heavy canvas laced to a metal ring. A person could stand in it, and the ring would come up to her shoulders if she were my height. Attached to this ring was a muddle of ropes which the dragon carrying the basket held in its claws. In this way a person could travel by dragon in relative safety, if not comfort, without the dragon suffering the indignity of carrying that person on its back.

As it turned out, even though Milain was a good deal slimmer than her mother, the basket could not be made to fit both of us. The solution Milain concocted did not please me: she sat on the metal ring with only her feet inside the sacking, holding onto the ropes.

"Goodness, Mother, calm down," she said in response to my concerns. "I've done this countless times!"

I need hardly point out this had the opposite of the intended effect.

It was with my heart in my mouth that Spheron took off with us suspended so hazardously below him. The storm of wind and magic whipped up by the dragon's wings was many times worse when stuck under it, and I was temped to crouch right down in the bottom of the basket. As it was I held on tight to the metal ring with one hand, and my daughter's leg with the other.

Milain tells me the mountains are a beautiful sight from the air, being able to look down between ridges and peaks to the narrow, glittering rivers and the tops of trees so distant they look like models on a child's play set. I have to take her word for it: I was far too terrified to notice any details beyond the great expanse of sky overhead that threatened to swallow us up, and the stinging wind in my face. For though the dragon used magic to augment its flight, this applied in no way to us, and I was overly conscious of the fact that only a layer of cloth and some hemp ropes prevented us from plummeting to our doom.

After a tumultuous flight, Spheron set us down in a remote valley where an ancient landslide had left a wide sandy beach pillowed up beside the stream. Beside this sat Tero, her large blue bulk standing out sharply against the yellow sand and stone of the canyon. She was watching Felpz, equally conspicuous in his purple suit, who in turn was regarding the center of the sand bar with extreme gravity.

Once I had extracted myself from the basket I could see why: it looked like a large animal had been slaughtered there. Old blood stood in pools and lay in streaks; the sand was turned and gashed so deeply even the more recent footprints of my daughter and her colleagues could not disguise it. Flies gathered profusely at the edge of the pools, and the whole place smelled vile.

It was late in the summer afternoon now, and the tall peaks rising on either side cast the whole scene in a soft blue twilight, yet still the blood glimmered in that way peculiar to the substance, and it was present in such volume that I felt my stomach clench. I am not by nature a weak-nerved person, but since my youth I have had an aversion to copious gore, and the sight put me off balance.

Milain, on the other hand, had banished any such weakness as she had apparently banished her fear of heights. She strode right up to Felpz, put her hands on her hips, and said: "Well? What do you make of it?"

For his part, Felpz did not seem at all surprised to see us. He looked up from his contemplation of the ground and blinked.

"Clearly, someone was killed here, or at least mortally injured," he said. "You observe the gashes in the ground, the disrupted soil?"

"Yes," said Milain, as if answering a painfully obvious question.

Felpz ignored her tone and carried on. "It crashed here. Attempted to take off again . . . failed. Then, it appears, someone came to its aid . . . " Felpz had circled the mess as he spoke, and now came to a halt beside a peculiarly smooth patch of sand. It looked as though something very large had blown on it, scattering the grains to cover any track. Felpz looked up at Milain, a hard crease between his eyebrows.

"Are all the resident dragons of Crogard known to you?" he asked. "Aside from this interloping elder dragon you speak of?"

"We have fifty-two adults on our books," Milain replied promptly. "But these are only the ones who have come forward and allowed themselves to be known. We estimate close to five hundred live in Crogard, but . . . " she glanced deferentially towards Spheron and Tero, who were standing loftily apart and not deigning to look at us, "dragons don't take kindly to their territory being invaded, and that is the last thing we want to do."

"Rather late to develop a sense of propriety," Felpz remarked with a sigh. "Still, late is better than never I suppose. Yet it doesn't help us now. There was a dragon here, I am sure. You see the traces of a body being dragged away? Yes, well, they go nowhere. They disappear into this . . . " he waved at the patch of wind-blasted sand, "obfuscation."

"You think a dragon carried the body away?"

"I am sure a dragon did," Felpz said. "The question is, which one? And why . . . is this a dragon's kill? Or is it something else . . . ?" He trailed off, letting his gaze wander over to the two dragons.

Felpz squared his shoulders and walked over to Tero and Spheron. Though they towered above him, Felpz somehow gave the impression of being their equal in size. The purple ghost of billowing sleeves and a trailing cape flashed on the edge of my vision, and I got the strangest sense of potential power, like water behind a dam, welling up behind him in this strange, distant way. Felpz, the man Felpz, was but the lid on a much deeper well—and we could only perceive its presence now because he wished us to.

Or at least, he wished the dragons to.

"You'll find it is in your best interests to answer my questions plainly," he said to both of them in such tones of authority that Milain's jaw dropped.

The dragons did not appear agitated; they regarded him impassively. Felpz took their silence for acquiescence.

"Do you have an interest in this matter?" Felpz asked, waving a hand at the nearby scene. "Specifically, do you have an interest in whether or not we learn the truth of it? If you are ignorant of the truth and have no objection to our untangling this mystery, please continue to assist us. If you are not. If you do not wish us to follow this trail to the bitter end, then I must request you remove yourselves and no longer provide us with false service."

Milain was staring in horror by the end of this speech, and I half expected the dragons to roast Felpz on the spot.

Instead they turned to one another, mantled their wings in a draconian shrug, and then as one leapt into the air, the force of their wingbeats like small thunderclaps as they soared away into the sky.

Felpz straightened the collar of his coat and smoothed his hair down.

"Just as well," he said, turning back to us. "Now we may make some actual progress."

I had never seen my daughter struck speechless, but there she stood staring at Felpz, her mouth still agape. I could see a torrent of outrage slowly building behind the shocked façade, however, and I hastened to intercede.

"Do I take this to mean those dragons are somehow involved in all this?" I asked.

Felpz dusted off his hands and returned to the messy scene. "Involved, yes, there is no doubt. But on which end I am not so sure. I see your daughter has inherited your talent for glaring holes in the side of my head. Please do not look so betrayed, Miss Birch. Once I get to the bottom of this I have no doubt your dragons' actions will seem perfectly reasonable."

"You sent them away!" Milain exclaimed, fighting back a slew of insults I could tell were boiling in her chest.

"I merely asked them to remove themselves if they were here on false pretexts," Felpz said rationally.

Milain looked ready to launch into one of her lectures on the proper treatment of dragons—powerful magician or no—when there was a shimmer in the air and the soft sound of feathered wings. A gust of wind smelling faintly of wet grass and flowers lifted the hairs on my neck, and Abharus stepped out of nowhere onto the sandy beach.

Or not quite nowhere. It appeared to be out of nowhere, but I got the distinct impression that he had just dismounted from a horse—or horse-shaped being.

He looked pale in the summer twilight, with a tightness about his mouth that boded ill for the news he brought.

"I found her," he said, gesturing at the blood. "The griffin, I mean. I found her body, or what's left of it."

Felpz's face darkened at that. "Near or . . . ?"

"Not far," Abharus said. "But hidden, and rather hard to get to. Hold on, Yuragorn can open a door on our end if you can do the rest here."

"Do so," ordered Felpz, and Abharus took firm hold of something invisible and vanished.

"Felpz," I said, laying a hand on my daughter's elbow. "Would you be so kind as to explain? What is this about doors?"

Felpz looked confused for a moment, as if surprised I should ask.

"Why, it's only a simple translocation spell. Similar to what I often do, but working with Yuragorn we can cross a greater distance in no time at all."

"And who," said Milain with steel in her voice, "is Yuragorn? I can't see him . . . her . . . it properly."

"Keep looking then," Felpz said, turning his back on us—but not before I caught the sly grin on his face. "When you see her you will understand."

The door that Felpz created was unlike anything I'd ever seen before. It was as though he pushed his hands clean out of the world and pulled aside a flap of curtain. From this breach a ring of light rose, sending out arms and tendrils like a spider's web, encircling him. At the center of this web, where the light was brightest, a small picture appeared: I caught a glimpse of a deep blue sky and high, red mountain peaks. A wind blew out of this image and brought with it that same smell of wet grass and flowers—a smell I was beginning to associate with the creature Yuragorn.

"After you," Felpz said, beckoning to us.

For once it was I who led the way, perfectly confident in Felpz's magic, and my daughter who clung to my hand—as she had not done in many years—as we walked down the glittering strands of web and into the picture.

We came out the other side into a gust of sharp wind. It was so strong I had to turn my face away in order to breathe, and I hunched my shoulders against it.

Abharus stood not far away, posed in a mimicry of Felpz, and beside him was the vague impression of wings and feathers and glimmering horn that was still all I could see of Yuragorn.

We appeared to be on a wide ledge near the top of a mountain: the evening sun was full upon us, but the air was noticeably colder and I felt light-headed. I was glad of my daughter's strong grip on my arm, and we steadied each other as Felpz came through, the closing of the portal causing the wind to back and buffet us irritably. I sank to my knees, all too aware of how much sky there was, and how little ground. This, however, only served to bring me closer to the reason for Abharus's summoning.

The bones and eviscerated skin of a griffin were laid out on the rocky slab.

Only the fear that I would tumble off into that great expanse of sky should I move kept me from writhing backwards.

The thing had clearly been dead for days and had been picked clean of meat and fat in that time. Only the skeleton, jumbled and scattered by the activity of scavengers, and pieces of hide, with here and there a few feathers, remained. The skull, which was as big as a horse's and had a beak a foot long, lay on its side near the cliff, and even from the distance of several feet I could see the movement of countless insects as they crawled over it, cleaning the curves and crannies of the bone.

Felpz came through so energetically that he nearly stepped right into the middle of this mess. He let out a surprised shout and danced sideways—towards the side of the mountain—and there crouched, observing the scene with grave eyes.

"I thought you said dragons only hunted when they had hatchlings to feed!" I exclaimed to my daughter, who was staring at the remains with equal surprise.

"So I said, but that hasn't stopped them poaching sheep," she said. "This is strange indeed. It could only have been a dragon that moved a creature of this size all the way up here, but why?"

"This death was not caused by a dragon," Felpz said from his perch by what had once been the griffin's tail. "And this"—he gestured at the scene—"was not the work of a predator." He leaned forward and began to crawl among the bones, turning them over and running his fingers across the sandy stone beneath.

"I don't believe I follow you," said Milain frankly.

Abharus, who had been standing very quietly with his hands behind his back, looked up at us with large, sad eyes.

"Dragons do not die," he said quietly. "They fly away into the sky and become stars. Griffins are creatures akin to dragons, being part bird—which are descended from the ancient dragons that once lived all over the world—and part cat—which have been friends of dragons since they first evolved. But a griffin cannot fly out of this world and rest in the ethereal sky—a griffin does die—so the dragons have done the next best thing." He waved a small hand at the bones scattered across the rock. "They gave her a sky burial."

"Some human cultures practice it as well," Felpz remarked from the middle of the bone field. "They lay out their dead on a cliff top, and the vultures come and eat it, carrying the flesh away with them . . . quite the kindest sort of burial, I always thought . . . " He was crouched on his tip-toes, running his fingers around and around, until with a cry of triumph one hand darted forward and snatched at something. Standing up, he leapt nimbly out of the bones and held out his hand to me.

There in his palm was the squashed remains of a lead bullet.

Milain stared at it, wide eyed.

"I don't understand," she said. "What does this mean? And . . . how do you know this individual was female?"

Before Felpz could answer, Abharus made an inarticulate gasping sound, and I caught a sharp whiff of Yuragorn's scent as the creature swept her wings out in alarm. A second later I smelled something else: something scorched and burned, hot and dry; the smell of a desert baking under the sun.

A new wind blew across the mountain. Where before all had been cool—almost chill—and smelling of clear mountain air with a hint of pine . . . now I felt a rough, hot wind on my cheek. It blew not up, from the canyons and valleys below, but down, out of that wide, blue sky.

A sky that had become much darker for the great shape that was sailing, like a spiky black thunderhead, down upon us. Its wings stretched from peak to peak across the nearest valley, and in its shadow Tero and Spheron, who were flying below, looked as small as sparrows.

"Felpz?" I said uncertainly. I was surprised I could speak at all; for I felt as though my heart was in my throat and beating fit to burst.

"Get behind Yuragorn," Felpz commanded, and he turned and leveled a piercing stare upon Milain. "For your future edification," he said
pleasantly, "that is not an elder dragon. That is what is called, by the
people who are in a position to call them anything, a Royal Dragon. A
ruling drake. They usually remain in the Dragon Lands."

"Then what is it doing here?" demanded Milain.

"That is one of the questions I will ask, when it arrives," Felpz
replied. "Whether it answers, that is another matter."

The dragon was definitely making for our mountain by this time. It
was circling above us, each circuit bringing it lower and lower. Every
time it passed, it brought another gust of hot, dry wind.

In colour it was a glossy, iridescent black, pricked with glimmers of
purple and blue. Its webbed wings, which must have been three hundred
feet long each, were slightly translucent, pale sky showing through them.
I could make out a dark latticework, like tree branches, that stood out
against the grey-blue of the membrane. It was soaring in the manner of
raptors, with its wings fully outstretched, and along with the sharp sting
of magic, I could feel waves of heat radiating down from it.

This dragon, I thought, did not need to breathe fire—it could set the
mountains alight with a beat of its mighty wings.

There was a gentle tug on my hand. I looked down to find Abharus
there, his face very pale but set in a determined expression.

"Come stand with me," he said. "Let Felpz do the talking."

He led us to a corner where the jutting ledge met the sheer rock
of the mountainside, beyond the remnants of the griffin. It felt just as
exposed—now the great dragon was level with us, circling the moun-
taintop and drawing ever closer—but then I heard the gentle rustle of
feathers, and a draft of cool air smelling of wet wildflowers washed over
us. By this time I could almost see Yuragorn's wings as they enfolded Abharus, Milain and myself, and I got the strongest impression of a large,
horse-shaped body. A long, jagged horn like a piece of starlight leveled
at Felpz, who stood brashly at the edge of the cliff, his purple coat-tails
flapping in the hot wind of the dragon's flight.

It passed before us once, twice more, the last time its wingtip grazing
the mountainside. Then it dropped out of sight.

I do not think the mountain actually shook when the great dragon
landed, digging its claws into the rock as if it were made of clay, but that
was my strong impression. Certainly there was a horrible, thundering
noise like several avalanches, and I felt the rock vibrate beneath my feet.

Felpz stood calmly through this all, his feet in a wide stance and his
hands clasped modestly behind his back.

Slowly, its horns like the masts of a sunken ship rising from the deep,
the dragon's head came into view. Up close I could see more clearly the
contrast between its shiny black, and iridescent blue-purple, scales that
shone in its dark skin like vivid stars. It had many rows of black horns,
all smooth and curving, save one or two that looked somewhat mangled,

and a string of plate-like protrusions that began between its eyes and dis-appeared behind the ridge of its head, creating heavy, forbidding brows.

Its eyes were deep blue pools set in black caves, and its thin-lipped mouth looked wide enough that, should it open, it could have swallowed all of us in one gulp. I could not see any teeth, but there were enough spines and spikes decorating its snout to make it appear as though it were snarling.

The dragon breathed out through its wide, flaring nostrils, and the air around us caught fire.

The sight of Felpz disappearing into those flames is not one I will ever forget, nor something I ever wish to see again. I felt my cry of horror die in my throat as the wall of fire hit us.

Then at last I saw Yuragorn. For the flames did not wash over us as they had Felpz, but hit an object that stood between us and the dragon, and there died. In the dying fire I saw the shape of a large horse, its limbs strong and graceful with thick feathers about its feet. Its tail was like that of a peacock, with long, flowing feathers, and in place of a mane, a crest of feathers. The wings spread wide above us to block the fire, and for a moment I saw its head, the profile of a noble equine with a jagged horn protruding from its forehead, its ears pinned back along its neck.

Then the shape against the fire turned. I saw its feathers, stretching like the fingers of spread hands, and the creature reared up onto its hind legs and beat its wings.

A rush of cool air came out of nowhere, the scent of wet flowers almost overpowering, and the dragon's fire rolled back, thinned, and died away entirely.

Felpz still stood at the edge of the cliff, his coat not even singed. The dragon's face regarded us, its eyes narrowed to glinting slits. Yuragorn was invisible once more.

"That was entirely uncalled for," Felpz said placidly, dusting off his shoulder.

The dragon snorted, sending jets of steam out of its nostrils. I saw Felpz move his hand over the jets of hot air as they passed him, and by the time they reached us the air was cool.

"We are not your enemies," Felpz said calmly. "We only wish to learn the truth."

The dragon stared at us. In its mountainous face I thought I could discern an expression of skepticism. Its breath washed over us, hot and clean and burning, like the first direct ray of sun on a desert morning.

"Will you not speak to me?" Felpz asked eventually.

The dragon's eyes flickered in their caves, and I felt the beam of its attention fall on me. Memories of the demon I had faced years ago rose in my mind, but the dragon was something very different. Where the demon's voice had felt like burning acid, the attention of the dragon felt like being dunked in a river of hot water. It made my mind sluggish and slow.

Then the dragon moved its attention to Milain, and while I was still reeling from the sensation Abharus jumped forward.

"I'll do it," he said loudly. "I will speak for you!"

There was a disturbance in the air around Yuragorn, and the dragon's gaze focused on Abharus like a searchlight.

What happened next I found difficult to understand at the time, but I now see it this way: the dragon beckoned to Abharus, even though its forelegs were currently clinging to the mountain. Abharus walked forward, stiffly, until he stood before the dragon's great spiny snout, and there turned to face us.

Only it was no longer Abharus. It was as though we only saw the shell of him, and something else entirely looked out at us through his eyes.

"I have read of this," whispered Milain, her hand clamped on my arm. "Some of the elder dragons cannot speak to humans at all, so they find one whose mind is attuned to theirs and use them as a translator!"

I shook my head, trying to clear it of the dragon's presence, and watched in mute horror and fascination as the dragon began to speak in Abharus's delicate, child voice.

"This . . . is not your concern, human mage." Abharus's mouth moved, and it was Abharus's voice, but it was the dragon's words and the dragon's will. It spoke slowly, as though getting used to this new, small mouth and tongue, but its words were quite clear. "Go back, humans. Go back to your cities and your little wooden houses. Go back. Play your music. Leave this place where my children live, and do not meddle in the affairs of dragons. If I catch you again, I will not be so gentle."

Abharus wobbled on the cliff edge, steadied himself, and then it was Abharus who stared back at us, his eyes wide and his mouth gaping open. It was undoubtedly Abharus who said:

"Felpz, she's got me. Her name is Kasarvo and she is very strong. Don't worry," he added, even as he walked backwards until he came up against the dragon's snout, hooking his arms over the two nearest spikes and holding on as if for dear life. I understood why a moment later when the dragon raised her head, lifting Abharus with her.

Abharus shouted something, something that was lost in the hot wind of the dragon's breath—which burned now more than ever, and I guessed Yuragorn had left us—and I saw Felpz run to the very edge of the cliff, clearly intent on catching Abharus's words.

With a mighty rumble the dragon leapt back from the mountain, her wingbeats hurtling air at us with such force that Milain and I were thrown back against the rock. In the strange way of things I did not feel the burst of magic the dragon used to propel herself upwards, but tasted it like hot sand in my mouth. The sensation was so intense that I actually bent over and spat, thinking I had somehow got a mouthful of dust, but nothing came out, not even spittle; my mouth was perfectly dry.

As the wingbeats of the dragon faded to distant thunder Felpz came back from the cliff, smoothing down his hair which had been blown all over by the dragon's breath and fire. He was frowning to himself, but did not seem particularly upset. Perhaps it was this relative serenity that caused me to fully realize what had just happened.

"That . . . that overgrown lizard!" I cried. "She took Abharus!"

"He will be in a better position than we," Felpz remarked, going over to the bones of the griffin—which had been blown up against the side of the mountain during the encounter. He took off his coat and laid it flat on the ground, then began carefully piling the bones into it. "This situation is indeed puzzling."

"P-puzzling?" cried my daughter, clearly thinking several steps ahead of us. "This is downright inconvenient. How will I explain this to the director? If we can find a way to get back—without Tero or Spheron to help it will be rather difficult." She looked accusingly at Felpz.

Felpz actually chuckled, and went right on collecting bones. I patted my daughter on the arm.

"Felpz has ways of making distance inconsequential," I explained. "Remember, he is a magician."

"Yes, yes, space folding," said Milain, looking bleakly around at the mountaintops surrounding us. "I can't see how that helps us here."

"You work with beasts who by nature are intensely magical," Felpz said, tying the sleeves of his coat together to secure the bones. Holding this odd bundle in both hands he stood up and smiled at us. "Have a little more faith in my magic. Corianne, be a dear and hold this." He passed his burden to me. It was large and bulky, but astonishingly light. "Now, it will be easiest if we join hands," he said, looping an arm through mine and extending the other to Milain. "Can you picture the landing field behind the abbey?" he asked as she took his hand reluctantly.

"Yes, easily," she replied.

"Good," said Felpz. "Imagine it in every detail—close your eyes if it makes it easier. Now hold that image in your head . . . "

There followed a jarring transition so abrupt it made my teeth hurt. It was as though the piece of the world we stood in were torn away, and behind that the field of Draco Abbey pushed forward. For one horrible moment I was uncertain whether I stood on the mountain cliff or on the singed grass of the field. Then the latter scene solidified, and I breathed in thicker, sweeter air and caught a whiff of horses from the stables. I found my feet planted in short, yellow grass, and a little ways off loomed the dark body of the abbey. The mountains were distant spires rising above us once more, silhouetted against the setting sun.

"Oh . . . my goodness," said Milain in a small voice. "You never said he could do that."

"He never has in my experience," I replied, once I could speak again.

Felpz, who might have taken issue with this conversation, appeared not to hear; he was striding away towards the abbey, beckoning to an astonished stable lad as he went. Finding I still held his bundle of griffin bones, I made haste to hurry after him.

Bouragner Felpz moved like a man on a mission, and we did not catch up to him until he was seated at the head of a long table in the reference library while young interns ran and fetched him book after book. A tall, grey-haired man with sloping shoulders and a burn scar on one cheek, whom I recognized as Dr Asifian Vayar, the director of the Draconian Institute, stood at his elbow looking bemused. His gaze hardened when he saw Milain, and he frowned disapprovingly at the bundle in my arms.

"We do not make a study of the griffins in this area," he said to Felpz, clearly answering a question that had been asked before our arrival. "They migrate through twice a year, but are not permanent residents. It would be highly unusual for one to be seen here during summer."

Felpz moved aside the book in front of him and picked up from the table the small lead bullet which he had found in the griffin's remains.

"Rare enough to surprise a farmer, already set on edge by having his stock in close proximity to dragons?" Felpz asked.

"That is an extraordinary claim," said the director uncomfortably. "What proof have you besides a lone bullet . . . " he trailed off as Felpz beckoned to me to hand over the bundle, and taking it he shook out his coat so that the scorched bones tumbled forth over the book-laden table.

A young intern cried out and snatched a particularly aged volume out of the way, but the rest were buried under the deluge of griffin remains.

"What is this?" cried the director, understandably affronted.

"These," said Felpz, spreading his hands over the bones, "are the remains of a griffin who came to these parts under duress and met with a very unfortunate end. It was shot, escaped, only to perish in the mountains. There the dragons found it, buried it after their fashion, and are in their way looking after its affairs."

"Its affairs? What affairs could these be?"

"My associate is looking into that as we speak," Felpz said placidly. "I expect an answer before morning. In the meantime, Miss Birch," his eyes rose and fixed themselves upon my daughter, "the first sheep that was killed . . . are you certain beyond a shadow of doubt that a dragon killed it?"

"I . . . " Milain seemed taken aback by this idea. She swallowed her initial affirmation, and a contemplative expression crossed her face. At last she sighed. "I assumed," she admitted. "The animal was well grown—nothing but a dragon could have carried it off."

"The name of the farmer to whom it belonged?" Felpz asked.

"Er, it was McMorris I believe?" she looked questioningly at her director, who nodded.

"Edther McMorris has the largest lease in the grass valleys," he explained. "We've had complaints from him before, but nothing as serious as this."

"And he reported the poaching of the first sheep? The one lost two weeks ago?"

"Aye, that is so," said the director. "It was he also who complained of losing one two days ago."

"Can you get a message to him? By human courier, preferably," Felpz said, scribbling a note.

In due course a courier was drafted and sent running with Felpz's letter. Milain, clearly impatient and uncomfortable under the disapproving eyes of the director, twisted her hands and muttered ominously.

"Wyvern would have been faster."

"Ah, yes, I nearly forgot," Felpz said, his face brightening. "Where is that charming fellow Radcliffe? I have a favor to ask."

Radcliffe arrived minutes later, accompanied by a small flock of other wyverns. They crowded onto the sill of the largest window and peered in excitedly as Felpz went to greet them.

"I need something found," he said frankly. "It may or may not be there, in which case I need to know one way or the other. You are looking for the remains of a sheep, well-grown, colour . . . " he glanced at Milain.

"McMorris keeps Borerays, most of them are white—he's very proud of them," she supplied.

" . . . likely dropped not too far from McMorris's farm. Give the mountains there a good sweep and report back. There will be—" he raised a finger at the ensuing clamor of high wyvern voices "—there will be biscuits for all who participate, whether a corpse is found or not."

The clamor's nature changed from protest to enthusiasm, and in a storm of leathery wings the wyverns scattered into the evening.

Felpz returned from the window and surveyed the table of books. He picked up his coat and shook it out, then put it on again and sat down. He looked up at our expectant faces with an expression of perfect innocence.

"Friends," he said, giving us a beatific smile. "Please, sit down. I imagine it will be a little while before Mr McMorris arrives, no need to pass the time on your feet."

So it was we were all seated around the table, which was still covered in old books and griffin bones, when a red-faced and breathless intern put in his head and announced, "Mr McMorris of Lower Rivenstone—" before Edther McMorris pushed him aside and entered the room.

He was a large man in both height and girth, with a forthright bearing and an expression that declared he was not best pleased.

Despite our visitor's daunting appearance Felpz leapt up and greeted him like an old friend; jumping out of his seat, he fairly danced across the room and clapped the man on the shoulder.

"Mr McMorris you are just the man I wished to see," he said jovially, shaking the astonished farmer by the hand.

"I have to admit you have me at a loss," McMorris said, with understandable reserve. He eyed Felpz's bright purple suit with distaste. "I'm here to answer a summons from Dr Vayar, who claims to have apprehended the one responsible for poaching my stock."

I did not bother to look, but laid a calming hand over the director's, who sat next to me. "Leave all to Felpz," I whispered to him. "He may be inscrutable, but he always has some clear end."

"A thousand apologies," Felpz said, throwing his hands up. "I did not mean to mislead you—for it was I who wrote that note, not the director. Forgive me, I am Bouragner Felpz, a magician of some small ability—but I do have your poacher."

"Indeed," said McMorris, narrowing his eyes at Felpz. "That news gladdens me." His manner was anything but glad; he made an involuntary jerk to put some space between himself and the magician. "Where do you have him restrained?"

"Restrained?" cried Felpz with a laugh. "No restraints are necessary. For you see, she—er, it is rather more likely that it was female, you see—is right here." He flung a hand out to the table covered in bones, the griffin's skull staring wanly from the center, and in that moment all his benevolent good nature quite deserted him. His tone grew chill and his face grave, and he looked very hard at McMorris as the man took in the grim sight.

I watched with interest as the farmer's ruddy expression went from suspicious to confused, and was just building into offended when Felpz spoke again.

"Mr McMorris," he said in that peculiar resonant voice that was quiet yet piercing at the same time. "Did you shoot a griffin that you caught hunting on your land two weeks ago?"

McMorris's head jerked up. He looked furious, but he said quite readily:

"Why, yes I did, the damn beast was harassing my sheep. She'd got one of my best ewes in her claws by the time I got there. I had my rifle with me, and I took a shot. The damn thing flew off but I'd do it again given the chance." The man's mouth snapped shut, and a look of panicked horror rose in his eyes as he realized what he had just said.

"That is . . . I meant to say . . . " he stammered. The words seemed to catch in his throat and drown in it. "How did you—?" he gasped.

Felpz smiled humorlessly. "I direct your attention to the contents of your left waistcoat pocket," he said. "Which contents, I admit, are entirely my doing."

McMorris groped in his pocket, his face now very pale, and produced the familiar vial of black blood.

"What—" his mouth worked wordlessly on lies the blood would not allow him to say "—is this?" he managed at last.

"A griffin's blood," Felpz said softly. "The blood of the griffin you killed. She may have flown on, but she left behind enough of herself to allow me to trap you."

McMorris gaped and stammered, clearly attempting to deny this accusation, but the vial of griffin's blood sat heavy in his hand and did not allow the lies to pass his lips. At last Milain went over and plucked the item off him.

"While I do not condone Mr McMorris's actions," said the director sadly, "by law he has done nothing wrong; he is perfectly within his rights to defend his stock, and griffins are not a protected species here; it is perfectly legal to shoot one."

"It is not the arm of the law Mr McMorris has to fear," Felpz said coldly. "It is the animosity of dragons, which I shouldn't need to point out are a law unto themselves."

"But the Institute said—" McMorris began.

"Have you forged a pact with their brood mother?" Felpz demanded, fury rising behind his eyes. "Have you sworn your soul to them under the old stars? Have you walked into the fire and called it friend? If not, then you mean nothing to the dragons. You are a pest, an intruder who has killed one of their allies, and no human promises can save you. There is nothing left to be said. I will not wish you a good evening, but I recommend you have a care on your way home."

McMorris was actually cowed by this onslaught, and seemed to shrink back in on himself. He turned to go and shuffled miserably out the door.

"You mean to just let him go?" Milain said indignantly.

"What else can I do?" Felpz said. "As your director says he has broken none of our laws. The dragons will deal with him in their own time."

The director blanched visibly at this thought, and after a moment Felpz took pity on him.

"Well," he said with a great sigh. "Perhaps Mr McMorris can be induced to move his farming elsewhere? To Gaela, perhaps? I understand there are no dragons on Gaela."

"None of this tells us what the dragons are doing," I pointed out. "Or what has happened to Abharus . . . "

"One, I hope, should explain the other," Felpz said cryptically. "But don't fret over Abharus; he's been in hotter places and has more experience in these matters than you might think."

Nevertheless I did fret over Abharus. All through supper and into evening I spun disconcerting narratives in my head, working myself into a shocking state of nerves.

We were seated in one of the small turrets that had historically been used for star gazing, but was now the wyvern's rookery, when events finally began to unfold.

Milain sat at a desk in the corner going over a pile of paperwork, while Felpz sat astride the windowsill, one leg dangling outside and kicking lazily at the stonework. With nothing better to do, I took a stool by the door and attempted to write in my journal, but found by this point I was too nervous to write anything. I had only got so far as "At least he has his Yuragorn creature with him . . . " when, as if in response to my thoughts, I smelled the scent of sweet grass and rainy nights, and a cool breeze blew into the little room out of nowhere.

Felpz kicked his leg inside and looked about alertly while Milain and I got to our feet. There was a whorl in the air by the wall, and I recognized the beginnings of another portal.

"Felpz?" I said tentatively. "What does it mean?"

"It means it is time to discover what this has all been about," Felpz announced, and strode through the portal almost before it finished forming.

Milain and I looked at each other across the space where he had been, then throwing aside our pens and paper, we dove after him together.

We came through into a confusion of darkness and hard stone. I groped about, grazed my hand on a sharp rock, and then found Milain's arm.

"Where is this?" she cried indignantly. "Mother, what has your magician gotten us into now?"

"Quiet," came Felpz's voice out of the darkness, and I swallowed back my reply.

I reached out, tentatively, hoping to find him, and instead felt a warm and furry flank which heaved under my hand. Whiskers brushed my face, and raising my hand to push them aside I felt the unmistakable shape of a horse's nose; soft and a little wet. It breathed out cool air that smelled of a wet night and flowers.

I remembered the shape in the flames.

"Yuragorn?" I said. "Where is Abharus?"

"Here," came Abharus's voice from somewhere near the ground. He sounded tired, but strangely triumphant. A tight knot that had been in my chest the whole evening finally loosened.

"Felpz, could you manage the light?" he asked. "I'm exhausted."

In response, a gentle yellow light bloomed, and by it I saw Felpz bending over the shape of Abharus, who was leaning up against the wall of the cave we appeared to be in. In his lap was sprawled a creature covered in downy white fur with short, stubby wings. Its beak was long and hooked, like an eagle's, and it rested comfortably across Abharus's right arm. It was fast asleep.

Felpz stood up and looked over at Milain with shining eyes.

"You were right after all, after a fashion," he said. "It was a hatchling."

"But not a dragon," said Abharus, gently extracting a hand and stroking the creature's feathers.

Responding perhaps to our voices, perhaps to the light, the creature made a crooning noise and lifted its head. It blinked, then stared up at us with eyes the colour of amber.

"A griffin kit?" Milain whispered in astonishment. "What on earth is it doing here?"

To her second question there was no immediate answer, but it was unmistakably a baby griffin which lay across Abharus. I could see now its front and rear legs, which were that of a cat, and its long feline tail which had not yet sprouted the stiff feathers that would enable it to steer in flight.

"Some crisis must have driven its mother to hatch her egg here," Felpz said, gazing at the animal with sad, fond eyes. "What that may have been, likely we shall never know."

The kit was not afraid of us; it got up — kneading Abharus painfully in the stomach — and walked on wobbly, uncertain legs towards Felpz.

Milain, with her natural affinity for strange animals, came forward and intercepted the griffin with wide, steady hands. She spoke to it softly, her voice low and cooing — not unlike a large bird. She dipped a hand into one of the pockets of her belt and produced a small strip of dried meat.

"I always keep some handy for the wyverns," she explained, offering it to the griffin. When the animal turned its nose aside Milain simply put the meat into her mouth, chewed it, then spat it back out onto her palm. Now the griffin found the food attractive, and snapped it up with a flash of beak.

"Have you ever cared for a griffin before?" Felpz asked.

"None as young as this," Milain admitted. "I usually see the regulars when they come through in the fall and spring. Sometimes we give them a meal."

"Griffins possess a human intelligence," Abharus explained, shifting into a more comfortable position. "This one is only a few weeks old. She keeps crying for her mother."

"Oh," I said, my heart sinking. "Oh dear."

"Is this what Tero and Spheron were hiding?" Milain asked, but without rancor; she was too distracted trying to measure the griffin kit while feeding it more chewed meat.

In response, a great noise filled the little chamber. It was not a roar: it was too calm and deliberate to be called a roar. It was merely a vast exhalation of air into a large and echoing chamber. For the first time I thought to wonder what lay beyond the sphere of Felpz's little yellow light.

"Oh dear, she's back," Abharus said, getting stiffly to his feet. "Kasarvo. Felpz, I meant to tell you. Kasarvo once served Eldis and Aldor — she knows griffins — that's why the other dragons called her in; they didn't know what to do with the kit after the mother was killed. Kasarvo has been protecting —"

He was cut off by a roar as the far wall of the cave burst into flames.

I looked again, and saw this was not quite so: the far wall was no wall at all, but a great window onto a vast cavern beyond. Something had just breathed a wreath of flames past the aperture.

Far from being distressed, the griffin kit squealed in joy and took off at an unsteady trot towards where the fire—now spent—had flared.

Milain, clearly expecting it to injure itself, followed hunched over, her hands hovering protectively around the animal's head.

"Oh, Milain!" I cried, as I had in years past when she had done unexpected and perilous things. But now—as then—she ignored me, and followed the little griffin until it stopped, propping its feet up on the ledge of rock that marked the end of our little cave.

Felpz moved his hand and the light grew stronger, revealing the great face of the huge dragon as it peered in.

Milain looked up, saw the mouth large enough to swallow her in a single bite, saw the deep, glimmering eyes, and put her hands on her hips. Then, to my shock and horror, she began to berate the dragon.

"Don't you dare think of breathing fire at me, drake," she said loudly. "Not with your little one right here. What have you been thinking? Leaving her all cooped up in the dark? Abharus seems to think you know a thing or two about griffins, but I'm not so sure. And what did you mean trying to roast us all earlier today? Did you really believe because one foolish and frightened human shot the mother we would only be interested in killing her child? Well! You may be a very ancient and learned dragon, but you clearly don't know much about humans."

She paused, her chest heaving, and still the dragon did nothing. The baby griffin mewled and pressed its feathery head against Milain's nearest hand.

"Abharus, what is she saying?" Milain asked, the tenseness audible in her voice at last.

"Nothing," replied Abharus from the back of the cave. "She is thinking."

With a faint shuffle Felpz went to stand across the griffin from Milain. He put a protective hand on her shoulder, then said:

"Forgive me, but there seems to have been a great misunderstanding here. We have no intention of harming this child. Indeed, I will do everything in my power to keep her safe."

The dragon's face regarded us with thoughtful, distant eyes. Then a white crack appeared along her snout, rows of pearly sharp teeth shining in the dim light as her scaly lips peeled back. Yet still no fire rushed out, and I realized with a jolt that she was smiling at us. Her mouth opened, but all that came out was a huge, satisfied sigh. Then the great head vanished downwards into the dark.

"I don't understand, what just happened?" Milain said in confusion.

"Kasarvo says, 'it is good,'" Abharus supplied. "She says she will take us back to your . . . um . . . lair. She says to wait."

"Wait?" cried Milain. "For how long?"

For answer there was a rumble from beyond the window, and the little griffin yipped excitedly. It scrambled up onto the ledge, and then jumped.

Milain shouted. I ran over, catching myself on the stone ledge, and gazed out.

The baby griffin was only a few feet away, apparently scrambling over a steep and spiky cliff. Felpz raised a hand, and his ball of light drifted free of the cave and shone more brightly.

I saw then that the dragon had not gone away, but merely turned about so that her great, wide neck was even with the cave entrance. The griffin sat atop it, its claws spread wide to grip the uneven surface.

While we stared in amazement, Abharus calmly pushed past us, making the short jump across nothing to land among the jumbled spikes and scales of the dragon's neck. He took up a perch behind the griffin and turned to us.

"She says to get on," he said. "Before she changes her mind."

I do not like to think of what followed. Even with Felpz in front holding my hand and Milain pushing me from behind I barely made it over the gap and onto the dragon's neck. Then I lay there gasping, clutching it with both hands. I felt ridiculous as Milain leapt over nimble as a mountain goat and came to sit behind Abharus, while Felpz sat comfortably beside me, but I was glad of my grip a moment later, when the great shape we were riding began plummeting through the dark.

Any cry of surprise that managed to escape my throat was quickly whisked away in the rush of air. I felt Felpz's steadying hand on my shoulder, and I reached out and grabbed his arm.

We fell through the black and empty cavern. The dragon's scales were warm to the touch, smooth as water-polished rocks, and smelled of a hot day under the sun.

With a great rush we came out of the cave and into the relative brightness of a night sky pricked with countless stars. By craning my neck I could look back far enough to see along the dragon's spine and down her tail, to where a huge, gaping maw of a cave in the base of a mountain yawned.

The wings of the dragon spread, and like dark sails they filled and we were whisked off over the mountains.

Strangely, now that we were out in the open sky my fear subsided. Having ridden magical flying animals before, I recognized the feeling of weightlessness I had experienced when riding a night mare, and I knew this dragon was using not only its wings to push the air about, but also a great deal of magic to make its substantial body much lighter, and by extent its passengers as well. However I still clung fast, as we were traveling at such speeds I feared the wind would blow me off otherwise.

The dragon's head was just visible before us as a large, black silhouette with craggy spires of horn jutting out from it. It eclipsed the starry sky and must have cast an even greater shadow over the land below.

After a time we were joined by two other dragons whom I recognized as Tero and Spheron. They twirled in the air about us like sparrows around a hawk. Milain laughed and shouted something at them, to which they replied by letting out piercing wails. To my consternation this caused the griffin kit to respond in kind, and the noise became truly terrible. It was almost a relief when the giant dragon let out a long, low, rumbling roar, drowning out the keening of its smaller brethren.

When the noise of that had faded away all was silent but for the swishing of the night wind, and we were descending low over familiar spiky mountains.

I heard later that the landing of Kasarvo at Draco Abbey sounded like a thunderstorm and woke the entire town. She came in so low her wings blocked out everything, and many people thought it was a cloud of black smoke. They said that when she touched down the ground shook, and several of the more delicate windows in the abbey were shaken out of their frames. The wyverns in the rookery were sent into fits of extreme agitation, and many of the animals not secured in their stalls bolted.

Dr Vayar tried to storm out onto the landing green to see what the commotion was about, but was prevented by Kasarvo's left forefoot blocking the door; the dragon was so huge she could barely fit in the field without crushing some fence or building, and so filled it entirely. Indeed, this was the reason for the small earthquake: rather than landing at a run as dragons preferred, Kasarvo had been obliged to drop vertically out of the air. We all felt it when she landed.

Abharus, moving in that strange, stiff way that suggested that the dragon was in control, not himself, dismounted and went to speak to the director, but not before he beckoned to the little griffin to come with him.

It took both Felpz and Milain working together to get me down off Kasarvo's neck, and for the final plunge off her foreleg Felpz was obliged to levitate me down.

I arrived in a storm of leathery wings. All the wyverns had focused on Felpz, yammering in their high, childlike voices.

"No sign of it?" I heard Felpz say. "Well, the dragons must have come back and picked it up. No matter. I shall speak to the cook about your biscuits, Radcliffe, now if you'll excuse me . . . " Felpz began forging a path after Abharus and the baby griffin, while Milain and I followed in his wake.

When we arrived, the director was speaking, somewhat distractedly, to some vague point halfway between Abharus and Kasarvo's face. He seemed to have realized Abharus was merely acting as the dragon's mouthpiece, and wasn't sure which entity he should direct himself towards.

"It's not that we don't like griffins. We are quite fond of griffins. I'm merely saying that we have no experts on griffin behavior."

"I should hope not," said Kasarvo through Abharus. "A griffin must learn to invent herself. What she must know about flying and hunting she can learn from us. No, I do not want you to teach her how to be a griffin. I want you to teach her how to be human."

"I'm sorry?" stammered the director. "Isn't that rather . . . um . . . presumptuous? Surely in time she may be reintroduced to her own family . . . "

"A griffin is not a dumb wild animal, it is an intelligent wild animal. Specifically, it has a human kind of intelligence. She cannot learn your tongue, your art, your music from us. This we entrust to you. We shall take care of the rest."

"Excuse me," Milain said, coming up and tapping at Kasarvo's claw, which was all she could reach (the dragon's head being a dark shape hovering two stories off the ground). "Do you mean to say, you want us to educate this griffin? But she's hardly a month old!"

"Griffins learn fast," came the answer out of Abharus. "She should begin early. It will be easier for her. Your language is harder than you think for one not born to it."

It was difficult to tell in the dark, but I thought the dragon's face took on a rueful expression at this.

"Well, in that case . . . " Milain looked around at the director.

"An elder dragon has just entrusted us with the care of a baby griffin," he replied with a stern glare. "Of course we accept."

"She's a Royal Dragon, really," Felpz sighed. "But that does settle things nicely, I think."

It was not quite so simple, of course. Farmers complained. There were concerns over the sudden and continued presence of a dragon the size of a small castle outside the town: for Kasarvo made it quite clear that she did not intend to simply abandon the griffin. She took to roosting behind the abbey, watching all the comings and goings with fascination. The positive aspect of this was that no one so much as commented on the arrival of the baby griffin — who came to be known as Rumpus, for obvious reasons — though McMorris did indeed sell his farm and move away after the first month — more likely because of Kasarvo than Rumpus.

Felpz and I stayed for a week. He spent a lot of time sitting with Kasarvo, speaking in a tongue none could hear but them. As a result, after six days Kasarvo could speak Kyrish in simple sentences — albeit in voice so rumbling and breathy it was almost impossible to understand — and Abharus disappeared with a sigh of relief.

To my delight Milain took charge of Rumpus's education, so I received a continual string of letters in the following months. She grew very well, her white down quickly shedding out to reveal a reddish brown coat with stark, black and white wings and tail feathers. Spheron taught her to fly by jumping with her off the highest tower in the abbey. By the time the fall migration passed through, she was more than ready to rejoin her tribe. It was a bittersweet day when I received the letter informing me that Rumpus had left Rivenstone, but a joyous one indeed when I learned the following spring that she had returned and decided to stay for the summer. Griffins were all well and good, she declared, but they did not have a library, and Rumpus wanted above all to learn to read.

As for Kasarvo? The great dragon remained at Rivenstone for Rumpus's first summer, and after the initial shock—after she showed no interest in raiding farms or setting the town on fire—the people accepted her as part of the landscape. She even allowed the dracologists to observe and study her, and I understand that the unique opportunity to see a living elder dragon—as the dracologists insisted on calling her—in the flesh more than made up for the disturbance that Rumpus caused.

Kasarvo left one night in early autumn, presumably returning to whatever distant world she originally came from, and has not been seen since.

Rumpus still lives at Draco Abbey, and though she is not strong enough to carry Milain about on her back as the dragons do, she follows my daughter on most of her expeditions. Milain tells me her intelligence rivals that of Dr Vayar, and that she wants to become a dracologist, like Milain.

"A griffin studying dragons!" Felpz exclaimed when I told him. He laughed. "That will be something. Oh, Corianne, can you not wait to see the books she will write?"

Author's Note

Eldis and Aldor, to whom Abharus refers in reference to Kasarvo's experience with griffins, are the legendary lieutenants of Bandur, one of the old Rian earth dragons. Eldis is described as a snowy white griffin while Aldor is pitch black. According to legend they are the mothers of all modern griffins. With this in mind it is not surprising that Kasarvo, having once served them, would be sympathetic to one of their descendants—no matter how much time had passed.

The Dragon Lands, which Felpz alludes to, are a hypothetical world that exists beyond the boundaries of our own. Very little is known about them, save that they operate by a very different set of rules.

Yuragorn is an alacorn: an extremely rare creature thought to be the origin of both unicorns and paragaids (winged horses). Alacorns exist on their own frequency, and so are difficult for most people to see. By all accounts they are intensely magical, and rarely form alliances with humans. How Abharus came to be such good friends with one is a story in itself, which shall be told another time.

five

The Three Fates of
TALIAS MINN

I T WAS IN THE EARLY HOURS of a wet morning in the autumn of 2316 that
the curious character of Talias Minn entered our lives. He did so quite
memorably, knocking the ancient Mrs Bryce over in his desperation and
bursting into the sitting room before we had even begun breakfast.

He would have been an ordinary and rather plain young man under
normal circumstances, but now his face was so flushed from exertion it
was red as a cherry, and he wore a bright gold and blue knit scarf wrapped
around his neck and thrown over one shoulder. This stood out against
his otherwise conservative attire and neat, sensible brown hair. His eyes
were very wide and darted about the room in frantic confusion before
settling on Bouragner Felpz, who was in the act of pouring tea.

"Oh, Mr Felpz! Mr *Felpz!*" he cried, darting forward. Then he froze,
his chest still heaving, and shut his eyes. With them still closed he said
in tones marginally more calm: "Please make no mistake: I am not a
lunatic, but I have been put through such unusual stress I feel on the
verge of losing my mind. Say you will help me, for I fear no one else
can!" He passed a hand over his face and wobbled on his feet.

I took the opportunity to leave the table and draw up a chair for him.

"Sit *down* young man," I said, guiding him into it. "It's not like me
to make promises on behalf of someone else, but rest assured Mr Felpz
will do all he can for you."

Thus reassured, the poor youth buried his face deep in both hands
and began to shake with silent sobs.

Felpz leant over and offered him the cup of tea he had been pouring for himself.

"See that he drinks this, Corianne," he told me. "And there is the bottle of whiskey on the mantel which may prove useful. Look after him while I see to poor Mrs Bryce, will you?"

Mrs Bryce, though aged, was a solid old woman and more amused by the incident than anything else. Once she had been set up in an armchair in her kitchen with a pot of her own and some biscuits, she sent Felpz right back up to "see that young one straight, like you always do."

By the time Felpz returned I had coaxed our new guest into drinking his whiskey-fortified tea, and he was more or less composed. He had taken off his scarf and now wound it nervously around his hands, while he looked up at us in hopeful distress.

"I am so sorry," he choked out at last. "It is only . . . the last few days . . . well, how could you know? My life flows in a very different channel from yours, and there is no reason that an important city magician should know about the trials and tribulations of a country bumpkin such as myself."

"Yet I am willing to learn," Felpz said, pulling up a chair and sitting down opposite. "Whatever could have caused you to alter the course of your life in order to interrupt my breakfast *must* be important. Now, the first thing you can do is tell me your name, and then explain very slowly and calmly exactly what has driven you into such a state."

The young man looked on the verge of tears again, but he mastered himself with a supreme effort and drained his cup before beginning.

"My name is Talias Minn," he said, a little shakily at first. "I live in Milton Drew, which is a little village outside Corvisgate. I am the son of the vicar, and have spent much of my life preparing to succeed him—or to move to a nearby town and perform the same duties. As a result I have little knowledge of practical magic—though I have a great deal of learning regarding the mystic acts of the saints—and I blame my ignorance entirely for allowing myself to become entangled in the unfortunate situation I now find myself.

"First, some background, which will help. Growing up in a small village, you must understand I had a very small social circle. There were my parents, my cousin Molly, who came to live at the other end of town when I was very small, and my uncle Samiel. I grew up playing with the other children my age, but as we have matured they have one by one left our village and gone to pursue careers in the cities. There was a good score of us when I was young, but now there is only myself and two others: Darik, who I was never very close to, and Falchone, who came to our village from Fortau two years ago. Her Kyrish was not very good at the time and, as the most learned person close to her in age, I nominated myself to tutor her. We found we got on very well. So well, in fact, that by the end of the first year we had determined to get married.

We have been engaged for three months now and plan to be married at New Year's. And this is where all the trouble began.

"Two weeks ago was the annual autumn festival, and my cousin Molly insisted on dragging me to the fair. Once there it was not enough for me to stand back and watch her 'ooh' and 'ahh' over the attractions; she took me to one of those cheap diviners with a crystal ball and demanded I have my future read.

"I tell you Mr Felpz, I have never believed in any sort of divination except that performed by the angels and the saints. Just as well, because the future predicted by the festival's witch was not at all attractive. She divined that my steps would be dogged by birds, every day a new bird, until the day when one hundred birds were following me at which time I would lose all my hair and come to a sudden end.

"Cousin Molly laughed at this and told me to try another witch to see if I didn't have better luck. And although I didn't believe a word of the prediction, I did feel it was an ill omen for a fellow about to get married, so I agreed. She took me to a witch who lived outside of town, and I sat down in her parlor and she gave me this prediction:

"I would live happily until the day before my wedding. However in the months leading up to that day I would meet a stranger in the village who would give me ten crests to hold for him until he returned. If I refused him I would die on the eve of my wedding. If I accepted and then spent the money myself, my fiancée would die on the eve of our wedding. And if I accepted and was faithful to him, my fiancée and I would have a long and happy marriage but without any children.

"None of these outcomes seemed at all desirable to me, and I was flustered by the certainty of the witch. When she saw how upset I was she patted my hand and told me to visit her mother who lived on the other side of Corvisgate.

"In my right mind I do not think I would have accepted, but I was already agitated from the first two predictions and now more than ever wanted some reassurance. Falchone thought I was being silly, but as I could not get the two predictions out of my head she agreed I should go, on the condition that once I got a favorable prediction I would cease talking about it.

"Well, I went to the witch's mother's house, which was on a modest farm outside Corvisgate. There she grew vegetables and kept chickens, and I was at first put at ease by the wholesome appearance of her home. No sooner had she got me into her kitchen, however, than I was gripped by an unusual fear. I could not describe it and so tried to ignore it, but as she began to tell my future it only grew and grew.

"This third and final witch—more aged than the other two—told me to stay away from dogs, because each dog from now on would be more and more aggressive towards me, until finally I would meet one that would leap upon me and tear out my throat. I asked her if there was any way to prevent this, and she told me that the only thing to be done was to avoid dogs.

"I went away very shaken indeed, but on the journey home I managed to convince myself it was only so much twaddle. I put the whole distasteful matter out of my head and began working on preparations for the wedding.

"But now . . . " The poor man leaned forward, covering his face with his hands. "Now I simply don't know what to *do* . . . "

Felpz put his head on one side and looked at our guest curiously. "Why such distress?" he asked softly. "Is one of the predictions coming true?"

Talias Minn raised his face, and his eyes were wide as saucers, his cheeks blotched white and red.

"No, Mr Felpz," he said in an agonized whisper. "They *all* are."

Such was my experience with my friend the magician that I could almost see the searchlight of his attention snap to Mr Minn; it was something in the sharpening of his gaze and a tenseness about his mouth, though to the casual observer he must have seemed unchanged.

Talias Minn certainly thought so.

"You *must* believe me," he said, extending his hands pleadingly. "My neighbor's little dog, which is usually the sweetest thing, has taken a set against me, and now I cannot pass their door without the dog running out and trying to bite me. The butcher's dog growls at me if I come too near. It has gotten so that I avoid dogs as much as I can, lest one of them attack me. Furthermore, ever since the day of the festival I have been followed by birds. More and more each day. And then, yesterday . . . yesterday I met a man in the village; a man I had never seen in my life before. He approached me out of the blue and handed me a ten crest note, saying he would have to go away for a time and he couldn't take it with him.

"I was so frightened I nearly ran off, but I remembered what the witch said would happen to me if I refused. After the dogs and the birds I did not find it so absurd."

"You took the note?" Felpz asked sharply.

"I have it here," replied Talias Minn, reaching into his breast pocket and drawing out a crisp, white bank note.

Felpz took the paper between his long deft fingers and held it up to the light. I saw his eyebrows rise, and he passed it to me with a low whistle.

"You have me at a loss, I am afraid," I told him, examining the note. "It looks perfectly ordinary to me." I handed it back to Minn.

"It *is* perfectly ordinary," Felpz said. "As ordinary as you could please. Just as I suspect this stranger is ordinary in his way."

"You think this is all a great coincidence?" Talias Minn exclaimed, a flush of anger in his pale face.

"I never like to rule it out," Felpz remarked pleasantly.

"Ha!" cried Minn, leaping up and darting to the nearest window. Thrusting open the blinds he pointed out into the street, where a healthy beech tree was in full, autumn splendor. Standing out sharply against the fiery foliage was a mass of black birds. Some were recognizably ravens, others smaller and sleeker—crows—and others were smaller still: blackbirds and starlings.

They sat eerily still, but I saw their little heads move to keep Talias Minn in their sight. The effect then was like dozens of eyes in a great bushy face, all staring at you. It was quite unnerving.

Felpz frowned. He got up and went to the window. Pushing it open he put his head out and called to the birds, as if they were a passel of children who had been misbehaving.

"Now what is this all about?" he asked. "Come, explain yourselves."

But the birds only shivered in the tree, and then they scattered, taking off in a mad whirring and whumping of wings, causing a shower of orange leaves to fall on the pavement below.

Felpz brought his head back inside, his frown even deeper than before.

"What does your fiancée, Miss Falchone, think of all this?" he asked, closing the window.

Poor Talias Minn, who seemed entranced by the departure of the birds, shook himself out of his daze.

"Oh, she thought it was nonsense at first, but recently she has become as concerned as I. It was she who recommended you to me. Apparently she read of your exploits in Elgany some years ago and was quite impressed."

Felpz raised an eyebrow at that and shot me a sardonic smile. "Ah, the matter of Kliser Kurn," he said. "I don't believe I told you about that one, Corianne. Too dark, too distasteful. Though I managed to sort things out well enough."

"If you could apprehend one of the most dangerous criminal magicians in modern history, surely you can tell me what is going on?" Talias Minn burst out. "My means are modest enough, but rest assured I will pay you whatever you deem worthy—"

Felpz raised a hand at this, and Minn's speech stopped abruptly.

"Let us not talk of payment," he said. "It can cloud one's judgment. Put that matter out of your head until this issue is resolved. And yes, I believe I can tell you what is going on, though at present I cannot tell which of the many possible explanations that have presented themselves is the correct one.

"You say that dogs have taken a set against you; you say that birds follow you—as we have seen—and now this mysterious stranger with his ten crest note. Have you considered the possibility that there are more mundane explanations for these events?"

"Mundane—how?" gasped Minn, perplexed.

Felpz came and sat in a chair opposite him, twisting his hands together expressively. "It is unusual for such prophecies to take root so strongly. Is it possible that someone has learned of these prophesies and is making them *appear* to come true? It is not as hard as I wish it were to place a spell upon someone that makes birds flock to them, or makes dogs dislike them. That stranger could have been an actor hired to be part of an elaborate prank."

Talias Minn looked flabbergasted. "But . . . but who would *do* such a thing?"

Felpz shrugged. "Someone jealous, or vindictive, or just plain malicious. Is there anyone in your circle who would or could harbor such feelings towards you? Anyone, perhaps, unhappy with your impending marriage?"

Talias Minn's whole face wrinkled in thought as he pondered this.

"No one that I can imagine," he said unhappily. "My family is overjoyed, and Falchone's relatives, though they are abroad, have been nothing but supportive." He ran a distressed hand through his hair and sank into his chair. He was such a pathetic sight that I felt my heart swell in sympathy.

"Well, that is hardly helpful," Felpz said, the picture of clinical disappointment. He went around behind Minn's chair and bent down, as if inspecting the back of our guest's head. "Don't move, I beg," he said when the man started in understandable surprise. "I can at least rule out the possibility that you are under an enchantment . . . " and so speaking he began to run his hands through the air a few inches away from Talias Minn, making short flicking motions, as if he was brushing dust off an invisible coat.

"Don't fret child," I said, trying to soothe our troubled visitor. "I've seen Felpz pull people out of far more perilous predicaments than this."

"That is some . . . er . . . some comfort," Talias Minn admitted, holding himself stiffly still as Felpz worked over his right shoulder and down his arm.

Felpz snorted, but it was only in frustration at his task.

"Nothing," he said, standing up abruptly.

"What does that mean?" I asked sweetly, for I could tell he would not explain himself without a little prompting.

Felpz turned around from heading into his own room, apparently thinking of something else already. His lavender dressing gown swirled about him.

"Oh," said he. "Well, you're not under any enchantment that I can see. The problem is, if it is fate, I can't read that either. To tell the truth you *look* like any other thread, as free as Corianne or I. That is to say," he went on, seeing our clouded expressions, "someone under as dire a fate—not to mention *fates*—such as yourself usually appears to have a . . . a sort of *weight* about their spirit. You do not. That was what led me to believe that your perceived fates might have been practical constructs . . .

but I cannot find any evidence of the spells necessary for that either. It's problematic. I need more time. But you will hear from me soon, have no doubt."

"Oh," said Talias Minn, sinking into his chair. I could see how much this worried him—it was thoroughly worrying, after all—and I could tell he had been hoping Felpz could give him some immediate assistance.

"Felpz," I said, catching him as he made another dart towards his room. "Is there nothing we can do for him *now?* Surely there is some charm or amulet you could give him that might alleviate the negative effects of the birds and the dogs?"

"Oh," said Felpz, and he actually stamped his foot—just like a child—in his impatience. "It is not as simple as that. I am not some general practitioner handing out placebos. No, it would be better to monitor their progression—we may learn something from it."

"In that case," said I, mentally striking the next week off as a loss on the writing front, "why don't I accompany him, so that I might observe the effects first hand? It would do well for him to have someone to confide in, at least."

Felpz blinked, as if this were the first thing I had said that he understood. His eyes sharpened, as they did when his mind was working furiously, and he looked from Minn to me and smiled slightly.

"Yes," he said at last. "Yes I believe that would work very well. You do not mind staying for a little breakfast, Mr Minn, while Corianne packs? It will not take long; she is really the most capable and efficient woman."

I could tell that Talias Minn was somewhat let down by this compromise, but he hid it well, and by the afternoon we were on our way out of Redling bound for Milton Drew.

Milton Drew, for those of my readers who have not had the pleasure of visiting the western lands of our country, is one of the many satellite villages surrounding Corvisgate, set among the rolling hills and hedge-lined lanes south of Barsbury Plain. In summer it is truly idyllic, but even in fall the place has a comfortable sort of beauty. Indeed, I found the country so delightful it was easy to forget what mission had summoned me.

I was reminded the moment we disembarked from our train when a large shaggy dog, who until then had been sleeping peacefully at the edge of the platform, roused himself and lumbered towards us, growling deeply with his ears laid back.

"Oh dear," cried Minn. "You see? You *see?* Even old Rumsfield now!"

I looked around, surprised to see that no one seemed at all concerned that a young man was being menaced by a large dog. I saw a middle-aged woman walk past and pause to stroke the beast on his reddish back, ignoring the malevolence he was radiating as he stalked towards us.

I do not have any unreasonable dislike of dogs, but I was not in a hurry to put myself in the way of such an ill tempered animal. Yet I still felt protective of Talias Minn, and I remembered how the birds had scattered when Felpz tried to speak to them.

Gathering up what courage I had, I stepped between Minn and the dog, and taking the firm tone I used on Felpz when he was being difficult, I said: "What is the meaning of this? Stop that growling nonsense at once and explain yourself."

To my intense relief—and Talias Minn's surprise—the dog stopped in his tracks, a startled expression on his wrinkled face. Then he shook himself and lumbered away.

Talias Minn let out a great sigh, and for a moment I feared he was going to swoon. I took his hand and flagged down a porter for our luggage, leading him into the station. Yet I glanced back as the doors closed behind us, and saw there, perched on the signal arm, a sleek black crow. It watched us intently until we passed out of sight.

In the cozy waiting room a tall woman with straw-colored hair leapt to her feet. She was young—about Minn's age—and quite handsome in a chiseled sort of way. Her clothes were well made but clearly old, dark and conservative with a high, stiff collar, yet she carried herself with such energy that she made them appear modern.

"Talias, Talias what happened to you?" she cried with a pronounced Fortaun accent, and I guessed that this was his Miss Falchone. She came forward and carefully took him off my hands, muttering soothing words in her native language.

"It's quite all right, Fal," Minn said, shaking himself out of her grip. "Just had a bit of a turn coming off the train." Clearly it was acceptable to show weakness in front of an old maternal figure such as myself, but not in front of one's fiancée.

Falchone looked at her betrothed in a shrewd way that suggested she knew exactly what had happened. "Didn't the magician help at all?" she asked.

Talias Minn brightened at that. "He has agreed to look into my case. And see, he has sent his friend Mrs Birch to look after us until he comes himself. Oh, Fal, you should have seen what she did to Rumsfield! Just one strong word and he slunk away like a chastised puppy!"

"Are you a magician as well then?" Falchone asked, turning to me. It was like being faced with a particularly rough-hewn marble statue: her skin was flawlessly smooth and pale, but the face it was stretched over was an angular one with high, jutting cheekbones like cliffs, and sharp curling lips. Her eyes, though I could see they were blue in color, remained dark, and so it appeared she had two black pools resting under her pale brows. This striking appearance was somewhat offset by her open and cheerful expression, and I took only a moment to collect myself.

"No, I'm afraid not," I said in answer to her question. "Merely an old friend. But I've assisted Mr Felpz on a number of cases, and I'm not inexperienced with this sort of thing. You may find me useful."

Falchone's face, which had darkened a little at my admission, brightened again.

"He has told you then, about the birds and the dogs and the stranger with the bank note? You still have it, don't you *chére?*" she asked sharply.

For answer Minn patted his breast pocket.

"Mr Felpz is pursuing many avenues of enquiry and hopes to have a solution very soon. In the meantime I am here to observe and offer whatever assistance I can."

"Oh, then you must come and see Miss Molly," Falchone exclaimed. "She was the one who got him into this mess. I've tried talking to her about it but she refuses to take me seriously. Perhaps now that the magician's assistant is here she will listen to reason!"

Smiling inwardly at the position that had been unilaterally assigned to me, I followed Falchone's tall, straight back as she led the way out of the station.

It was late in the afternoon and growing dark when we reached the vicarage where Minn and Falchone lived. This was a large, sprawling estate near the center of town guarded by rows of birch trees and flanked by two evergreens that stood on either side of the gate.

"It is good to have a guest," Falchone said as she let us in through the kitchen door. "Talias's father is away visiting his mother, and the place is too big and rattling with only the two of us. Here, come and sit. You find us in such a distressful time I don't see the point of hiding anything from you. Would you like tea and biscuits? Oh, I also have Hersian coffee—we have it all the time in Fortau but I must order it specially here—it is much stronger than tea though."

I sat a little bemusedly in their modest kitchen, gazing around at the blue and white plates on the wall and the faded salmon wallpaper. Here and there more exotic knick-knacks could be seen—evidence, no doubt, of Falchone's foreign roots. All in all it struck me as a good and unpretentious place—very much like what I had seen of the people who lived in it—and I felt it was a shame that their lives should be so disrupted.

Coffee was eventually agreed upon, to revive us from our journey, before we called upon Molly Minn. ("She lives close by, will be an easy walk. Good for your legs.") And as we sat and drank, Talias Minn began to recover somewhat. He was almost jovial when we left the vicarage, bundled tight against the cool autumn night.

Molly Minn lived at the top of a large house and turned out to be an older woman, closer to my own age. She was a little irritated at being roused from her relaxing evening, and even more irritated with Falchone, who let herself in without so much as a knock. When she saw Talias, however, she softened.

"Is this about those silly predictions?" she said, wringing her hands. "I told him not to take things so seriously, but it is all my fault really: I should never have taken him to see those witches."

"It is no good to make self-recriminations now," Falchone said briskly. "You can at least help us solve the problem. Look, here is Mrs Birch, who has come in place of the magician who is helping poor Talias. Tell her what you did."

Molly Minn, who was in her way quite a handsome woman with dark hair salted with grey and very large brown eyes, glared at Falchone. But she came around and said to me, quite civilly, "It began as a harmless enough joke, I assure you. Everyone knows these carnival witches do not *really* tell the future, but instead give positive, if vague predictions. I thought, with Talias so excited about his upcoming wedding"—here a sharp glance in Falchone's direction—"that hearing some reassurance would do him good. But instead the witch began spouting this nonsense about *birds* and suchlike.

"Well, I assumed it was malicious nonsense, but Talias took it mightily to heart—"

"I never did," interrupted Talias. "Until the birds started to follow me!"

Molly Minn waved a hand as if this were nothing important. "So I suggested he see a *second* witch, who would be more agreeable. But she was as disastrous as the first, rattling on about strangers and ten crest notes. I thought, this is getting ridiculous! I took him over to Corvisgate to see Mrs Dolhume—who I *know* is the best witch in the county and doesn't make up silly predictions—and *she* comes back with this thing about the dogs. Which I don't know what to make of. Dogs usually get along fabulously with Talias. But now all they do is growl at him. Is it true then, and those *really were* predictions?"

"It certainly looks that way," I admitted, at which the woman's shoulders sagged.

"Oh . . . I *am* sorry love," she said, patting Talias on the hand.

Falchone sniffed.

I glanced from one woman to the other, and decided a change of tone was in order.

"Nevertheless, I am *sure* Felpz will be able to sort this out. He's very good at solving magical problems."

"Oh, I do hope so," said Molly Minn anxiously.

In truth I was hoping Felpz would turn up sooner rather than later. I had not the foggiest notion of how to proceed, and the effects of Minn's fate made themselves noticeable as soon as we left Molly Minn's house. The tree outside her front door was filled with the round, dark shapes of owls, and these watched us intently as we left, before following us silently through the town. I tried shooing them off, but they only scattered to the nearest rooftops and sat there, waiting until we had progressed farther down the street.

We walked fast, wishing for the relative safety of indoors, but not fast enough to outpace the lean dog who fell in behind us after a few yards. Hearing its growl I steeled my nerves and turned around, prepared to scold it away, only to find it was actually three dogs, with a fourth lurking in a nearby alley. Their ears laid back along their heads and all of them growling low, they made a truly sinister sight. I did not blame Talias Minn for giving out a despairing wail, but I did wish he hadn't. At the sound of their quarry all the dogs darted forward.

"Get him away!" I cried to Falchone, waving in the direction of the vicarage.

The woman, bless her, did not have to be told twice, and Minn not at all. They pelted up the lane, while I put myself firmly in the way of the dogs.

"Now see *here*—" I began, but then they were already upon me.

Then they were past me, lunging silently through the night. I cursed, and turned to run after them, and found myself staring up at a jagged roofline covered in birds.

"You!" I shouted, forgetting how silly I must have looked in my frustration. "Why can't you do something *useful!*" I strode towards them, and they fluttered away.

All but one. This one was darker and leaner than the others, and I saw with surprise that it was no owl, but a raven. It looked down at me out of beady black eyes, and I remembered how Felpz often received messages via raven.

"You could at least tell Felpz about this," I shouted up at it. "I need him here *immediately.*"

The raven put its head on one side, as if considering. I thought to add, just in case, "I would appreciate it very much!" and then hurried after the stricken couple. I heard the sharp whir of its wings as it passed by overhead, and I wondered whether it would deliver my message or if I had just been playing the fool.

When I arrived at the vicarage it was to find a crowd of dogs sitting silently around the front door. They were arranged in a semicircle and were staring at the door as if they were cats watching a mousehole.

Thinking better of attempting to reason with them I went around to the kitchen door and let myself in there. I was confronted immediately by a white-faced Falchone wielding a carving knife, which she lowered as soon as she saw me. Behind her, in the hall, they had pushed the sofa against the front door and piled chairs on it. Minn sat halfway up the stairs looking down on the scene, huddled in a blanket but apparently unharmed.

"They aren't mad anymore," I explained. "They're just waiting around the front door. Still, I wouldn't recommend venturing outside until they leave."

Minn whimpered and put his head in his hands. Falchone set down her knife and went to comfort her fiancé, while I secured the back door.

It turned out to be a long night. Minn refused to go to bed, and so we were obliged to sit up with him in the parlor all night. This was a cozy little room well equipped with soft, comfortable armchairs, but even the most comfortable chair in the world can become a torturous device if sat on for too long.

Such was my fate, and I spent the night awkwardly dozing until, in the wee hours of the morning, my body succumbed to exhaustion and I fell asleep despite it all.

I was roused by an almighty crash from the hallway as the pile of chairs toppled. Half asleep and disoriented I could not remember for a moment where I was. Then I heard the familiar sound of Talias Minn's moan, and it all came back.

Minn was standing on the chair that had until recently served as his bed. Falchone had picked up a lamp and was hefting it menacingly — truly a most competent woman — before I managed to lever myself out of my own chair, which seemed to have half-swallowed me during the night.

There was a desperate scraping as the sofa was pushed aside, and I leaned into the hall to find none other than Felpz standing in the open doorway, the morning sun shining in behind him, as he surveyed the pile of furniture with some perplexity.

"Felpz!" I cried indignantly. "You could have *knocked!* You'll frighten Minn to death at this rate!"

Felpz's features sank into a tired, long-suffering expression, and he called out over his shoulder to someone unseen:

"Quite lively as I see. Thank you, and I apologize if she was rude."

There was a muffled *cawing* and the flap of wings. Felpz picked his way inside.

"My raven, it worked?" I asked in surprise.

"Rork is not 'your raven,'" Felpz explained. "She is a very kind and generous friend. I asked her to keep an eye on you during my absence, which she did most faithfully. Apparently you had some trouble last night with the town dogs? You may come out now, Minn, I can assure you *they* are not here anymore."

Talias Minn crept forward into the hall on tip-toe, clearly prepared to flee at the first sign of anything canine. When he saw it was only Felpz he relaxed slightly and let out a long breath.

"Are *you* the magician?" Falchone said, striding forward. "Does your presence mean you have a solution to our problem?"

I saw Felpz's eyes widen at the sight of her, but otherwise he remained unmoved. He put his hands in his pockets and cocked his head at us in a quizzical manner.

"Not a definitive solution, I'm afraid. I was hoping to make a few more advances before joining you, but Corianne's call from last night sounded so urgent I thought it would be best if you accompanied me for the remainder of my investigation."

"Investigation?" Minn said. "What is it you have been investigating?"

Felpz shrugged. "The witches, of course. They were a little hard to track down, and none too obliging when I did find them. I am satisfied, however, that the two I have managed to interview did not intentionally cast malicious fates upon you, nor do they have the skill to do so even if they wished to."

"But *Felpz*," I interjected. "There is something *very* strange and quite dangerous going on here."

"No doubt," Felpz said, wincing a little at my tone. "As I said, I *had hoped* to make further advances before I saw you. You remember I have only spoken with two. There is still the third witch who lives on the other side of Corvisgate. I had intended to visit her this morning, and if there are no objections I do not see why you should not accompany me."

"Excellent," said Falchone before either of us could reply. "Is a splendid idea, but first we must have breakfast. At least let me pack something for the train."

Felpz gave her an amused look, and at the challenging expression she threw his way he turned to me and shrugged dramatically.

Taking his meaning, I said to Falchone: "Felpz does not travel by train for such short distances. He has a much swifter means of transport. We might as well have a comfortable breakfast here before we set off."

It was late in the morning and the sun was peeking over some low clouds in the south when we again left the vicarage. Felpz strode in front, as was his wont, with Talias Minn fairly clinging to his coat-tails. Falchone and I took up the rear, and as we walked I attempted to explain the spatial folding magic Felpz performed in order to speed us on our journey.

"Imagine our world laid out on a sheet of cloth," I said, remembering the manner in which this practice had first been described to me, so many years ago. "We are like ants creeping across this cloth. Normally, it is stretched smooth and tight. What Felpz does is to create a fold in this cloth so that two points that would normally be far apart are now close together, and the ants—that is to say, *us*—may step from one point to the other and pass over all the distance in between."

Falchone's eyebrows went up at this, and she looked around at the little village intently.

"I see no folds," she said, a little skeptically.

"I've never actually *seen* it happen," I admitted. "But I've felt the effects. You will notice something, I am sure."

We reached the edge of the village, and though I noticed nothing odd, Falchone and Minn each exclaimed and pointed. According to them, it appeared we were now outside Corvisgate itself—not Milton Drew—and were heading down a narrow country lane leading away from that town.

It was a short walk from that point to the bottom of the lane where the witch kept her farm. Though Minn told me it was a full morning's journey when he went with his cousin, we arrived at the high, wooden gate within minutes. It appeared to be an ordinary farm at first glance, with a little barn and a cozy-looking house nestled in the fold of a hill. The drive was a dirt track, heavily rutted from the recent rains, which wound between low fences made of piled stones. On the other side a trio of goats watched us curiously.

Though the place had an aura of comfortable dilapidation, the wooden gate swung open at our approach as smoothly and silently as the best oiled steel door. Felpz gave it an approving look as he passed inside, and we followed close behind.

The door to the house itself opened in a similar fashion as we drew near, and Felpz walked boldly inside. When we entered, however, we discovered that the door's mystical action was explained by the presence of the witch herself, who had been standing behind the door and was revealed as she closed it behind us.

Mrs Dolhume was a short, wide, grandmotherly woman with a head of thick, silvery hair piled in a lopsided bun. She wore a faded blue dress under an apron with little dogs and cats printed on it, and large gold rings in her sagging ears. These glittered at us as she wagged her head in greeting.

"I can't say this is a surprise," she said in a cheerful, creaking voice. She shook a bony, bulbous finger at Felpz. "And I have to say it's a relief to see it's *you*. When Mirabell told me there was a *magician* asking after the fates of the Minn boy I worried he'd enlisted the help of one of those hard-mouthed college men who can't tell a rune of fire from a pig's arse. But now *you're* here, Mr Felpz, maybe we have a chance of sorting this mess out."

"My dear Mrs Dolhume," Felpz said, so startled by this greeting that he let slip a surprised smile. "It appears you already have intimate knowledge of these events. I have been hard pressed to find any concrete evidence, perhaps you may be able to enlighten us?"

"Come in then, come in," said the witch, leading us briskly through the little parlor and into a kitchen so large and cavernous I could not credit it with fitting into such a modest building, and I wondered if the witch had enchanted her house so that it was bigger on the inside.

This kitchen had a huge, wood-burning oven taking up an entire stone-faced wall, and a high ceiling strung with ropes from which hung bundles of herbs and strings of drying fruit. A long, wooden table ran the length of the room, and Mrs Dolhume rattled down it, scooping off dirty plates and mixing bowls and cutting boards, piling them on top of each other, and setting the lot unceremoniously next to a deep, stone sink. The whole place had a strange, uneven feel to it, which I soon realized was due to fact that the entire floor (paved with tightly fitting stone slabs) sloped down towards the center, where a thick, iron grate covered the aperture of a drain, half hidden by the table.

At the very end of this table sat the most unusual thing yet: a tall, slender person with the head and face of a deer, and a pair of large, impressive antlers. They wore only a simple loincloth, bound about the waist by a belt containing many pouches, and they were completely covered by a coat of fine, honey-colored fur. They were hard at work shelling nuts into a large bowl, and looked up at us with huge, dark eyes for only a moment before dropping back to their work.

"Sit, sit," commanded Mrs Dolhume. "Don't mind my assistant, Jeserry. Now, I think tea is in order, and then talking. Biscuits, anyone?"

It was some minutes before we were settled to Mrs Dolhume's satisfaction, but once we had been provided with piping-hot cups of tea, and a plate of biscuits each, she got down to business with the same brisk efficiency.

"I knew there was something strange the moment Mr Minn walked in my door," she said. "It was as though his destiny—which ought to have been in a state of constant flux—had divided and hung in two ghostly clouds above him, as if he had the *potential* for two fates, neither of which had crystallized yet. I thought to myself, I thought: what is this young man, who ought to have no very strong fate at all, doing with *two* potential ones hanging about?

"I should explain, as I believe I did the first time Mr Minn came here, that what I do is merely *read* the fate that is already there. I don't *lay* destiny upon anyone. The only difference in a person after they have been to see me is that they *know* what their fate is—which can itself drastically affect how events play out, let me tell you. So I sat down, intending to muddle through and hopefully dispel these clinging half-fates, as they did not look at all nice, when the most peculiar thing happened.

"I set about drawing up the strings of fate, as I usually do, and I came across a knot of sorts. It was this knot that contained the information about the dogs that so upset Mr Minn. Really it shouldn't have had such a pronounced effect, but as soon as I told him, it was as though all three fates—the two which had come with him and the one I had just foretold—suddenly solidified and became equally real.

"It was the most peculiar thing, and I'm afraid to say it so surprised me that I could not at first articulate what had happened. It wasn't until the next morning—long after Minn had left—that I managed to puzzle the thing out with Jeserry's help. Even then I could not imagine what could have led to such a ridiculous circumstance, until yesterday when my daughter came to visit me all in a fluster.

"My daughter, as you already know, is Mirabell, a witch herself. She came to me in such a state as I haven't seen her in since she was a child. 'Mother!' she cries to me the moment she's in the door. 'Mother, I have done something utterly foolish and I don't know how to fix it!'

"So I sits her down, like I have you, and she tells me about how, maybe a month ago, this young man comes to her and pays her a great deal of money so that, should a Mr Talias Minn come asking for his fortune told, she would read the most dire fate she could imagine.

"Now Mirabell's a good girl, and she would never do such an underhanded thing—there's enough charlatan witches out there to give us real practitioners some problems with credibility—but the young man was ever so insistent and made it to sound as if the whole thing was a great joke and he would reveal it to his friend later and they would all have a good laugh. Mirabell was still reluctant, but there's not a lot of money floating around in the life of a young witch, and so she took the job. She saw Mr Minn, told him a fortune she thought was safely ludicrous enough never to come true, and then tried to forget the whole nasty experience. But then, oh, but *then*—then yesterday she gets a call from a fearsome magician who is working on behalf of Mr Minn, and *he* says not only has the fate she predicted come true, but so has the one predicted by that poser, Narla Roost, *and* the one foretold by me, her own mother!"

Mrs Dolhume sat back in her chair and sipped her cup of tea serenely.

"She hadn't the heart to admit to you what she had done, poor child," she went on. "But now you're here be sure I've told you the truth, and perhaps we can set about clearing this mess away."

Felpz leaned back and crossed his legs, looking down the table at Talias Minn, who was sitting like a statue, holding Falchone's hand as if it were a lifeline.

"Thank you, Mrs Dolhume," Felpz said after some thought. "This has been immeasurably helpful. Yes. I do believe it explains what is happening to Mr Minn."

"It doesn't explain it to *my* mind," I pointed out. "You'll have to clarify, Felpz."

Felpz snapped his fingers in impatience.

"Have a little sympathy with those of us who do not have your vast experience," Mrs Dolhume chided, endearing herself to me in an instant. "I'm afraid I am still rather at sea over this myself."

Felpz stared at us in amazement.

"Is it not *obvious*?" he asked. "Why, it's as clear a case of the female trinity phenomenon as I have ever seen."

"The female what?" Falchone asked, speaking for both myself and Minn.

Mrs Dolhume, on the other hand, let out a sharp breath and said, "*Oh!* Now why did I not see that?"

"Likely because you were yourself a part of it," Felpz said mildly. "Practically the vertex, in fact. But let me explain properly or Corianne will have my hair. The female trinity effect, which is also called Shovid's Law—after the three-faced goddess of witchcraft—is the otherwise unexplainable sudden increase in the power and efficacy of magic when

performed in concert by three women. It can also be used to describe
that particular kind of magic that is attendant on groups of women who
work in threes. Trios of women are often more successful and more powerful than the sum of their members. Strangely, it does not affect men—
though there is a male equivalent, which applies to men who work in
teams of two—hence the *female* trinity effect.

"What we have *here,* in this particular case, are three prophesies made
by three witches. Each one, with her prophesy taken individually, should
not have been able to influence Talias Minn's fate—since two were false
prophesies and therefore no more indicative of what would happen than
a layman's fantasy, and the third should have been an honest reading; that
is to say, *descriptive* rather than *prescriptive.*

"However, because there were *three,* well, what Mrs Dolhume saw
hovering over Minn when he entered her house was clearly the potential
for these fates to become real—should they receive the boost of power
they needed—and this they received when Mrs Dolhume performed her
own fortune telling—because of Shovid's Law. Also, because Mrs Dolhume alone was attempting to perform a true reading, that trueness managed to bleed into the false fates, thus overwriting whatever mild, muta-
ble destiny Talias Minn ought to have.

"Is that clear enough for you?"

Talias Minn stared at the table for some minutes, apparently puzzling
through this. Then he looked up, and there was an odd kind of light in
his eyes. That of fever and panic, but also threaded with wild hope.

"So . . . " he said. "These fates . . . they are not my *true* fates?"

"Very few people have true fates," said Felpz. "In reality, we con-
struct and reconstruct our fate every day. What you have, to be more
precise, are artificial, malevolent destinies. They are not uncommon—
some curses use them—but I've never seen three of them at work at the
same time."

"But . . . but they weren't real?" Minn asked. "Were not *intended* to
be real? Not until Mrs Dolhume completed the triangle and then this . . .
this *Shovid's Law* came into effect and made them real?"

"That is a simplification," Felpz said blandly. "But more or less accurate. Ironically, one could say you brought them on yourself; if you had
stopped at one witch or two, their false predictions would have remained
merely suggestions."

"Felpz!" I cried. "That is *not* helpful."

"What *would* be helpful," said Falchone, a steely glint in her eye,
"would be to know who this young man who wished to frighten my
Talias was. I should like to have words with him!"

"I should like to have a great deal more than that!" Minn said, a touch
of color returning to his face, even if it was the flush of anger.

"He is undeniably important," Felpz remarked, turning to Mrs Dolhume. "He is the ultimate catalyst for these events—for I have no
doubt this mysterious young man who bribed Mirabell also bribed Narla

Roost—and if we are to untangle Minn from his unwanted fates, we will need his cooperation. I do not suppose your daughter described him to you?"

Mrs Dolhume looked up in surprise. "Described him? Why, she knew him. Did I not say? It was Darik Shaw."

"Darik *Shaw!*" Minn groaned, and not for the first time.

We had left Mrs Dolhume's farm and were walking back the way we had come. The witch accompanied us ("It's partly my fault you're in this mess, love, must do what I can to clean it up"), while her assistant, Jeserry, followed at a respectful distance. He carried a large sack strapped over his shoulders and walked with a long, twisted staff hung about with crystals that swayed and clinked as it moved.

"I have only met *Monsieur* Shaw once," Falchone stated. "He did not strike me to be very much of any sort of man. Not memorable, I mean to say."

"Perhaps Mr Minn knows more about him than he has divulged," Felpz suggested.

"About Darik?" said Minn distractedly. "We were at school together years ago, grew up in the same village, but you know I don't think I've exchanged more than a dozen words with him? He was always about riding his father's horses while I took a more scholarly interest."

"So you can think of no reason why he would wish such ill luck upon you?"

Minn stared off into the distance, his eyes wide and tired. "Not a reason in the world," he said.

Darik Shaw lived in a grand old house on the edge of Milton Drew. When we arrived, however, we were greeted by his housekeeper who told us Mr Shaw was not at home.

"Been out with his horses all day," she said, eyeing Jeserry with some curiosity. "Must say he hasn't quite been himself this past week. Better not to disturb him." And she shut the door on us.

"Queerer and queerer," Felpz murmured.

"Shall we wait?" asked Falchone.

Mrs Dolhume chuckled. "My dear child, you are not in the company of people who wait, not when they have a means to find what they want." She made a clicking sound with her tongue, and Jeserry came over, bending his antlered head until it was level with the witch's shoulder. Mrs Dolhume spoke to him in a low voice, full of clicks and hisses, and then Jeserry nodded. He walked out into the middle of the drive and turned around in a slow, full circle. Then he gave a little shiver, and with a bound, took off across the lawn, using the staff he carried like a third leg, the crystals clinking and flying, the sack bouncing on his shoulders as he went.

We followed his dark, cloven tracks at a more sedate pace, though Minn looked as if he wished to run—perhaps for fear of losing Jeserry.

The creature waited for us, however, whenever he reached the edge of our sight. Like this he led us in a jerky sort of way across a field and down into a dell where there was a large stable with an adjoining house. There we met a group of people, who stared when they saw Jeserry, but nevertheless came plodding up the hill towards us.

They appeared to be stable hands and groundsmen, from the way they were dressed, each one in a state of dejected frustration.

"See here," cried Minn, recognizing one—an older man with a short, grey beard. "Mr Kilnner, what has happened? Is something wrong?"

Mr Kilnner shrugged unhappily. "Wrong indeed, Master Minn," he said. "That there Mr Shaw has given us all the sack. Up and turned right to the devil, and there we were all going 'bout our business all good and proper."

"But he is still there?" Felpz asked intently.

"That he is," said Mr Kilnner, giving Felpz a strange look. "But good luck getting much sense out of him. And mind he may call the constables on you!" This last was shouted after us, as Felpz, not waiting for Jeserry's lead, had bounded off down the hill towards the stable.

He did not get far; at the bottom of the hill, just before the stable, was a veritable sea of dogs. They crowded round, all shapes, sizes and colors, and when they saw Minn, they growled.

Felpz stopped in consternation, and Jeserry understandably hung back. On their heels Minn steadied himself and glared back at the dogs—but from the safety of behind Felpz's elbow.

"Can't you send them away?" he was asking when I arrived, slightly out of breath.

"I'm afraid I already did," Felpz said, a little chagrined. "As soon as I received Corianne's message, in fact. I laid it on whatever was assailing you to return to its source. A long shot, as I was unsure how well the magic would work when performed at such a distance. But see? It has worked perfectly. Oh, Mr *Shaw!*"

The stable had a high barn of the sort with two stories and a door opening on the gable end—presumably to drop hay through. Beyond the crowd of dogs I saw this door open, and a disheveled, dark figure appeared.

It was hard to make out much of Darik Shaw from this distance, but I could see he looked to be in rather worse shape than Talias Minn had been when he'd first called upon Felpz.

Then, suddenly, the figure crumpled in on itself, and a flock of birds came swooping out of the door.

Minn flinched visibly, and Falchone, Mrs Dolhume, and I all raised our arms in defense. But the birds fluttered harmlessly into a nearby tree and from there watched us curiously.

"Did you lay it on *everything* that was assailing Mr Minn?" I asked Felpz, unable to keep the accusing tone out of my voice.

"From that distance I was unable to be specific," Felpz replied sharply. Then, turning back to the barn, he called in a much more soothing tone: "Oh, Mr Shaw. Do come down, Mr Shaw. There has been a grave mistake, but with your cooperation I see no reason why we should not be able to put all to rights."

The figure of Darik Shaw, still just visible in the open door, shuddered and unfolded into view. He wore good clothes, I saw, but these were so tattered and misused I wondered what sort of fit had come upon him, or if the birds, in their frenzy, had injured him. Yet when he came closer to the edge I saw no blood on him, and he appeared to be unharmed.

"What do you want?" he called out in a broken, anguished voice. "Go *away*. I told them all to go *away*."

"I am afraid that won't be possible," Felpz said. "Not until this is resolved. Mr Shaw, you *do* know why this is happening, do you not?"

"Stupid witches," mumbled the figure in the barn. "Stupid, *sodding* witches"—Beside me, I felt Jeserry stiffen, and Mrs Dolhume laid a hand on his arm—"it's all their flaming *fault.*"

"Fault may be assigned evenly, in this case," Felpz said mildly. "However, the credit for the instigation still rests squarely on your shoulders, Mr Shaw, and I am going to need your help in order to undo it. Tell me, why *did* you wish to frighten Talias Minn?"

This question gave Darik Shaw pause. He peered out at us, and for the first time seemed to realize we were not his employees. He stared past Felpz to Falchone. His hand rose, pointing a shaking finger.

"It was your arrogance that drove me to this!" he cried, his face red with emotion.

Falchone gaped at him in response, utterly at a loss for words.

"Why did you pick that wretched, sniveling little rat over *me?* You should have been *mine!*"

Talias Minn sputtered indignantly at this, but Falchone looked from one man to the other with complete composure. She looked from Shaw, red-faced and overcome with emotion, to Minn, white-faced and shocked.

"I should think," she said in a softly dangerous voice, "that would be obvious to anyone with a shred of common sense!"

Darik Shaw grimaced at her. Falchone folded her arms.

"Now will you do as the magician asks and help us?" she asked.

But Darik Shaw was already shaking his head. "No . . . no . . . " he groaned.

"Do you not wish the fates lifted?" Falchone pushed on.

"No!" cried Darik Shaw, and began to laugh hysterically. "No, no, you're welcome to them! If they drive you half as mad as I, it would be worth it!"

"Please stop that," said Felpz.

The crazed laughter stopped with a choke, and Darik Shaw stumbled backwards into the barn and out of sight.

Felpz rubbed his eyes, as if the whole situation were giving him a headache. From the trees the birds watched, and the dogs began to sit or lie down.

"What an inconsiderate young person," Mrs Dolhume said.

"He is certainly not making my life easier," Felpz replied tiredly.

Falchone, who seemed to have been doing some hard thinking, turned to face us and clapped her hands dramatically.

"I see what we must do," she said in her decisive way. "He will not help us undo the fates, so we must do it *ourselves.*"

"That will be easier said than done," Mrs Dolhume began to point out, but Falchone cut her off.

"You say this happened because three women predicted fates for my Talias? Because of this Shovid's Will they are all coming true? Well, what I see here is that *we* are also three women, and *we* don't want the fates to be true. I don't see why three women can't undo what three other women have done." She put her hands on her hips and cast a challenging look at her audience.

Felpz, who had listened to this announcement with moderate surprise, now began to smile. He was positively grinning when he turned to Mrs Dolhume.

"She makes an excellent point," he said. "That you were also one of the three original witches should help you in undoing it."

"I'm still not sure it can be done," Mrs Dolhume said skeptically. "Undoing fates as strong as these, when the instigator is so set on them, would be very dangerous. However, we might *move* them. Transfer them to another person, that is."

"Excellent," said Falchone. "Then we move them to Darik Shaw. That is as good as reversing them."

"But," said Talias Minn. "I don't wish these fates on Darik Shaw, much as he's proven to be a scoundrel."

"Then it shall be easy for me to dispel them, once they are shifted." Felpz said, patting him comfortingly on the shoulder.

"If I may," said I, speaking up at last, "I would draw your attention to the fact that, aside from Mrs Dolhume, neither of us has any practical magical skill."

And do you know, they all turned and laughed at me? Quite kindly of course, but I was rather affronted by it. Seeing this, Mrs Dolhume touched me gently on the elbow and said, a twinkle in her eye, "Don't you worry about *skill,* I've got enough skill for the three of us. No, it's power we're wanting, and between you and Falchone, if I do say so myself, I think we have enough power to move mountains."

"Particularly if you're working *against* the nature of the fates," Felpz added. "Corianne doesn't like to mention it, but she has a natural talent for rejecting malevolent magic."

"Then it is settled," said Falchone. "How do we begin?"

Feeling somewhat ridiculous, I allowed Mrs Dolhume to guide me into position alongside Falchone. We stood before the crowd of dogs—who seemed oblivious to our presence—and joined hands. I felt Falchone's wiry grip and the witch's hard boney one, and tried to not let my hands be crushed between them.

Mrs Dolhume began to rock forwards and back upon her heels, her head weaving about, as if searching for something.

"Oh!" cried Falchone. "I've *found* it!"

And suddenly I could see what she meant: the fates were tied around Minn like a knot of fine, almost transparent filaments, drawn impossibly tight. The ends stretched out of him, over our heads, and into the barn.

"Don't try to to untie it," Mrs Dolhume commanded us. "Help me shift it. *Slide* it."

Sliding is a good word for what we did, as little sense as that makes. Imagining myself taking firm hold of the knot of fates I pulled, and pulled, and slowly the knot did begin to slide along the translucent strings.

I know it may seem confusing to think we did all this while standing still and holding each others hands, but that is how we did it. It was as though my mind put out hands and arms of its own, and that was what I used to drag the knot away from Minn.

We had got it roughly halfway when all of a sudden it became much easier, and the knot fairly slipped along, disappearing into the barn. I realized it must have switched to Darik Shaw, like a magnet turning, and let go just in time.

There was a snap through the air like an invisible whip-crack, and suddenly all the birds gathered in the tree turned their collective attention from us to the open door.

At about the same time all the dogs—held at bay by Felpz's magic—turned and rushed towards the building, growling and barking.

"Quickly, Minn!" cried Felpz, urgently. "Do you wish your fates upon Darik Shaw?"

Minn wavered for a moment, but only because he had not seen what we had done and so was confused.

"N-no, I said so. Of course not!" he stammered.

And I saw how the string of fates—their ends still attached to him since Darik Shaw held the knot—broke free and spiraled through the air.

Felpz reached out—in the same manner as we had—and I saw him take hold of the loose ends and unravel the knot of fates bound to Darik Shaw, like someone pulling a thread out of a sweater. He pulled and pulled, casting the strings free into the sky, where they hung briefly before dissipating into the open air.

The baying of the hounds stopped abruptly, and the birds took off in a great rush of flapping wings. One by one the dogs left the barn, disappearing into hedges and through the surrounding fields, returning to their ordinary, inoffensive lives.

Lastly, Darik Shaw himself emerged from the barn, blinking and bleary eyed. Talias Minn marched up to him, and for a short moment I feared he would do the other man violence, but he only reached into his breast pocket and, taking out the mysterious ten crest note, thrust it into Shaw's hand.

"There," I heard him say. "You can riddle what to do with it. Good-day, sir. Good-*bye.*"

He left Shaw staring bewilderedly at the note, and taking Falchone by the arm began leading us in the direction of Milton Drew.

After seeing Mrs Dolhume home and Falchone and Talias safely installed in the vicarage, Felpz and I decided we would better serve everyone by going home again—it still being fairly early in the afternoon. But the couple insisted on seeing us off, and as we waited for our train, Falchone took me aside, a strange pink tinge to her otherwise marble complexion.

"You must forgive me, Mrs Birch," she said. "I feel so very silly. I only just remembered—I must have been more distracted by Talias's fates than I realized—but I think I've *read* one of your stories before. That's how I knew the name Felpz. But it was so wild and fantastical, though I knew the magician was real I doubted the story was. Let me assure you I harbor no such doubts *now.*"

I laughed and told her I was merely pleased one of my narratives had been of help.

"Do you think," asked Falchone with a sly twinkle in her eye. "Do you think, one day, perhaps this will make another story?"

"Well, that entirely depends," I replied. "Would you and Minn terribly mind being the subjects of one of my little ramblings?"

Talias Minn, who was standing nearby, only shrugged and smiled at Falchone, who clapped her hands delightedly.

So although in the past I have been obliged to change the names of the participants in order to protect their identities, in the case of the protagonists here I have made no such alterations. The reader will be pleased to know that, not only did the mysterious stranger never return, but the couple never received any trouble from Darik Shaw either. I am happy to say that Talias Minn and Falchone deQuivier were successfully married the following spring and are currently raising their first child. But if you visit Milton Drew you will not find them there; after the wedding they decided to move away, and where they went is one thing I have promised not to say.

six

THE STONE MAN

IN THE LAST DAYS OF 2317, leading up to Chandarmas, the whole of Kyreland was hit by a series of snowstorms. These were spaced such that we had a day or so of bright sunshine in which to enjoy the wintry scene, and before it could begin to wilt it would be renewed by another storm.

Snug in my rooms in the house between Kings Street and Bridgeton Way, I watched the snow flurry and cheerfully wrote seasonal letters of greetings from our fire-warmed sitting room.

It was from this happy pastime that I was roused by a banging on the front door. Being between housekeepers at the time (the much-lauded Mrs Bryce having retired that fall and moved to live with her niece in Burrock on Reid) I was obliged to climb out of my chair and tramp down the stairs, in no fair frame of mind.

Much of my sour mood vanished, however, when I opened the door to find my old friend Milky standing on the threshold—Milky, whom I had first met as a thieving street urchin, and whose adventures during Felpz's absence still remained a mystery to me. Now a solidly middle-aged man, lean and weathered but bristling with energy, he made his living—when not running errands for Felpz—as an antiques dealer and wood worker. Although he was bundled tight against the winter weather in a thick coat and hat, I recognized his scarred hatchet face at once.

My exultations of surprise and delight were, however, abruptly cut short when I saw what he dragged behind him.

It appeared to be a heavy burlap sack, of the sort used to deliver presents, but instead of the hard shapes of packages, it was soft and lumpy with a familiar head of dark hair protruding from the top.

"My dear Milky," I cried, "whatever is going on—and what on earth are you doing with *Felpz*?"

For it was the head of Bouragner Felpz, my childhood guardian and current benefactor, that I had recognized, and it followed that the corresponding body must occupy the rest of the sack.

"A favor he probably won't thank me for," Milky grumbled. "'Tis a favor nonetheless. Can you get a fire going in the moss? He needs a good thawing."

By *moss* I assumed Milky meant our kitchen, which was something of a muddle—its usual keeper being gone and a succession of less-than-adequate housemaids having done it little good. It had, however, the advantage of not being separated from the front door by two flights of stairs, and so it was in the kitchen that we gathered around my newly lit fire, propping Felpz up in front of it across two chairs.

Two chairs were required, and the burlap sack explained, by Felpz being frozen solid. Stiff as a board he was, and breathing so faintly as I nearly thought him to be dead.

"Not this one, and not so eas'ly," Milky said with grudging admiration. "But he got right up to the wall this time. I should give him a good kick in the shins if they weren't hard as rocks."

"That's less than charitable," I said reproachfully. "What on earth drove him to this? And where did you find him?"

Felpz had been absent from home for the past couple of days, but since this was his standard behavior I had not bothered to trouble myself over it. Now I wondered if he had been out freezing while I sat snug and warm at home.

"In Cawmeadow's Park," Milky said. "He'd fallen across the path, and the shovelers didn't know what to do with him. Recognized him right enough and sent a man 'round to my shop, they as knowing me and knowing I was a friend of his. Well, I took an old sack and went to save everyone some bother and took him home. As for why he should do such as daft thing as to freeze himself I can't poss'bly imagine."

"Oh, I can imagine some possibilities," I said shrewdly, putting a kettle on to boil over the fire. Despite the soft living I had enjoyed since returning to live with Felpz, the skills I had acquired as a single mother continued to serve me well, and in no time I had us outfitted with cups of tea.

We were sitting thus, drinking companionably, when Felpz's rigid body gave out a convulsive shudder, and he coughed violently.

"Easy there Mr Felpz, sir," Milky said, holding his shoulders so Felpz did not rattle himself clean off the chairs. "Have a care or you'll ruin Miss Cor's lovely fire."

"Blast the wretched fire!" Felpz wheezed, and though his voice was wrecked and hoarse I could tell his faculties had not been damaged in the least.

"Good to have you back Felpz," I said, pouring him a cup of hot water. "Give this to him, would you Milky? If it spills I doubt it will do him any harm—he's still cold to the touch."

He was, too; there was even frost on the lapels of his coat and the tips of his boots. This did not prevent him struggling (with Milky's support) into a sitting position and grabbing the cup I offered him and draining it in one gulp.

"That's better," he said with a satisfied sigh. "Another, if you please, Corianne, and I will be fit as a fiddle."

More hot water was procured, and I poured him a cup of tea without asking. By this time Felpz was sitting up on his own with one leg resting on the other chair. Briskly he shook out his coat, and I saw the frost disappear in the blink of an eye. Color returned to his pale cheeks, and his lips—which had been frighteningly blue—were now healthy and red again.

"You may ask yourselves—*thank you*," he said, accepting the proffered cup of tea, "why I should attempt to freeze myself overnight, for I admit it is not a pastime I normally engage in."

"Oh, we assumed you'd have some daft reason," Milky assured our friend. "Though we did hope you'd tell us about it."

"Verily, verily," said Felpz with good cheer, and Milky and I arranged ourselves in attentive positions accordingly.

"A few days ago—what was it? Wednesday? Yes. Wednesday I received a visit from a most precocious young woman. Maybe you remember Miss Sutherhand, Corianne? The clockmaker's daughter from Endless Street? Well, I shall explain for Milky's sake. Quite a character, Miss Hilaria Sutherhand. *Robust* I think they are calling women like her these days, with thick round glasses and a penetrating voice. I remember she drove Corianne and her writing clean out of the sitting room with it.

"As it stood, Miss Sutherhand had been put through a most trying experience over the last few weeks. She is of that age—you will remember, Corianne—when young women are most susceptible to losing their heads and all the good sense that is normally contained therein over handsome young men. In this case Miss Sutherhand had been under additional pressure from her family to marry, given that she is an only child and her father is old and frail. They subscribe to the ridiculous notion that a woman cannot inherit her father's business, you see.

"To this end they had been introducing her to a veritable parade of young men, and she in the infinite wisdom of youth chose a young sailor of pleasing build and manners who had recently retired from the sea and was looking for shore work and was eager to learn the craft of clock making. A fine match, or so her parents thought, and the man was invited to live under their roof—he having no family living—in the days leading up to the wedding. This, as Miss Sutherhand impressed upon me many times, is next Saturday. It was also during this time that events took a change for the macabre.

"At first all went sunnily: the man was everything he appeared to be and took readily to her father's trade and soon began doing work for him. This required that he spend a certain amount of time at their workshop, which is around the corner from the family's house, and necessitated that he walk home in the dark most evenings. Not a problem for this man—whose name I should say: Jethro Waterworth—who was strong and energetic.

"One evening, however, he was missed at supper, and Miss Sutherhand herself went in search of him—imagining, I suppose, that he had become entangled with a project at work and simply forgot the time. This was on one of our recent bad nights, when it was snowing so fiercely no one went out if they could help it. Miss Sutherhand, bundled up in all her coats and armed with a storm lantern, reached the shop successfully only to find it dark and closed. Perplexed, she turned to make her way home. It was on this return journey that she stumbled into a strange figure cloaked in snow.

"He stood outside her house, and Miss Sutherhand was afraid he was some poor soul who had frozen to death in the night. However, when she held up her lantern to his face she found it was her own fiancé—not merely frozen, but turned to *stone.*"

"Stone?" I echoed, bewildered.

"Yes, *stone,*" Felpz assured us. "Miss Sutherhand ran away inside and got her mother up, and together the two women went out to see what could be done. Yet when they arrived at the same spot they found no man—stone, frozen, or otherwise—and the snow already filling in the place where he had stood.

"There being nothing else they could do at that hour the women went back inside, but for understandable reasons they were unable to rest easy. Then, after midnight, there was a thumping on the front door and who should come in but Mr Jethro Waterworth, quite cold and hungry but apparently flesh and blood.

"He was greeted with joy and relief, and upon hearing of Miss Sutherhand's misadventure, laughed it off as a foolish mistake. Miss Sutherhand returned to her room, much upset by all this, and tried to put the matter out of her head.

"The next night, however, she was unable to sleep, and in her restlessness she went to her window. That night the snow was thinner, but the stuff upon the ground reflected the weak moonlight brightly. In this she saw clearly the shape of a man standing below her window, looking up at her. In her fright she shut the blinds at once and remained in bed until morning.

"Mr Waterworth, all this while, was dismissive of her concerns, putting it down to hysteria and bad dreams. He was also spending an increasing amount of time at the shop—sometimes even spending the night there. None of this helped Miss Sutherhand's mood, but she endured it, until something truly disturbing befell her.

"As she described it, she was woken from a fitful slumber by a draft on her cheek, and sitting up she saw her door open. Knowing it had been shut when she had lain down she took up a match and lit her lamp, crossing the cold floor quickly to shut it again. Before she did, however, she took a quick glance out into the hall.

"That was when she saw him . . . or it. She was a little confused on that point. She said it looked like a man all curled up on himself with his head on his knees. Even as she stared, this strange person moved and raised its head to look at her. From what I can tell, its face was that of Jethro Waterworth but streaked and speckled as a piece of granite. It stared at her with blank eyes and from its mouth came not words, but a grinding noise.

"Miss Sutherhand admits she did become hysterical then, and in her upset she dropped her lamp and struck her head hard on the door frame, causing her to lose consciousness. She came to in the morning to find herself lying in her own bed, and not even a scorch on the floor from where the lamp had hit. But Jethro Waterworth has not been seen since."

Felpz had become more and more animated during the course of his monologue, and by now nearly all trace of snow and frost was gone from his person. Even his clothes were clean and dry once more.

"That is quite astonishing," I said, gathering up our empty cups and refilling them with tea. "It does not, however, explain how you came to freeze yourself overnight."

"Doesn't it?" Felpz said in surprise. He took his tea and sipped it. "No, I suppose it does not. I'd have to give you an account of my own actions of the previous days for that to become clear. As I am already overdue for an appointment with Miss Sutherhand, I suggest you come along and hear the whole story. I would be grateful for some steady characters by my side."

Naturally I agreed on the spot, and after some grumbling Milky allowed himself to be led along as well.

The weather had turned while we sat by the kitchen fire, and now dark blue-and-grey clouds hung overhead like a cold blanket. Sharp flecks of snow danced through the air on fitful winds, and the streets were empty save for the most courageous of travelers.

This included our three heavily wrapped forms, as we made our way out to the street, where plowing from the night before had left it more traversable than the pavements to either side.

I had expected Felpz to employ the sort of travel magic he usually did whenever there was a walk of more than a few minutes ahead of us, but to my surprise the clock maker's residence was hardly a hundred steps from our own front door.

"The shop is around the corner that way." Felpz indicated the direction down the frosted street after he had rapped firmly upon the clock maker's door. "And you may be interested to note, through that alley behind us is the back of Cawmeadow's Park, where you discovered me this morning, Milky. Bear that in mind—ah, here is Miss Sutherhand."

The door had opened and a charming young woman appeared. In person Hilaria Sutherhand was rather more attractive than Felpz's ungenerous description led me to believe, and I'm afraid Felpz was mistaken in the assumption that her emphatic voice was what drove me from the room: for I was certain I had never seen her before in my life and must have been inexplicably absent when she first presented her case to Felpz.

In height she was a touch shorter than I, with light brown curls piled clumsily on top of her head. She wore thick-rimmed spectacles and an awkward checkered dress that only served to make her appearance more endearing.

"Thank the Lady you're here, Mr Felpz," she said upon sight. "Father's taken badly since this morning. It was the shock, I am sure. As I was truly shocked as well, but my heart is stronger than his."

Felpz, who had been on the verge of introducing us, paused.

"Beg pardon, my dear," he said. "Do you mean to say some new calamity has befallen you?"

Miss Sutherhand waved her hand, ushering us in. "It is past now, but you come at a ripe time. Mother!" she called up a flight of narrow stairs as we entered. "Mother! Tell Father it is only the magician. The magician and his . . . er . . . " she trailed off at the sight of Milky and myself, who must have appeared to her an odd couple indeed.

"Miss Sutherhand, my friends Mrs Corianne Birch and . . . "

"Edder Thorn, ma'am," Milky said, dropping a polite bow. Felpz took this interruption in good grace, however, and continued smoothly:

"They are here to assist me and witness the resolution of your problem."

"Resolution?" echoed Miss Sutherhand, with the air of someone who has long given up on such a thing. "You may be less confident after you have heard what I have to say."

"That is as may be," Felpz allowed, removing his hat and shaking the snow off it onto the doorstep. "But I fear we are in danger of getting our narrative out of order. Will you sit down, Miss Sutherhand, and hear of my progress first? It may shed some light on the matter."

"Whatever progress you have made I would be glad to hear," Miss Sutherhand said agreeably, and led us through into a comfortable parlor heavily decorated with tinsel and ivy wreaths. Everything was remarkably festive, and I belatedly remembered that, were it not for this upending of their plans, the Sutherhand family would be preparing for the double holiday of Chandarmas and their daughter's wedding.

Miss Sutherhand sat us down on big, comfortable chairs and set out a plate of soft, buttery scones while she poured tea.

"First I must explain for Corianne and Mr Thorn's sake," Felpz began, "that I approached the disappearance of Mr Waterworth as I would any other missing person. You remember, Miss Sutherhand, how I asked for a piece of his clothing? I was able to use that to follow his trail to the shipping docks, where it then vanished. I searched the place with every spell I knew and still found nothing. Perplexed, I did some mundane searching and discovered a surprising thing. No one there had heard of Jethro Waterworth, not even the record keeper whose job it is to record the personnel of incoming and outgoing ships. As far as the books are concerned, Mr Jethro Waterworth never set foot on Redling's docks.

"Naturally this intrigued me, and I tried the passenger yard across the river—but with no success. Eventually I resorted to combing the records of every ship that came in shortly before you first met Mr Waterworth. I used some very complicated and tedious magic to make a thorough search that would tell me if he had been on any of those ships—even in an unofficial capacity. The results were troubling: on no ship had Mr Waterworth arrived in Redling. But I did find a ship that had carried him *away* from Redling. The brig *Marilda* had employed a sailor by the name of Jethro Waterworth, until he was lost overboard in a storm off the coast of Handmark last year."

At this Miss Sutherhand made an involuntary motion of alarm, and Felpz nodded consolingly.

"Do not doubt that this Waterworth they presumed drowned and the one to whom you are engaged are in fact the same person. Stranger things have happened. The question was *how did he do it?* To find out I would need to speak with him—or at least set eyes upon the fellow. To do this I began with the presumption that, if he had true feelings for you, he would not be able to stay far away, and if I positioned myself accordingly I would be able to get a glimpse of him.

"To this end I set up my vigil in Cawmeadow's Park, where I have been for several days. I became so absorbed in my task, I admit, that I quite forgot to care for certain physical concerns and in the end caused Mr Thorn here some trouble and Corianne an unwarranted shock. It was a foolish oversight. Had I been attentive to my own condition I could have solved this matter already, but as it is I can only report partial success."

We all looked at him expectantly. He looked back at us, clearly relishing the attention.

"I have seen your fiancé, Miss Sutherhand," Felpz said. "I saw him last night, in Cawmeadow's Park. I saw him break the ice from beneath the surface of Throttle Creek and walk out of the dark water beneath, moving stiffly through the snow. You may ask why I did not accost him. I am ashamed to say that by that point I had allowed myself to become so chilled that I could not move. It was thus how Milky—er, Mr Thorn found me, and having now been thawed out I come to you only to find there has been a new development."

"Indeed," said Miss Sutherhand. From her perch on the settee she knotted her hands in her skirt anxiously. "And I believe what you say, Mr Felpz, outrageous though it might be. For it explains why, when I saw him last night, he was soaking wet."

Felpz actually started out of his chair in his eagerness. "He has been here? Last night? Did he leave anything?"

Miss Sutherhand, a little put out by my friend's enthusiasm, pulled her arms close in at her sides. "It is a queer thing you should ask," she said. "For he did leave something on the doorstep—mother would not let me touch it so I took a pair of tongs from the kitchen and left it in a washbasin."

"Really? Oh that is *most* gratifying," Felpz said. "But would you tell me the events in order? Spare no detail!"

Miss Sutherhand sighed, but she bore my friend's insensitivities with fortitude. "I have not been sleeping well," she said, "as you can probably imagine. Last night I found myself jolted into wakefulness in the early hours of the morning for some reason unknown. I lay in my bed for what felt like hours, tossing restlessly, until I gave up the fight and lit a candle, presuming to go downstairs and read for a while.

"Almost as soon as the light had done flaring I heard a pounding on the front door. It nearly shocked me out of my own skin, and woke Father and Mother as well. They made me stay upstairs while they went to answer, but I opened my window and looked out, and saw all that happened.

"When the door opened I saw by its light that Jethro was standing there, in a puddle of dark water and quite bedraggled. I saw him reach out imploringly to my parents, heard my mother scream, and then the door slammed shut on him. It was only in the morning when I could see he had gone that they would let me go out. It was then I found what he had left: a rough copper ring, so rusted it bristled with blue-green stubble, holding a whorled piece of shell. Under it was a note in such a scratchy hand that I could hardly recognize it as Jethro's. The ring Mother did not allow me to touch, but I have the note here . . . " She fumbled at a pouch on her sash and eventually produced a stiff, ragged piece of paper, which she handed to Felpz.

"'My dearest Hilaria,'" he read, a frown creeping over his brow. "'It was never my intent to cause you grief. Even if you can never forgive me, I beg you accept my sincerest apologies. I had hoped my nightmares were over, but as it appears *she* will not let me go so easily, I have chosen to take my cursed self away rather than allow it to stain your life. The water does not forget. Yours ever, Jethro.'" He turned the paper over, sniffed it, then felt along its edge with his fingers. Then, with a small, triumphant smile, he said: "I have you!"

"You have him?" Miss Sutherhand said. "Do you know what is going on?"

"I have what I fancy is a fairly accurate idea," Felpz said. "But I'd much rather hear it from *him*. Come, Miss Sutherhand, show me this ring he left—that shall dispell any remaining doubts. Then, I think, we shall pay Mr Jethro Waterworth a visit." He stood up suddenly, slipping the note into his pocket and gesturing to Miss Sutherhand.

Understandably confused, the young woman led us into the kitchen, where she took a bowl down from the counter and presented it to us.

There in the bottom was a ring matching her description. Felpz gave a little ejaculation of joy and snatched it up immediately. As he turned it before his eyes, I saw the bit of shell glint like mother-of-pearl. Felpz squinted at it, tapped it with a finger and then blew on it. He rubbed it briskly on his sleeve and, holding it out, we all saw how the copper now gleamed rosy with no sign of rust or discoloration.

"It was prudent of you not to touch it," Felpz said. "As it happens, however, there is nothing dangerous about *this* ring. In fact, I believe you should wear it. It may help our case."

"Our case?" Miss Sutherhand said, bewildered. But she took the ring and slipped it on her finger. She had to wear it on her index finger, because it was so large. "Won't you explain?"

"It is not I who need do the explaining," Felpz said. "Won't you take word up to your parents that you are going out—in company of friends, assure them. Assure them also I will have you back for tea, and that they can expect this whole matter to be resolved—one way or the other—by that time."

While Miss Sutherhand went pounding up the stairs to deliver this message, Milky and I waited with Felpz by the front door, each of us on edge with anticipation.

"Mr Felpz," Milky began to whine, then caught himself. "Are you planning something, Mr Felpz?" he asked solemnly.

Bouragner Felpz shifted on his feet and gave us a sidelong glance. "Well, perhaps I am," he admitted. "But can you blame me? The whole matter is far too fantastic to be resolved in the mundane way."

I was about to make the case that Miss Sutherhand might appreciate a mundane conclusion, but was cut off by the reappearance of that person descending the stairs in a flurry of skirts and coat.

"Mother has decided to stay with Father," she relayed. "I am in your hands, magician. Lead the way."

Felpz did, out the door and through the snow, forging a path to Cawmeadow's Park, with Miss Sutherhand striding by his side. Milky and I followed at a little distance, walking in their tracks.

As a place of recreation I do not care much for Cawmeadow; I find it gaudy and pretentious, but that may be the fault of my own bias. That day, covered in snow with the metal railings studded with frost it did present a certain chilly beauty, and it also had the advantage of being quite deserted.

The centerpiece of Cawmeadow is doubtlessly Throttle Creek, that once-infamous tributary of the Reid that has confounded watermen and agents of the law since the founding of the city. Where it flows through Cawmeadow, however, a good deal of effort has been made to clean up the bank and do what can be done to prettify its noisome flow.

When we approached it through the frigid park that day, I saw with some surprise that it had not frozen entirely over. Its center was black and white reflecting the snowy banks, while the deep current which prevented it from freezing was visible only as a slight roil on the otherwise smooth surface.

"Before we proceed," Felpz said, coming to stand at the very edge of the water and turning to face Miss Sutherhand. "I must ask you a question, and see that you answer it frankly."

"Indeed, sir," said Miss Sutherhand gamely.

"While I do not see why your fiancé should not continue to be as you knew him, agreeable and kind," Felpz said. "It is quite likely—almost certainly so—that he is not the man you first took him to be. You may—*will* certainly—find him much changed. With this in mind, do you still consider it in the realm of possibility that you should take him for a husband?"

Miss Sutherhand appeared understandably taken aback by such a question. She stiffened under her thick coat and regarded Felpz critically.

"You put me on the spot, Mr Felpz," she said. "I can hardly answer that without knowing what these changes are."

"Yes, yes of course," Felpz said, a little impatient. "I only ask, would you dismiss him out of hand?"

"I would hope not," Miss Sutherhand said. "Mr Felpz, what on earth is going on?"

Felpz raised a hand, one finger extended, and brought it around in front of him to point at the dark water of the creek.

"Magic," he said, "always complicates matters. If magic had not been put to use here, your current predicament would have been cleanly avoided. However, in this case, I feel justified that a little more magic will help smooth the way to a resolution."

He fixed his eyes upon Miss Sutherhand's hand then, on the copper ring she wore, and then transferred his gaze to the water. His pointing hand turned so that it was palm up, and he *beckoned* with it, moving his arm in a strong arc.

Even though we stood behind him, Milky and I both felt the pull, and I saw Miss Sutherhand sway forward on her feet.

"Good gracious!" she exclaimed, and then stopped to stare. We all stared, save Felpz of course, who only smiled in satisfaction.

From out of the water a dark shape appeared, sending ripples outward to lap at the bank. It moved towards us, slowly rising, and I soon recognized it as the head of a man, dark grey and speckled, glistening wet.

He must, I reasoned, be walking along the bottom, for as he approached the shore, slowly his shoulders emerged. Then he bent forward, as if taking a step, and all at once the rest of his body surged upwards, the water sluicing off sopping wet clothes and raining upon the surface of the creek. He stood there in the shallows, among the broken ice, only his feet hidden beneath the surface, and stared at Felpz reproachfully.

In build he was a mid-sized man, not too tall or wide, and he wore what might have once been a good set of coat and trousers, but which were now draggled and ripped. His skin, everywhere it showed, was the shiny, dark, speckled grey of wet granite, his eyes polished orbs with black holes bored in them. His hair was a delicate filigree of stonework, and his mouth as it opened revealed similarly grey lips and teeth.

Miss Sutherhand, to her credit, only let out a small gasp, and staggered a little. The stone man's head swiveled to face her, and his features contorted into a look of concern. He made an involuntary movement, as if to take her hand, and at that she stumbled backwards and would have fallen in the snow had Milky not read the scene and come forward to steady her.

"Easy there, miss," he said, leading her in the direction of the nearest bench. I saw his meaning and went over to dust the snow off it.

"That was hardly fair, Felpz," I said reprovingly. "You could have given the poor girl *some* warning."

Felpz gave a little shrug, as if conceding this point, but he only said: "She would have needed no warning had Mr Waterworth here given her an honest account of his ... hmm ... curious predicament."

The stone man—Mr Waterworth—still with his feet in the creek, raised a hand and coughed. "You may scold me all you like, stranger," he said. His voice was a little raspy and hard, but not unpleasant. "Now you see me for what I am, could you blame me?"

"Oh ... oh, Jethro." Miss Sutherhand, sitting on the bench, clutched her arms around herself and shivered a little. Milky took off his coat and draped it over her shoulders, but Miss Sutherhand pushed it off. "Jethro, what on earth has *happened* to you?" she asked.

Mr Waterworth gazed back out of his stone eyes unhappily.

"Come, Mr Waterworth," Felpz said gently, extending a hand. "Sit down and give us a full account of your history, and I promise to do all I can to set matters right."

Waterworth looked skeptically at Felpz, and did not move.

"I'll stay here, if you please," he said. "The water is ... it helps me stay ... er ... fluid."

Felpz nodded assent, and went to stand a little way between Waterworth and the bench where we had gathered.

Jethro Waterworth hung his head and shuffled his feet, sending more ripples splashing up onto the shore. "I tried to tell no lies," he said. "I still think of myself as a man, even if I'm not much of one any more, and a man ought not to tell lies.

"I was a sailor, true enough, and worked aboard the *Marilda* five years. Maybe you've already found that out, and if you did, you know I was lost overboard in a storm last year. This is true, and if I left it out of my original story it was only because I wished it had never happened. But I will tell you now how it did, and how I came to be here . . . like this.

"The water was dreadful cold when I hit it—colder somehow than the stinging wind and rain I had already endured—and as it closed over my head I fought to claw my way back to the surface. But it was as though the waves were pounding down on me, and with all my clothes now soaked and heavy I began to sink.

"I've never been a particularly religious man. Is that an odd thing in a sailor? Perhaps. In that moment, however, I did pray. I prayed to whatever merciful god looks after drowning sailors desperate to be saved. I felt myself sinking farther; the light was gone entirely, and in the darkness I lashed out. My hand brushed something soft, and I felt something smooth with sharp pricks in it—like a cat's paw—close around my arm. I thought it must be some sea monster come to eat me—they have some mighty big ones up north—but then a low greenish light bloomed around me, and I saw it was not a monster at all, but a *mermaid.* She had a cloud of yellow hair that floated around her face, and though her hands were webbed and her skin mottled like that of a fish, she was in other respects perfectly humanlike—at least above the waist. Below it I caught a glimpse of fins and scales and some wicked-looking spines.

"She whispered to me through the water, asking if she should save me. Unable to speak at this point I nodded fiercely, and she drew me into her arms and pulled me down. My world went black, and I thought I was a goner."

Jethro Waterworth clenched his fists, making a grinding noise. "I should have been a goner," he said bitterly. "She *didn't* save me, not in any meaningful way. She took a fancy to me for some reason, and decided she would keep me—like a child finds a pretty crab or other creature on the beach, and thinking what a nice addition it would make to their home takes it with them, away from its rightful place in the world. Only the mermaid, knowing I would die and rot otherwise, turned my flesh to stone and my blood to water. So I awoke at the bottom of the sea, unable to breathe—but not *needing* to breathe—and before my eyes the darkness took form, and I found myself shackled to a rock on a vast and desolate landscape, while above, the mermaid and her kin swam like sinister birds, soaring on the currents of the ocean. They laughed at me when they saw my confusion and fear turn to anger, and though I found

I could speak now, no matter how I shouted and pleaded with them to let me go they would only giggle and wag their fingers.

"They were not intentionally cruel," Jethro Waterworth allowed grudgingly. "They brought me food—freshly slaughtered fish, mostly—but I found that in my new form I could not eat. They took my disinterest for disdain and eventually the food stopped. My clothes slowly frayed and rotted away, and then they dressed me after their fashion: in plates of shell and rope woven of seaweed. Sometimes my mermaid—the yellow-haired one who had captured me—would unhook the chains that secured me to the rock and take me for walks along the ocean bottom. This seemed to delight her, but for me the abyssal plane looked all the same, and it only served to remind me how complete my isolation was.

"I thought at the time I must have spent aeons on the ocean floor, and that my existence would stretch out forever into this dim and bleak monotony. It came as something of a shock then, when on the return from one of these walks we found, waiting for us at my crag, a person I had never seen before. Like the mermaids he was half fish, but recognizably masculine. Also, the pattern of scales which decorated his tail continued up over the rest of him, and his face was fierce and alien, covered in spines and little fins. His tail too, rather than being smooth and shimmering like the mermaid and her sisters, was ridged with spines, and there were tendrils coiling around his underside. And though he was the most unnatural creature I have ever seen I could also tell that he was unspeakably angry.

"My mermaid saw it too and shrank away from him, her hair going slack and limp. The merman shouted at her fiercely in their language. He seemed to be admonishing her. He pointed at me several times with one spiny hand and made slashing motions with his arms. The mermaid, after meekly accepting this tirade for some minutes, eventually spoke up, and it appeared she was just as angry as he. They argued together, floating in the water over me, for what felt like a long time. Then the merman, clearly out of patience, darted down and raised an arm as if to strike me. Surprised and terrified I cowered away from him, but my mermaid dove in between us and the merman held his blow.

"She spoke again, pleadingly, and after a while the merman went away, muttering something threatening. Then my mermaid turned to me, and I saw there was a strange coloration around her eyes, as though she had been weeping. She embraced me with her smooth and prickly arms, kissed my cheek, and then undid the shackles from my leg. Then, grasping me under the arms she lifted me off the ocean floor and swam with me, farther than we had ever walked. We passed over deep trenches and mountains of rock. Eventually we came to a cliff where the water was lighter, and there she set me down. She stroked my hair lovingly and murmured something in her own tongue, and then she was a flashing streak disappearing into the murk.

"As you can imagine I was entirely at a loss for what to do. For many days I sat at the edge of the cliff, pondering whether to throw myself off it. Not needing food or sleep, I felt in no hurry to make a decision. After a time, however, I became aware that the murky light surrounding me dimmed sometimes, even when it was clearly day upon the surface. Straining my eyes I found I could make out dark shapes passing overhead, impossibly far above me. It took me some time to recognize their shape, as in my previous life I had never seen them from such an angle.

"They were ships, I tell you. Ships! And they passed with such frequency that I guessed the mermaid must have left me right in the middle of one of our shipping lanes. For the first time since I felt myself plunge into the icy water a hope flared in my chest, and I got to my feet and began following the shadows along the ocean floor.

"It was a long and weary walk. I later estimated that I must have walked along much of the coast of Kyreland, down past Gaela, and right up to the mouth of the Reid. I trudged over deserts of sand, and crept through strange canyons carved of rock. I climbed, steadily, and the floor became thicker and siltier. I began to come across pieces of debris, and the unmistakable detritus of human beings. I passed one or two sunken vessels, gutted and crawling with fish. At last I reached a place where all the dark shadows of the ships converged, and here I felt a change in the water, a heady sweetness that made me feel drunk. It quite took me off my feet, and I lay in the sands feeling the tides wash over me, slowly burying me, until at last my head cleared a little, and I found the strength to dig myself out. I suppose that must have been my body adjusting to the fresh water, though I couldn't imagine what it was at the time.

"I continued following the ships, walking up the bottom of the river. Now more than ever I had to navigate between discarded pipes and wire fencing; I passed many a rusting bicycle and once the corpse of an animal.

"Though the water was much shallower here, and I could even see the surface glittering above me, I still did not leave the water. Since I had given up all hope of seeing land again, now that it was a distinct possibility I found I was terrified of it. I continued walking upriver, until I found myself at the docks of Redling.

"There I stayed, hunched under a pier, until at last I summoned up enough courage, and one night I walked up a boat ramp and out of the water for the first time in what felt like years.

"I cannot tell you the horrible, bittersweet joy that filled me, to see my city as I had left it, but through stone eyes that saw through the darkness as easily as you see by sunlight. I could not return to my family like this, nor could I go back to work. Then I thought of returning to the water, and I could not bear it.

"Now without fear of any mortal disease I visited the lowest parts of the city and there acquired clothes. I learned to paint my face and hands so that in passing I appeared human. I found work, for in this vast metropolis there is work enough for someone with a strong back who asks no questions, and eventually saved enough to go to a witch whom I knew of old who makes a living off enchanting sailors. I put my case before her, and though she couldn't break the curse the mermaid had put on me she gave me a spell that would make me appear human. This I took, and under its guise I set about starting a new life for myself. I had not intended to fall in love or take a wife, but when I found Hilaria it was as though all the cold water in my veins turned to steam, and I felt warm for the first time in ages."

Jethro Waterworth hung his head, looking a bit like a kicked dog. On the bench, Miss Sutherhand clutched her breast, one hand covering the finger that wore the copper ring.

"It was foolish of me to think I could ever have a happy, normal life. As you discovered, if I remain out of water for any length of time I feel my muscles stiffen and my body freeze. The first time it happened I was horrified, for I could see all that happened around me, but could not move myself an inch. Hilaria found me once in this state, and it was crushing to see how she recoiled. Eventually I managed to break myself free, and through supreme force of will I staggered to the nearest body of water and threw myself in. Almost at once my body came to life again, and I was able to return. But I had to keep going back to the water, otherwise I would freeze up again. To make matters worse, not long after that, the spell the witch had given me began to wear thin, and when I went to her for a new one she was unable to help me. Apparently her spells are not the sort that you can simply recast if they wear out.

"Needless to say I was utterly distraught, and argued within myself back and forth over what I should do. I had thought I had decided I would tell Hilaria the truth, but when I came to her I found I had not the heart, and I sat in the hall outside her room cursing myself and my wicked life. I had no idea I had woken her, and to my horror I looked up and met her eyes as she gazed out into the hall. I cannot tell you how distraught I was to have frightened her, and when she hit her head on the door frame as she fell I cursed myself harder than ever. But I caught her lamp before it reached the floor, and I carried her back to bed before taking myself away. I decided I should leave her, and take myself and my curse out of her life. But I could not go without a word, and so I left her a note and my ring—the one piece of my old life the mermaid hadn't taken from me. I had thought I would return to the river, perhaps find myself a secluded spot in the country and leave myself out to dry . . . "

He rounded on Felpz accusingly. "But now *you* come and drag me from the water! Who are you to think bringing up my sad past will solve anything? Can you break the mermaid's curse? Can you give me my life back? For I tell you now, I want nothing of the one I have!"

Felpz, who had listened to the man's appalling story in silence and with gravity, endured this outburst serenely. He drew in a deep breath and looked the stone man over with a critical eye, folding his arms and cupping his chin in one hand.

"My dear Mr Waterworth," he said mildly. "While I can appreciate the trials you have been through, I cannot help but feel you have not given Miss Sutherhand the credit she is due. Certainly *she* should have some say in whether her marriage should be called off. Have you not seriously considered that, even though she has acted in fear and alarm, *you* have also been acting in a frightening and alarming fashion? If what you say is true—and I see no reason why it should not be—then you have nothing to be ashamed of and everything to gain by accepting this new life that has offered itself to you."

Jethro Waterworth glared at Felpz, then cast a beseeching look at Miss Sutherhand.

"You must understand," he said, grinding his hands together, "I *cannot* ask that of her, not in my current state."

"By refusing to ask," Felpz said, "you are robbing her of the chance to say *yes.*" He looked over at us where we sat on the bench, and shrugged. "I realize this is not what you may have had in mind, Miss Sutherhand, and I certainly do not wish to put you on the spot, but if you remember my earlier question to you: *do you* still think it is within the realm of possibility?"

Steadying herself on Milky's arm, Miss Sutherhand rose shakily to her feet. Slowly she walked through the snow to the water's edge, where she reached out and hesitantly touched the stone man's cheek. She turned to Felpz, a frown creasing her forehead.

"You are said to be the greatest magician in this country," she said, a little accusingly. "Even *you* cannot turn him back?"

"The thought had occurred," Felpz conceded. "And had it been that simple I would have done it already. But the more I see of you, Mr Waterworth, the more I think you are better off like this. I believe you had already drowned when the mermaid cast her spell on you, and I fear that if I turned you back you would revert to that state: a dead, drowned man. Not something either you or Miss Sutherhand would find at all agreeable. As for the difficulty you have remaining out of water . . . I think it is merely a problem of lubrication. *Drink* more, Mr Waterworth. I know you have gotten out of the habit of it, but I think you can manage a dozen glasses a day. A dozen glasses of water will do the trick nicely, I believe."

Jethro Waterworth blinked at Felpz. He turned and blinked down at Miss Sutherhand, who was scrutinizing him through her glasses.

"Well, Jethro," she said, and by her tone I could tell she had got herself under control once more. "You've made about as big a mess of this as possible, and by rights I should cast you off. Not for being made of stone, mind, but for being such an utter *coward* about it. I should give you a sharp slap, I think, but that I imagine it would hurt me more than you."

Jethro Waterworth hung his head, and made a motion as though he were going back into the water, but Miss Sutherhand caught him by the sleeve.

"I did not say I *am* casting you off, you great fool. Come back with me, we'll get you changed into some dry clothes, and if you can stand to come upstairs and explain this—*calmly*, like a gentleman—to my parents, we'll see if we can't keep our appointment on Saturday."

And taking him by the arm, she led him out of the water. Pausing as she passed Felpz she tipped her cap to him. "Thank you for finding him," she said briskly. "It is not the outcome I would have wished, but at least it is not outside the realm of possibility."

Wandering over to stand by Felpz, Milky and I watched them go: the straight-backed woman and the drooping, dripping man, as they walked arm in arm through the snow.

"Do you think they'll make a go of it?" Milky asked, putting his coat back on.

"I hope so," I said. "I rather think he's a better man than the one I married. What do you say, Felpz?"

Felpz, who had been gazing into the depths of Throttle Creek, looked up at us and shrugged. "I don't see why not. There have been stranger couples, after all."

I wish I could tell my readers that Miss Sutherhand and Mr Waterworth did go on to marry, but as this is a true account I cannot tack on whatever ending I like. In fact Miss Sutherhand's parents did not take the news nearly as well as their daughter had, and Mr Sutherhand died of a heart attack not long after. Following this calamity Miss Sutherhand and Mr Waterworth were obliged to postpone their nuptials indefinitely, and it would be almost three years before Felpz received a small parcel in the mail, attached to which was a brief note saying that the clock maker's shop on Endless Street was changing its name to Sutherhand & Waterworth's, after the marriage of Miss Hilaria Sutherhand and Mr Jethro Waterworth. In the parcel was a beautifully carved pocket watch with mother-of-pearl lining and a note from the new couple, thanking Felpz for his assistance.

"'You will be pleased to know,'" Felpz read aloud to me, "'that the watch is fully waterproof. Jethro made certain of it.'"

"How thoughtful," I said, turning the piece over in my hands and thinking back to that cold winter day. "Though it might serve you better were it proof to freezing."

Felpz laughed, taking the little clock and swinging it by its chain. "Well," he said, "rest assured I do not intend to *test* it any time soon."

seven

THE WITHERED HAND

WHEN I TURN TO MY NOTES concerning the macabre incident of the withered hand and the incredible events that followed, I find it was in the autumn of 2321. How long ago that seems now, but at the time I was so well bundled in current matters that I hardly noticed the passage of time. When I did it was with increasing alarm that I found myself advancing steadily towards the midpoint of my sixth decade. I had at times in the past considered myself *old.* At twenty I felt old in comparison to myself at fourteen; at thirty I felt old in comparison to myself at twenty-three; at *forty* I thought of myself as an imposing and ancient matron. When I discovered I had vaulted clean past fifty — an age I now think the very picture of youthful energy — I no longer wished to think of myself as old, and only acknowledged my age inasmuch as I complained at length about any physical inconvenience affecting me. This, however, became more and more difficult, due to interference from my friend Bouragner Felpz.

Whenever I complained about any of the frequent indispositions attendant upon a woman of my age, Felpz would suffer nobly for a week — and then the attacks of discomfort would cease abruptly. When I began to complain of the arthritis in my ankles he put up with it for all of two days, and then my joints inexplicably improved. And I had only mentioned offhand how my near vision was not what it had once been, when the very next day a package arrived for me containing a pair of thick, ugly, round glasses, which rendered my vision sharper and more accurate than it ever had been.

I am sorry to say I was unreasonably annoyed by this. Having had to bear with persons older than myself airing the grievances of their age all my life, I now considered the one advantage to my slowly failing body to be the privilege of complaining about it. But I did not wish to seem ungrateful to Felpz, who I knew was behind all my miraculous recoveries (one does not live with a magician for the better part of twenty years and not become aware of the signs). The conundrum made me irritable in a way that physical discomfort never could and was therefore beyond Felpz's ability to correct. I regret to say we took to snapping at each other relentlessly, and anyone privy to our private interactions would have wondered why we still suffered to live together. Indeed, the state of our combined tempers was as dry as tinder, and I fear a conflagration would have been kindled had not the events I alluded to in the first paragraph taken place.

They were heralded, as many of our adventures were, by an unusual letter. It came with the morning post on a chilly autumn day, and I noted its presence between a parcel from my daughter and the paper purely by reason of it slipping from between the two and onto the stairs as I brought the mail up to our rooms. Picking it up I was surprised to find that it was hardly more than a scrap of soft, grey paper folded over upon itself. Its front was almost entirely covered in penny stamps, as though the sender had not been sure of the postage required, and all it bore for an address was: *to le Viole Magicien du Felhass,* which was such a queer mishandling of Felpz's name—and his original, lesser-known one at that— that I marveled at the letter being delivered at all. The writing was sloppy and spidery, with many slips and slides as if the writer had not been in full control of his quill.

Such was my fascination with this curious piece of post that I brought it straight to Felpz, completely forgetting the argument we had been in the middle of when I'd stormed out to bring in the mail. I found him at his bench, which took up the better part of his workroom. This place had, in my early days, been the only area of our flat off limits to me, but when I returned to live with Felpz as a grown woman he generously offered to give me a tour, and I had been welcome in it ever since. Save lately, when we were at each other's throats, and he retreated into it in order to escape me. This had doubtless been his motivation on this occasion, and he reacted to my presence in his retreat of magical artifacts and oppressive clutter by letting out a cry of frustration and turning perfectly invisible.

"Felpz, you must see this," I said, hardly noticing the absence of his visual form and heading unerringly to the one empty spot on his bench where I knew him to be sitting. "It must be the queerest letter you've ever received and I know I shall die of curiosity if I don't learn what's in it." So saying I stretched out my hand, holding the grey paper gently between two fingers, as if offering a nut to some exotic bird with a powerful beak.

Felpz faded back into view bending forward to peer at the letter. Gone was any trace of sour temper, and he seemed wholly enthralled by the sight of the writing. He brought his hands up swiftly as if to snatch the paper from my fingers, but then stopped himself and let me place it gently in his waiting hand. With careful fingers he folded back the edges and flattened the letter over a silver plate on his bench, this being the closest thing to a clear area. He leaned forward and read what was written there with narrowed eyes, then shut them entirely and breathed in a long, deep inhalation. Then he picked the letter up, held it before the light, turned it upside down, and finally took a corner into his mouth and nibbled at it. Taking it from his mouth he looked at it in some perplexity, a line of worry creasing his brow.

"I know the owner of the hand that wrote this," he said at length, softly and uncertain. "But I do not know how he should come to write me such a thing."

"What is wrong?" I asked. "What does it say?"

For answer Felpz handed me the limp sheet of paper. I took it, and had to look twice in order to find the words in such a wild and raggedy hand. It appeared they said:

Old friend, please help. Come at ons.

And below that an equally ragged and spidery drawing of a manse, surrounded by a shaky scribble that seemed to suggest greenery and a garden.

"What on earth could they mean by that? 'Come at ons?'" I mused, passing the letter back.

"I expect it was meant to be 'Come at once,'" Felpz said, and he tapped the drawing on the bottom with his thumb. "There, it seems, is the place the writer wishes me to go. It is certainly not *his* house—that I should recognize."

"It could be any number of country mansions," I conceded.

Felpz waved a hand sharply. "No, it is one in particular, one where I am needed urgently. Corianne, do bring me that frivolous volume of illustrated houses that Mrs Bryce sent us last Chandarmas."

I knew the book he meant precisely, and went and fetched the thing from where it had lain, brick-like, at the foot of my writing desk all summer. It was a marvel of a tome indeed, with entries on all the large and majestic houses of Kyreland and Torland, with huge glossy photographs of each, and until that day had been perfectly useless. I laid it heavily on a hastily cleared corner of Felpz's workbench, and he laid the letter, without opening it, face down upon the cover.

The magic he did then was quiet and subtle, and I felt it only in the rising of the hairs on the back of my neck and a faint chill in my spine. He simply held his hand flat, palm down, over the letter and the book, and shut his eyes for a few moments. Then he lifted the letter and, opening the book flat, held the edge of the letter up to the edge of the pages. Immediately they began to fly across, as if whipped by a strong wind, and then abruptly stopped and lay still again. Felpz brought his free hand down on the open page with a triumphant smack.

"Asterly Hall," he said, pointing. I leaned forward and saw there the accompanying photograph for that entry, and found it indeed bore a striking resemblance to the drawing on the letter. It might have been difficult to tell—the house being in many ways a typical Warken mansion—except for the singular detail of the windows, which were arranged in a diamond orientation rather than a square one, and this detail had been preserved in the drawing—though when I had first seen it I thought it due to a quirk of the artist.

"Odd," said Felpz, and I could not tell whether he was relieved or frustrated at the finding. "Really it is the *oddest* thing."

"What is?" I asked.

Felpz looked up at me in surprise, as if he had forgotten I was there.

"It is only that, unless my magical sensibilities are wildly out of whack, the person who wrote me this note should not be at Asterly Hall."

"Yet it seems clear they wish you to go there," I observed.

"Indeed," said Felpz, his brow furrowing. Then, as if the cogs in his mind had finally aligned and engaged the rest of his body, he stood up abruptly, slipping the note into his breast pocket and reaching for his coat—which he'd lain casually over the back of his chair. "The only thing will be to *go* and *see*," he said, shrugging the garment on. It was a rich violet today with a delicate magenta filigree pattern around the collar and in the lining. This was in contrast to the dull greyish purple—nearly navy—that the very same coat had been yesterday. The changes his clothing went through was something I had come to accept about my friend, but this change seemed to indicate a fundamental shift in his mood; where before he had been bored, lethargic and a little displeased with the world in general, now he was excited and interested in something, and this in turn excited and interested me. Bending low over the book I noted the address of the mansion.

"It is only just outside Briarford," I remarked. "We can have a bite of breakfast at Webley Square and take the Dartfordale Regular from Peddlefield and be there before noon. I'll pack you an overnight bag, however, just in case this turns out to be something more involved. I know how things like this can distract you." I gave him a firm pat upon his shoulder as I slipped away, leaving him unable to respond before I was out the door and busy assembling our travel things.

Felpz was uncharacteristically mute on the journey out of Redling. Had it not been for the vibrancy of his clothes I would have thought him melancholy, if not outright depressed. He kept touching the pocket of his waistcoat where the letter was stored, as if to assure himself of its presence, and stared out the window with a blank, vacant expression.

All of which, I felt, was rather a pity, it being one of our glorious fall days, with the trees like bonfires of gold and orange and red, their leaves lying in drifts beside the tracks. The sky was alive with birds, and in the fields the sheep and cows and horses were looking exceptionally soft and fluffy in their new winter coats. The few clouds were high, unobtrusive white things, providing no impediment to the bright slanting sunlight.

We reached Briarford easily enough, and I was a little taken aback to find it a much more bustling and urban place than I remembered from my youth. Though farms and fields still separated it from the metropolis of Redling, the Great Kyrish Railway had brought the throbbing pulse of the city to this small hamlet, and we emerged from the station to find ourselves on a street lined with busy shops and offices, loud with the clop of shod hooves as horses pulling everything from sleek black cabs to huge hay wagons trotted past. One such cab pulled up to a stop right beside us, and a distraught young woman tumbled out. She was wearing a neat black dress with a black collar and matching black hat—but of the modern sort fashioned out of felt after men's hats, with only a modest bundle of rooster tail feathers affixed to the band. She saw us and, clutching at her breast, staggered over.

"Oh, thank goodness you are here," she said. "I do hope you were not waiting long; you understand Asterly Hall is very upset at the moment. I had no idea his will would be so particular. If you'll come this way . . ."

She trailed to a stop, for Felpz had raised a hand and was taking off his hat.

"Madam, I'm afraid you mistake us. We are bound for Asterly Hall, but we have no knowledge of recent events there. Whomever you presume us to be I assure you we are not them."

The woman appeared to trip, even though she was standing still. "What? Then you are *not* the solicitors?" She sounded rather accusing, as if we were doing her a disservice by not being what she expected.

Felpz and I looked at each other, and I had to repress a laugh until I remembered that I was wearing my sharp new traveling coat and, if the color of Felpz's costume were ignored, we made a very dignified and respectable-looking pair.

"No, madam, we are not," Felpz replied with perfect gravity. "I am Bouragner Felpz, a magician from Redling, this is my friend and confidante Mrs Corianne Birch. I recently received a communication suggesting all was not well at Asterly Hall, and I am here to discover why that is and to improve matters if I can. If some calamity has befallen you, I would like to lay my services and expertise at your disposal—if the skills of a magician are something you require."

"A magician?" the woman said, and her face shifted violently. It was as though her nerves, already strung high, took a bit of a turn and veered off in another, no less unpleasant direction. "That is . . . most extraordinary. Unexpected. I should not know what to say. My grandfather died last night, you see, and this morning we are like an overturned beehive— his passing was not expected. Family matters have become more complicated by the minute, and I had to summon his solicitors up from Redling. That is who I was expecting to meet, but perhaps I missed their train. Oh, dear. But we *do* have need of a magician, sir, I believe that no matter what my brother says. Here, you take this cab back to the hall—he's been paid—and I will meet you there as soon as I have located Kellard and Mikkel. Tell Barrydew—that's our butler—what you are and that Miss Asten sent you. Try to avoid my brother if you can, but if you should meet do *not* let him turn you away until I've had a chance to speak with you."

Felpz took this outpouring with stolidity, and touched his brow to the young woman as she hurried past us into the station. With a shrug to me he put on his hat and approached the cab.

"Straight to the hall then, gentlefolk?" the cabbie said, tipping his cap to us.

Felpz paused with one foot on the running board. "Yes," he said. "But not up the drive. Leave us at the gate, if you please."

"Curiouser and curiouser," he said to me as we rattled off through the town.

"It is quite a quandary indeed," I agreed, with perhaps more cheer than was tactful. Felpz raised an eyebrow at me.

"You are enjoying trampling through this tangled web?" he asked.

"I look forward to watching you unravel it," I replied primly.

Felpz smiled, but it was a tight smile and gone almost as soon as it had formed. "I hope I can bring this to a satisfactory conclusion," said he, and glanced sharply out the window. "I fear . . . no. No, I will not dwell on that. No use fearing the worst without concrete evidence. First, we must see what Asterly Hall has to say."

Asterly Hall turned out to be a large and rambling estate not far from the bustle of Briarford, but the gate the cab dropped us at was clean and modern and stood open. Far from walking up the wide gravel drive, however, Felpz immediately veered off through a thicket, and we ended up approaching the residence from across a field of neatly manicured lawn. When I expressed surprise at this choice of route he held up a hand to silence me and marched on. In this way we passed through a small grove of brilliant orange-and-red-leafed trees and eventually arrived at the back of the house, where we surprised a footman and a housemaid smoking in the rear courtyard. By the way they guiltily hid the ends of their cigarettes I assumed they mistook us for someone else, but upon seeing we were strangers—and well-dressed ones at that—they became even more flustered.

"If you'll 'scuse my saying so sir, ma'am, but I'm afraid you've got the wrong end of the house," the footman said stiffly as the maid hurried inside. "If you'll follow me I'll lead you 'round to the front."

"Not at all," said Felpz congenially, lodging himself firmly beside a cart loaded with empty glass bottles and clay jugs. "It was this end I was aiming for. You'll do me a greater service, young man, if you would inform your butler that a pair of visitors have arrived at the behest of Miss Asten, and wish to share a confidential word."

"Just so sir," said the footman, his creamy-pale face going poker blank. "If you'll step with me I'll take you in via the drawing room . . . " and he made a move as if to lead Felpz out of the courtyard.

"No, thank you," said Felpz, and a rather dizzying thing happened. Felpz was suddenly farther along the cart, and the footman, rather than leading us out of the courtyard, was walking away into the house saying, "I'll only be a moment, thank you."

"Felpz, what in the worlds—" I began, but once more Felpz silenced me with a gesture. He ran his hands briskly over the cart, lifted the lid of a jug and sniffed the contents. Shrugging to himself he went over to the waterbutt and peered inside. Shaking his head he replaced the lid and was just going to peek into a broken-down shed standing in the corner when again the rear door opened and a short, roundish person dressed in immaculate black tails and pinstriped trousers stepped out. Seeing Felpz engaged with the shed they cleared their throat disapprovingly, and I was obliged to step forward to introduce us.

" . . . and you are Barrydew then?" I finished.

"It is *Mister* Barrydew, if you please," said the odd little person. He had a highish, throaty voice, and I would have been hard pressed to put a sex to it had I not been given the preferred pronoun. "You'll forgive Jakob, but you must admit this is somewhat irregular. Err-*herm*," he finished pointedly, and Felpz at last withdrew his head from the shed. There was a spiderweb stuck to one ear, which he flicked away impatiently.

"This is not the house I feared it would be," he said, as if he had not heard the butler arrive. "But that does not help me in my quest. Barrydew? Oh good, perhaps *you* can tell me what has been going on here."

"If Miss Asten sent you I assume you'll have been told more than I can say already," Barrydew said, tightlipped.

"It was more an accident of chance," Felpz said with a wave of his hand. "I was summoned here by a third party, and Miss Asten sent us along from the train station. She said we were specifically to speak to *you.*"

Barrydew looked at Felpz skeptically, then turned to me.

"A magician, you say?" he said, unimpressed.

"One of the best in the country," I replied. "Have you never met one before? They are all a bit eccentric."

Barrydew gave a little wiggle about his shoulders that might have been a repressed shrug, or might just have been him settling his coat. "Come inside then," he said. "If you won't at least go around to the drawing room, you'll have to come in through the downstairs."

He made this sound as if it would be some hellish ordeal, but the corridor and pantry we passed through were very neat and clean, if a bit plain and worn—but the good, honest wear of a place well-used. I caught sight of a pair of inquisitive eyes gazing up at me from waist level, and turning I saw a mousy little girl with a wild head of brown hair and an even darker face staring back at me. Aside from this vision, however, we saw no one else, though I could hear the thumping and hammering of feet running about floor above us. We climbed a set of stairs and passed through a narrow passage before emerging into a light, tasteful room decorated with sofas and draperies in soothing moss green.

Barrydew crossed at once to the only other door and pulled it gently shut, then he checked out the window and finally came back and ushered us into chairs.

"I believe they can spare me for two minutes," he said, swiftly and quietly, and in tones far different from the ones he had employed in the courtyard. "The facts, magician, in the extreme brief, are these: Miss Asten's grandfather, Lord Asterly, passed away yesterday evening. And in the time since I laid him out then and this morning when the doctor arrived to sign the death certificate, his left hand has gone missing."

Felpz, who had been examining an arrangement of autumn branches set in a vase beside the sofa where he sat, looked up abruptly and fixed the butler with a penetrating stare.

"Gone missing," Felpz echoed, but not as a question. It was as if by repeating the words he was driving the facts further home inside his brain. "His left hand . . . " he murmured. Then, with a full-body convulsion, snapped to his feet and paced to the window. He pulled aside the drapes and checked behind them, as if he expected to find someone hiding there.

"Yes," said the butler tightly. "Gone clean off at the wrist, leaving a fairly well healed stump. It was no prosthetic hand, I assure you: I saw the man use enough cutlery with it."

"No," said Felpz, and there was a bubble of excitement in his voice. "A prosthesis would be problematic. But a real hand . . . and a *left* hand . . . "

Whatever he was about to say was interrupted as the outer door—the one Barrydew had shut upon our entering—cracked open and the footman, Jakob, put his head in. "Flares up, Barrydew, his young lordship wants you urgently."

"I must go," Barrydew announced. "Pray, do not leave this room. I will send Miss Asten in directly when she returns." And with a swish of fine black coat-tails he was out the door, leaving the footman to close it behind them.

"How very *peculiar*," I murmured in their absence. I turned to Felpz and found him standing by the window, his cheeks flushed with color, practically hugging himself in relief and joy.

"Not at all," he said distractedly, when he noticed me looking. "This sort of thing happens all the time. The trick will be figuring out *how*, and where the wretched thing has got to."

"The what?" I said.

"Why, the *hand* of course—the missing *hand!*" He fairly leapt over to the nearest bookcase, and began running a finger along the spines on the shelf. "I may be getting ahead of myself. Better to familiarize ourselves with the history of this land and family. We may be dealing with a more entrenched servitude than I hoped. A history of the family's lands and titles, if you please," he said, very firmly, to thin air. Then, a moment later, he pulled an old volume off the shelf that had not been there before. "Thank you," he said, flipping through it as he walked back to the sofa.

We were in the moss-colored room for almost an hour, during which time Felpz summoned several more books relating to the family's history, and I grew hungry. Eventually he gave a deep sigh of satisfaction and leaned back, holding a battered old journal in his hands.

"You have a great gift of patience, dear Corianne," he said, gazing up at me from where he sat on the floor, surrounded by books.

"Hardly a gift," I replied. "I fought for it dearly. Are you able to shed some light on the matter now?"

Felpz raised a hand, one finger extended, as if requesting yet more patience, but he said: "First, allow me to walk through the history of this estate, as it has been presented to me by their own records—partly for my own benefit."

"I am all ears," I said readily.

"Good. Then I shall begin by saying that there was nothing particularly of interest about the Earls of Asterly up until a century ago. Then one of them, through a combination of bad luck and personal vice, managed to lose the greater part of the title's wealth. The hall and lands remained, but with no money to run and maintain them, they fell into a sad state. It was into this low point in the family's history that the previous Earl, one Wallard Asten, was born. Things are a bit muddled here, but it appears that in his youth he was able to locate and dig up what is referred to only as 'Halliard's Legacy,' and used it to restore the monetary wealth of his family. When he came into the title he expanded his affluence further by the traditional means of prudent book-keeping and sensible investments. He married, had one son, who in turn married and sired two children. The son died unexpectedly some twenty years ago, and Lord Wallard was, for the better part of their lives, the primary caregiver to his son's children. These are undoubtedly the Miss Asten and her brother who currently reside beyond—" he waved a hand at the door. "What interests *me* is 'Halliard's Legacy' . . . " he set aside the journal and pawed through the books until he came to an ancient red tome with peeling gold leaf on the cover.

"According to this compendium of Asten ancestors," he continued, opening the book, "'Halliard's Legacy' refers to one Halliard Asten who, in the 2140's, acquired what is described only as 'a great treasure' and buried it on his home lands. The writers of this useful volume assume it is gold, which seems to be borne out by the use to which Wallard Asten put it some hundred years later, but I think it was something else entirely. Something altogether more powerful and dangerous than gold. Because Halliard Asten, it is said, acquired his treasure . . . from *Amstrass*."

I confess this pronouncement did not evoke quite the realization and awe in me that Bouragner Felpz desired. I was still too caught up in the mystery of the disappearing hand, and could not fathom what connection it had to the turn in a family's fortune or to the mythical vampire, Amstrass. I began to point this out, but was interrupted by the door banging open violently and a young man striding into the room.

He looked enough like Miss Asten—wavy chestnut hair and high, aristocratic cheekbones—that I guessed this must be the promised brother, the new Lord Asterly, and made to get to my feet. The young man paid me no attention, however, and aimed his assault purely at Felpz.

"What is this, sir? I ask you! It is entirely impertinent and disrespectful—do you not know we are a household in *mourning*, sir? I'm afraid I must insist you *leave*, immediately."

Felpz looked up at the boy serenely from within his circle of books. "I answer to Miss Asten," he said calmly. "It is by her request that we are here. Hers, and an old friend of mine. Until affairs are settled to their satisfaction you will find me quite immovable."

He spoke frankly and without rancor, which only served to enrage the man further. It was quite a stroke of luck, then—or perhaps it was Felpz's magic; the timing was so spectacular that I imagined it was so— that Miss Asten herself entered the room. She was breathless and a little flushed, and carried in her wake the butler Barrydew and two dour-faced lawyers in black. I saw the footman Jakob behind them, his face a contortion of confusion as he was drawn into the room as well.

"Reginald, that's quite enough," Miss Asten said shrilly. "I still live here—they are my *guests*."

The young lord rounded on his sister. "Hickory," he said, the figurative steam rising from his ears almost visible to the naked eye. "If this is more nonsense concerning your midnight hallucinations—"

"But they were *not* hallucinations, as you well know!" the young woman returned hotly.

Barrydew came over and began neatly picking up the books Felpz had piled on the floor. "If you're done with them, sir," he said deferentially. "And a word of warning; they may be at it a while."

"As long as they do not block the door," Felpz said pleasantly, still sitting cross-legged on the carpet.

More people were filing into the room as the two siblings argued. Behind Jakob came the little dark girl I had glimpsed in the kitchen, and behind her a wide, matronly woman in a dirty white apron. An old man with wavy, white hair who looked like a valet squeezed in behind her, followed by the housemaid whom we had surprised in the courtyard, and finally a rail-thin woman in a tidy tweed dress.

"Right," said Felpz, standing up. Immediately the volume of the arguing voices dropped sharply, and into the relative quiet he said: "Is that everyone?"

No one answered. They all stared at him with varying degrees of confusion and—in the case of Lord Asterly, the footman, and the housemaid—anger. Felpz took it all in with his same bluff pleasantness, and clasped his hands modestly behind his back.

"First, allow me to introduce myself, as some of you may yet be unaware . . . " he began.

"This is most—" Lord Asterly said, and then his mouth shut with a snap as Felpz's beam-like focus turned on him.

"I am Bouragner Felpz," my friend continued, as if he had not been interrupted. "You may already know the name. I am a magician of some means, and I was summoned here by *this note.*" He reached into his breast pocket and removed the folded piece of soft grey paper. Holding it delicately between two fingers he presented it to the crowd as he went on. "Which I am certain none of you wrote, by the way. Yet it indicates that someone in this house is in distress, and so I have called you here: Everyone who has knowledge of the goings on relating to the writer of this note: I would request you tell me everything you know, as that will allow me to resolve the matter in the most timely fashion, and allow you to get back to your peaceful, ordinary lives." He said this last with an arch look at the Asten siblings, who gazed back unlovingly.

"First," said Felpz. "I already know about the late lord's escapade in his youth and Halliard's treasure. I have also been informed that, after his death, his *left* hand has gone missing. What I wish to know, now, is whether anything extraordinary relating to his left hand was noticed while he was *alive.*" His eyes scanned the crowd invitingly, and I felt the pull of the magic he was using to encourage anyone with such knowledge to come forward and share it.

At first there was no response, but then the tidy woman in the tweed dress exchanged a look with the footman and the housemaid, and took a cautious step forward. "Mrs Beller, sir," she said, her voice deep and dry. "Housekeeper. The young lord and lady will forgive me saying this, as it was not to be common knowledge beyond the family, but the late lord was *left handed*, sir."

Felpz nodded encouragingly. "It has been known to happen to the best of us," he assured the woman. "Personally, I believe there ought to be no shame in it."

"That's most generous of you," the housekeeper said, her own hands folded tightly together in front of her stomach. "But I mean to say, he *wrote* left handed. Signed his letters left handed. Why, we had to make sure all the maids knew to set his place mirrored from what was proper, for he even *ate* left handed."

"And that is all?" Felpz said, a hint of disappointment in his voice.

The housekeeper exchanged another look with her fellow adult servants, but it wasn't until the aged valet nodded firmly that she replied: "That is all we *saw,* sir. All we saw."

"But there was more to see?" Felpz asked, and again cast his gaze over the assembled crowd.

This time it took longer, but at last there was a nervous shuffling, and the dark little girl, eyes wide in fear, made her way to the front of the crowd. With her wild dark hair she looked almost like some fey child, and she glanced about at the surrounding adults, clearly in awe of them.

For his part Felpz went down on his knees so their faces were even. Gently he said: "And who are you?"

"Pattiny, m'lord," she said, her voice small and lisping.

"I am no lord, not any more," Felpz replied, a small smile flitting about his mouth. "But it is no matter. What did you see, Miss Pattiny?"

Pattiny looked around again, and I saw both Barrydew and the white-haired manservant staring at her sternly. Clearly the poor girl was intimidated by them, but then the matronly woman in the apron, who I assumed was the cook, came forward and patted her on the shoulder.

"You g'on and tell the magician, luv. He'll understand."

Pattiny swallowed, twisting her boney, dark hands in her skirts.

"I din't *see* so much," she whispered. "Not as awake I din't. I could never *see* it with my eyes open. Only dreaming, like, with them shut."

Felpz nodded. "That is true to its nature," he said. "Nothing to worry about."

"I always thought it was some sort of spider," Pattiny admitted. "So I tried to kill it at first. Mighty big it was too, for it knocked over a vase in Miss Asten's room. But it weren't no spider m'l—sir. It only had five legs, an' I know all the spiders have *eight.* I saw it in a dream once, and it came and climbed up my window trying to get out. I tried leaving my window open after that, and from then on it would come down to the kitchens at night and help me with the washing up."

"During which time you never saw it?"

"Not as I see you," the girl said quietly. "But I saw the things it moved, and it left tracks in the flour."

"And this happened . . . ?" Felpz trailed off.

"A year," Pattiny said in her brief way. "At least a year."

"Pattiny here starting speaking of it to me about eight months ago," the cook supplied helpfully. "Goodness knows I never saw anything, but I don't doubt her word. Our Pattiny has always had a special touch about her."

"Thank you," said Felpz respectfully, getting back to his feet. He turned and looked at Miss Asten, who was staring at the girl with her mouth slightly open.

"You saw it too!" she cried suddenly, her hands flying to her face. "Why didn't you speak up *sooner?*"

Pattiny looked terrified at this, and backed away into the cook's skirts as if to hide herself in them.

"She did, ma'am, she *did*," the woman said. "But who listens to the nattering of a simple kitchen maid? Why, I only believed her because I walked in one evening and saw the dishes dancing in the sink, as if held by an invisible hand, and Pattiny here giving it directions as to the proper washing. Gave me quite a turn it did, but I believed. Oh, never doubt *I* believed."

"Barrydew!" cried Miss Asten, rounding on the butler. "Why was I never told this?"

Barrydew, his arms full of books, pursed his lips and looked deferentially at the young Lord Asterly. "I was given to understand," he said in a pinched voice, "that the late lord wished his peculiar shortcomings kept an utmost secret."

"*Grandfather's* shortcomings?" Miss Asten gasped. She turned to Felpz. "Magician," she said. "The reason I wanted you here was this! For the past year I have been plagued, like Pattiny, with strange visions and half-dreams of a disembodied white hand that crawled along the floor and battered at the windows. I would have dismissed them as nightmares but that one morning I woke to find handprints fresh upon my window frame. It is a *hand*," she said, turning to Pattiny. "The five legs you saw were *fingers*. Very long and boney ones too, quite like spider legs. And the hand itself was all withered, and the skin wrinkled and dry. Sometimes it even appeared bluish, so I never associated it with my *grandfather's* hand . . . until last night, that is."

"And what happened last night?" said Felpz, his voice gone sharp as a knife.

"Oh, don't tell me this is all about that silly dream of yours," Lord Asterly began, but his sister turned on him.

"For the last time, it was *not* a dream, Reginald!" she more or less screamed, and the two lawyers drew back in surprise.

"Please tell me," said Felpz, his soft voice cutting through the clamor and bringing silence with it. Miss Asten checked herself and took a deep breath.

"Last night grandfather died," she said, a little shakily. "It was not entirely unexpected, him being so old, but it was still a shock, you know. Why, I had thought the old man would live forever. It was quite upsetting, anyway, and it was near one in the morning before I was at last abed. Once there I found it impossible to sleep, but lay restless with my eyes closed. And I dreamed, or thought I dreamed, in the way a nervous mind does, while still being partly awake. I heard the creak of my door open, and a skittering of nails on the wooden floorboards, and I smelled something . . . hard to describe now that it is day and I am surrounded by living souls. It reminded me of wet grass and night sky, and put me in mind of old books—the sort with spines so stiff they are fused shut.

"All this I thought of as a dream, but I was rudely awoken by the feel of cold, twig-like fingers gripping at my face, and I opened my eyes to find my vision blocked by a dark object. I believe I screamed, and pulled at it with my own hands. It came off easily enough and landed softly at the foot of my bed. I sat there, feeling the cold air rush in at my back and my heart thudding in my chest, and as surely as I see you now I *saw*, for it glowed ghost white and pale blue in the dark, a withered, disembodied *hand*. It lay there, twitching, for some moments, before it righted itself and, like a spider, scuttled off into the darkness.

"I struck a light and called for Flowers, my maid, and when she came we made a thorough search of the room but found nothing." Miss Asten raised her chin in defiance at her brother, and looked upon Felpz. "Yet come morning we discovered Grandfather's own hand had gone missing! That would have been enough to send me on a search for a magical consultant, only I had to deal with his solicitors, who were needed on account of his will not being entirely complete."

"I quite understand," said Felpz. "Thank you for being so frank, Miss Asten. You have been most helpful. And I am sorry to hear of the fright you were given last night. If it alleviates your discomfort at all, know that I do not believe you were in any real danger."

Miss Asten did not look convinced, but Felpz had already moved on to the two solicitors, who were looking increasingly uncomfortable.

"Which brings me to you . . . Kellard and Mikkel, was it?"

The man cleared his throat ponderously. "Yes, yes, we are," he said. "I am Kellard, and I would like to say we have no knowledge of any of this strange business concerning missing hands. We are only here to deliver the missing portion of the late Lord Asterly's will."

"Ah," said Felpz graciously. "Can you tell me what is in it?"

Both the solicitors inflated indignantly.

"We are the custodians," said the woman. "We were involved in its drafting and would never violate a client's confidentiality in such a way."

"Indeed," said Felpz agreeably. "However, as the relevant heirs are present now, perhaps you would be so good as to read its contents—with their consent, of course."

The lawyers exchanged looks, but Miss Asten spoke up at once.

"If you think it will have some bearing on this mystery, then I would greatly appreciate this," she said. Her brother, however, looked troubled and reluctant. Kellard gave us a grave look and frowned.

"It was impressed upon us that the matter contained herein was of a most intimate and confidential quality, for the eyes the next Lord Asterly only," he murmured, glancing at the young man.

"If it had nothing to do with the matter of the withered hand," Felpz said relentlessly, "then you would not be standing here. As it is, whatever is contained in that missing portion has direct relevance on my investigation, so I must insist."

"Oh blast it, Kellard," said Lord Reginald, "give it here and let me read it. Perhaps it will get them to go *away*." He shot the last words pointedly at Felpz, who received them in good grace and nodded, smiling.

The solicitors did not look best pleased by this, and cast disapproving glances at the servants—who seemed to be using the excuse of Felpz's magic to shamelessly indulge their curiosity—but they came forward, and the woman, Mikkel, laid a slim black briefcase on a nearby table. Kellard produced a key and unlocked it, gently lifting the lid and withdrawing a thin, paper folder. This he passed without opening to Lord Reginald, who briskly flipped it open. He made a little noise of surprise at finding a single sheet of paper contained therein, but held it up and, squinting rather, began to read.

"'To my rightful and legal heir, the next Lord of Asterly. You hold in your hands the last will and testament of Wallard Asten, seventh Earl of Asterly. In it you will find no provisions for land deeds, titles or other practical matters, but rather this concerns the most important artifact of the Asterly Title. That is the peculiar matter of Halliard's Legacy which I, Lord Wallard, did unearth and uncover in the year 2246. I have used it faithfully since that date to repair and restore the glory of the Asterly title, and I hereby call and command you to do the same. Use it well, and allow it to guide you in all things, and as surely as my life is testament, your lordship will be as successful as mine. I hereby entrust the legacy to you, that on my passing it will leave my body and become one with yours. This has been the ultimate will and testament, made by Lord Wallard Asterly, being of sound body and mind, on September the 18th, Year of our Lady, 2292.'"

The young lord looked up, a bewildered expression on his face. "Why this is most vexing," said he. "It does not help us at all with the problem of the missing bequeathment lists."

"I expect the problem there is entirely a mundane case of misfiling," Felpz said dryly. "However, that letter does bear directly on the matter at hand. You'll note the curious turn of phrase at the end: '*on my passing it will leave my body and become one with yours.*' Keeping that in mind, consider the mysterious loss of your grandfather's left hand, and the upsetting experience Miss Asten endured last night—not to mention the testimony of Miss Pattiny, and one cannot help but become aware of a great, nebulous web coming slowly into focus."

There was startled gasping from the servants, quickly hushed by the housekeeper, and slowly Lord Reginald lowered the letter, staring at Felpz aghast.

"Do you mean to say . . . that . . . that *hand* these women have been hallucinating—that was grandfather's *legacy*? And now it is coming for *me*?"

"That would be what is implied by that statement," Felpz said. "Although the fact that the hand went to Miss Asten first suggests that it might have its own ideas of who should be the next Earl of Asterly."

"Well," said the young man, the color rising in his cheeks. "I want no part of it. Sounds downright witchy to me. Hickory can have it."

"*I* don't want it!" Miss Asten proclaimed, eyes gone wide. "It frightened me half to death!"

"That is just as well," Felpz said mildly, gazing around the assembled room. "For I do not believe the legacy should go to *anyone* save its original owner."

"And how do you suggest we do *that?*" Lord Reginald said, somewhat accusingly.

"Oh, that should not be too difficult," Felpz said. "If you would leave matters *completely* in my hands, I can assure you the case will be settled and done before the sun rises tomorrow."

Relief flashed across the face of Miss Asten, but Lord Reginald narrowed his eyes suspiciously.

"How surprising," he said cynically. "The magician will make all our problems go away . . . for what fee?"

For the first time the good humor that had flowed in an undercurrent beneath Felpz's manner evaporated completely. Something hardened behind his eyes and he looked as close to being offended as I had ever seen him.

"My *fee,*" he said, dropping the word as if it scalded him, "is your quiet and docile cooperation, *Lord Asterly.* What I do, I do on behalf of an old, old friend—not for any reward a human peer could ever grant me."

I could see Asterly bristle at this, but for once he thought better of antagonizing my friend, and held his peace. His sister, meanwhile, came forward hopefully.

"Whatever assistance you require, I will be more than happy to provide," she offered graciously. "If only I could have some sort of an explanation of these extraordinary events as well, that would settle my mind greatly."

Felpz looked round at her; the cold fury melted away, and he smiled briefly. "A full explanation indeed, my lady," said he. "But as I can do nothing further until tonight, I suggest you put the matter out of your mind until then. Let us all meet again in this room, after sunset. Kellard and Mikkel, I need not keep you, but in addition to Miss Asten I will need you, Lord Reginald, and you, Miss Pattiny. You have been touched by this hand, and you would do well to witness this. As for the rest of you, let me detain you from your valuable work no further. Corianne, I think we shall walk back into Briarford and find a bite to eat—the colors are astonishingly bright this year—and return here by six, when, I hope, I will be able to give you all a satisfactory explanation."

This was, more or less, how events unfolded. We had a good luncheon at a charming inn in Briarford, and were back at the hall before sundown. The house had settled somewhat by then, and this time we entered properly through the front door—much to Barrydew's relief.

We gathered once more in the moss-colored sitting room, and in addition to myself, Felpz, Miss Asten, Lord Reginald and the girl Pattiny, I got the impression that a number of the staff were crowded around outside the door. Barrydew stood defiantly just inside it, his face blank as a poker player's, but Felpz only shrugged when he noticed, and set about clearing a space in the middle of the room—pushing chairs and sofas up against the wall and tucking the tables in between them. Barrydew and Pattiny tried to help at first, but eventually gave up when it became clear their efforts were not appreciated.

"I think our appetites are thoroughly whetted, Felpz," I said, once he had the furniture to his liking and we were all seated, facing the open area that had been cleared in the center of the room. "You did promise an explanation."

"Mr Barrydew, would you be so good as to turn down the lights?" Felpz asked. Then, as the butler obliged, he went on: "An explanation, yes. Thank you, Corianne. Well, as we have a little time I suppose now is as good an opportunity as ever."

He rested himself on the edge of a nearby table and crossed his hands. "The crux of the matter is this legacy. Corianne and I have recently familiarized ourselves with your family's history, and perhaps you remember the stories of Halliard's Legacy?"

"Indeed," said Miss Asten. "I was given to believe it was gold."

"As was I," admitted Lord Reginald. "Why, I dug up half the grounds as a small boy searching for it. Quite a tongue-lashing I got for that, too. Now you mean to say this mysterious, magical hand . . . *that* was Halliard's Legacy all along? What the Devil *is* it?"

"Something almost as far from a devil as it is possible to get," Felpz said mildly. "It is an object of great power and potency. That it came into the hands of a Kyrish Earl is remarkable indeed, especially considering it came from *Amstrass.*"

"You'll have to elaborate on that," Miss Asten spoke up. "For I always understood it to mean he found it on a journey to Svenia."

Felpz gave Miss Asten a disappointed look.

"Corianne, *you* know who Amstrass is, I pray," he said tiredly.

"Near enough, I should think," I said, and turning to Miss Asten I explained. "You may know her as the *Vampira d'Amstrass,* or the Red Vampire. She turns up all over the place in legends from that area, and even makes an appearance in some Kyrish literature. She's known for riding a giant stag and keeps a hellhound at her side. Though I must admit," I added, turning back to Felpz, "I always thought she was a myth."

Felpz nodded and smiled. "A myth, yes, and so much more. Never doubt, however, that she is very much a real person. How Halliard Asten managed to get the hand away from her is a mystery to me, though knowing her, it is possible she simply became bored of it."

"This hand," said Lord Reginald. "You said you know what it is?"

Felpz nodded assent. "It's a tricky matter to explain. Put as simply as I can manage, that hand is a piece of a *lamphra*. Lamphra, as I can see you do not know, are the lords of the great realm of Dream that lies between ours and oblivion. They are primordial creatures, not bound to any one shape; they also gave vampires many of their powers, along with their weakness to sunlight. A lamphra cannot appear in daylight except under special circumstances, which is why we are holding this gathering after dark. They do, however, possess many extraordinary powers, which your grandfather, as bearer of the hand, would have been able to use to restore the fortunes of his estate."

"And how do you know," the young lord pressed on, "that it was this hand that Amstrass passed on to Halliard Asten? Why should she have it in her possession?"

Felpz leveled a steady, dark look upon the young man. "I knew she had it because I was there when she took it," he said blankly, in tones that forbade further questions. Then he sighed and went on: "The hand of Halliard's Legacy once belonged to a particular lamphra I know rather well — hence my involvement in this matter. Being first in the possession of a powerful vampire, then locked in a box and buried, and finally affixed to the arm of a living human — I can only assume it drew on the life of Lord Wallard's own left hand in order to be visible in daylight, hence the disappearance of his left appendage entirely — the lamphra hand having completely consumed the human one. At the death of its human master it took the first opportunity it could to escape. Indeed, has been trying to escape for at least a year, according to Pattiny's testimony." Felpz nodded at the little girl, who shivered. "But on every occasion it found itself blocked by the power of that curious testament Lord Reginald carries. Although . . . " and now his eyes, dark in the dim light, swung to Miss Asten, "the fact that it went to *you* on the night of your grandfather's death seems to indicate it has a different notion as to who should inherit the Asten title." Felpz shrugged. "In any case, it took advantage of its limited measure of freedom to write a note to me, I being its closest ally. So I am here, with those who hold the power to free it, and the one who was closest to a friend it had in this house, and I have been calling the hand, gently, all this time I have been speaking. I feel it drawing close now, and provided no one does anything rash, we should not have long to wait."

Felpz's voice faded into silence, broken only by the sound of someone — I believe it was Lord Reginald — breathing heavily. Despite Felpz's optimistic words we waited in the dark and the quiet for almost twenty minutes before the monotony was broken.

Felpz uncrossed his hands, letting them fall to his sides in a low swish of cloth. Turning in his direction I saw him outlined against the dim glow of Barrydew's lamp, his head erect and his neck arched. He was staring very intently at a corner of the ceiling, and at once I cast my gaze in that direction as well.

"Can you see it, Corianne?" he asked, his voice low and unusually hoarse.

I strained my eyes, but at first could see nothing but the seam of the wall where it met the ceiling in a tight corner. I fancied I saw a tiny crack in the plaster there, but the light was so bad that even with my enchanted glasses I could not be sure.

Then, and I cannot describe how this set my heart pounding and my hands shaking, I saw a pale finger, as thin and knobby as an oak twig and the color of milk, creep out from the corner where the wallpaper met the plaster. It was soon joined by another, and another and another. They gripped at the wall, and slowly the whole hand emerged: veined and faintly blue-tinged, the thumb supporting the palm as the hand stood there, like an alien spider. It ended neatly at the wrist, where the skin was pulled down to cover the bones and flesh beneath.

Slowly it crept down the wall, climbing awkwardly on its five limbs. The nails looked chipped and torn, as if it had been through some hardship lately, and it walked with its pinkie raised, as if that finger pained it.

Still none of the others in the room reacted as if they could see it, though Pattiny's head came up, and she said: "Is here now."

"Yes," said Felpz, coming forward into the clearing and going down on one knee. "You have very good witchsight, Pattiny. Better trust it over your own eyes."

The hand was nearing the floor now, and disappeared behind the back of a chair. At once I began scanning the carpet, trying to catch a glimpse of it between the chairs and table legs.

Lord Reginald and Miss Asten—not to mention Barrydew—though they could not see what we did, were still following our gazes in the direction of the hand.

Eventually it emerged. Pale and timid as a newborn lamb, it rocked on its destroyed fingernails, and slowly crept forward into the clearing.

Felpz, now on both knees, held his own left hand out towards it, his fingers open and inviting. I had been impressed before at the spidery grace and delicacy of Felpz's hands, but in comparison to this withered thing they looked quite thick and meaty, full of blood and flesh. The disembodied hand was clearly something dusty and dry, shriveled and discarded like the shell from a molting insect.

Yet on it came, growing slightly transparent in the light, and when it reached the tips of Felpz's outstretched hand it seemed to hesitate. Then, almost unbelievingly, it slid first one and then another finger over Felpz's palm, until it was pressed against his in a bizarre handshake. Felpz's fingers closed around it and he stood up, the withered hand held limply in his own.

The hand must at that point have become visible to Miss Asten and Lord Reginald, for they shot backwards in their seats and exclaimed. Barrydew's face twisted in alarm, but he was master of himself a moment later. Pattiny, however, leaned forward, a look of fascination on her bluff, dark countenance.

"Now comes your part," Felpz said, turning to the Asten siblings. "The hand has chosen you, Miss Asten. Do you accept it?"

"*No!*" cried Miss Asten, bringing one of her own up to cover her mouth. Then, seeming to realize how this reaction could have a negative effect, she cleared her throat and added: "I would not wish to take advantage in such a way."

Felpz nodded, and turned to Lord Reginald.

"You are the legal heir," he said. "The hand is still bound to you, as long as you keep that testament. Do you wish this?"

Lord Asterly looked at the hand in outright horror, thinking, no doubt, how it had consumed his grandfather's own hand.

"Not at *all,*" he said, his voice a little strangled. "If only I knew how to break that testament!"

"Fire is the standard method," Felpz said. "But in this case, I think if you simply broke the words, that would suffice."

"Break the *words?*" Lord Asterly said, but his sister had already reached into his coat pocket, where the testament had lain, folded, and taking it out she began to rip it to pieces, carefully shredding it so no word remained intact. Miss Hickory Asten, I thought, would probably become the true lord of Asterly Hall, title or no title, just as the hand had implied.

There was no noticeable change in the hand once she had finished, the testament lying in shattered leaves at her feet, but Felpz smiled and gave her a little bow.

"Now what?" the woman asked briskly. "Now what will you do?"

Felpz seemed surprised she should ask. He closed his right hand protectively over his left, and I saw the withered hand curl, like a satisfied cat, against his palm.

"I will take the hand," he said, as if this should be obvious, "and return it to its rightful owner."

Barrydew drove us back to town, and though Felpz insisted we go at once, Barrydew and I found ourselves waiting on him in the drive. When he did appear, it was from around the side of the house, having clearly just come from the kitchens.

"Remarkable girl, that Pattiny," he said, climbing in beside me. "You'll do well to heed her words, Mr Barrydew. Particularly after she finds her name."

Barrydew gave him an odd look, but said nothing. He flicked the reins, and the coach lurched forward into the night.

I was surprised, once we reached Briarford, to find that there were not one, but two trains to Redling that night. Felpz and I boarded the earlier of these with time to spare, and soon we were on our way home.

The adventure of the night, however, was far from over. Felpz, though he seemed altogether less nervous than he had been on our journey of the morning, was in no way relaxed.

"I confess," he said, gazing pensively out into the passing night, "I was not certain it was not Madgrin *himself* who was confined within that house. Such things have happened before. It was one such instance that resulted in his loss of this . . . " he patted the breast of his coat, beneath which the tips of the hand's fingers were just visible.

"Madgrin?" I repeated, puzzling at the odd-sounding name.

"The lamphra in question, and a very old friend," Felpz said. "One of the better dream lords, if a trifle too kind for his own good. It is him I intend to summon tonight. If you can bear with me a little longer Corianne, you may find the interview a pleasing finale to the day's events."

As you can imagine, the prospect of meeting such a mysterious person served to keep me well awake for the duration of the journey home, and upon reaching it I sat up with admirable fortitude while Felpz assembled the necessary items for the summoning. These were surprisingly simple, consisting only of a candle and a long mirror he pulled out of the closet and propped against the wall.

"Ordinarily I would go to *him*, but events of recent years have made it difficult for me to reach his house. However, with sufficient effort on my part he should be able to find *me* with little to no trouble. Do you just sit there, Corianne, and have a little more patience yet."

At this point I was pleasantly full of patience, warming myself by the fire with my feet propped up. Felpz could have taken the remainder of the night to perform his spell, and I would not have cared. As it happened, the magic worked perfectly and immediately, but without the intended result.

I remember it like this: Felpz stood before the mirror and lit the candle. He brought it to his face, staring intently at the glass through the flame. Then he gripped the base of the wax cylinder in one hand and threw it at the mirror. I could not suppress a flinch at this, as I fully expected the flame to bounce off the glass and burn the carpet. Instead, however, it passed clean through the surface of the mirror as if it were made of water, and I saw it travel in a graceful arc into the reflection of the room. This had gone suddenly dark and dim and a bit twisted, and with a jolt I realized it was no longer a reflection of our sitting room at all! Gone were the comfortable maroon carpet and the gentle drapes, scuffed armchairs and the litter of books and papers that persisted no matter what I did; in their place was a dark and lonely corridor made of stone slabs, with a pricking around the top that suggested a starry night sky. The candle I could still see, hanging as if in midair, until I realized it was held in the hands of a dark shadow, who stood in the corridor looking back at us—though they remained invisible, cloaked in the dark and masked by the light of the flame.

For a moment nothing happened. Then there was movement in the mirror, and the shadow grew suddenly larger. The surface of the mirror rippled, like the surface of a dark pond disturbed by a stone, and the candle re-emerged, now held in a small but robust hand, white as marble but tinged blue at the tips. A moment later the shadowy figure stepped out of the mirror, coming fully into our view at last.

My first thought was surprise: in all his references Felpz had clearly stated that Madgrin was *male,* yet the person who stood before us now was obviously a woman. Or at the very least, woman *shaped.* She stood about a head shorter than me, with such a round, full face that her cheeks turned her eyes into smiling crescents. She wore a simple, loose dress made of flowing, velvety fabric that draped around her rotund figure and swirled at the bottom, hiding her feet. Her hair was a tangle of gold and silver, and her lips were sky blue. Lit from below by the candle she carried, it was difficult to tell her age: she might have been ancient, or she might have been hardly more than a girl. There was a confusion of movement behind her, and I saw that her shadow did not keep the shape of the body that cast it, but writhed about, sometimes sprouting great, creeping spider legs, sometimes throwing up the head and flying mane of a horse, sometimes a slithering whip like a snake's tail. She brought with her into the room a smell like that of fresh grass after a summer rainstorm, and under that a dry, musty smell of old books.

She looked about the room with pleasant expectation, and when her eyes landed upon Felpz her face burst into a wide smile.

"My dear magician!" she cried, and blowing out the candle, she tossed it aside and threw herself at him. Felpz, surprised yet clearly delighted, laughed as he caught her up into his arms and swung her round. This caused her shadow some excitement, and I saw the silhouettes of horse, spider and snake all thrown against our wall in turn.

"Badgrave," said Felpz, setting the unusual woman down again. "You were not the one I was expecting, but I am glad to see you nonetheless. Please do not tell me your being here means the old master has got himself into another pickle, it would entirely ruin my night."

"Not in the least, not in the least," said the woman Badgrave, settling her garment. I noticed that now she stood still again, her shadow gathered as a lump around her feet, shooting curious tendrils out towards me and Felpz. "He is beyond well, only I was the nearer when we heard your call, and it is easier for me to cross the bounds these days." Her voice was light and airy, pleasant to listen to even though she had a strange lilt to her words that suggested an old accent that had not quite let go yet.

"I am glad to hear it," said Felpz heartily. "It is fitting enough, however, that you should play a part in the return of this, being as you were also present at its taking." As he spoke, Felpz reached inside his coat and removed the withered hand, presenting it to Badgrave.

The woman blinked and stared at it, a look of wonder crossing her bluff countenance.

"By Grimby's boots," she breathed, taking the hand reverently in both of hers. "Yes, I remember that day well, as I do this hand. I see Amstrass was not very careful with it after all. I do hope it did not cause much trouble."

The hand, I noticed, was the exact same blueish white as Badgrave's complexion, and as soon as it was placed in her hands it came to life, crawling up her arm and twining itself into her trailing mane of hair. Badgrave hardly batted an eye at it, merely stood still while the hand got a good grip on the strands of silver and gold.

"Hardly any," Felpz said, watching the antics of the withered hand with amusement. "Indeed I think it might have done some good. I'm afraid it was the hand itself that suffered most, in the end."

"Well, all that is over now," Badgrave said, patting gently at the hand currently knotted in her hair. "I shall see it gets back to Madgrin, though what he will do with an extra hand is beyond me. Still, I'm sure he will find some use for it."

"I have no doubt," said Felpz, giving her a bow.

Badgrave turned to leave then, but caught sight of me. I had remained mute in my chair the whole time, feeling that this meeting of old friends should not be interrupted. Now, however, I felt a strange thrill course through me, and cleared my throat to introduce myself.

There was no need, however. With a crooked sort of smile, Badgrave said:

"You must be his storyteller! Corianne, is it not? I have heard much of you—that is, I have heard much of your stories. Very fine things they are, too." She came forward and shook my hand. "If it is not too forward of me to offer, I find myself upon the verge of settling down into a house of my own soon, you see, and as such I will be in need of a staff— particularly a *librarian*. If that sounds at all appealing to you, please consider it an open invitation—after you are finished here, of course."

She beamed at me, radiant and blue, squeezed my hand—hers felt like the cool caress of river water—and then sailed back through the mirror, taking her oddly twisting shadow with her.

The lights in our room flared brighter upon her leaving, and I saw now the mirror was back to its ordinary self. A gentle murmur from the window suggested that the earliest of risers were getting about their business, and checking my watch I was astonished to find that four hours had passed.

"Felpz," I said, my voice weak in my throat. "Who on earth was that?"

"That was Badgrave," Felpz said, smiling fondly at the mirror, as if he could still see into that dark and stony corridor. "Another lamphra, though a young one—comparatively speaking. You could say she is the daughter of Madgrin."

"And she will return the hand?"

"As sure as you can be of anything," Felpz said, and there was a note of pride in his voice. "Trust nothing but that Badgrave will look after her old master."

"It is as well," I said, levering myself out of my chair. "For she seems to have taken the remainder of the night with her."

Felpz waved his hand dismissively at this, and wandered off towards his own rooms. "Lamphra have a different handle on time than we do. Never fear, where once they take they give back in dreams."

There was a rustling, and the sound of pouring water, and I guessed Felpz was readying himself for bed despite the imminently rising sun. I went over to where the candle had fallen and picked up the extinguished stub. Puzzling over the magic I had seen done, I went on to puzzle over Badgrave's words to *me*.

"Felpz, whatever did she mean by '*after I have finished here?*'" I called out to my friend.

Silence fell in the next room, as though Felpz had frozen in his tracks. Slowly his head reemerged, and he stared at me, wide-eyed. "I beg your pardon," he said. "*What* did she say?"

"You did not hear?" I asked.

Felpz shook his head. "Her words were for you, I only caught the general intent."

"It was the most curious thing," I said, punctiliously setting the candle on a bookshelf. "She offered me the position of *librarian* in her new house, provided I was 'finished here.' Whatever did she mean by that? Do take me seriously, Felpz, I am not joking." For Felpz, upon hearing my words, had burst out in delighted laughter.

"I have never been more serious!" he cried, darting back into his room. He emerged moments later, now dressed in a brilliant lavender suit with matching top hat and mauve boots. "Do you fancy some breakfast, Corianne?" he asked, his face aglow with cheer. "The Caison Patisserie will be opening soon, have I never treated you to their croissants? Their eclairs are the most marvelous things as well. Yes, we can let Caison serve us breakfast for supper and then dream the day away, content in the knowledge that all will turn out well in the end. Take my arm, Corianne, and come along."

Seeing I would get no solid answers from my friend, I nevertheless accepted his arm, and set aside the words of Badgrave as a mystery to be solved at a later date. I contented myself with the knowledge that the immediate future held fresh baked goods and the promise of sleep. Which was, I thought, as much as anyone could hope for.

Author's Note

The characters of Madgrin and Badgrave, and indeed Felpz himself, all appear in the novel, *Lucena in the House of Madgrin*, which explains in more detail how Madgrin came to lose his hand in the first place, and why Badgrave's shadow behaves the way it does. It also sheds some light on the curious offer Badgrave makes to Corianne, and why the news of it makes Felpz so happy.

eight

The
MOONFOOT PROBLEM

THE OTHER DAY I RECEIVED A LETTER from Felpz. In it was a clipping from the *Times* of Redling, containing an obituary for Lord Farrod, Earl of Moonfoot, and a note attached in my friend's own hand saying: *I think it's high time you told the story of Lord Nickel and Medrova. They are well beyond the reach of Kyrish law, and it can't hurt that terrible old man now.*

I was surprised and a little excited by this, as I had thought those events would remain buried until the time of my grandchildren or later. I was still skeptical of Felpz's assurance—being that the events in question compromised the virtue of a very grand old Kyrish family—but since the last lord of that line is cold in the ground, and having ascertained that the only people living whom this story could touch are safely on the other side of the world, I feel relatively comfortable in recounting them now.

Shoveling through my veritable snowdrift of notes, I find it was in the summer of 2322, over ten years ago, that my attention was brought to the astonishing murder of Lord Nickel Kellsbrook, only son and heir to the Earl of Moonfoot. To say this was where the story began, however, would be misleading. In truth the first I heard of the curious string of events—though I would not connect them until later—was at a casual lunch with my old friend Milky.

"Mrs Grissom told me the most incredible thing," he mentioned offhandedly one afternoon at Valaire's. We had taken to meeting there for lunch about twice a month, as otherwise our lives did not intersect save on the occasions when we were both caught up in Felpz's adventures, and then there was no time for innocent pleasantries. It was through these regular visits that I first learned of Mrs Grissom, the tailor who rented the shop next door to his carpentry business, and his other mercantile friends: Mrs Dolnir, a potter, and Miss Valaire, who ran the very same Valaire's Café and Chocolaterie where we held our semi-monthly meetings.

It amused me that Milky, despite cultivating friendships with mature and intelligent women, had managed to remain perennially single throughout our acquaintance. It could be argued that this was *because* they were mature and intelligent women. I certainly had no inclination to marry anyone, not even Milky—fond as I was of the man I had had enough of marriage to last a lifetime, and though I confess I did puzzle over what *his* reasons for singularity could be, I never was impertinent enough to ask.

I was, however, happy to listen to his recounting of Mrs Grissom's tale, which he told with an odd mix of amicable irreverence and acute attention to my reactions, as though he hoped to read something more out of them than what I would openly say.

"She has a remarkable new client," he told me. "A foreign gent, but she tells me no more of him. 'Parently he has been in and out of her shop for the past few months, always ordering some fine new garment or other, but with the most exacting measurements."

"That cannot be so unusual," I said. "A gentleman will want his suits to fit as perfectly as possible."

"Ah, but they're not *suits*, is the bargain of it," Milky said, dipping into his old slang in his excitement. "They're all *dresses*. A lady's wardrobe, from what Mrs Grissom can tell. Which wouldn't be so strange on account of itself—a man's got every right to order fineries for his lady to wear—but if these dresses are for a woman then she's a very peculiar shape."

"Why?" I asked with a laugh. "Have they got an extra sleeve or some such?"

Milky frowned at me, as if pondering how best to phrase his next words.

"Nothin' so fantastical," he said at length. "It's just . . . well, Mrs Grissom explained it better, bein' a tailor and all she knows about the shapes of people's bodies, and *she* says they don't seem like women's dresses. Something about the hips being mighty narrow and the shoulders unusually wide . . . also, whoever they are for, it's someone nearing six feet."

"That can't be so astonishing," I said, pouring myself another cup of tea. "Women are not cut out of dough by the same stamp, as you should well know, and some of us are quite tall."

Milky wriggled uncomfortably and appeared to hide behind the teapot.

"You cannot mean to suggest that you believe these dresses are being ordered for the gentleman *himself*?" I asked.

Milky, if possible, shrank further behind the pot.

"Not the gent what's been in there," he mumbled. "Mrs Grissom says he's a completely different size—much smaller than the measurements."

"Oh . . ." I said, thinking the matter over. In truth I found the idea of a man in women's clothing somewhat less shocking than my peers did. Having been exposed at a young age to women who preferred to dress in traditionally male costume, I now supposed that the reverse might also be true. I said as much to Milky, and added: "Though why a man would voluntarily submit to being laced into a corset and to wearing layers of cumbersome petticoats is beyond my imagination. Why not have a nice suit made with a few frills and floral patterning as a compromise?"

To which Milky laughed, and all the tension went out of the air. Our conversation turned down other avenues, and soon we were engrossed in picking over the reports, freshly appearing in the day's papers, of the extraordinary and gruesome murder of Lord Nickel Kellsbrook—the odd eccentricities of Mrs Grissom's clients clean forgotten.

Since it has been so long I see no reason why I should not recount the details here—though in their full and validated form, and free of the speculation added into accounts of the time for drama.

Lord Nickel Kellsbrook, as has been mentioned in this narrative before, was the only son and heir to Lord Ferrod, Earl of Moonfoot. A popular young lad, clean and handsome and dazzlingly charming, he had long been notorious for cavorting around the Redling clubs and getting into all manner of scrapes—though these were always of the amorous, rather than violent, variety. Even so it was a known shame to his father, who was rendered beside himself with grief and fury when the young man eventually fell ill as a result of his wanton lifestyle. The Earl responded by having the lad sent away for a year's voyage in the south seas, which the doctors prescribed as the best medication for his ailment. Much to the surprise of fashionable society (and the delight of Lord Moonfoot), young Nickel returned from this voyage fully recovered and with a much more sober bearing. He had arrived back at the family seat of Moonfoot Manor the summer previous, and to all appearances seemed content to remain there—eschewing his former haunts in the city and concentrating on fulfilling his duty as the heir of a major estate. Indeed, little had been seen of the young man since his return to Kyreland, and some rumors speculated that he had not in fact recovered from his illness and was on his deathbed at Moonfoot Manor.

The rumors proved both false and true, after a fashion, when his body was discovered, clubbed to death and throat cut, on the floor of the manor's dining room. The young man was certainly dead, but just as certainly due to no illness. Unless, as some of the more irreverent papers proclaimed, it was the illness of having half one's brains scattered across the hearth.

It was a shocking state of affairs, and the country was waiting eagerly for the report of the necromancers, who had descended upon the corpse like vultures the moment the Earl declared he wished to have the case settled as soon as possible. It had been two weeks, however, and not a word from any of the necromancy houses either in Redling or in the country.

"I wonder what Hydegan would have made of this," I pondered, referring to our old friend who had been instrumental in popularizing the use of necromancy in murder investigations. He had long since retired to raise bees in Duscany but had left behind a force of young necromancers to take his place. Their practice had proved useful in cases where the victim had seen their attacker—though some legal gymnastics had to be done before courts would accept the testimony of a dead person—but not useful at all where the murderer had succeeded in hiding themself.

In this case, however, there had been no word—either of useful testimony or lack thereof—and the public's opinion of necromancers was becoming a trifle strained.

"I can't begin ter imagine," sighed Milky. "As I can't know what's stopping the ones we've got now. If it were the fact that his head was compromised that's preventing his corpse from talking, then I 'spect they'd 'ave just said so. What could be flummoxing them so good that they can't even *admit* they're flummoxed is beyond me. Though I'da guessed that, were it a really bad tangle, Hydegan as likely have sent off for Felpz by now, asking for help. But I fancy these new ones are too proud. It would be like running home to mother to get her to sew yer trousers shut. Nice thing to be able to *do*, but no one likes to admit it." He shrugged, and there we left the matter for the day. Milky retuned to his shop to finish a commission, and I returned to my own lodgings, looking forward to a pleasant afternoon spent writing in the seclusion of my study.

Which plans were dramatically overturned the moment I stepped into our entry hall and found Felpz lying in a truly alarming posture at the foot of the stairs. I shall not describe it, for I shall be describing enough unsettling sights herein, and I do not wish to torment my readers with ones which turned out to be completely benign.

At the moment, however, the sight of my oldest and dearest friend, apparently dead of a broken neck, sent my heart plummeting and a terrible wail out of my throat. Gone were any assurances that Felpz was a magical immortal whose physical form could endure the onslaught of centuries, scorching fire and freezing cold, for there he lay on the floor— as clearly deceased as a carcass at the butcher's—and all I could find it in myself to do was scream and scream, turning my head away as if to deny the universe this truth.

"Well at least *you* find it convincing," said the voice of Felpz from the top of the stairs.

I whipped my head around and there was my friend, full of life and light and wearing a deep plum-colored suit with matching leather shoes, filling the space at the top of the stairs with his warm, commanding presence.

"*Felpz,*" I gasped, my voice a mere rasp. I was not certain whether I wished to embrace or shake the man. Not being close enough to do either I shook my fist at him as I struggled to catch my breath. "Felpz — what is the meaning of this — *this* — " I gestured at the terrible form upon the floor.

"You mean my simulacrum?" Felpz asked, waving a hand. As he did so his fallen double dissolved into a dusky purple mist and then vanished altogether. "I wanted to see if I could make one in that state. Not something I've ever had to do before, but that is the joy of our ever-changing world: new sights, new challenges, new *tricks.* Oh, step up here my dear Corianne, I did not mean to shock you so. Come in and I will make you some tea. Then I will explain the matter in full."

I must have appeared more upset than I felt — indeed I mostly felt anger at Felpz for his insensitive behavior — for my friend turned hennish for a few minutes, guiding me gently to an armchair and seeing me comfortably settled. When I had gotten over my shock and began to snip at him like an impatient horse, he took the cue and cast himself back across our sofa with a grand sigh.

"Oh, it is all due to this blasted Moonfoot case, Corianne," he moaned. "If you must blame someone, blame those wretched, incompetent necromancers!"

"They have asked for your help," I remarked, with only a little surprise.

"If only they had been so deferential," Felpz snarled, unbuttoning his coat and casting it open so he could stretch his shoulders. "No, I have been retained — *retained,* Corianne, like a civil servant! — on behalf of the Great Kyrish Police, to sort out the mess *their* necromancers have caused by botching what should have been a simple waking. It has taken me *days* to work back to this solution, and I am still not sure it is the right one. Pray, do you feel strong enough to bear the weight of my unburdening? I feel I must talk this through with *someone,* else my head will explode."

"By all means," I said, settling back in my chair and sipping my tea. Now that the shock had worn off — Felpz being so vividly and clearly *alive* — I was dreadfully curious about the whole matter. It was not often Felpz volunteered such candid discussion of his work before a problem was solved, and I relished the opportunity to attempt to solve it with him.

"Pray," I added with a grin, "leave nothing out."

Felpz smiled shortly, a brief flash of humor before his face fell back into gravity. "You may not thank me for that. Well, you must by now have heard of the unfortunate demise of the young Lord Nickel?"

"Oh yes, Milky and I were just discussing it," I assured him.

Felpz gave out a little *hmph* noise and twined his fingers together. "Then I shall pick up with events that first included *me*. You may recall, dearest and most long-suffering Corianne, how I was summoned away quite abruptly after dinner some weeks ago? Well, that was at the behest of our old friend Cullins—you remember Constable Cullins, who was so impetuous as to bring me in on the matter which you so fancifully titled *The Twisted Unicorn?* Well, he is *Captain* Cullins now, and quite a grand old captain he is—who more less begged me to have a look at a matter which stumped his necromancers. 'They are very good at getting the dead to talk, but if they *don't* talk then they're little more useful at solving a murder than kittens.' I protested that where specialists such as necromancers had failed he could hardly expect a general practitioner such as myself to have better luck. To which he replied that that was *precisely* why he wished for my assistance. Do you know what he said to me, Corianne? It was perhaps the most flattering thing I've ever heard: 'You are only a *general* practitioner,' he said, 'inasmuch as your specialties cover every vein of magic under the sun. You may not fare better than a necromancer at coaxing words from a corpse, but *you'll* see things in the situation that they, lacking your universal knowledge, would miss.'

"As you can imagine this outpouring of praise disarmed me, and I agreed. Much good it has done me to succumb to flattery." He twisted his face in disgust. "So I found myself summarily briefed on the state of the investigation. Which, for your benefit, is this:

"They are relatively certain of the time of the murder, the time of death being the one thing the necromancers were able to divine from the body, and from the testimony of the housemaid, who heard a ruckus in the dining room at a little past eleven. Since it sounded especially violent she, being a sensible young woman, fetched the butler and a footman before leading them into the dining room. By the time they arrived, however, the deed had been done, and Lord Nickel was already dead. Cullins told me a full examination of the room turned up a wealth of footprints and the residue from a sharp blast of magic—presumably behind the blow that destroyed the poor man's head. A few obvious valuable pieces—plate and a pair of ornamental swords—were also missing, and as the man had no known enemies the whole mess was presumed to be the work of burglars. Moonfoot is known to be a wealthy estate, and the earl is not particularly popular with the townsfolk, so it seemed to fit well.

"Seemed, I repeat. The chief inspector on the case, a small shrewish woman named Halfway, was puzzled over the matter of the footprints. *She* felt there were too many of them, considering the size of the room. Something about diverting forces to act as watchdogs. Anyway, that point is not immediately relevant so I will leave it for now. What *is* relevant is what happened when they brought the body back to the necromancers. I must admit, on the whole they have not been too much of a disgrace to Hydegan's name, but three young and impetuous—if largely talented—individuals do not make up for the careful purity and grace of form that marked Hydegan's work. They also have the regrettable tendency to argue amongst themselves. So it happened that the initial examination of the body, as it was reported to me, was a fractured affair—each necromancer having scribbled their own notes over the official write-up, and sometimes over their colleagues' notes. They do seem to agree, however, that the damage to the head, though quite extensive, was reconstructable provided they could recover all the pieces of brain matter. As this was not the first time they'd been asked to wake the victim of a head trauma, the request had been anticipated by Inspectrix Halfway, and the missing pieces duly provided. And do you know what they found when they'd got the head reassembled and the corpse awake and talking?"

"Pray tell me," I encouraged him.

"Nothing," said Felpz. "Nothing whatsoever. The corpse rose, all right. It took breath and it answered their call, but of its life it would say *nothing.* Not even that it had no knowledge of its death. *It could not even tell them its name.*

"Well, at the time the necromancers understandably assumed that the problem lay in their reconstruction of the head, so they promptly put him out again and messed around *some more.* They tried this three times, and each time the corpse would say *nothing.* Finally they tried a fourth time, and that time they failed. The corpse would not stir. At this point Cullins thought to call me in, and though it is flattering to be considered a universal specialist, I can't help but wish I had been there from the beginning.

"I did, however, strive to learn from the mistakes of the necromancers. Rather than attempt a simple waking of my own, I approached the body as if I had been first called to the scene. I made an entirely mundane examination of it—just as doctor would have done—and I discovered a number of interesting things that had not made it into the official report.

"For one, the devastating blow to the head—which was no doubt the cause of death—was not the young man's only injury. Far from it. He bore a great number of smaller, yet altogether more sinister wounds. Multiple bruises around the ribs, a few of which felt broken, ranged from old and fading to brilliant and purple to new and red. And there were other marks: the small, circular holes caused by that of a hat pin or a needle along his upper arm and down his thighs, and multiple scars from similar wounds, long healed over."

Felpz leaned back upon the sofa, his twining fingers gone tense and angular. "All situated such that, when clothed, nothing would be visible. Indeed, since necromancers are not in the habit of stripping their subjects—in fact it is considered a terrible violation in their profession— they had no knowledge of the extent of the abuse the man's body had suffered. At the time I was hard pressed to say how it related to his ul-

timate fate, and I was as stymied as they were. Eventually I came to the
decision that, as his death was of no help to me, I might as well make a
study of his life. For if his death had been as random and violent as it
appeared there was nothing I could do. If, on the other hand, there had
been something in his life to precipitate its violent end I might unravel
the mystery that way.

"In this matter I was aided with surprising vivacity by Inspectrix
Halfway, who, being neither mage nor necromancer, had lighted upon
my train of thought from the very first, and was delighted to have the assistance of one versed in the magical arts at her disposal. She brought me
over to Moonfoot Manor and showed me around the crime scene, carefully reconstructing it over the cleaned and tidied room. She showed me
photos of the prints they had been able to isolate, and I had to agree they
were a curiously diverse and varied selection of burglars, ranging from
a great, striding heavy fellow, to prints as light and delicate as a child's.
She also had me interview the servants who had found the man, and here
I ran up against a curious thing: though they were all more than forthcoming about the events of the night—and with such ardent honesty I
could not doubt them—they were singularly repressed when it came to
matters of the *house*.

"'Was Lord Nickel often up late?' I asked.

"'Why sir, I couldn't say,' was the answer, and this coming from the
man's *valet*. And a thread of fear ran through them all, as though they
were intentionally shielding someone—not out of loyalty or love, but
out of *fear*. I confirmed this when I asked after the relationship between
the earl and his son, and they all but shut down on me.

"'Was the earl a loving father?'

"'I'm sure he was, sir.'

"'Was there ever any disagreement between father and son?'

"'I really couldn't say, sir.'

"The more I questioned the more I became convinced that they were
holding something back, a dark secret that they dared not reveal for
fear of losing their livelihoods. I shared this suspicion with Inspectrix
Halfway, and we found ourselves in complete agreement. She had in fact
already interviewed the earl and come away profoundly unimpressed.

"'He speaks of his son almost as though the man were a horse or
hunting dog,' she confided in me. 'He mourns his loss, but only because
it is an inconvenience since now he must find a new heir. As though he
has lost a piece of *property*, not a member of his family.'

"'Grief does manifest itself in a myriad of different ways,' I allowed.

"'Wait until you've met the old boulder,' she told me firmly.

"Before I continue, let me give you my first impression of Lord
Moonfoot, so that you may judge what transpired in context. When
Halfway described him as an *old boulder* she was not being entirely po-
etic. The man struck me as having a hard, cold, immovable quality, and
he is indubitably quite old. His son Nickel was the only offspring from

his third marriage, which ended in divorce when the lad was sixteen. He has, in fact, three daughters from the two previous wives, all of whom were grown and married off before the son finally arrived. So the boy was raised as an only child by a string of nannies, as his mother was a sickly woman, and as soon as she got her strength up she left the old man—though she had to leave her son behind to do it. All this may give you a singularly uncharitable view of his character, but I can say that it would pale next to the revulsion you would feel were you to actually meet him.

"He is, it must be said, a handsome old man, with a fine head of silver hair and bright blue eyes. But whatever superficial beauty he has managed to retain is spoilt by his icy and venomous character.

"'I must wonder what a *magician* thinks he may accomplish in a matter not even the necromancers can untangle,' was his way of opening our interview. He then proceeded to ask me what my qualifications were, how I intended to catch his son's murderers, and whether I had found his missing valuables yet—as though I were coming to him in supplication, requesting the honor of serving him. I answered these questions with as much honesty and as little anger as I could manage, the result being that he took an immediate dislike to me. Perhaps this was unwise of me, for if I had bothered to curry his favor he might have been more forthcoming when I began bombarding him with my own questions. Then again, he might not have, and as it happened I learned a great deal more from his reactions and subconscious movements than I ever did from his words.

"When I asked, for example, how his son had come to be covered in small, hidden injuries, there flashed across his face as strong a look of contempt and guilt as I had ever seen. He made some excuse, of course, about his son's wild youthful adventures and not being able to exert the steadying influence that had been required. I became convinced, however, that he knew exactly who his son's tormentor was—if it was not in fact *himself*. When I pried more about the nature of the illness that had necessitated a year-long voyage for recovery he began elaborately obfuscating—at times contradicting himself. When I continued to press the matter he eventually allowed that it had been an illness of the *mind* rather than of the body, leaving me to assume that his son had been caught in some horrifically perverse act and only by removing him from Kyreland was a scandal averted. As an honored member of the peerage a *scandal* was to him a disaster even greater than losing his son entirely.

"I left his study, where our interview had been conducted, with the feeling of having been thrown against a board of nails, and was tempted to examine my own person for wounds similar to those of the dead man. Yet I now had a picture in my head of what Lord Nickel's existence in the manor must have been like, and I had to wonder if he had not bashed his own brains out as a means of escape.

"How all this leads to me creating a dead simulacrum of myself is a labyrinthine path so follow closely: I returned to Redling at this point,

uneasy in my mind about the matter. It could yet have been a simple robbery and murder, for I am no expert at unraveling crimes, but I found I
had become deeply interested in the life of this young man who, it seemed
clear to me, had suffered a miserable existence in his short time. I felt immense sympathy for him, and wanted at least to uphold the truth of his
fate, so that he might in death receive a validation that he had been denied
in life.

"To this end I began to examine his history in more detail. I hunted
down his old nannies, and found them for the most part to be good, kind
women who — being no longer in the employ of that prickly old man —
were altogether more willing to talk about Lord Nickel than any of his
servants. To his credit the young lord had kept in touch with them, so
from them I was able to glean a picture of an intelligent, sensitive young
man with a taste for fine things and an appreciation of the arts. What did
they think of his amorous exploits in Redling? Vicious lies, they said.
Dear Nickel would never debase himself in such a way. Who spread
them? There they were at a loss. Not his father, surely, for it would
serve him no purpose. Perhaps some jealous peer who envied his popularity with the young ladies. So he was popular with the young ladies?
Oh, *very* popular. Did he ever show them any favor? Nothing beyond
what propriety would allow, he was a *perfect* gentleman. Then why was
he sent away under such dubious circumstances? Well, there they hesitated, for he had never said — and they had heard nothing from him since
he embarked on his voyage, but the consensus was that he must have
fallen in love with some unsuitable woman. Perhaps a maid, perhaps a
simple flower girl. For whatever reason she was not the woman his father
wished him to marry, and in order to separate the two he had drummed
up the story of his son's illness and sent him away. They feared at the
time that his father would try to isolate him from all his old friends, and
this fear was borne out by the events that followed. Lord Nickel returned, but not to the regular correspondence with his old caregivers
that he had previously enjoyed. Their letters went unanswered, or were
returned unopened. They were quite dejected about the whole matter.
Had they any suspicions surrounding his death? There they were confounded. They all agreed that the old man held no great love for his son
beyond that of a possession, but they could not believe he would have
the boy murdered — as it would not serve his interests.

"I left them in no greater a state of enlightenment than when I had
found them. In fact I felt myself heavily weighted by all the information
they had laid upon me. It was at this point, dear Corianne, that I disappeared for a few days. Did you happen to notice? You *did?* Well, I
hope I did not worry you. Anyway, it was during this time that I found
myself drawn back to the problematic body — both of my own accord
and because the Kyrish Police were anxious for me to resolve the matter
and would not stop pestering me.

"I came into the necromancer's workshop late at night, when the place was deserted, and sat there alone with the corpse for some hours, turning over all the information in my head. I considered what I now knew of this man and what I knew of his family, and I decided the only way to untangle the mess for good would be to *talk* to him. You may point out that this is what the necromancers were trying to do from the beginning, but it is actually another thing entirely to summon the *spirit* of a dead person and converse with it, rather than simply to re-imbue a dead body with enough life that it may answer your questions. It is much more difficult to do the former, for example, and requires a certain elasticity—a disregard for the rules of life and death—on the part of the summoner, which not all magicians possess."

"But *you* do," I pointed out.

"Yes, *I* do," Felpz sighed, running a hand through his hair. Today this was a salt-and-pepper mix of dark brown and streaks of grey, but I knew it could turn all white or all brown at the whim of his mood. The same could be said for the bags beneath his eyes and the wrinkles of his brow. All could be gone and his face young and smooth were the right stimulation to be had.

"Even so it is not an easy task, and not something to be undertaken lightly. In this case, however, when all else had failed, I deemed it worthwhile. I set about summoning the spirit of Lord Nickel Kellsbrook, and do you know what happened?"

"I cannot imagine," I admitted readily, only wishing for the next piece of the story.

"Nothing," whispered Felpz. "Nothing *at all.* There was no answer from beyond the wall—not even a *rejection* of my summons. It was as if . . . as if I were summoning the spirit of one who was still tied to his body. In other words, the spirit of someone who was still *alive.*"

"But the body!" I cried.

"Yes!" Felpz echoed, leaning forward eagerly. "The *body!* Suddenly I looked at it again, really *looked,* and found myself doubting for the first time whether or not this was the *right* body. What if, I thought, Lord Nickel had faked his own death, and the corpse on the table was not, in fact, *his*? What if it had been tampered with, somehow, so that it could not speak and thus reveal its secrets? The best way to find out, I decided, would be to put the body back into its *original* state, *before* its head had ever been clubbed open. I could not bring it back to life that way, but I could at least examine it for signs of disguise—magical or practical. You may remember the magic I used ten years ago to restore the gold hair of that Cairdrian ghost?"

"I shall never forget," I assured him.

"Well, I did more or less the same thing to the corpse. It was significantly easier because the time that had elapsed since its death was not as much as in the case of the ghost. It took effort, yes, but I managed to run events backwards, effectively undoing the necromancers' muddling and reconstruction of the head. I saw it come apart, go back together, come apart, over and over, until at last it came apart and stayed that way. This time, however, instead of the careful dissection used by the necromancers, it was violently smashed open. A few pieces of skull and gore had even deposited themselves around the room, in effect recreating their positions in the dining room at Moonfoot.

"I then proceeded to do what I imagine Hydegan would have done from the start: I rolled time back *further,* so as to force the head into its original form, whole and intact. This is an even more difficult thing to do, as it requires crossing back into a time when the body was alive, but I expected I could hold it that way long enough to get a good look at the undamaged body.

"In this, however, I failed. Not through any lack of skill or power on my part, but because the body, when forced back along its own timeline to its form prior to that horrible blow, did not reconstruct itself as it should have. Instead . . . it *dissolved.*"

I started in my seat, nearly spilling my cold tea.

"I'm sorry," I stammered. "It *dissolved?*"

"Into a cloud of mist and vapor of pure, undirected *magic,*" Felpz said, his eyes shining with intensity. "The reason the necromancers hadn't been able to get a word out of it was because it wasn't a body at all—it was the *simulacrum* of a body! Like the one you saw me produce earlier. The reason it had been so difficult to push it back beyond the state of the head trauma was because that *was* its original state. It had been *created* dead. It had never *been* alive and so had no living memories to relay. It had no spirit. No . . . nothing. All its original, base components were simply this nebula of magic which, when I ceased to hold it, reshaped itself into the form of the murdered corpse once more."

"Why, Felpz," I gasped. "This is most extraordinary! But . . . what does it *mean*? Beyond the obvious, I should say, that there apparently has been no murder after all."

"And I reckon there were no burglars either," Felpz said, leaning back and smoothing down his hair. "As I think these events through I fancy more and more that the items really *were* stolen—but not by burglars. By Lord Nickel himself."

"To escape his abusive father," I said, speaking as the thoughts came to me. "He faked his own death and made off with a few valuable items, perhaps to aid in starting a life elsewhere."

"And that is where this whole matter breaks down!" Felpz cried, springing up from the sofa and beginning to pace about the room. "The motive and the evidence all points that way, but the *means*—where is the *means* by which he constructed such an incredible simulacrum?"

"Pardon?" I asked.

Felpz made a snatching motion with his hand, his fingers snapping, as though to catch the words he needed out of thin air. "To disguise the body of a real person would not be so remarkable," he said. "Distasteful, but it would be doable by the sort of disreputable jobbing wizard who might take such a commission. Where the body would be obtained is a further problem. But that is not what happened in this case. Here the body was constructed purely from magic, out of scratch and ether, and in such detail that it fooled all the best police officers and the necromancers *and me.* We all knew there was something wrong with it, but it never occurred to any of us that it was not real. To make something of that quality, that fine craftsmanship, with that sheer *realism*, would require a truly masterful magician. I know, because I've spent the last day trying to make one myself. The best result I managed was what you discovered on the floor when you entered a few hours ago, and that was after several attempts. If it is so difficult for *me* . . . then what magician could Nickel Kellsbrook have convinced to make *his?* For it would have taken a magician of my caliber to create such a thing, and I happen to know that there is maybe . . . *one* other such magician in all of this hemisphere capable of such a thing, and Nimbastula is such a wholesome soul I can't imagine her stooping to such a level. I have written and asked anyway, but I seriously doubt she had anything to do with this. You see . . . " and here he paused, having come around to rest himself against the back of the sofa. Crossing his arms he nibbled nervously at his fingertips for a moment before snatching them away. "In order to make a truly accurate simulacrum, one that recreates *exactly* the body it is meant to imitate . . . well, the magician in question must have intimate access to that body. Just as an artist who wishes to make an absolutely realistic portrait needs a life reference from which to work. I could make a convincing simulacrum of *my own* corpse, but I could not do the same for any other person— not even you or Milky. One would require a degree of knowledge of the subject's body that . . . well, to put it frankly, Corianne, the kind of knowledge that only mothers know of their children or lovers do of each other—and then only the most trusting and uninhibited of those." He shrugged unhappily. "I know exactly what I am looking for," he continued. "A extraordinarily talented magician who is intimately related to Lord Nickel and who has somehow *escaped* my notice. For be sure if one had been born in Kyreland, nay, anywhere across Thamber, I would have felt it."

"How are you so certain it is a *human* magician?" I asked. "Could not a fairy do something similar?"

"Oh, if it were a fairy that would broaden our prospects greatly," said Felpz. "But no, alas. From the feel of the magic I know the caster to be human. A young human, too, which inclines me to believe it is *not* the boy's mother. Though female magicians have, through sad necessity, become quite good at hiding their powers. Which leads me to believe . . . "

"His unsuitable lover?" I suggested.

"It does have a singularly romantic ring, does it not?" Felpz said, managing a grin. "A pleasant reversal of the knight in shining armor.

Here we have a prince, not a princess, imprisoned and helpless, and a brave hero come to rescue him—not with arms and armor, but with clever spells and creative magic. But why did it take her so long? A full year he was away at sea—surely to someone powerful enough to create a simulacrum of that quality, crossing a mere ocean and stealing your prince away off a boat would have been much easier! It is what I would have done. No . . . wait . . . *yes!*"

Felpz raised his head, and I saw his eyes were shining brilliantly. "The *boat!* Of course! It would explain why I have no knowledge of this mage! Ha *ha!*" he cried jovially, and danced around, gripping my arms and sweeping me to my feet. He kissed me on both cheeks and danced away to the door before I'd caught my breath.

"Oh, talking candidly to you is the best for clearing a troubled mind," he said, pulling down his hat and dusting it off.

"I am glad I could assist," I said, sinking back into my chair. "But Felpz, where are you going? Have you solved the mystery yet?"

"The *boat,* Corianne!" he cried, now halfway out the door. "The *voyage!* It all began there! Expect me back in time for supper—order enough for four, we shall be having guests tonight."

"What?" I said, bewildered. "Who?"

"Why, Lord Nickel Kellsbrook, of course," said Felpz. "And his brave enchantress!"

And with that he was out the door and down the stairs, leaving me alone and almost as confused as when the afternoon had begun.

Nevertheless I did as my friend had asked, pondering over what he could be up to. When dinner arrived I set it out while I puzzled over the implications of his last words.

"The lord must have met someone on the ship," I said to myself as I laid out the plates. "But if he were so madly in love, why not fly off there and then? Why come back to his father—who sounds like such a brute? Perhaps they didn't realize just how in love they were until later? *Pah.*"

At last I heard a touch of the bell, but when the housemaid showed the visitor in it turned out to be a pagegirl, who bobbed her head eagerly before handing me a letter.

It was a note from Felpz, and read as follows:

> C, *please bring dinner to the dockyards at Shiner's Head. Will be waiting for you aboard the* Emmiran. *Say your name and the captain will let you aboard.*
>
> ~F

"*Oh!*" I broke off in frustration. "And I just got everything unpacked!"

There was nothing for it, however, but to repack the food and hire a cart.

The docks, calm in the steeply angled sun of that summer evening, were a particularly beautiful sight: the ships sitting like dark waterfowl upon a river that shone golden in the reflected light. I found the *Emmiran*—a steamship of modest size—after only a little difficulty, and the captain—who surprised me by being a stern woman with brick-red skin—let me aboard with a gruff welcome, leading the way to one of the larger cabins. There I found Felpz, sitting with his feet up on a dining table reading a novel of all things. He leapt up at the sight of me, and thanked the captain profusely before helping me lay out the dishes all over again.

"You left me at something of a chasm in your narrative," I chided him. "Surely you could string me a bridge now, as it were."

"Yes," said Felpz, distractedly straightening the silverware to his satisfaction. "I suppose we do have the time. Although we won't know the whole story until our guests arrive—they are not due aboard until nine o'clock—but I can tell you my train of thought, and how it influenced my actions of this evening. Please, sit."

"When I last saw you, Corianne," he continued once we were seated at the far end of the table, facing the door. "I left you with a somewhat confusing reference to a ship and a voyage. You may have already connected the loose threads yourself, and will not be surprised to hear that I suspected that this unusual mage who facilitated Lord Nickel's improbable disappearance was someone whom he met while on his voyage. Naturally the first thing I did was go down to the docking office to check the passenger manifests on all the ships during that time, and soon found the one that carried the ailing Lord Nickel. The *Nabasca*, it was, out of Minton's Yard. She made a cruise down through the Shinasian Strait and around Idria before working her way north again around the far east coast of Aurasia and thence back to Kyreland. A straightforward enough journey, and no unusual hardships. The *Nabasca* has been in and out of Redling's docks five times since, and—according to Minton's records—is currently somewhere in the Ardaman Ocean, heading south for Soloran. This brought my line of reasoning up short, as I had assumed the timing of Lord Nickel's disappearance—if his confidante was indeed someone he met at sea—would coincide with the *Nabasca's* presence in Redling, and therefore the presence of that person. Was it a fellow passenger then? That would have made things rather difficult. However, I thought to examine the crew of the *Nabasca* and discovered that, though its officers are all the same as they were two years ago, one member of the crew left not long after Lord Nickel's voyage. Imagine my excitement when I discovered it was none other than the ship's *wizard*. One Wizard Medrova, according to the crew's list. Tracking this wizard's movements from ship to ship, I discovered that she has not been back to Kyreland since the *Star of Idria* docked here three months ago. At that time she transferred to serve the *Emmiran,* but as that ship—*this ship*—was currently en route from Azo, she was obliged to spend the last few months on shore. This puts her firmly in Kyreland during the time of Lord Nickel's supposed murder—and more, it allows her time to have planned this admirable stunt. Her being a ship's wizard also explains why I should be unaware of her presence—for I have been unable to discover any clue as to her nationality."

"I see," I said. "So you believe Lord Nickel fell in love with his ship's wizard, but still returned home?"

"I can only imagine the condition of their parting," Felpz remarked, "but I can suppose that, when she discovered the deplorable condition of his home life, this enterprising lover struck up a plan to free him. To that end they faked his death and now intend to flee the country. I checked, and indeed Wizard Medrova is bringing a guest with her on this voyage—though, no doubt as a means of subterfuge, they are listed on the passenger manifest as one *Miss Brodelia Summers*. It is for this couple that we are now waiting."

I found myself looking around the cabin with renewed interest—and not a little bit of alarm.

"If that is indeed who you are expecting," I said, "then why have you not brought Captain Cullins along?"

Felpz raised a curious brow. "Why, because I do not see how this concerns him," he said blandly. "No one has *actually* died, after all. I seriously doubt Lord Nickel is leaving against his will—though if that is the case of course I will prevent it. At this point I merely wish to meet this remarkable magician. Mostly just to see if I am *right*." His eyes twinkled, and I suddenly thought: *there must be something more! He suspects there is more, otherwise he would not be here!* And I felt a thrill of nerves run through me, tingling in my limbs and making me feel momentarily weightless.

The evening wore on, the sun finally sinking below the horizon. Felpz lit the lamps, and we waited in their soft, warm glow. The little room rocked gently as the boat rode the swell of the river's current, and I began to grow drowsy from the motion. I was just beginning to worry that the dinner would be spoilt from the cold when there was a noise outside and we jumped to attention.

I was aware of voices on the other side of the door, too indistinct for their words to be made out, and then the handle turned and a couple bustled into the room.

A woman and a man, they appeared. He had the same brick-red skin as the captain, with short curly black hair and a clean-shaven chin; he wore a neat blue suit with the silver cloak of a sea-wizard thrown over one shoulder. The woman was a striking creature of unusual height with a delicately coifed head of golden hair and beguiling dark eyes. She was wearing a remarkable gown and a coat of fine brocaded cloth. Though both fit her well and were quite flattering, they were also clearly brand new, and were something of a contrast to the wizard's well worn coat.

They stared at us in shock, and for a moment I had the terrible feeling that we were in the wrong room and that we had interrupted a honeymooning couple—for they had that air about them of newlywed lovers—and Felpz was staring back in equal surprise. But then he leapt to his feet and beckoned to them in welcome.

"Come in, come *in*," he said. "You will forgive the intrusion—but I saw no other way in which we could be certain of meeting you. I am Bouragner Felpz, and this is my friend Corianne Birch. Please be assured we come here in all goodwill, and grant us the pleasure of your company at supper. You must forgive me," he continued, coming around the table to approach the wizard. He made a short bow. "I had no *idea* you were Azoan, and your name quite threw me off. Corianne, if I ever give the appearance of being an insufferable know-it-all, please remember this as one of the times I failed *utterly*. I got entirely the wrong impression of you, Wizard Medrova."

I found my gaze snapping around to the wizard, and then across to his companion with new shrewdness. Now I looked closer I noticed all over again her height, the broadness of her shoulders, and the somewhat awkward way she gripped her handbag. Then I looked back at the wizard, recalling that peculiarity of the Azoan language, where their boys' names were long and fancy, and the women's short and blunt.

"*You* are Wizard Medrova?" I couldn't help gasping. "But then—" I cut myself off before I said something regrettable.

"I *am* Wizard Medrova," the young man said, straightening his shoulders. "This is my fiancée, Miss Summers, and I'd thank you to remove yourselves from our private quarters, *sir*," he added, casting a scathing look at Felpz. He spoke Kyrish well, but there was an odd clip to his words and a cadence which I'd never heard before.

"Oh, well that is too bad," Felpz said. "I had hoped to hear the story from you, as I could never be sure otherwise. One question, then, and we will make you an engagement present of this dinner."

Wizard Medrova raised his chin challengingly. "Ask it," he demanded.

"Was it your idea, or Lord Nickel's, to use an inert simulacrum to fake his death?" Felpz asked, all innocent curiosity.

The effect of his question, however, was dramatic.

Wizard Medrova sucked in a breath so sharply it whistled, and the tall lady—whom I was beginning to suspect was a lady only in dress—made an involuntary motion as if to flee. Finding herself caught by the wizard's hand, she cast her head down and murmured something in his ear.

"No," said Medrova in answer. "I expect he has constables lining the gangplank."

"What?" said Felpz. "Nothing of the sort! If you're determined to be so unfriendly we will, naturally, leave. It is only I've never *seen* such a fine simulacrum, and I just *had* to meet the magician who created it. Of course, I am also curious as to what has taken you so long to leave the country. You've run quite a risk, staying so long after you pulled that magnificent stunt."

The two looked at each other, and I noticed how Medrova was not really so short; it was only the extreme height of his companion that made him appear so. Then with a sigh Medrova turned and shut the door firmly behind him and released Miss Summers's arm. Miss Summers, now putting herself to no effort to appear ladylike, fairly dumped her handbag on the table and drew out a chair, roughly grabbing her skirts to yank them out of the way as she sank into it.

"Well Med?" she said, in a voice so rich and deep it rivaled that of Felpz. "Why not just give him the whole story, if he's so persistent? Knowing him, if he wanted us caught we'd already be in shackles."

Wizard Medrova still hesitated, and his eyes went distrustingly towards me.

"I'll tell them then," said the lady, who I presumed was actually Lord Nickel. "The truth is, we had planned to wait until the night before the *Emmiran* sailed. We would be halfway to Azo before your necromancers puzzled out his simulacrum—which was *his* idea, by the way. Med is quite a brilliant magician, you know."

"Downright extraordinary," Felpz agreed. His head snapped around to gaze searchingly at Lord Nickel. "What happened?"

The man—and I could see clearly that it was a man now—sighed heavily, then winced a bit. "Well, I suppose I should begin at the beginning, otherwise you'll keep peppering us with questions, won't you?"

"Let me," Medrova said, coming around and laying a protective brown hand on Lord Nickel's shoulder. The man looked up at the wizard and then put his own hand over his companion's, holding it as if it gave him strength. Perhaps it did.

"I'd better tell the first part, though," he said softly. "It is mine to tell." He shrugged, a little sadly. "Whatever you have heard of me, or perhaps read about in the papers, I assure you it was all lies. My father saw to that. He would have preferred any lie, no matter how distasteful, rather than the truth."

"Which is what, Lord Nickel?" Felpz asked gently.

Lord Nickel tilted his impeccably coifed head and raised a perfect eyebrow, as if wondering why Felpz would even ask such a question. "I should think that would be immediately obvious," he said with a wry smile. "I shall not inflict upon you an account of the miseries of my childhood, however. But I will say this: I was never ill, and I never mistreated a woman. I *believed* I was ill for a time, and I tried—I tried very hard—to please my father. To find a wife. But the fact of the matter was, though it was laughably easy for me to befriend charming young ladies, I could never stomach the thought of marrying one. I backed out of several arrangements, which angered my father—he had it put about that I had committed some . . . indiscretion. Anything to cover up what was really going on. I managed this way for some years, simply putting off the inevitable, when at last I took a fall. I made an overture—an act of desperation, more like—to someone I thought I could trust. I was wrong about him, however, and he went straight to my father. The result was ... well, according to the papers I had either contracted syphilis or had gone mad, when in truth I had only developed an unwise infatuation with my valet. The upshot was my father packed me off onto a wretched little boat for a year with a handpicked counselor. His purpose was double-ended, you see—get me out of the public eye, and away from any friends or influences. I confess the first week was terrible. The counselor was very persuasive, and for a time I thought I really was going mad. Then ... then I met Medrova." Lord Nickel looked up at the wizard adoringly, and gently brought the hand from his shoulder to his lips and kissed it, before letting go.

Medrova, not leaving his post, squared his shoulders and turned to Felpz. "I wasn't aware what was happening at first. Azoans have a different attitude toward male lovers, what with the way our marriage system works. I suppose you could call it *polyandry,* but that's a bit of a simplification. Let's just say, there's many Azoan women who prefer some of their husbands to show interest in *each other* rather than themselves. It's nothing to be ashamed of, as long as you don't deceive anyone about your preferences. It was something of a shock to me to discover foreigners who held quite negative views on the matter. I was still feeling my way around the crew of the *Nabasca* when Nick came aboard, and I'm sorry to say I didn't wise to what was going on right away."

"Oh, but you put a stop to it as soon as you did," Lord Nickel said, smiling ardently up at him. "He was so very clever about it, too."

"I am sure," Felpz said, a twinkle in his eye. "Please go on."

"Well," said Lord Nickel, casting his gaze aside, and blushing such that he almost looked like the maiden he was dressed as. "We became friends," he said. "Very close friends."

"We became lovers," Wizard Medrova said dryly, gazing across at us as if issuing a challenge. "It was not in the best judgment of course, but ... " he sighed. "I still cannot bring myself to regret my choice."

"Darling," said Nickel with gentle reproach. "I do not believe there was much choice about it. On either side. Oh, but it was *wonderful.* And right under that dreadful counselor's nose, too. We got to see such sights: calling at ports all throughout Aurasia and Idria—I even got to ride an elephant. I wished the voyage would never end."

"But it did," said Felpz, and looked accusingly at Medrova. "And you did not take him away with you. Why?"

Medrova, after a moment of shock, pursed his lips. "I was in no position to offer him a good life," he said. "I'm a ship's wizard, not a captain. And at the time I was serving on a *Kyrish* ship. And ... and he's a *lord.*"

"Not anymore," Lord Nickel pointed out happily.

"You were *then*," Medrova insisted. "Frankly, sir, I didn't know what kind of life he would be returning to. I thought . . . well, I don't know what I thought. I certainly never imagined it would be this *bad*."

"We did agree to see each other whenever he put into port," Lord Nickel said. "It was my sole consolation. But I thought, with that, I could manage. I went back to Moonfoot and redoubled my efforts to please my father. None of which were sufficient, however. I think he knew I had not changed. He hadn't, either. In some ways it was even worse than before, since I now had thoughts of Medrova constantly on my mind. It made seeing the prospective brides even more painful, because I recognized in them the same desire I had for love and affection— and I knew all of mine was already bound to another, oh, it was *awful*. I couldn't; I just couldn't, and it made me sick inside that my love was somewhere out on the far seas. My father knew it, and he . . . well . . . he expressed his displeasure."

"If you discovered the simulacrum," said Medrova coldly. "Then you no doubt examined it close enough to see the evidence."

"Oh, I saw," said Felpz quietly.

"He was worse when I found him," the wizard went on. "Two years I'd been out of Kyrish ports and hopping ships looking for one with a friendly crew. I finally get back in and discover an *Azoan* ship in need of a wizard. I could hardly fathom my good luck. Better yet, the *Emmiran* also needed refitting and would not be ready for two months, giving me enough shore leave to make a proper visit to Nickel. I knew I couldn't walk up the drive and present myself at the front door, but I had no idea it would be so bad. What do I find left of the man I knew aboard the *Nabasca*? This battered mess, all torn to shreds inside and out and more blue than pink below the neckline. I told him I would not stand for it. Whether he loved me or no I was taking him away from that wretched place, and I set about making plans to do it.

"I could not, of course, simply spirit him away. Being the son of an Earl that would cause us problems. I needed to extract him, but in such a way that no one would think to pursue us. A disguise, I knew, would be in order, and what better way to disguise a man than to dress him up as one of your Kyrish ladies? They wear such complicated outfits and makeup—even more than Azoan gentlemen—I knew Nickel would be unrecognizable. I was able to contract, through a sympathetic soul in Redling, the services of an understanding tailor who made the clothes for Nickel's new wardrobe—I did not dare enchant them, as I worried even the scent of magic would arouse suspicion.

"It was actually Nickel's idea to fake his own death, but as we both agreed it would not be convincing without a corpse and as we would not consider using a real one, I had to come up with the simulacrum. We originally planned to stage the murder the night of our departure, so as to provide no time for the police to catch on . . . but . . . well . . . "

"Some crisis occurred," Felpz finished.

"You saw the simulacrum," Medrova said grimly, and gazed sadly at Lord Nickel, whose shoulders drooped.

"I may look all right now," he said quietly. "But when Med found me I could barely breathe."

"That awful old man had hit him with a poker. An *iron poker.*" Medrova's soft, foreign voice pitched up in anger and he clenched his fists. "His own *father!* I could have banished him to the outer darkness—the one with *thorns* in it—I really could have!"

"I'm glad you didn't," Nickel said quietly. "He is my father."

"From my point of view that makes it rather worse," Felpz said, folding his arms. "However, I'm glad you restrained yourself, Medrova. It would have made things difficult for me."

Medrova muttered a word I didn't recognize except I fancied it was an insult.

"Med insisted on getting me out immediately, even though the *Emmiran* wasn't due to sail for another two weeks. I've been living as Miss Summers during this time, and we had expected to depart at dawn. We still intend to, unless you mean to stop us."

"You may *try*," Medrova said, with a grim smile.

Felpz only leaned back in his chair and laughed. "My dear young men," he said. "Such a thing is furthest from my mind. Not only do you have my sympathies, but I could never bring myself to wreck such a brilliant scheme. No, at this point I only wonder what you intend to *do* when you get to Azo. Lord Nickel, surely you must realize none of your titles or rights will hold any power there."

"I realize this," Lord Nickel said. "In fact, I wish it. They have only brought me misery. I am quite looking forward to being plain and simple Nickel. Have even been considering taking an Azoan name."

Felpz raised his eyebrows and looked at Medrova, who shrugged.

"We will live as best we can," he said simply. "Azo does not offer the same opportunities for men as Kyreland does, but it is getting better. Perhaps we'll find a woman who will take us both. Whatever the case may be, we will not have to *hide* who we are."

Felpz regarded the couple with a placid smile. "Then I can only wish you the very best of luck," he said. "Though with your capabilities, Medrova, that hardly seems necessary. Oh, and you can be sure I shall keep the police chasing their tails for weeks to come. You shall have no fear of pursuit. Unless, of course, *Corianne* has some reason to object."

Suddenly I found myself at the center of attention, not all of it friendly. I glared back at them.

"What?" I exclaimed. "Of *course* not!"

As we disembarked after a leisurely and considerably more amicable dinner, Felpz paused on the gangway and rapped his hand against a plate of wood on which was inscribed the ship's name.

"A more fitting vessel to take them I should not believe exists," he said.

"Why not?" I asked.

"The name *Emmiran*," he said, taking my arm and leading me up away from the docks, "belonged not only to one of their queens—*Azrans* they're called—but to one of the royal husbands. Sumér Emmiran, who became the equivalent of a Prince Consort, was originally a slave from Niérlind. Brought to Azo by centaurian traders he was freed and eventually married Azran Raion. And although our Lord Nickel is giving *up* his title by going to Azo, I cannot help but think he will find his own sort of freedom there."

"Did you suspect Medrova was a man?" I asked.

Felpz snorted and ducked his head. "That was an oversight on my part, I regret to say. The name sounded Hyberian to me, because of the ending. I quite forgot that Medrova is also a traditional Azoan boy's name. It just goes to show you, Corianne, that you can live a thousand years and *still* be surprised. Though the revelation didn't change my feelings on the matter. No, they didn't change one jot."

"How do you suppose the earl will react when he eventually finds out?" I asked.

"I am not convinced he will ever find out. Certainly I think the former Lord Nickel would be safer if he did not. No, I think I shall have to make certain he never finds out, and I'm afraid that means you'll have to wait to tell this story until death carries the old man off. Hopefully by that time this country will have progressed to the point that it will be able to accept Medrova for the hero that he is. For he is a hero, Corianne, if not quite the one we were expecting."

That is all there is to the story of Nickel and Medrova. My story, however, continues on a little longer, and finds its end two weeks later, when I once again sat down to lunch with Milky on the upper floor of Valaire's. As I felt I could rely on him to keep the secret—and since I suspected his Mrs Grissom was the selfsame tailor that Medrova had gone to—I told him the entire story of the remarkable man for whom those dresses had been meant. When I had finished he stared at me for some moments over his untouched meal, his mouth agape, and then burst out:

"And . . . he let them *go?*" He seemed torn between amazement and a sort of stunned hopefulness.

"Of course he let them go," I said. "They were clearly madly in love with each other and besides, they hadn't done anything *wrong*. Quite the opposite, I think. Why, I should have liked to have gone straight to Moonfoot and given that horrible old man a right thrashing. To treat your child in such a way—it's *repulsive*."

"Is that what you think?" Milky asked, his voice as stiff as a board.

"Of *course* it is," I said, too caught up in my own emotions to notice. "Why, don't you agree?"

Milky looked down at his plate very suddenly then, and said in a rather choked voice: "No, no, I agree completely. I just . . . well I weren't sure you or Felpz would feel that way. But I'm glad you do."

I stared at him, hard, my mind slowly fitting together the bits of evidence that had been piling up around my friend for decades. I remembered Medrova's allusion to 'a sympathetic soul in Redling' and all at once they fell into place like the pieces of a puzzle, and I was stunned by the picture I saw.

"Oh, Milky," I said. "Don't tell me *you* would have liked to have been on that ship to Azo as well?"

Milky's head jerked up in surprise. His eyes were red, but he had so far regained control of himself that his voice came out quite normal when he said:

"What? Lady no, Miss Cor! A scratched up old alley-cat like me? I'd ruin their fun. Besides, all my friends are *here*."

I looked at him and felt a great swell of pity for the man, and at the same time a sort of fierce protectiveness.

"Quite right," I told him. "Besides Mrs Grissom and Mrs Dolnir *and* Miss Valaire, excellent guard dogs that they no doubt are, if you ever find yourself in any serious trouble I am sure Felpz would be more than happy to sort it out. Just don't expect him to create a perfect simulacrum of your dead body."

Milky closed his eyes and shuddered. "Good *Lady*," he groaned, lowering his head into his hands. "Let us hope it never comes to *that*."

And to my certain knowledge, it never has.

nine

The CASE of
COUNTESS BARONIA

Author's Note

This story contains two names whose pronunciations are not obvious and whose spelling could lead to some confusion. To prevent this, remember that the name *Merodite* is a four-syllable word pronounced with an *ee* sound at the end, similar to the name "Aphrodite." Conversely, the terminal *e* in *Calamite* adds no additional syllable, and that name ends with a sound identical to the word "might." The fact that both names are spelled with the same three letters at the end is an unfortunate accident, where the limitations of our alphabet have become sorely apparent.

—G.O.

THE YEAR OF 2323 WAS A MEMORABLE ONE in the house of Bouragner Felpz, not for the repetitious alignment of its number but for the sheer volume of cases Felpz handled. Hardly a day went by, it seemed, that he did not field some request for aid or provide consultation on a magical problem. Why then, asks the reader, do I not have volumes worth of stories from this year? The sad truth is that, while Felpz was very busy, the cases that kept him so were not memorable. A misplaced relative here, a cursed tree there . . . Felpz applied himself to all the problems with the same vigorous fervor, and as a result they were usually solved in a matter of hours—if not minutes—and oftentimes without Felpz needing to leave the comfort of his armchair.

I confess I lost track of my friend's activities, being hip deep in a project of my own, until the late fall, when I realized we had somehow contrived to drift as far apart as two people living in the same quarters could. I was appalled, but so busy wrestling with my novel that I had no energy to spare to do anything about it. Once I had beaten the book into some state of presentability, however, I decided to give myself a holiday and determined that Felpz should share in it.

I approached him with the suggestion that we take the month of Chandarmas off—perhaps to visit my daughter and her family—during which time he could read my novel, and I could go over the notes from his cases to see if there was anything of interest worth publishing. To my delight he was of the same mind as I, and we were on the verge of making more substantial plans when our morning was upended by the arrival of Lady Emalta, Countess Baronia.

She swept into our sitting room like a tidal wave, the effect heightened by the frothing white skirts that escaped from under the severe navy-and-teal traveling coat to trail artistically behind her. These surged around her legs before stilling in a flutter of chiffon and lace when she stopped to survey her audience, while her upper body—encased as it was in the aforementioned coat—remained erect and rigid, stiff as a ship's prow. A middle-aged woman, though her features were not particularly striking, now as then I do consider her to have been the best dressed of all our visitors. Everything from the fluttering, light skirts, to the elegant leather boots beneath them, to her coat, to her tasteful hat and her soft gloves was perfectly coordinated on a theme of sea greens and blues, with just enough contrast to keep it visually interesting. The cut of her costume was similarly artistic: it ranged from the soft, flowing tresses of her skirts to the hard lines of her coat and back again to the frills peeking out from her cuffs and collar, altogether enforcing my initial impression of her as a great, white wave breaking on sharp, dark rocks.

"Magician Felpz," she announced in stentorian tones.

The man in question, who was no less strikingly—if less elaborately—dressed in a morning coat of plum silk with a brocade collar and matching slippers, rose to his feet and bowed graciously.

"I am Emalta Tragansea," this impressive woman continued. "You may know me better by my title, the twelfth Countess of Baronia. I require your assistance in a matter most urgent."

"My dear . . . Lady," Felpz replied, taking special care of the honorific. "If the matter is indeed so pressing that you have arrived in advance of your card I shall naturally hear your case, but you must allow for the presence of my friend Corianne as well, for you did interrupt our business."

Lady Emalta had the grace to look a little ashamed—but only so far as a dusky blush across her wide cheeks and a slight suppression of her chest. The next instant her natural confidence reasserted itself, and she took another stride into the room, bringing herself into the center of our little world. She stood there, with such erectness and majesty that I forgot my disappointment over the interruption and turned to give her all my attention—as indeed Felpz was doing himself.

"Magician," said this imperious woman, "I shall not waste your time. I *am* sensitive to the needs of others. But my case is of such immediate import that you will no doubt forgive me for intruding so rudely. My situation, therefore, is this: a necklace of great value has gone missing from my house, and I desire you to find it for me."

There was, I'm afraid, a rather impudent *clink* of porcelain as I fairly dropped my coffee cup onto its saucer in surprise. For although I had witnessed my friend take on all sorts of cases, none of them had ever appeared so patently mundane.

Felpz must have felt so as well, for he sank back into his chair with a look of incredulity.

"My Lady," he said, and I could not tell whether he was reining in anger, disappointment, or laughter with his restraint. "I have been asked to do a great many things during my time, but finding a piece of lost *jewelry* has never been one of them."

"I realize my request may seem . . . somewhat below your standard," said Lady Emalta contritely. "But this is no typical necklace: it is an heirloom which has been in my family since the founding of our house. Its worth is beyond that of sapphires. Furthermore, I do not believe it has merely gone missing: I am certain that it was, in fact, *stolen.*"

"The worth of the artifact is unimportant to me," Felpz said with a wave of his hand. "If you believe it to be stolen then surely the *police*, or even a private detective, would be of more help than I. I deal in *magical* conundrums, Lady Emalta, and I am under no illusion as to my ability to act as an agent of the law. No, what you want is a detective, milady, not a magician."

Lady Emalta smiled at this self-deprecating excuse, as if she half expected it. She reached into a pocket of her coat and removed two small velvet bags, one of which chinked faintly as she laid them both on the nearby side table.

"There are two hundred Kyrish crowns in gold, eight hundred in verified bank notes," she announced. "They are yours if you will but come with me to Baronia and consider my case. No, do not argue," she said, seeing Felpz's mouth come open—though I believe it was only in astonishment. "You shall have a thousand more—in whatever form you like—if you do manage to find my necklace. I hope, magician, that this will convince you of the sincerity of my request."

Felpz's eyebrows climbed right up his forehead, pushing wave upon wave of surprised wrinkles ahead of them, as he looked from the neat little bags to the countess and back again. Yet I could see how his jaw had set obstinately, and I could tell he would throw away this unasked-for windfall purely because of the pride he took in his craft.

"Oh, why not find the necklace for her?" I asked him. "It will not be so hard for you. I will come, and we can spend our holiday at the seaside. I daresay it'll be a trifle warmer down there than our dreary Redling winter. Think of it! Reading in the morning, walks along the beaches and the sandy cliffs in the afternoon, and hearty southern suppers in the evening. It will be marvelous. And all you have to do is find the lady's necklace—is that so much to ask?"

Felpz crumpled back into his chair to stare at me in consternation, while the Countess Baronia gazed in open surprise. Taking a cue from her I held my chin up high, defying either to contradict me.

Neither did.

Which was how Felpz and I found ourselves bundled into a private, first-class compartment on the western express that very afternoon. The skies over Redling were grey and murderous cold, as indeed they had been all autumn, and persisted thus all the way to Greywall, where we switched to the coastal line and began winding our way south. In all, the trip lasted well over six hours, during which time Lady Emalta gave a full account of the circumstances surrounding the disappearance of her necklace. This she did, but not before she also gave us a brief history of the Tragansea family, with which, she assured us, the necklace was inextricably linked.

"It belonged to Amariel Tragansea, you understand," she explained, when we were hardly out of Redling. "She was the wife of Roderick Tragansea, first Count of Baronia. It passes to the eldest daughter of each generation, you see, along with the title of Countess."

"I'm sorry," I said. "Isn't that a bit odd? I thought titles usually went to the eldest child, whatever its sex."

"That is how the modern Kyres do it, yes," Lady Emalta said. "But the Tragenseas have always been a matrilineal line, sort of a reverse of that archaic practice of male primogeniture. In fact, when the title was founded that was the fashion, and Lady Amariel caused quite a disturbance when she insisted upon a *female* primogeniture. Now, of course, things have been going this way for so long hardly anyone pays notice to it."

"You were telling us about the necklace?" Felpz said, steering our topic gently back on course.

"Oh, yes, yes of course," said the current countess, rearranging her skirts. "The necklace. It came with Amariel Tragansea and has been passed from mother to daughter down that line directly to me—and I would pass it on to my own daughter, if only I still had it. It has great . . . sentimental value."

"Clearly," said Felpz in a wry tone.

Lady Emalta shot my friend an uncharitable look but made no comment. "I only wish to make its importance clear," she said, with admirable self-control. "So that you may take its disappearance as seriously as I do."

Felpz, who had been sitting slumped against the window, propped his head up on one hand and gazed across at our employer. "Then tell me of it," he said.

"The necklace disappeared two days ago. I regret to say it has taken me that long to get the straight story from the servants, who were greatly confused, and my daughter, who took the whole thing as a practical joke at first. As far as I can tell, after stitching together their disparate accounts, what happened was this:

"The last time I saw the necklace, it was in its box on my dresser, where it had been since my mother's death. I noted it particularly when I was dressing for dinner that night, as my maid—Liriel—had been asking if she could take it out and clean it. Its box has a glass front, you see, with a steel frame and lock, so although it is quite secure it can also be admired. Lately, however, it has begun to tarnish a little from lack of attention, and I gave Liriel the key to the box so that she might clean it before I went down to dinner.

"Now, from my perspective it was a perfectly ordinary, quiet evening. No guests in the house, and so my daughter and I dined alone. Falling into a lengthy conversation we were both late to our beds, and when I returned to my rooms I noticed at once that the box containing the necklace had been moved. Thinking only that Liriel had failed to put it back where it belonged, I went to correct its position. That was when I discovered that the necklace which should have been inside it was gone.

"I summoned Liriel, to ask her what was taking so long, but when she arrived she was as mystified as I. She had been planning to clean it the next day, she explained, and had not so much as touched the box during supper. Then I began to feel a twist of anxiety in my gut, and asked her what she had done with the key. She assured me she had it safe about her person, but when asked to produce it was unable to do so.

"Well, this as you can imagine upset the poor girl something awful. Being newly employed in my service she had been eager to prove her worth, and such a disastrous failure on her part was a crushing blow. I do think she expected to be sacked on the spot, but it was her utter and abject despair that convinced me of her innocence. I sat her down and had her recount the events of her evening exactly as she could remember them. I took notes," the countess assured us, producing a sheaf of papers, "so I might repeat her story to you.

"According to Liriel, after she had finished her own supper she sat up in her room working on a piece of mending I had assigned to her the day before. She had only one visitor during that time, our new improver who came in to borrow a needle and thread. She also answered a call from the housekeeper about breakfast for the next day, but other than that she did not leave her room. She insisted she had the key on its chain around her neck the entire time and offered to scour the steps between her room and the housekeeper's quarters in search of it—thinking, no doubt, that the chain might have broken and the key dropped off without her knowledge. I pointed out that this was a futile effort, as clearly someone had *already* found the key, and used it to make off with my necklace.

"At this point I called my daughter in and explained the situation to her. She is a feisty young woman, and I've known her to pull practical jokes before. I hoped, I suppose, that she had conspired with her own maid to play a trick on me, but she was just as surprised as I had been — and a bit more quick to pin the blame on Liriel. She was convinced, however, that *someone* was playing a very naughty trick on me and had the entire staff out and lined up so that she could lecture them. No one volunteered any information, which led me to believe that they either knew nothing, or that someone had indeed stolen my necklace. Perhaps both, if it had been done by someone from outside the house. Further adding to the mystery, not a single soul had been seen in the vicinity of my rooms that entire evening. It was as though a ghost had been through and spirited the thing away.

"Nevertheless I had the police out the next day, and though the detective they sent was quite energetic and eager to help, she was unable to uncover any more evidence than we had. Which was why I determined to enlist *your* aid, magician. Since it seems the mundane methods of investigation are utterly powerless to help me."

Felpz considered our client from his post by the window, with thoughtful expressions drifting over his face.

"Is there any reason to believe this *might* be the work of a ghost?" I asked.

"None that I can think of," the countess admitted. "I only meant it *seemed* that way."

We both found ourselves looking expectantly at Felpz after this exchange, but the man gazed out the train's foggy window into the ominous winter sky, and had no answer for us.

The weather lightened noticeably after our change of trains and grew steadily sunnier the farther south we went, so that by the time the sun set it was sending strong rays of gold across a pale blue sky, and I was most sorry to see it go. We finished the final leg of our journey in darkness, lit only by the yellow lanterns of the station and the harsh electric torch wielded by the driver who awaited the countess's return.

I was a little disappointed in our timing, since the House of Baronia lay at the center of Old Baronia, the last holdout of what had once been the most powerful kingdom of ancient Kyreland. Its crooked streets and pale-gold stone houses were much admired in the rest of the country, and I did long to see it with my own eyes. But I consoled myself with the assurance that I would have plenty of time for sightseeing after Felpz had sorted out the matter of Lady Emalta's necklace.

The House of Baronia itself was raised somewhat above the town in the manner of the old castles. It had originally been one itself, but long ago its wall had been torn down to supply building material for the town, and now only a single tower and part of the courtyard of the original structure remained, the rest having been renovated by a Tragansea two centuries earlier. It perched on a headland of stone overlooking the sea, and was something of a jumble, being built across many different levels so as to accommodate the natural terrain.

In the dark, from within the carriage, I could see little but got the impression of a high, turreted building with many lights around its base, the towers standing as dark silhouettes against the starry sky. Even through the padded walls of the coach I heard the wind howling in its heights, and smelled in faint gusts the tangy swell of the ocean nearby.

We were greeted at the front door by an iron-faced man and a distraught young woman who ran down the steps and pulled open the door of the coach all in a rush. She was a wild, pale-faced thing with dark hair that had contrived to wriggle out of the tight bun it had been put up in, falling haphazardly around her ears.

"Milady, *milady*," she was saying as the countess gathered her sea-foam skirts and swirled out of the coach.

Such was her concern that for a moment I took her to be Lady Emalta's daughter, but then saw the plain black dress she wore, and concluded this must be the maid.

"Never fear, Liriel," the countess was saying, confirming my suspicions. "You were in such a state last night I didn't think the trip would do you any good. And look, I have brought help—Mr Bouragner Felpz, the magician from Redling, is here to find the necklace."

The maid's large, dark eyes turned to Felpz, pleading.

"I *didn't* take it," she said to him, her voice a whisper.

Felpz gave her a keen look, and after a moment he gave a little shrug. "No, no, I believe you did not," he said. Then, to the countess, he went on: "I would like, however, to question the remainder of your staff. Particularly this new boy—the, er, *improver,* you called him? And if you have a picture or photograph of the necklace, that would be helpful. I'll need to know *what* I'm looking for if I am to find it, after all."

"Yes, of course," Lady Emalta said, and turned to the iron-faced man, who nodded and retreated up the steps without a word.

By this time the maid Liriel had composed herself enough to take the countess's travel case, and a pair of footmen had trotted up to unload our bags. In this way we were ushered up the steps to the front door of the hall and inside, where we found ourselves in a veritable blaze of lights. This area was clearly part of the old castle, for the ceiling stretched up above us in a high arch of stone, which had been hung with strings of electric lights. The walls were decorated with tapestries and portraits, and the stone floor covered in a magnificent ultramarine carpet. In the center of this stood a young woman—hardly more than a girl, but with such poise and confidence that she projected the bearing of someone much older.

"Welcome back, mother," she said, dropping a neat curtsey. "I take it your errand was a success?"

"Merodite, my dear, come meet the magician and his assistant. Mr Felpz, this is my daughter, Merodite."

Felpz, however, had wandered over to the far wall and was studying a line of oversized portraits that ran the entire length. These showed, upon closer inspection, woman after woman, beginning with a painting so dark and stained with age that the subject was barely discernible.

"A pleasure, I am sure," Felpz said distractedly, not taking his eyes off the paintings. "You'll forgive me but . . . who are *they?*"

"They are our ancestors, magician," said the countess, a trifle coldly.

Ignoring her tone Felpz went to stand under the nearest and pointed up. "And this one?" he asked.

"That is Amariel Tragansea," Lady Emalta said. "Next is her daughter, Corialla, and . . . "

"Next is *her* daughter, so I see!" said Felpz, sounding delighted. He moved away down the line, leaving me to pay my respects to Lady Merodite, who was looking a trifle sour.

"He may have a brisk manner, but he means well," I assured the young woman, but she did not appear impressed.

"My lady," Felpz called from some ways down the hall. "Are *you* in this collection?"

"Indeed I am," said Lady Emalta tiredly. "At the very end. Merodite . . . " but Felpz had already turned and hurried off. Gracefully, as if this had been her intention all along, the countess turned to me and finished her sentence. "Merodite has a portrait too, but it hangs in a different part of the house. Only countesses are hung in the hall. We have a separate room for the Lords of Baronia as well."

"I'm sure Felpz will be pleased to learn that," I assured her.

However, once he had been down the line of portraits and back again, Felpz showed no desire to see any other Tragansea family members. "The necklace," he said. "I am so sorry for letting myself be distracted. To find your necklace I need to know what it *looks* like. Have you a detailed drawing or even a photograph I could work from? Also, the box in which it was kept. That would be helpful."

"Both will be supplied," Lady Emalta assured him. "If you'll come through into the library, that will doubtless be more comfortable."

In due course we were led out of the hall and up a flight of marble stairs, through a high wooden door and into a round, comfortable room lined with books. Here a wide table sat in the center, covered in a crimson cloth with matching upholstered chairs set around it. A footman was just laying out a tray of tea and coffee and arranging a trolley filled with cakes nearby. Having had nothing since the rushed dinner between trains at Greywall I felt my attention drawn inexorably to that trolley, and could not understand how Felpz kept himself away from it, marching up and down the length of the table while we waited for the requested items to be brought. He condescended to receive a cup of sweet, milky tea, of which he took two sips and no more, while I piled my plate high with scones and, after the tea, took a serving of coffee.

I had only begun upon my plate of refreshments when Liriel entered, bearing in her arms a silver box with a glass lid and a small, framed picture. These she laid by the countess's elbow, bobbed a curtsy, and then went to stand demurely in the shadows by the door.

Hastily brushing away my accrued crumbs I leaned over to get a better look as Felpz opened the box and examined the picture.

The box was roughly the size of a large, thick book and had, as I have said, a glass lid. This was framed in silver, cast into the shape of breaking waves. In fact, the whole box was decorated along similar lines: the sides showed waves crashing upon a shore, flecks of foam and seaweed artistically fashioned into feet. Though the metal was blackened with tarnish in the crevices, the raised surfaces were brilliantly polished. All in all it looked to me like a much-loved artifact that was nonetheless seldom used.

The picture, in its elaborate, gilded frame, had a similar feel. Felpz turned it over in his hands and examined the back of it before looking at what the picture actually showed. When he saw it, he gave a small, inward sort of nod, and passed it to me.

It was another portrait of a woman, and showed her face and neck down to the point where the latter was crossed by a necklace, thus giving her the appearance of being a floating, disembodied head. It was, if I am any judge of such things, a very good little painting, and the woman it depicted bore a remarkable resemblance to Lady Emalta—if perhaps a trifle more austere.

"Another one of your ancestors?" I asked her.

"My own mother," replied the countess, tersely. "Lady Istel."

"Mark that she wears the necklace, Corianne," Felpz told me.

Mark it well I did, for it was a remarkable thing: at first glance it appeared to be a string of pearls, but upon closer inspection these resolved themselves into tiny, perfect skulls. Glinting from each eye socket was a shard of diamond, and the artist had rendered the reflected light such that some of the skulls appeared to be staring back at the viewer.

"That is the most unique and beautiful thing," I told Lady Emalta, though in truth I found the piece rather unsettling. Some of the skulls struck me as being of a sour disposition, and I did not like the way they looked at me.

"Many have thought so," said the countess with a stiff bow of her head. "You see why I wish to have it returned?"

"Yes," said Felpz, who had picked up the box and was sniffing it curiously. "I am beginning to see why, though it might have helped, of course, had you told me right away that your family has *merfolk* ancestry."

At hearing this I looked up from my study of the portrait sharply, in time to see the two noblewomen freeze. But while young Merodite

appeared purely surprised—and perhaps a trifle disbelieving—Lady
Emalta's hands grasped the tablecloth convulsively, and I saw a trace of
fear in her eyes.

"Why ever should you believe *that?*" she demanded, coldly.

"The legends about Amariel Tragansea coming out of the oceans are
just that—*legends!*" said Lady Merodite, with a nervous glance at her
mother.

"So it *was* Amariel Tragansea. I wondered, you know," Felpz said
with a twinkling smile.

"Mother, what *is* he talking about?"

Lady Emalta unclenched one hand from the tablecloth and lifted it
to silence her daughter. The young woman obediently fell back in her
seat, but her eyes were alight with curiosity. When the elder woman
remained mute, glaring at Felpz with pursed lips, it was he who answered
the question.

"That necklace," he said, gesturing at the picture I still held. "And
this box. Both are of merfolk make. I have seen their like before, and it
is most . . . distinct. The portrait of Amariel in your hall also contains
certain clues, though she had disguised herself well enough that I could
not be sure if she was a mermaid, or merely the daughter of one. You
told me yourself that you are a direct descendant along the matrilineal
line from her, therefore I reason, *you are both*, if only the slightest bit,
part mermaid. Although, unless new sea-blood has been introduced in
the interim since Amariel, it is likely the two of you are more or less
human by this point. But I think you may find yourselves quite unable
to *drown*, if it ever comes to that, and you may experience a slight ringing
in your ears if a ship ever wrecks upon these shores."

Merodite laughed at this, but her mother's face remained closed and
grave, and Felpz looked across at her with a pleasant, expectant expression. Eventually the ice of her countenance cracked, and she spoke—in
a resigned tone—the following:

"It is not a topic I like to discuss. The legend—and it is as Merodite
says, a *legend*—tells that the first Count of Baronia stole that necklace
from a grotto, and that Amariel came out of the sea and offered to be his
wife in exchange for it. In the way of tales this came to pass, and Amariel
ruled Baronia well, but was ever found to be wandering the beaches in
the moonlight, and would on occasion disappear—only to return in the
morning, sopping wet and smelling of the sea.

"But all old families have granules of mythology embedded in their
history," she said with a stern frown. "Who is to say this one is true?"

"I do," said Felpz. "At least, I hope it is true. It would explain, for a
start, why your necklace is currently *at the bottom of the ocean.*"

This caused a great stir, and even I found myself surprised.

"You found it already?" I asked.

"I have been casting my consciousness outwards as we have been
speaking," Felpz said dryly. "The necklace was not hard to locate, once

I knew what I was looking for. It quite *reeks* of magic, did you know? I hope you were never so foolish as to actually wear it."

"It is on the *bottom* of the *ocean*?" Merodite said, flabbergasted.

"Not far west from here," Felpz said, but he did not take his eyes from Lady Emalta, who had grown pale at his words.

"All the portraits in the hall," he continued, fixing the lady with his stare. "The ladies in them are depicted wearing this necklace—it was too difficult to make out in detail, but I am satisfied the necklace they wear is this one—all of them, save the last. You. You have kept it in this box— quite wisely, I must say. Was it by chance, or do you know more of its powers than you have told us? Tell us now, Lady Emalta, for it may shed some light on why the necklace was stolen—and who it was that took it."

Lady Emalta rose from her chair in a majestic flow of sea-foam skirts. For a moment I thought she would sweep out of the room in a great huff, but she only took to pacing up and down the length of the table, one hand fisted on her breast as though she fought some internal battle.

"The truth is I know nothing for certain," she said at last, drawing up to stand next to Felpz. "That is part of what vexes me so. For I only know what I have seen with my own eyes—all else is supposition based on old and questionable legends."

"Then tell me what you have seen," Felpz requested patiently.

"What I saw," said the countess, a faraway look about her face. "What I saw was my mother, day after day, wearing that necklace. She would never take it off, not even to sleep or to have it cleaned. But rather than become tarnished or dirty—or even wear down and break—the necklace only looked more and more spectacular. Yet at the same time, my mother grew more and more frail. By her forty-second year she was so decrepit that people thought her a woman twice her age. By forty-three she was bedridden—and *still* would not take off the necklace—and by forty-four she was dead, the necklace gleaming at her throat, shining with a radiance that was not to be believed unless you saw it. I can prove nothing—the doctors said she died of natural causes—but I am convinced that the necklace stole her life away. So I had it removed and put into that box, where it has remained these past twenty-five years."

"You never told me of this, mother!" Merodite said.

"Like I said before I know none of this for certain," the countess snapped. "It has been something of a superstition of mine, and I do not like to admit to it."

Felpz tipped the box closed with a soft *snap*, and held up the portrait for a better look.

"And this is she? Your mother, Lady Istel?"

The countess gave a curt nod.

"Well, well," said Felpz with a sigh. "This is a trifle messier than I had anticipated. Though I may yet get it sorted in short order. You are a very astute woman, Lady Emalta, and quite right: I rather fear the necklace *was* responsible for your mother's death, and that you kept it safely locked in this box—which has a pretty strong containment charm on it—was most fortunate for all your family."

"What, do you mean to say the thing was cursed?" Merodite asked.

"Not cursed," said Felpz. "It merely . . . *is*. Being created by merfolk it has certain . . . properties. There is magic in it which, though harmless to merfolk, has serious detrimental effects on anyone who is *not* a merman or a mermaid."

"But our ancestors have been wearing that necklace for *ages*," Merodite protested. "I never heard of it giving any of *them* problems."

Felpz did not answer immediately but smiled kindly at the young woman, while her face went from flushed to pale and her expression from incredulity to shock as she realized what her words implied.

"It would not have," Felpz said at length. "As long as they had sufficient mer-blood in them, the magic would not affect them. It seems, however, that with Lady Istel the line has become sufficiently humanized that it is now susceptible to the necklace's magic."

Lady Emalta came around and sank into a chair.

"Then what are we to do? Once we have it back?" she asked.

"Put it away in the box again, I should think," said Felpz.

"But why—" Lady Emalta began, but was cut off by a commotion at the door.

This had been growing slowly for some time, beginning with the frequent opening and closing of the door as servants came, saw us engaged, and went. This escalated to hushed conversations in the hall outside, which in turn grew more heated, until at last the iron-faced butler came into the room and bowed.

"Apologies m'lady, ladies, sir," he said. "Something dire has happened; I must speak with you at once."

Lady Emalta drew an indignant breath, but something about the man's manner piqued Felpz's attention, and it was he who responded first:

"What have you found?" he asked.

This startled the butler somewhat. He took a half step back before he regained his composure. He looked shaken, I now realized—almost sickly.

"It was what we *didn't* find at first," he began, his voice a wheeze. He coughed. "I assembled the staff, as you requested m'lady, so that the magician here might interview us. Come to find the improver, Combs, was *missing*. It then came out he had not been seen since your necklace was stolen. We've been searching the house all this time."

"Well?" said Lady Emalta. "Did you find him?"

The butler's iron face cracked, but he pulled himself together. "Yes, m'lady, we just found him. And . . . it is with the deepest regret . . . I must inform you that he is *dead*."

"Dead!" cried Merodite. It was not even a question.

"*Dead?*" repeated Lady Emalta, incredulously.

Felpz rose in a swirl of purple coat and stood there, very still, while we all looked at him. Then he gave a little twitch, as if shaking himself out of a dream, and said: "In the under-cellar." Then he took off out the door, brushing past the butler and the servants beyond, and was gone.

"What did he mean 'in the under-cellar?'" Merodite asked in the confused silence left in his wake.

"I expect that is where they found his body," I said wearily, heaving myself out of my chair. I made it all the way to the door before the other two women started after me, they were so taken aback.

"Lead the way," I told the butler.

The under-cellar turned out to be located at the very bottom of that great house, set deep into the bedrock. At high tide it was easily below sea level, though it was so well insulated by stone and mortar that nothing could be heard of the outside, and it was easy to believe you were deep in the heart of some isolated mountain.

Though our way was well lit—first by electric torches and later by gas lamps—the stairs were roughly cut and very worn, and I soon grew weary of them. Natural curiosity, however, spurred me to pass my usual tolerance for physical exertion.

I was rewarded, at the end, by a scene out of nightmares. In the dance of dark and light thrown by the lanterns we eventually came upon a small storeroom where Felpz and a male servant crouched over a fallen form on the stone floor. Something dark was puddled beneath it, and I found I had to steady myself against a nearby wall.

"Magan, notify the police," I heard Lady Emalta say in a choked voice, and there was a hushed "Yes m'lady," and the patter of feet away up the stairs.

"Who found him?" Merodite asked, pushing her way into the room.

The unknown man by the body stood up, revealing himself to be a dirty but fair-faced young man. Hardly out of his teens, I thought.

"That would be me, milady," he said, with a respectful touch of his forelock. "It was a mad errand, only we'd searched everywhere, and Magan was ready to send to the village to see if he'd run off to visit his mum, and I thought . . . well, there's *one* place we haven't looked, might as well check that so's there'd be no door unopened and . . . " he trailed off dejectedly, looking down at the boy on the floor.

This one was truly a boy, still with the soft, smooth face of youth, evident even contorted by death. I felt my heart ache for him, and more so for the poor woman he'd left behind, but whatever emotional upheaval my soul intended to experience was put on hold when Felpz leapt up and went over to what appeared to be a solid brick wall and began pawing at it.

"Felpz," I said heavily. "*What* are you doing?"

"Salt water," replied Felpz, not turning away from the wall. "That is not blood—he was strangled—it is *salt water*. How did *salt water* get here?"

"How do you know—*oh* . . . " said Merodite in a small voice.

Cautiously I came forward, and indeed the dark liquid was not blood—it only gave the impression of being dark because of the bad light. Now I saw it was too thin, too transparent to be blood, but the pitiful figure on the floor was enough to keep me at bay. I did not try to ascertain for myself that he had been strangled, but trusted my friend's assessment.

Felpz was murmuring to himself, strange words I only half caught, but understood them to be in some mysterious language.

"Magician, what are you—" Lady Emalta began, but then there was a *snap* in the air, as though my ears had popped, and a grinding sound as a section of bricks fell away under Felpz's hands. Their movement revealed a small, dark passageway, out of which a draft of cold, wet, salty air blew, along with a faint rushing sound.

In that grim little room all was silent, and when Felpz turned away from the wall his eyes were gleaming.

"It is an escape route," he said. "Built into the very foundations of this house. Oh, Corianne, I must thank you for convincing me to take up this case. It is proving *most* interesting."

"Would this have anything to do with Amariel Tragansea?" Lady Emalta asked, sounding resigned.

"I think it has everything to do with her," Felpz said. "This portal leads to the sea. What more perfect way for the merfolk employed by her to slip away home for their holidays, without revealing their true nature? It's been sadly neglected, I fear—you have not employed mer-servants for many generations, it seems—but it still responds to the correct words. Now, however, it has served as an escape route for our thief."

"Thief *and* murderer," I reminded him.

Felpz glanced back at the body on the floor, and he sighed. "No, I do not think this was murder. Not as it could be described by you or I. This was a tragic and entirely avoidable accident. One that, I hope, will never be repeated."

With these words he turned to the wall again and climbed into the hole, shoulders first.

"Felpz!" I called after him, indignantly. "What are you *doing*?"

There was some thumping from within the tunnel, and eventually Felpz's head reappeared. "I am going to retrieve Lady Emalta's necklace," he said, innocent as a babe. "Expect me back by morning. Good night!"

His face disappeared into the darkness, and no amount of calling was able to bring him back. After a couple of minutes, distant but distinct, I heard a splash echo up the tunnel.

"He is a most *peculiar* man," Merodite said faintly, and though none of us replied verbally, I think we were all of her mind.

The remainder of the night was no less busy, if rather more mundane. First a constable and then a detective arrived and had to be shown the body. I left after giving my own limited statement and allowed the head housemaid to lead me up to my room. This was a comfortable apartment in the modern wing of the house, and it was so far removed from that cold, eerie cellar that I put myself to bed quite easily. Though my mind was initially plagued by the events of the day—the fate of the boy had deeply upset me—soon it all faded into pleasant blackness, and I slept.

The morning came, and with it the cries of seabirds, which served to shake me from my rest rather earlier than I would have wished. I had begun to dress, and to push my hair into some sort of order, when there was a knock at the door, and the maid, Liriel, put her head in.

I confess I was surprised to see her, but more surprised, I think, at the sight that was revealed in the morning light—which had, I could only assume, been invisible in the artificial light from the torches the night before.

The girl was older than I had first thought, and there was a strong ovality to her face that caused the features to slope somewhat toward the center. Her dark hair had been bravely pinned up under a cap, but a few wriggling wisps still escaped around her ears. The most peculiar thing of all, however, was that her skin had the faintest greenish tinge in the corners and the crevices of her face. It was enough to make me hesitate before addressing her, and to forget the words she had greeted me with.

"I'm sorry," I said. "My mind is all in the clouds this morning. What did you say?"

"Beg your pardon, ma'am," said the girl. "But breakfast is ready in the dining room, and the countess is requesting your attendance. The magician is not back yet, and she wants you to find him."

"Oh . . . " I said. "Well, I'm afraid I can no more bid that magician than I can bid the tides of the sea, but I'll come down to breakfast, and see if I can't settle her feathers."

"Very good, ma'am," said Liriel, bobbed, and left.

I went down to breakfast very slowly, for I was still not easy in my mind over the recognition that had stirred within me when I had looked upon the maid's face. I felt, strongly, that I had seen those features before—though in a different configuration. I might have tormented myself over this puzzle for hours had I not passed by the entrance hall en route to the dining room. There I caught a glimpse of the portraits lining the wall, and one about halfway down provided all the answers I needed.

I must have had a strange expression on my face when I entered the dining room at last, for Lady Emalta—assembled in a magnificent costume of burgundy wool with chocolate silk lining and layered skirts of mint and sky blue—greeted me most courteously and expressed concern over the quality of my night.

Marshaling my features into an expression of idle pleasantness, I assured the lady all was well with me, before filling my plate at the sideboard.

"And the magician?" the countess asked, folding her hands over her half-empty plate. "Any word from him?"

"Alas," said I. "I know no more than you do, milady. Felpz goes and does what he will, and I find the best course is to relax and wait for him to bring the answers to you."

Lady Emalta's face pinched, but she swallowed her disappointment and resumed her meal. In time we were joined by her daughter, and the three of us were still seated around the table when there was an almighty hullabaloo from the front door.

I heard it bang, and then raised voices and a thundering of feet. A rushed conversation just outside our door, and then it opened to reveal the butler, Magan, his iron face rust red from exertion and his chest heaving. Nevertheless, he had composed himself enough to speak fluently, though his words were somewhat forced.

"My . . . ladies," he said. "I am pleased to announce that the magician has returned. He is . . . on his way. Up the drive. As I speak. And, m'lady, he has someone with him."

"Someone, Magan?" said Lady Emalta.

"Someone, m'lady," the butler repeated. "We cannot be sure what they are . . . but it looks to be a mermaid. Or perhaps a merman. To own the truth it's hard to tell from this distance. But if you come to the front door you may see for yourself."

Needless to say we all rose—the two fine ladies in a swirl of skirts—and as one made a rush for the door. Coming out onto the front steps I was immediately struck by the majesty of our surroundings—which I had not been able to fully appreciate the night before.

From where I stood the promontory fell away before us in a tumble of pink and grey stone to the village nestled at the foot of the cliff. To our right stretched the sea, cool and misty grey on that winter morning, with the sky fading to a delicate blue above our heads.

The road we had climbed in the carriage the night before was now visible as a dark stripe crisscrossing the tumble of stone, sometimes disappearing behind a crag, and upon it I saw two figures moving. They were well over halfway up the ascent and drawing steadily closer, but it took me a moment to recognize Felpz, and his companion fairly baffled me.

The reason I had difficulty identifying my friend was because he was soaking wet. His hair was plastered down across his head, smooth and shiny as a seal's back, and his normally fluttering coat hung, stiff and dripping, at his side. In its wetness it appeared more black than purple, and this also served to confuse me.

The person he had with him—and I saw now how he clutched their arm and forced them to walk a little in front of him—was as strange a creature as ever I saw. Slinky, with greenish blue scales that caught the light and sparkled with iridescence, they were so covered with spines and fins that it was difficult to make out the shape beneath it all. They walked with a stunted, stuttering gait, and relied upon Felpz as much to keep them upright as anything else.

Quite a crowd had gathered upon the steps of Old Baronia by the time Felpz and his unusual charge crested the final rise and trudged across the wide stone terrace before the house. Lady Emalta and her daughter stood at the head of us, but turning to the side I saw the butler Magan, both footmen, the servant from the cellar last night, and the maid Liriel, all crowded around the door.

Felpz drew up in front of this audience and bowed. He did so rather jerkily because the person he held made a determined effort to get away just then. Coming upright once more Felpz tugged at their arm.

"I said I would return you safely to the sea," he said, a little snappishly. "The *least* you can do is cooperate."

The creature snarled and shook its arm out of his grasp, but made no move to flee. Instead, it drew itself up, the fins and spines around its neck fanning out and revealing its face, which was a most interesting combination of human and fish. Almost draconian in its construction, it had an eerie beauty about it, and glittered from all the fine, translucent scales that served in place of skin. The eyes were perhaps a little large, and when it blinked there were not eyelids, but pale membranes that pushed in from either side. The nose was very small and the mouth very wide, and the whole face had that same, slanting ovality that I had noted in the maid Liriel and the portraits in the hall. It sneered at us, and so fascinated by it was I that I didn't even notice that it was wearing the necklace of pearl skulls until Lady Emalta cried out and pointed.

"There!" she exclaimed, half in alarm and half in triumph. "A thief! I knew it all along!"

A strange gurgling, hissing sound bubbled up from the throat of the mer-person, and their mouth split asunder revealing twin ridges of sharp, triangular teeth. They were laughing, I realized with a cold chill, just as they began to speak.

"No thief," they said, their voice as hissing and gurgling as their laugh, but still understandable. "Never a thief. One cannot steal what one already *owns*."

"But that is *my* necklace!" Lady Emalta declared, and looked so fierce saying it that for a moment I was unable to decide who looked more threatening, the woman or the mer-person.

At her words the latter straightened up, the spines across their shoulders lifting to provide an even stronger impression of height and size, and their eyes narrowed to slits — which, due to the arrangement of their membranous lids, were *vertical* slits rather than horizontal ones. It was a truly unsettling sight.

"It was Princess Amariel's necklace," they said, their voice like steam flying from a hot iron. "And you, though you bear her title, hold none of her blood! The necklace rejected you a generation ago. Now the ownership returns to me, and I shall take what is mine: first the necklace, and then the house of Old Baronia."

"You shall do no such *thing*," said Lady Emalta, coming down the steps. "You've no *right*."

"I'm afraid Calamite here has every right," Felpz said heavily. Even in the cold morning air he had begun to steam faintly and was becoming visibly drier. "The rights and legacy of the countesses of Baronia are tied up in this necklace. As has been explained to me, the necklace was a betrothal gift to Amariel Tragansea from a sea lord. She took the necklace, but instead went ashore and married a human. She tied his lands and title to her necklace, so that she could pass them down to her daughters through the piece of jewelry. An ingenious way of circumventing the traditions of the time, but now that the blood of the merfolk has dwindled so far as to be imperceptible in your generation, the necklace can no longer be safely worn by the countesses of Baronia. So Calamite, as a descendant of the original owner of the necklace, has some claim to it. The necklace, and through it, thanks to Amariel's enchantment, all the lands and titles of Old Baronia."

"This is outrageous," declared Lady Emalta, and I had to admit I partly agreed with her. "He killed *Combs!*"

"I killed no one," hissed Calamite. "The necklace saw to the boy. You've your own human frailty to thank for that."

Lady Emalta looked so angry at those words that I thought fire would leap from her eyes. Seeing her so, however, only made the mer-person chuckle.

"Don't be so angry," it said. "I agree it would be unfair to pull your home out from under you, as a riptide sweeps a swimmer out to sea. Which is why I propose a compromise: give me your daughter to wed, and our children can carry on the line—yes, and the necklace as well."

Lady Emalta turned white in fury and shock, but it was Merodite herself who replied.

"I shall *never* in a thousand *years* marry anyone as despicable as *you!*" she cried, her eyes flashing like thunder. "Neither shall I let you steal mother's necklace! We may be humans, but we're still *Traganseas*. We are the ladies of Old Baronia, and we will not give it over to you!"

Calamite laughed again. "If you want it, you may come and take it off me. Though I highly doubt that will do you any good," and the creature smiled at us, broad and satisfied and so smug it truly began to wear on my nerves.

"Felpz," I said. "Can't you *reason* with him? Er, it?"

"I have spent all *night* attempting to negotiate a mutually acceptable compromise," Felpz said wearily. "Convincing Calamite to come ashore was the most I could do. Even now, I dare not take the necklace by force. Were I to touch it, I very much doubt you would ever get it away from me again, and this would prove disastrous for all parties."

"Oh, *yes*," Calamite fairly cackled. "The necklace has a power. In the hands of the merfolk it is tamed, it is *obedient*. To a human it is unquenchable lust and a consuming fire. To see it is to desire it; to have it is to die for it. So you can take me as the new Lord Baronia, or you can take the necklace back—and in doing so, throw away your lives."

I could have slapped it, spines and all, I was so frustrated. But it was Merodite—young and impetuous, with all the pride of her ancestors behind her—who strode down the steps, across the short expanse of gravel, and took hold of the creature by its neck and began to pull at the necklace.

Her mother and I both shouted—inarticulate noises of protest, as we were too surprised for proper words—and Calamite, far from allowing the necklace to be taken, grappled with Merodite and bared its teeth.

The young woman might have come to grief then, had Felpz not intervened. He pushed an arm roughly between the warring parties, and there was a sharp *snap* of raw magic that sent the two staggering backwards from each other.

There was a twinkle in the air, and something landed with a delicate *clink* upon the ground. I blinked and looked more closely, and realized that the snap I'd heard had not just been from Felpz's magic: the clasp of the necklace had also broken, and in Merodite's contortion as she stumbled backwards it had flown out of her hand and now lay among the rocks, gleaming and shimmering.

What came over me then was the strangest feeling. As I looked upon the necklace I felt a great rush of desire within me, while at the same time the reaction left me cold in the pit of my stomach. A sour taste grew in my mouth, and altogether I felt quite ill. Where the necklace had looked eerily beautiful in the painting and upon the mer-person's neck, now it appeared the most horrible and evil thing imaginable, and I wanted nothing more than to crush it beneath the heel of my boot.

Judging by the reactions of the crowd, however, I was alone in this revulsion. When I chanced to look around, I found them all gazing at the thing as though they were besotted. Even—and this was most terrifying of all—Felpz himself, who clung to Calamite as though they were an anchor.

It was Lady Emalta who came forward, stumbling a little, and picked up the necklace. She cradled it in her hands reverently, an odd light dancing in her eyes.

"Best put it away now, my lady," Felpz said in a strained voice. "You had the strength to shut it away once. Shut it away once more. The box!" he barked. "The silver box! Why does no one have it?!"

But Lady Emalta said nothing, and no servant went to fetch the box. Instead, as one in a trance, she put the necklace round her throat and held it there—for the clasp was still broken.

"*Mine*," she said, her eyes shining and shimmering. "I am Lady Emalta Tragansea, Countess of Baronia. You have no claim and no power. *Go back to the sea!*" She pointed with her free arm, forcefully, towards the cliff.

Calamite sneered at her, at all of us, and then shrugged. "I shall be back," the mer-person said. "Upon your death I will return. Again and again I shall. And I won't have to wait long—the necklace will see to that!"

The creature took three lunging, awkward strides, and then cast itself into the air beyond the cliff's edge, whereupon it disappeared.

My first instinct was to run and see how it navigated the tumble of rock that lay between it and the sea, but at that moment Lady Emalta gasped, clutched at her neck with both hands, and fell to the ground.

We all rushed towards her, but Felpz reached her first.

"Ease up, my lady, let it go," he was saying, and I saw with horror that the necklace had tightened considerably around the woman's neck. Her skin was standing out around it in angry red, and she was clearly suffocating. Her mouth worked, forming words for which she had no air, and her eyes bulged.

"Yes, this is exactly what Calamite hoped would happen," Felpz said. He looked up, cast around, and for a moment settled on me. "Corianne," he said. "I cannot risk touching the thing. You'll have to take it off her."

"No!" I cried, for I had the sudden unshakable knowledge that were I to touch that horrible thing I would be sick.

"Oh, will you both stop dallying and *help her!*" someone shouted.

To my surprise it was Liriel, the countess's maid. She who had stood behind me quietly for the whole ordeal had now come forward and was gently lifting the countess's head into her lap. "Have *none* of you worked a clasp before?" she said, her pale little hands running around to the back of the older woman's neck. There was a neat *click,* and then the necklace came away and Liriel was scrambling backwards, holding the artifact as though it were a live snake.

As abruptly as a candle being snuffed the sickness in my stomach left me, and Felpz's face lost that panicked, strained look. The crowd fell away as Merodite came forward and took her mother's hand, and the countess coughed and gasped and drew in much-needed air.

Through it all Liriel stood with the necklace in her hands, its skulls faintly gleaming—but only as much as any pearl would in that bright winter sunshine. It appeared to me nothing more than a curious bauble now, and I could not imagine why it had elicited such strong feelings.

"Could I trouble someone for its box?" she asked faintly. "It's put away on milady's dresser. Ordinarily I'd go, but I don't like to leave her now."

Felpz himself went for the box, returning in a matter of seconds. The necklace was placed in it, and the lid sealed. Then at last Felpz seemed to relax. He handed the box respectfully back to Liriel with a short bow, looked around at us, and said:

"That turned out as well as could be hoped. Is there any breakfast left? I am *famished.*"

"You must thank Liriel not me," Felpz said later, after he had breakfasted. Lady Emalta had been put to bed, but was now sitting up and insisted on seeing us. We were seated in her room along with Merodite, and Liriel herself was standing modestly by the door.

"If it pleases you, milady," said the young woman, her face still downcast. "Think of it as reparations. It was my weakness that allowed Combs to get the key off me in the first place. If I hadn't been so wrong in the head over him I should have noticed what he was up to."

"Oh, I imagine he would have got it eventually *some way,*" said Felpz magnanimously. "Merfolk are notorious for getting what they want out of humans. Including myself, I confess. When I brought Calamite to Old Baronia I hoped that they could be reasoned with. I see now I was overly optimistic. Without Liriel's intervention I shudder to think what would have happened. You'll want to give her a raise, I believe. A promotion, too. You'll need someone to be the keeper of the necklace now that you yourself cannot handle it, and it seems Liriel is more than a match for the task—she is, after all, more than meets the eye."

"Traganseas aren't the only ones with family legends about merfolk," Liriel said modestly. "It's quite common 'round here, actually."

"Oh, *good,*" wheezed Lady Emalta. "Do you know if any of them contain eligible bachelors? I've been thinking, you see, about what the creature said, and it was right about one thing: perhaps Merodite *should* marry someone who, if not a *merman,* is at least closely related to one."

"*Really,* mother?" said Merodite, aghast.

Felpz shrugged. "That is a possibility, I suppose. In the meantime, however, I recommend entrusting all duty concerning the necklace to Miss Liriel. Now, I believe our task is complete. Corianne, I promised you a holiday, and I do not see any reason to delay."

So it was we left the three women there, and I am happy to say the following two weeks proved to be as enjoyable and excitement free as ever I could have hoped. Felpz read my novel, and I compiled this neat little account of our adventure, which now needs only one or two words to make it complete.

It is my understanding that Merodite did not marry a man of merfolk descent, but chose instead a decent gentleman from Greywall who took the eccentricities of the family he married into very much in stride. It is Liriel who keeps the necklace to this day, and she is training a young boy—the orphan of a fisherman father and a mermaid mother—to be her successor. Lady Emalta remains a steadfast fixture at Old Baronia, and Calamite has remained in the sea.

As to the exact powers of the necklace, Felpz and I compared notes about our experiences the following week.

"The machinations are simple," he told me. "The necklace makes itself irresistible to anyone without sufficient merfolk blood. It then proceeds to kill them. Because it is magic, however, and powerful magic at that, what it would have done if brought into contact with *my* magic. . . . " He trailed off and shuddered. "*Perish* the thought."

"But I felt no desire to put it on!" I pointed out. "Quite the opposite, in fact."

"You are a rather special case, dear Corianne," he said, twinkling a smile at me. "I was counting on that, not being certain of Liriel. You have, after all, a knack for subduing powerful magic. Look at the effect you had on that fairy when you were but a girl, or the demonic lamp you still keep in your bedroom with no ill effects. No, I was—and am—confident that you would have had no trouble with the necklace of Amariel Tragansea."

"You flatter me," I said with a wry grin. And I was very flattered, and deeply touched that he trusted me so. "However, I must say I'm glad I never had to touch the thing."

"As am I, dear Corianne," said my friend heartily. "*As am I.*"

Note On the Gender of Calamite

In my first draft of this narrative I identified Calamite as male—as most people had assumed based on its behavior. Felpz corrected me, however, and explained that the creature did not have a human gender. Merfolk, it seems, are more fluid in these matters than humans, and unless explicitly stated, they should properly be referred to by gender-neutral terms. Though some merfolk will take on the characteristics of human males or females and then may be gendered accordingly, this is a conscious change and one they make the same way they can take on legs, lungs, and other aspects of humanity. So Amariel is female because she felt that presentation was the best way to achieve her ends. Had Calamite succeeded in marrying Merodite they would undoubtedly have made a similar adjustment. Since that did not come to pass, happily, I have chosen to render to them in their natural, ungendered state.

ten

THE GOBLIN'S FIDDLE

IT NOW COMES FOR ME TO TELL of that most bizarre escapade concerning the Goblin's Fiddle. Those of my readers who read the Elgan papers in the spring of 2325 may remember the sensational story of a passenger train inexplicably disappearing from its tracks en route to Redling, and then just as inexplicably reappearing in the middle of Hexenwald forest—forty miles from where it had last been seen. No one on the train could give a clear account of what had happened, save a particular magician whose explanation was discounted on the grounds that it was "too incredible to be believed."

Well, it should not surprise any of my readers to learn that the magician in question was none other than my friend, Bouragner Felpz, and that what he said was completely true. I would have told the authorities the exact same story (having also been a passenger on that train—the now infamous Rotgreif Express) but none of them thought to ask me.

I shall tell the story now, in its entirety, and while some may find it fantastical, to those familiar with the adventures of Bouragner Felpz it should not be beyond the realms of credulity.

I unwittingly entangled myself in the affair—and, it followed, Felpz—by having the gall to take myself away on a foreign holiday. I made the trek all the way to Milany before working my way north around the Crowan Sea, visiting the grand old cities of Frazia and Amaris, and staying a spell in Schüle. It was entirely delightful and quite an adventure considering I did it all by myself—though my daughter flew down to visit me in Schüle at the end of my stay. We spent an enjoyable week taking in the sights of Elgany's brightest city, before we came to the end of our mutual vacations and turned homeward. My daughter, true to her nature, rode home on the back of the dragon that had carried her to Schüle in the first place, while I took what I thought at the time was the much safer route: that of the Rotgreif Express, which joined Schüle, Glossen, and Redling by way of reliable iron train tracks.

When I boarded the train on the evening of April 13th, I was in that exhausted but happy state that follows three weeks of travel and sightseeing, and was prepared to sleep the two days it would take for the train to reach Redling Central Station. My daughter, bless her, had insisted on buying me a first-class ticket, and so I treated myself to a decadent complimentary supper after seeing my luggage satisfactorily stowed.

I'll admit, I found my fellow travelers almost as interesting as the sights of those famous cities, and lingered over my coffee to indulge in a bit of innocent eavesdropping.

It appeared that my neighbor—a tiny old woman bedecked in pearls and heavily embroidered clothes—was an Aldonican countess, and she spent the entire meal deep in conversation with a statuesque Milanian woman with iron-grey hair heaped in an impressive bun. This woman, I gathered, was the mother of a young musical prodigy, whom the countess was most insistent give her a private performance while we were en route.

I sipped my coffee, both amused by the Milanian's attempts to politely decline the countess's request, and also sympathetic when it appeared the countess would not be put off. She was a woman of that pointed, wiry variety who asked for things by making it sound as though whatever it was she wanted was actually in her target's best interests.

"He should be a *star*," she said, her Aldonican brogue barely noticeable under the authority and force with which she spoke. "It would be a wonderful opportunity for him to perform in front of a peer of the land—and before he ever reached it, no less. That way, when you get to Redling, you can tell everyone that he is Elzarino Cappofazi, charmer of royalty!"

Mrs Cappofazi made dubiously appreciative noises, and by an inspired maneuver managed to turn things around on the countess by stressing that her son was very tired and would likely not give a good performance while traveling.

"I would not wish you to hear him at anything but his most magnificent," she assured the countess, who was forced to accept the implied honor by dropping the matter.

I chuckled inwardly to myself over this, and after I returned to my compartment I made a note of the young man's name—so that I might, if he was indeed bound for Redling, attend one of his scheduled performances.

Then, feeling the effects of the stress of traveling and the generous meal I'd recently consumed, I curled into my bunk and went fast to sleep, lulled by the gentle clacking and rattling of the train as it hurtled on through the night.

I was woken sometime in the wee hours of the morning by the sound of music, soft and mournful, emanating from somewhere down the carriage. It followed no clear path or melody, and yet I was certain the tune had meaning. In my somnolent state I believed it had a great deal more meaning than any music I had ever heard. In some ways it reminded me of the song of the firestones I had heard in my youth. Loyal readers may recall this song, which when sung properly became a door to another world. This music had a similar quality, though what its purpose was I could not tell. Wondering on this, I fell back to sleep and did not wake again until I heard someone rapping on my door.

I awoke to find light full upon my face—not the warm, golden light of dawn, but the cool, bleached light of the moon. And the tapping, I saw when I blinked the sand out of my eyes, was coming from my window, not my door.

Light poured in from a crack in the curtains and lay in a pale stripe across my bunk. Pulling my dressing gown more tightly around myself as I sat up, I noticed with alarm that the gentle rocking of the train had ceased; we were apparently stopped.

Going to the window I pulled back the curtain and felt my heart leap to my throat at what I saw on the other side.

A huge face, like something between a lizard and a bird of prey, gazed back at me. The face was ringed with feathers and had a short, hooked sort of beak—which had been the source of the tapping. Its eyes were very dark and green, and blinked slowly at the sight of me.

"*Need help?*" the face asked, its voice light and chirping, like a parrot's, though faintly muffled by the glass separating us.

I was so surprised that it took me a moment to realize what it had said.

"I am fine, thank you," I told the face, firmly. I knew that many strange creatures lived in the Hexenwald, which lay not far from the tracks, and supposed that the stopped train had attracted attention from one of its residents.

"*I'll stay near,*" the face said. "*Just in case.*" Then it peeled away from the window, and I caught a glimpse of a long, snake-like body twisting through the air as it writhed away. Its absence revealed the landscape beyond, and I felt my jaw drop open at the sight of it.

We were no longer in the forested mountains of northern Elgany, but on a wide, flat plain of bluish-green grass. It stretched away to a distant horizon where steep, spiky mountains capped with white, like rows of sharp teeth, cut into a deep, dark blue sky. In this sky was no sun, but a huge ivory moon that shone with a soft brilliance. It lit the plain like daytime, but was dim enough that I could look directly at it, and saw there a range of mountains that formed the shape of a dragon wrapped across its surface.

I staggered back from my window, shook my head violently, and questioned whether I was really awake. This was certainly strange enough to be a dream, but as I stood there and felt the cold air clinging to my ankles, and heard on the other side of my door the shocked gasps of my fellow passengers, I began to realize that I was very much awake, and something very strange had happened indeed.

Seeing that I would likely get no more sleep that night, I dressed with the intention of going out to see what my companions had to say, only to find when I slid my door open that the corridor was jammed with people, making it impossible for me to leave my compartment.

This makes it sound as though there were more people than there actually were: the corridor was sufficiently narrow that it was difficult for two people to pass one another, and so what first appeared to be a crowd was in fact a line of about twenty people making their way slowly past my door. They were all in their nightclothes, and appeared understandably worried.

"Excuse me," I said, catching a young man by the sleeve of his nightshirt as he inched by. "Can you tell me what is going on?"

"That's the question we've all been asking, hasn't it, mum?" he said dryly. "The conductor's just opened up the dining car, and we're hoping he'll have an explanation."

I doubted that, but I joined in the line at the next opportunity, and so made my way with the rest of first class back to the carriage I had so recently quitted.

The conductor was a tall, dark man with a fine white mustache and a snowy head of hair. Upon first impression I had taken him to be the sort of steadfast, unflappable man who would remain calm in any situation. This impression was borne out now, when he stood at the head of the dining car, very neat and composed in his blue-and-gold uniform, and ponderously cleared his throat.

"Ladies and gentlemen," he said, inclining his head ever so slightly in the direction of the countess. "It appears we have lost our way in the night. I beg you all to remain calm and patient while the captain and I attempt to get us back on the right track."

The room exploded with questions. *Where* were we? made up the bulk of these, but I also heard a few voices, raised in alarm over the others, asking *how would we get back?* and *how did we get to wherever* here *was?*

The conductor raised an implacable hand for silence and waited stoically until the clamor died down.

"I wish I had answers for you," he said. "At the moment, we cannot be certain *where* we are, though it seems to be some sort of alternate dimension. We have no knowledge of how we came here, but we have several ideas for how we might return. Our primary concern, however, is your safety. Which is why we ask you to return to your quarters and to not, on any account, step outside the train. Thank you, that will be all."

This only caused more clamor, but seeing I would learn nothing of value I turned to leave. In doing so I caught a glimpse of the Milanian woman, Mrs Cappofazi. She was standing behind me, near the door, clutching herself tightly around the midsection, and staring with stricken horror out the nearest window. Sensing my gaze upon her she turned her face to mine, and I saw her eyes were wide with despair and horror. Then she shook her head and darted off through the door and down the passage.

I chose not to pursue her but returned instead to my own compartment, hoping that I might find something in my belongings which I could utilize to contact Felpz, or perhaps Abharus, who would likely have better luck sorting us out than the poor conductor.

I had not yet managed to get my trunk down, when I heard the soft thump and slither of something on the roof of the car. At first I worried it was some sinister monster, but then my mind went to the odd feathered serpent that I had first seen upon waking.

Bearing in mind the conductor's sensible instruction not to set foot outside the train, I opened my window as far as it would go and pressed my face to the resulting aperture.

"Hello?" I called. "Is that you?"

Immediately the light from the ivory moon was cut off as something dark dropped between my window and the sky. Green eyes glittered and a beaky mouth smiled.

"It *is* me," the creature chirped. "Do you want my help? I could fetch my mistress."

"No, thank you," I said, as I had no idea *who* would be mistress of such a creature and did not wish to find out under current circumstances. "But do you think you could fetch someone *else*? A friend of mine, he is a magician. He is called Bouragner Felpz. Or Felpass, sometimes," I added, in case the creature might know my friend by his older name.

The face twisted almost upside-down, like an owl, and frowned.

"He is also called the Purple Magician," I added, a little desperately.

At once the expression on the birdlike face cleared, and its eyes twinkled.

"Oh, I *know* the Purple Magician," it said. "I will fetch him. Fetch him at once!"

"You needn't," I said hastily. "Just tell him Corianne is stuck on the train, and the train is . . . well, wherever *here* is. Do *you* know where we are?" I asked, struck by a sudden inspiration.

"Corianne is stuck on the train, which is lost between the teeth and the throat," recited the creature. "I will tell him!" And with a flick of its long tail the creature was twisting up through the pale sky, and I was left pondering its last words. I only hoped Felpz would be able to make more sense of them than I.

Having done all that I could towards resolving my predicament, I settled myself to wait, but found I could not sit still for the shivering excitement that continued to rush through my veins. Though the walls and furniture of my little compartment were perfectly unchanged, in this strange moonlight everything took on a slight shimmer, as if seen through a pane of lightly smoked glass. The light was also strange in that it penetrated even the darkest shadows, and so in a way I could see things rather better than I had by the ordinary lamplight. It gave the world a dreamlike, uncertain feeling, which led me to feel similarly uneasy.

Then I felt a curious shiver, like a breath of cold air on the back of my neck, and a moment later I heard a faint sound, high and mournful, like the whine of an injured animal. This slowly grew and strengthened, until it finally lifted to become the haunting melody from the night before. Distant at first, it soon penetrated my compartment, and it was only by assuring myself that I was still alone could I convince myself that the player was not in the room with me.

The music had not been playing for more than a minute when the train surged into motion again. Glancing out my window I saw the vast field of blue-green grass creeping by, and it appeared the spiky mountains were drawing slowly nearer.

Rising carefully I opened my door and put my head into the corridor, only to have it nearly taken off by one of the porters flying past. In his wake I saw my neighbors emerging, some shouting questions, others looking around for the source of the music.

This now seemed to be coming from all around us, and was growing loud enough to be uncomfortable. Before it became unbearable, however, it was cut off in an abrupt screeching, and a moment later the train slowed and came once again to a halt.

"What in the great beyond is going on?" came a shrill voice from the direction of the countess's compartment.

"That *is* a pertinent question, my lady, but I'm afraid the answer is somewhat beyond me," came the reply, almost at once, from the shadows at the end of the carriage. Though the speaker was yet invisible, I felt my whole body relax, and a warm feeling of reassurance swelled in my breast: for I recognized that voice immediately as belonging to my friend Bouragner Felpz.

The door to the dining car was flung open, and there was the conductor—rather more ruffled than the last time I had seen him—with the porter behind him, gazing timidly from under one elbow. They stood there, struck still as the tall form of Bouragner Felpz, his coat vividly purple even in the washed-out light of the ivory moon, emerged from the shadows at the far end of the corridor. His eyes found mine immediately, and he smiled jovially.

"Corianne, how happy I am to see you—even if it is rather earlier than I expected. I confess, you were right to worry about losing your way on your travels, though you've managed to do it in an entirely unique way."

"Do you know this person, ma'am?" the conductor said, and I turned to find myself face-to-face with his humorless gaze.

I refused to be intimidated, however, and drew myself up proudly before I answered.

"This is no ordinary person," I told him. "This is the renowned magician Bouragner Felpz. As he is a *particular* friend of mine, I thought it would do us all good if he lent us some assistance in getting out of our current . . . predicament. So I called him."

The conductor looked at me, disbelieving, but was forced to turn his attention away when the countess's door slid open and her voice could be heard echoing into the passage.

"—magician? Bring him here at *once*. He'll be much more useful than these mundane blue-sleeves. Perhaps *he* can tell us where we are."

I saw the porter wince, and the conductor turned a stormy glare upon the countess's poor maid, who was just shutting the door behind her, her face dark with shame.

Felpz had already raised a hand and was shaking his head.

"All in good time," he said. "*Where* you are is no mystery. The problem will be getting you all *back* to more or less the right place."

"Felpz," I said, reaching out to tug his sleeve. "*We* still have no idea where we are. The odd creature I sent to fetch you said it was somewhere between the teeth and the throat, but I'm afraid that means nothing to me."

Felpz turned a surprised look at me. "Really? Do you not recognize it? All of you?" He looked around at us, apparently astonished at our universal ignorance. He gestured expansively. "You are in *Dream*, my friends. Between the teeth and the throat of it, to be precise. Now, it will be impossible for me to get you back to where you belong without knowing what brought you here in the first place. You, conductor . . . ?"

"Jamison," said the conductor stiffly.

"Jamison," said Felpz. "If you would, gather the crew in the . . . have you got a dining car? Oh good. Yes, the dining car. I suppose you have too many passengers to fit them all at once . . . better have them brought in one at a time. But first, I must speak to your crew. And have a look at the engine. I take it you will want to come, Corianne? Just so. How was Schüle? No doubt you wrote to me of it, but your letter had not yet arrived when I was called away."

Staggered by this abrupt change of topic, I endeavored to dredge up some of the memories of my visit as we made our way slowly down the passage—squeezing past the countess's maid—and once more into the dining car.

Felpz listened attentively as we were then shown into the galley beyond, and thence to the foremost reaches of the train: the little cabin where the staff would squeeze themselves when not on duty. Here my words petered out, and just as well, for Felpz strode forward and opened the door that would lead us out of the train—it being the only way to reach the engine.

I saw the conductor give an involuntary twitch, though the man clearly thought better of warning a magician off his job.

"You may step out as well," Felpz assured us as he climbed down. "This is a singularly benign section of Dream; as long as you remain in sight of the train I anticipate no problems."

"Felpz you really must explain better than that," I said, following him out the door. "Do you mean to say we are *dreaming?*"

"Nothing of the kind," said Felpz, who had reached the ground and was inspecting the wheels of the coach. "When I say Dream, I mean the *place.* That wondrous, maddening, inscrutable place where conscious and unconscious thought take form. Where stories exist as islands, and the foundations of history lie sunk in the sea of memory. If you'll remember, our adventure with the withered hand of Asterly Hall introduced us to one of its residents: the lamphra Badgrave."

I did indeed remember those events, and the singular character of Badgrave, and paused to wonder whether that had anything to do with current events, but I was distracted when I reached the ground and saw why Felpz had been examining the wheels.

There were no iron tracks beneath the heavy metal rims, and they were sunk deep in the lush green grass. Tracks of another sort—crushed stems and gouged earth—stretched out behind them, clearly the marks of the train's recent journey.

Raising my eyes I saw we stood in view of the engine. When last I had seen it, this impressive boiler on wheels had been belching steam and smoke, its headlamp blazing proudly, its huge steel form vibrating with power.

Now it was dark and cold and silent, a lump of metal crouched on that surreal landscape. The only movement was a flicker of denim as the enginemaster put first his head, then his upper body, out of the little window to the driver's cabin and called down to us in Elgan.

Felpz's head went up at once, and he answered the driver in kind. They conversed thus for some minutes, and since I had only the crudest grasp of the language I soon gave up following the thread of their conversation and turned my attention to our surroundings.

Now that we were out in the open air, the feeling of looking through a pane of frosted glass had evaporated, and I could see clearly every blade of that wondrous, blue-green grass. The mountains in the distance appeared more jagged and sharp than ever, and a faint breeze wafted down from their direction. It smelled of old, dry, unopened books, but that was almost overpowered by the fresh, pungent smell of the damp grass.

Felpz, meanwhile, had progressed down the engine, inspecting the driving wheels and eventually the cowcatcher. I drifted after him, not wanting to let even the smallest distance grow between us—for I felt this was a place where things could easily be lost or forgotten. Indeed, since I had been out in the air I had felt a deep calm come over me, a complacency similar to the feeling of drifting off to sleep, and I worried that if I did not keep moving I might stand there, ankle deep in the blue-green grass, forever.

At the very least, Felpz was easy to keep track of: his purple coat seemed to glow in the light of the huge ivory moon, and I could find him even out of the corner of my eye. When he finished with the train and came marching back down its length I saw his brows were furrowed in thought. He waved at the enginemaster and offered a few words of reassurance, but spoke no more until we had climbed back into the coach.

"This is most remarkable," were the first words out of his mouth. The conductor, the porter and I were pressed into the small free space around him, and our anticipation must have been palpable. "You can absolve your engine of any wrongdoing. There is nothing about it to suggest that the machine is under any direct enchantment. Although the good *motormeister* tells me the train ran smoothly into this realm, and they were only able to stop it by dousing the engines and applying all the brakes. Even so, moments before I arrived, they said the train moved of its own accord."

"Yes," we all cried at once. "I felt it," I added.

"It seems to have stopped at the first hint of my arrival," Felpz murmured with an amused quirk of his lips. "This suggests to me that there *is* something facilitating your journey, but it is certainly not based in the engine. How are the passengers, Mr Jamison? I think it is time I spoke to them. I shall start with you three here, if you don't mind."

"It was a little past midnight that we noticed the change," the conductor volunteered. "Though I can't say when it actually happened. It being night we weren't exactly glued to the windows."

"Of course," said Felpz, nodding encouragingly.

"I was first aware of the light. The moonlight. Knowing we were still in the first quarter, when it suddenly came blazing in through the windows it was a shock. It was about that time that all the gas lamps went out as well."

"And the train continued to run smoothly?"

"For a bit, sir, for a bit. We began to decelerate immediately, however, as the engineers noticed the change as well and got the train to stop."

"Yes, that tallies with what the *motormeister* told me," Felpz said. "And you, mister . . . ?"

The porter, a young freckled lad, jerked himself to attention. "Sterngarten," he offered. "It is just as *Herr* Jamison says."

"And you noticed nothing out of the ordinary in the hours previous? How was the run from Amaris to Schüle?"

"Our journey up until now has been perfectly ordinary," said Jamison stiffly. "No disturbances."

"Except the music," I put in.

"You heard it?" Young Sterngarten said, his eyes very large and bright with something like relief.

"We do have a violinist on board," Jamison allowed, but Felpz had already turned away from him to concentrate on me.

"What music?" he asked, very intent, and I knew I had not been wrong to speak up.

"When I first woke—" I began, but Felpz interrupted almost at once: "This would be at what time?"

"Oh, I don't know. It must have been after midnight, as we had already left our iron rails. Anyway, I heard music. Fiddle music, to be precise." I proceeded to describe in detail my impression of the music, helped along by Sterngarten's encouraging nods. Jamison, however, only frowned more and more as I went on. I would have found it off-putting, but my experience with Felpz told me that this would likely prove critical to finding a solution, and so I forged on.

"You say the sounds held meaning?" Felpz echoed.

"I would not have dared put it that way," Sterngarten said. "But now that she says it so, I have to agree."

"And you have not heard this music since?" Felpz asked.

"In fact I *did*," I said, feeling triumphant. "Just before the train began to move again. I heard it stronger than ever."

"I did hear complaints of a noise," Jamison allowed. "But was somewhat distracted at the time, you understand."

"It stopped with your arrival," I added.

"Ah," said Felpz with a sage nod. "That is very helpful, thank you, Corianne. Mr Jamison, I believe you mentioned something about having a violinist on board?"

"Just so, sir," said the conductor. "A Mr Cappofazi, traveling with his mother. Something of a child prodigy, I understand."

"Would it be possible to interview him *sans* maternal interference? No? No, I suppose not. Then I will interview them together. *Herr* Sterngarten, would you be so kind as to fetch them? I don't think we need disturb the other passengers, but if they ask, tell them they need not worry. We should—*should*—be able to set all to rights by morning. And in the meantime, Corianne, this will prove to be a most memorable finale to your holiday. Now come, let us leave these cramped quarters."

The drama of the night was not yet over, however. Once we had installed ourselves in the dining car we had to wait for some time before the efforts of young Sterngarten produced Mrs Cappofazi and her son. Far from being in their bedclothes—as all but the staff, myself, and Felpz were—the mother and son were dressed in finer clothes than they had dined in, though these were now somewhat rumpled. But while Mrs Cappofazi strode imperiously into the car with the air of one about to conduct an interview rather than be the subject of one, her son merely drifted in her wake. A small, pale boy with lank dark hair, he had a nose that would have been striking on a marble statue but on a child seemed cumbersome and out of place.

Mrs Cappofazi appeared ready to take command of the proceedings, but Felpz spoke before she had time to open her mouth.

"It is good of you to come, madam. Please believe, had I been able to rectify our situation without rousing you from your . . . " he paused to take in her evening gown and neat calfskin boots, " . . . rest. But I have discovered, through my investigations, that you and your son are partly responsible for the current state of affairs."

I could see the woman's breast swell indignantly at this, but her son tugged earnestly at her sleeve and spoke softly, causing her to deflate a little. She turned to him, and spoke very quickly and quietly in Milanian. Despite my recent immersion in that language I caught little of her meaning, but by the way Felpz's eyes followed them, and by the twitching of his brow, I guessed he had little trouble surmounting the language barrier.

"It is not *our* fault," Mrs Cappofazi said at length, her manner having softened somewhat. "It is his *violino* . . . "

"Fiddle," provided the boy.

"I thought it might be," said Felpz. "I don't suppose you have it with you?"

The young boy shook his head vigorously, his dark hair flapping. "It flies away," he said. "Somewhere on the *treno*, er, the train."

"How do you know it is still on the train?" Felpz asked.

"Because I hear the music, *mago*. Don't you?" The boy asked this, his eyes very wide and open and innocent, but I felt a shiver run down my spine as I realized the train was not as silent as I thought it had been.

Beneath our voices, beneath the rustling of Mrs Cappofazi's dress, was a faint hum. A whine, like a lost animal. It seemed to resonate up from the floorboards, and only by holding my breath was I able to make out the haunting melody that had crept into the sound.

Sterngarten muttered a curse in Elgan, and the conductor, Jamison, turned around very sharply, as if he expected to find the source of the music around his feet.

"What in the blazes is that infernal thing?" he cried.

"Nothing infernal," Felpz said mildly. "Though . . . I understand it was well received by the Prince of Hell. No, I believe you somehow managed to lay your hands upon a most extraordinary instrument. I should like to have the story, if only for my own satisfaction, but first I believe we had best get it back to its rightful owner.

"I am speaking, of course, of your violin, Mr Cappofazi. Tell me, what does it look like?"

The boy appeared taken aback by this question, but his mother stepped up promptly and began to explain:

"It is a very old instrument. Dark mahogany in color, with a unique carving upon its surface."

"Does it not have teeth?" asked Felpz.

"Teeth?" cried the woman. "I should think not. No violin has teeth!"

"I know of one that does," Felpz said. "And it is the only violin—nay, the only *thing* that could possibly cause the kind of trouble we are currently experiencing."

For once Mrs Cappofazi was silent. By her side her son had gone even paler than before and looked ready to topple over.

"You saw it," Felpz stated, but gently, and he stepped over and guided the boy into a chair.

"I thought it was a dream," moaned the boy, and finally the whole picture snapped into focus.

"Good gracious, Felpz," I said. "It's the *Goblin's Fiddle,* isn't it?"

Felpz looked up and positively beamed at me. "*Very* good, Corianne. You'll be able to start your own consulting business at this rate."

"The Goblin's *what?*" said Jamison, and the Cappofazis looked at me in confusion.

"Is it anything to do with the *Wichtelschneider*?" Sterngarten asked.

"Corianne," Felpz said, standing up abruptly, "you may explain."

"It's a bit of a misleading name," I admitted, as Felpz went over to the door and began feeling around the frame. "It doesn't belong to a goblin, nor was it made by one—to my knowledge no one knows who made it. It is the instrument of . . . well, this is going to sound downright fanciful, but it's the instrument of Grimbald, the Queen of Dreams. Surely you've heard of her . . . " I trailed off. My audience was rather more interested in Felpz, who had now moved his examination to cover the coach wall. Sliding around the windows and inspecting the floor in places, he made for a distracting sight.

"As such, it is a powerful part of Dream itself," Felpz said, no doubt sensing that the tide of attention had turned to him. "It would be completely within its power to transport a train—nay, an entire city—into Dream. All it would need is a player. Someone to unlock its power." He shot a glance at Elzarino Cappofazi, and the boy hung his head.

"No, do not be ashamed," Felpz assured him. "Worse things have befallen those who played the Goblin's Fiddle. Count yourself lucky."

"But how on earth did it fall into the hands of a human?" I asked, feeling a little frustrated. "From all the stories I read, Grimbald was quite attached to it."

"She was—is," Felpz corrected himself, gently coaxing Sterngarten and Jamison aside so he could examine the wall behind them. "But she is also easily distracted. She has a habit of leaving it in odd places—sometimes I think she does it on purpose just to see what happens."

"How did you come by this violin?" I asked, turning to the Cappofazis.

To my surprise Mrs Cappofazi colored, and cast her eyes downward as she answered:

"My family was not rich," she explained. "When Elzarino wanted to play the violin we had no money for lessons, but I thought, if he had at least a toy violin then he could pretend to play. But I had not the money even for that. Then I found this old *violino* at the *avanzo negozio*—er, what you would call a junk shop? So I bought it for my son and bring it home. And we put some cotton strings on it and made him a bow out of a piece of old broom handle and some more string. And he played with it, and to our astonishment it made music! We took to standing on the street corner every *Sabato*, and in time he earned enough money to buy a real bow. Later, we put real strings on the violin, and cleaned it and polished it, and to our surprise we find out it is actually a very good old violin. He gives performances, and people like his music because it is like no music they have ever heard. It has never done anything like this before," she finished earnestly.

"Except," said Felpz from the other end of the coach, "make music with cotton strings. That should have been your first clue. But do you mean to say you noticed nothing out of the ordinary tonight?"

The boy went red in the face at that, and his mother looked indignant. Eventually, however, he explained:

"I take the violin out to practice. I always play a little before I go to bed. But when I have it out and tuned I was suddenly tired, and I sit down to rest. The next thing I know, I am waking up on my bunk, and the violin is gone. I hear it playing, though, and the music is so strange I can do nothing but listen. Then it stops, and I get up to tell Mamma—and that is when I notice that the outside is gone wrong."

"And you did not alert anyone to the fact that your violin had gone missing?" Felpz asked. He was now wandering back and forth along the coach, apparently at random. Yet I couldn't help be reminded of a cat, casually herding its pray into a corner, and felt my heart begin to beat a little faster.

"We tried!" protested Mrs Cappofazi. "But all they say is, 'go back to your compartment, madam. We are doing everything we can, madam.'"

"Also," her son put in, quietly, "we began to suspect my violin was being . . . used somehow. I kept hearing it play. Sometimes it sounded like it was in the room with us."

"No doubt it has been moving all over this train," Felpz said tiredly, "trying to find a way to get the thing started again. Now I am here, however, its options are limited. Would you just take a step to the side, Madam Cappofazi, and I think I shall be able to put a face on tonight's troubles."

So saying he made a little dart past the Milanian lady, nearly clipped one of the tables, and sent a chair crashing to the side. Ignoring it, he dove into a shadowy corner and, after a slight scuffle and some grunting, re-emerged, triumphantly carrying something at the end of his outstretched arm.

"There," he said, pausing to nurse his free hand. "Is this not your violin, Master Elzarino?"

To say it was a violin would be to put entirely the wrong idea into my readers' heads. In general size and shape it was quite like a fiddle, but around its edge were studded horns and curving claws, and in place of gracefully curving F holes was a gaping mouth lined with teeth. There were little stones set on either side of the fingerboard, and what with these and the toothy mouth it was easy to see a face on the instrument—and it was not a pleasant one. Across the body were carved runes—some large and angular, some small and curling, like the trails an insect larva makes as it bores through wood. The whole thing was of a dark, radiant wood, with a faint reddish tinge around the corners. What was left of its strings hung limply below the scroll, for they had all been cleanly severed.

What made us recoil, however, was the violent snapping of the violin's toothy mouth. So vigorous was it that I saw how Felpz's shoulder jerked as he held it.

"Mr Cappofazi," he said, a little out of breath. "Correct me if I am wrong, but this *is* that same violin, is it not?"

The boy, half hidden behind his mother's skirts, nodded shakily.

"It is not meant to have teeth, though," he said in a small voice.

"You mean it never bit you?" Felpz asked in some surprise.

Elzarino Cappofazi shook his head.

Felpz laughed ruefully. "Count yourself lucky, then. Count all of you lucky, in fact, that Corianne had the wits to summon *me.* I shudder to think what would have become of you had this . . . artifact . . . been allowed free roam. But that is all speculation; now we should have little difficulty in summoning its master—which may bring about its own set of problems, but I am optimistic as to our prospects."

"Its master?" I repeated. "Didn't you say it belonged to the Queen of Dreams herself?"

"Indeed I did," said Felpz. "A little room, please. Mind your fingers. Yes," he said, edging his way towards the door, "I said the Queen of Dream, and that is who I intend to summon. It is *her* fiddle, after all, and the only right thing to do with it—as with so many objects of power—is to return it to its rightful owner."

He had reached the door by this time and, holding the snapping violin well clear of it, pushed it open with one hand.

"I should mention, for those present, not to try to attract attention to yourselves. Above all do not try to be clever. Grimbald likes clever people, and if she likes you, it will be much more difficult for you to return to your normal lives."

So speaking he carefully stepped off the train and hopped to the ground. As one we crowded 'round the little aperture and peered out, only to see him wading away through the blue-green sea of grass, the violin—now thrashing vigorously—still held safely at arm's length.

When he was easily ten yards from the train he stopped, turned around in a slow circle, and then, very calmly and politely, said:

"Grimbald?"

Nothing happened. All was silent.

"Grimbald?" A little louder this time, but still nothing.

Taking a deep breath, Felpz raised his head to the huge ivory moon and shouted "*GRIMBALD!*" into the dim blue sky.

At first, I thought nothing had come of it this time as well. Then someone behind me, whose voice I did not recognize, said:

"Oh, *this* is interesting."

Slowly, we turned our heads and found someone new had joined our number. In height she was half a head shorter than I—shorter even than young Elzarino—with a bush of wildly curling dark brown hair. In the uncertain light of the ivory moon this appeared to twist and curl around her face as though it were alive. This face was not one I would soon forget: round as an apple with a soft nose and dimples, it was made subtly sinister for being the color of the deepest blue sky, with dark blue shadows—like patches of midnight—around the eyes. These shone like little glass orbs, and it was difficult to tell where their gaze fell, as they had neither pupil nor iris. The unsettling effect was compounded by the wide smile that stretched from cheek to azure cheek, indigo lips drawn thin across bright, white, square teeth.

It was an odd sensation; for I have confronted demons, fairies, ghosts and dragons, and though each of these pressed their presence upon my consciousness in different and discomfiting ways, this person presented nothing more than an unusual sight. Yet she was all the more frightening because of this, for I had no idea what her intent could be. Was she malevolent? Kind? Did her presence portend nightmares or salvation? As her face, with its blank, colorless eyes, rotated slowly towards each of us in turn, I was put in mind of a wildcat—something that appeared benign enough, but could at a moment's notice turn into a fierce force of chaos.

"Yesssssss . . . " said the little blue woman, the *s* trailing off into a soft hiss, and I caught a flick of her shiny, dark blue tongue between the white teeth. "This is *very* interesting."

"Grimbald," said Felpz, warningly, and I heard the rustle as he waded back towards the train through the grass. "Come away from them. I have what you want."

The woman took no notice. Her black dress, which hung snugly over her squat, plump figure, fluttered around her blue knees as she took a step towards us. She wore heavy, brown leather boots, and their soles looked as though they had dried mud on them.

We drew back, and Grimbald laughed.

I thought at first the laugh echoed, back and forth until there were three or four voices laughing. Then I noticed that they all differed in pitch, tone, and pattern. One was a chuckle, one a guffaw, one a sinister cackle, and one a disarming giggle. But they were all unmistakably the voice of the blue woman in the black dress.

"Sorry, Felpass," she said with a grin, even as the other laughing voices faded away. "This is *too* much fun to pass up. Now—what have we here . . . "

All at once I found myself staring into milk-white eyes—they reminded me of twin moons of the kind one saw on winter nights—and I felt a tickle as a tendril of Grimbald's curling hair brushed across my brow.

"*You're* a bit early," she said. "I'll leave you . . . for now. And *you* . . . "

She whirled away, crouching before Elzarino Cappofazi. "*You'd* best learn to think for yourself, young man. Can't have mothers and fiddles running your life. Why, it'd be all the wrong sort of play, day *in* and day *out* . . . " She swung out her bare, blue arms, waving them back and forth as she spoke. "Carpe noctis, and so on. You've got a deep well, see you don't poison it."

"Grimbald!" Felpz said abruptly, now standing directly outside our door. "Will you have the decency to take your trouble-mongering fiddle *back* now? It's giving my arm a dreadful ache."

"It's only because you haven't been *polite* to it," Grimbald said, not turning to look. "You should have taken me up on violin lessons when you had the chance."

Felpz let out a heavy sigh. "Grimbald," he said, in the tones of one trying to coax a cat down from a tree.

Grimbald, however, was patently not listening. She had straightened up and was sniffing the air, dog-like, while she turned in a slow circle.

"Pearls?" she said, slow and disbelieving. "Sterling silver . . . oh, and *pale* gold. Very nice . . . most of the diamonds are glass, but one is real. Why . . . that is *lovely* . . . "

"Grimbald," Felpz said sharply. "Do not. Don't you *dare* . . . "

At last Grimbald turned to regard the magician, and her eyes fairly blazed.

"I never dare!" she cried, still grinning cheek to cheek. "I am *Grimbald!*"

The air around her blurred, her dress flared, billowing like smoke, and when it cleared, the space she had occupied was empty.

"Felpz," I said, a little shakily. "What did she mean going on about pearls and silver and gold?"

Felpz let out a frustrated groan. "It is one of her favorite . . . *hobbies* . . . " he said disgustedly. "To steal crowns. Comes of not having one herself—though she *could* if she ever spared a thought to it. GRIMBALD!" he shouted, his voice amplified so that we all put our hands over our ears.

"The countess!" gasped Sterngarten, and Jamison cried, "She will never ride with us again if we allow her crown to be stolen!" And in a tumble of uniformed limbs the two men went running off down the coach.

What they hoped to do against the Queen of Dreams herself I could not fathom, but from the expression on Felpz's face I guessed he foresaw some dire fate. Taking a step back from the door he angled himself down the train—towards the countess's compartment—and holding the fiddle high above his head he spoke, with perfect composure and gravity:

"Grimbald, if you do not take your fiddle back *this instant* so help me I will . . . I will *feed it to the Arkengal.*"

Another blur of blue and black, a puff of smoke and a wriggle of hair, and Grimbald was standing directly in front of Felpz. There was a thin circlet of silver set with glimmering pearls and glinting stones tucked crookedly amongst her dark curls, and though she stood up straight the highest of these barely cleared Felpz's chest.

"You wouldn't," she hissed.

"I would," Felpz whispered back.

Grimbald snorted. "You're no fun. Who put ice in your bed this night?"

"And I'll take the countess's coronet back," Felpz said, extending a hand.

Grimbald glared up at Felpz, and for a moment I held my breath, certain something unexpected and awful would befall him.

Then Grimbald laughed. Not her eerie, multi-voice cacophony, but a simple, good-natured laugh.

"It's not *hers*, though," she said. "It was given to her by a not very nice man who stole it from a princess of Carndül. I'm just *returning* it."

"Then why are you wearing it?" Felpz asked tiredly.

"Because!" said Grimbald, raising a hand, one finger extended. "I *need* both my hands . . . to *play* with!" And with these words she reached out, and though Felpz was holding the fiddle high above his head, she somehow managed to snatch it from his hand.

Felpz let his arm drop in relief, just as Jamison and Sterngarten came bursting back into the dining coach. A shrill cry from behind them heralded the appearance of the countess, and the stunned Cappofazis found themselves pushed aside by the wiry little woman.

"*You!* I'll have your neck, you blue, thieving *tart!*" cried the countess, red in the face and bristling with anger.

Felpz turned a truly horrified expression upon the woman, but Grimbald only smiled. Slapping her hip with one hand, she tucked the belly of the fiddle—now quiet and docile—under her chin, and drew a bow out of thin air.

"Dreams, my little lady lord," she said. "Get too deep in them, and you can lose things. But consider it payment—and a bargain at that—for the violin performance you were so set on having! And never say Grimbald takes without giving *back!* You've heard my fiddle whine, and you've heard it moan, but count yourselves among the lucky few to have ever heard it *sing.*"

She raised her bow. Felpz nearly tripped over his own feet as he darted back to the train, half stepping onto the running board.

"What do we do?" I whispered to my friend.

"The only thing one can do when Grimbald plays," he said with a wry grin. "*Listen.*"

"You can also *dance!*" Grimbald called, beginning to tap out a beat with the tip of her bow. "*I* intend to!"

It should not, by rights, have been possible for that stringless fiddle with a gaping mouth full of teeth to make a sound—yet in the way of that strange place it not only happened, but made perfect sense.

Grimbald drew her bow across the fiddle and it produced a deep, resonant chord—more akin to a 'cello than a violin—which hung in the air, vibrating, long after the melody had moved on. It swooped and soared, dipped and scattered into countless notes that fell on us like a gentle rain. Around her in the grass little balls of light winked into existence, and as she played they slowly rose and hung in the air around her, gently bobbing to the tune of the music.

And how shall I describe such music? It was not meant to *be* described, I think, but I can give my reader some idea of it by describing how it affected me.

It was the sort of music that stirred feelings of excitement and anticipation deep within my heart—similar to the feeling of sitting down with a good book. It put me in mind of dark, beautiful and mysterious places, of lonely towers where magical things lived, and vast cities underwater that spread out like a filigree of golden light.

At the same time it filled my limbs with a bright, white-hot energy, and without any conscious thought I found myself nodding and bouncing in place. I was appalled when I discovered this, until I noticed that everyone else in the train was doing likewise. Young Elzarino was fairly capering about, and his mother did nothing to stop him. The only person who seemed (literally) unmoved was Felpz, but I noticed how the knuckles of his hand, where he gripped the doorframe, had gone white, and I guessed it was taking an immense effort to hold himself still.

Out in the field, under the huge ivory moon—which seemed to have gotten bigger while Grimbald played—the cloud of lights had risen into the air and begun swirling around her. She laughed and threw up her leg, beginning to stamp and kick even as she played. Her black dress swirled and her hair twisted out, catching the orbs of light like dew in a spider's web.

The music grew faster and faster, the visions it conjured swimming before my eyes, and at a certain point Grimbald tossed her fiddle and bow clean into the air, where they hung suspended, playing themselves as if by some invisible hand. Meanwhile, on the ground, Grimbald began to twist and jump, her strange laughter joining in with the music.

At the sound of her laugh, the land began to change. The moon re-treated, growing paler, and the sky grew darker, darker, until it was al-most pitch-black. Columns of darkness erupted from the sea of green grass, putting out thorns and bushy leaves. The smell of pine sap and oak, wet moss and earth overpowered the gentle scents of Dream, yet still I could see Grimbald—she seemed to occupy a separate level of reality from the dark forest springing up all around us—dancing and laughing, her violin playing itself in the air above her head.

"What is she *doing?*" I hissed at Felpz.

Felpz groaned, looking a little green. "She is sending us *back*," he said. "I was *afraid* of this—who *knows* where we'll end up!"

His words were drowned out, however, as Grimbald took her fiddle back and changed the tune. Now the music was gently receding, the tempo slowing, but her laugh remained.

One of her laughing voices spoke then, and its words wove in and out of the laughter like a strain of music.

"*Dreams take and leave you, little earthlings,*" said the voice. "*Be-fore the beginning, and after the end, Dream will have you. Go out, go out, go out into the day. But you will come back, come back, night after night, until the great endless night swallows you all. Dream will have you, before the beginning, and after the end.*"

And when the voice had finished speaking I found I could no longer see Grimbald, or her fiddle, or the moon, or the distant mountains—and the sea of blue-green grass had been replaced by an impenetrable forest, dark and damp and smelling sharply of sap and moss.

I felt myself come awake then, the mist clearing from before my eyes, and I realized the music had ended—it only echoed like a fading mem-ory in my head—to be replaced with the real sound of crickets in a wet wood at night. Soon these noises were joined by a clamor of voices as my fellow passengers realized what happened—and that we had *still* not been returned to our proper place.

"Now this," said Felpz tiredly. "*This* is what I was afraid of. Do your best to calm them down, won't you Corianne? And I will see about divining where in the world we are."

Despite Felpz's doubts, and as my readers no doubt remember, it turned out we were still in Elgany—a mere forty miles from the nearest train tracks. We were also, however, deep in the Hexenwald Forest, with no conventional way of obtaining help. It might have evolved into some-thing terribly ugly had not Felpz expedited our rescue by sending an obliging owl to the nearest village with a message. The bird returned at the first light of dawn, bringing with it a stout Elgan matron on a broomstick. Apparently there was no pre-existing task force devoted to putting wayward trains back on their tracks, but after some consul-tation with the staff of the train it was decided the witch would muster her colleagues, and return with a means to airlift the passengers to her village—from whence coaches could be arranged to rejoin them with the Rotgreif Express.

Sadly, I was not present for this spectacle—though I heard it involved several enchanted hot-air balloons and was most impressive—for Felpz and I left as soon as the witch returned at the head of a flock of reinforcements.

This was in the early afternoon, however, and we waited out the morning—after an improvised breakfast—by keeping the Cappofazis company.

Mrs Cappofazi seemed understandably contrite, but her son was downright despondent.

"What shall become of us now?" he moaned, propping his elbows on the window of their compartment and staring out into the trees. "I thought I was an excellent *violinista*, but it was the instrument all along, not me."

"Not necessarily," Felpz said, crossing his legs and folding his hands over his knees. He leaned back against the headrest, his eyes closed. "Did you have a dream, Signor Cappofazi? Any ambition of your own?"

The boy drew his eyes away from the window and frowned at Felpz. "Dreams? Yes, I dreamed of making music. Making music for people to dance to, sing to, weep to. But how am I to know that was me at all and not the *violino?*"

"Because of the nature of the Goblin's Fiddle," Felpz said, still with his eyes shut. "It does not put ideas into people's heads—merely brings out what is already there. Did you not read what was written on it? The runes were quite clear."

I nudged my friend gently with my elbow. "Not all of us are as astute as you in those matters," I reminded him.

Felpz cracked an eye open at us, raised an eyebrow, and sighed. Lifting one hand he traced a pattern through the air as he spoke:

"*I am the Fiddle of Grimbald,*" he said. "Those are the big ones across its face. But if you read the fine print near the bottom, you'll find it says, *by the power of my voice, let dreams conquer all.* The fiddle is remarkably perceptive. If it brought something extraordinary out of you, Signor Cappofazi, it is only because there was something extraordinary within you to begin with. You've been given quite the leg up, really. And though you may find your natural talents lie along different lines than that of the violin, have no doubt that you are capable of remarkable things—magic fiddle or no."

"Do you really think she might have left her fiddle in that shop on *purpose?*" I asked him. "I mean, *anything* could have happened!"

"Precisely," said Felpz, closing his eyes once more. "That is one of the quirks of Grimbald—she revels in the unknown. In *possibility.* But is it not true of dreams as well? They intrude upon our ordered lives, show us possibilities we might never have thought of on our own, and

in time they vanish as we drag ourselves back to wakefulness—or when they have run their course. Is it not fitting, then, that an instrument of Dream should behave in a similar way?"

As none of our company could come up with a satisfactory answer to this question, the compartment fell into silence as the remainder of the morning dragged by.

The brigade of witches arrived just before one in the afternoon, and in the chaos and confusion of flying robes, voices yelling in Elgan, and the frantic passengers, Felpz took me by the elbow and led me off into the forest.

"I have every faith in *Frau* Schwarzstamm. She is quite a powerful and resourceful witch," he explained. "They have no real need of us anymore, and to be honest I am tired. I took the liberty of arranging for your luggage to meet us in Redling—I hope you don't mind—for I think we can make our own way home from here."

So it was that I missed the spectacle of the witches and their hot-air balloons, as Felpz and I walked through the Hexenwald Forest, our way truncated by Felpz's magic, until we reached Lundberge. There we caught the first train to Redling, upon which Felpz announced he was finished for the day and promptly fell asleep.

My readers will be glad to know the remainder of our journey passed in perfect peace, and the rescue efforts by the witches of Hexenwald were entirely successful—though I understand their largesse extended only to the crew, passengers and their effects; the train itself they left in the wood where Grimbald put it. It is still there, for all I know, the great green expanse of the Elgan forest having swallowed it up like the sea swallows a sunken ship.

As for Elzarino Cappofazi, he never made it to Redling. He turned around and went straight back to Milany, where he promptly gave up the violin and turned his hand instead to composing. Though there were some rough years early on, lately I hear he has been meeting with increasing success.

eleven

THE SILVER CHIMERA

For all the long years we spent living in close proximity, I seldom heard my friend, Mr Bouragner Felpz, voluntarily speak of events from his youth. The fact that his youth was shrouded in the mists of the distant past led me to imagine many reasons for this reticence: a distaste for dragging up events so long gone, sorrow at the memories of lost friends, or plain and simple forgetfulness. I never questioned his cause, however, nor asked him to share his memories, and I do believe this was one reason for the strength of our friendship. I did not even try to determine his exact age, though I guessed he had seen more centuries than many of us see decades. Just how many centuries I had no way of knowing, until one summer evening in the late 2320's, when to my surprise and excitement, he began to talk of King Arell.

It was brought on, prosaically enough, by a play we had seen that afternoon in which the nineteenth-century monarch had a supporting role. It was a good piece of dramatic fiction, performed by an enthusiastic group of actors in Griffinsgate Park, and the setting—open air with strong, slanting sunlight—had served the story perfectly. Afterwards, as we walked back through the long summer twilight, I could not stop singing its virtues. And as to one who has enjoyed something there is no greater delight than in sharing that joy with another, my happiness was punctured by Felpz's distinctly sour attitude; he walked in silence, barely responding to my words, with a pinched look on his face, as though he had bitten into a pear and found it a lemon instead.

"Whatever is the matter, my friend?" I asked him. "Did you not like the story?"

"The story was serviceable, with a predictable but satisfying ending," he allowed.

"Did you not like the actors?"

"The actors were delightful."

"The costumes, then? The choreography? Was there someone in the audience who distracted you?"

"The costumes were ingenious," Felpz said briskly. "The choreography was charming, and the audience singularly well behaved."

"Then what pebble has gotten into your shoe?" I asked. "For you look as though the characters had done nothing the whole time but insult your mother."

That at least caused his grimace to break as he let out an involuntary laugh. He quickly sobered again, however, his face settling into an expression of dissatisfied contemplation.

"It is nothing so much to do with the *play* but with *history,* and this country's blatant disrespect for the accuracy of the latter," he said.

"Felpz," I said, biting back my own annoyance. "It is a work of *fiction.* You can't expect the writers to slavishly serve events from over five hundred years ago."

"No, but I would have wished they had the decency to *respect* them. Respect them for what they *were,* not paint it over with pretty pastels."

"I'm afraid you've lost me," I admitted. "What *was* it that bothered you so?"

"Their choice of actor to play King Arell," he admitted at last, "looked *nothing* like him."

I found myself a little taken aback by this. First by the implication that Felpz had seen Arell the Great in life, and second by the sheer ridiculousness.

"Felpz," I said gently. "You cannot expect a modern actor to look exactly like a historical figure—or anyone else, for that matter."

"Nor do I," Felpz announced. "But there are characteristics, Corianne, that become intrinsically linked to one's person. Imagine, for example, if I were a character in a play and the director was thoughtless enough to cast someone with *blond* hair for the part. Why, it would be laughable. Bouragner Felpz does *not* have blond hair, save when it serves me as a disguise."

"Is *that* your problem?" I asked, for indeed the actor playing Arell had been a handsome, blond man. "Is it so important Arell not have yellow hair?"

"Goodness, *yes,*" sighed Felpz, his whole being seeming to shudder. "He had black hair. Black as coal and ink, *and*"—he raised a finger and wagged it at me—"his skin was not much lighter!"

This made my step falter, it came as such a surprise, but Felpz did not notice. Now he had begun, he seemed unable to stop.

"And he was not some willowy, graceful boy. It's true he was quite young when he was crowned, but he was already a head taller than me and twice as wide across the shoulders. Yet for all that he was gentle as a lamb, no malice in him, and his honesty was so blunt you could use it to hammer nails. There was a reason I simply handed my kingdom over to him when the time came."

If the first revelation had made my feet falter, this one nearly tripped me.

"You had a *kingdom*?" I stammered.

Felpz glanced down at me in vague surprise, as if confused why this should startle me. Then his face softened, and he smiled.

"Only a very small one, a long time ago. Many people did, in those days. Anyone with enough power, in one form or another, could take a piece of land and call him or herself monarch of it. And I had more power than most. I flatter myself I took to ruling out of concern for the people of my birth country, who I found beset by all manner of troubles. I'd even go so far as to say I improved things a little. In truth, however, I fear I was as intoxicated with power as any, and it wasn't until I met someone frighteningly sober that I realized what had happened to me. Then, in disgust, I threw away all the fine things I had acquired during my short reign, and might have thrown my magic away too had Arell not convinced me otherwise."

He fell silent, and I, holding my breath in anticipation of more, could barely contain an outburst of frustration.

We walked on, and I noticed Felpz was not shortening our journey by magic, as he was wont to do, but taking us the long way home, as though his legs were restless and needed the exercise. We were nearing our street at last when my patience was rewarded.

"He gave me a silver chimera, out of gratitude for my services," Felpz said, his voice quiet and his eyes distant, gazing off over the steep roofs of the city houses, with their fat, squat chimneys like pots, to some place beyond the pale pink-and-yellow sky. "A token, really, but a meaningful one. I wonder if I still have it." He fell silent again, and I resigned myself to wonder what story might lie behind this reference, but upon our return he spent the next two hours turning his study inside-out, searching for the elusive keepsake. And as he searched, he began to talk.

Settling myself innocently in a corner, I organized the detritus cast aside by the whirlwind that was my friend, and I listened.

"Of all the things he gave me, it was one people never mentioned. The importance was all between the two of us," he said, picking up where he had left off. "Do you know Arell's coat of arms? They are unlike any other Kyrish monarch—either before or after. Only his bear the chimera volant above the crown."

"I seem to remember something to that effect," said I, recalling with difficulty my knowledge of the Norumblanain dynasty. "It is because Arell owned a chimera, did he not?"

Felpz paused in his search to shoot me an arch look. "No, he did not own her. He never owned her. In fact, the whole point was that he did precisely the opposite. I see there are still some holes in your education that need filling, so make yourself comfortable; this may take a little time. Yes, you may take notes, if you must," he added, seeing my hands dart involuntarily for the pocket in which I kept my notebook and pen.

"It was in winter," Felpz began, leaning back on his heels and casting his eyes up to the ceiling, "some years after I ceded what authority I held over the northwestern corner of this country to King Arell. That much I remember clearly. It followed some unpleasant business with the half-dragon Machalion—he was my rival in many ways, and I believe a large part of my decision to hand over my power to Arell was so I wouldn't have to deal with *him* anymore—so it must have been some time during the eighteen-seventies. Yes, that seems about right. It was when Arell came to Kyremouth and began building what is now Kingstower. You may have seen illustrations or even photographs of it and know it as the towering monument that stands over the Kyre delta—part colossus, part lighthouse—signifying the northern extent of his country. When I arrived, however, on a muddy winter day so very long ago, that bustling city was still in its infancy, a collection of timber houses that had been hastily thrown together in advance of the king's court, and as likely to burn down as they were to get swept away in a mudslide. And the tower was two scaffolds tied together with string, a mere placeholder amongst the rush of buildings.

"I came out of a sort of morbid curiosity, if I came for any reason at all. I was in a very low state at the time; I had become disillusioned with things I once held in high esteem, and I still bore an emotional wound from the loss of Machalion. It is an odd thing, Corianne, how having some form of consistency in one's life—even if it is only the consistency of a rival—can provide a much needed anchor. My volatile relationship with Machalion had been such an anchor for the better part of the previous hundred years, and the loss of it left me adrift in a swiftly changing sea. Worse, I had become disgusted by my own magic, and took to excising it from my person—akin to an animal that develops a nervous habit of pulling out its own feathers or hair. As a result I was but a pale shade of myself, hardly recognizable, when a cold wind blew me into Kyremouth.

"I did not go down to the King's Docks, as they were called then, but stayed up on the western swell where the old village of Kyremouth—built sensibly of stone and populated by hardy fishermen—used to stand. Since wind and water magic were some of the few things that still felt clean and good to me, I quickly made myself useful as a weatherman, and once people grew to trust me enough, I was even allowed out on the boats. I pride myself that I never let a ship run afoul, nor by my workings did I cause anyone else trouble, and it seemed the people liked me for it—though I believe my habit of standing at the stern, in nothing but my tunic and short leggings, letting the frigid winter wind whip through me, was unsettling to them.

"It was by chance that I found myself on the King's Docks one day, having been attached to a boat whose duties brought her there. It turned out the crew's business would keep them all day, and I was given leave for the duration to take what joy from the new town as I could find.

"I did not expect to find much. The streets were all of mud and the buildings damp and cold. The population had been whittled into hard, sharp people who seldom smiled and went about their work with a grim determination which, though admirable, was not conducive to good humor. Finding the people unwelcoming I allowed myself to drift through the town, letting my feet choose which path to take. This eventually led me to the little headland where a patch of ground had been cordoned off, and the foundations of the Kingstower were just being laid.

"I wandered around the perimeter of this, taking in with dull curiosity the piles of timber under canvas sheets, the immense coils of ropes, and the shipments of stone which were slowly but steadily being carted in, and wondered at the audacity of the young king, who thought he could build a tower in such a place.

"Having satisfied my curiosity, I made to leave, only to find my way blocked by a huddle of people. These were no common townsfolk, nor were they my local seamen: two wore arms openly, and one was very tall and cloaked in a fine fur cape and hood. They appeared to be arguing over something, but I knew they could not help but notice me. This being the very last thing I desired, I dragged up some of my vestigial skill and attempted to slip by them in the form of a fine mist.

"It must have been a very poor attempt, for I had barely passed the group when the tall figure in the cloak reached out a hand and hooked me neatly by the elbow, causing the illusion to drop, and I found myself wheeled round to stare up into the great black, bearded face of none other than King Arell himself.

"How shall I describe him? None of the portraits do him justice. The best I can say is he looked like a polished, black stone that glowed faintly with a reddish blush. His hair, which had been a great black mane the last time I'd seen him, had been neatly plaited into countless rope-like braids which fell in a thick tumble around his face, disappearing into the collar of his cloak. Extraordinarily, his eyes, though they appeared as black as his skin, were in actuality an abyssal indigo, and sapphire sparks would flicker in them if the light was right. I could see those flecks of blue from where I stood gazing up at him, and found myself—as I believe many were—rendered immobile at the sight.

"'How now, it is the Purple Magician, is it not?' he said, his eyes widening in surprise. 'What winds have whipped you, mage? For you look closer to the lavandil than the iris.'

"In this I could not argue, for in my desolation even my color had weakened, my clothes bleached to the palest hues of mauve and

grey-lavender. Combined with my ragged appearance, it must have reminded Arell of that rare form of daffodil, sometimes called a lavandil,
that is pale lavender instead of gold, with a heavily serrated trumpet. In
response I could only shrug and nod toward the foundation of the tower.

"'The winds brought news, and I wished to see,' I told him simply,
wanting only to get away. His knights, whom I did not recognize, were
eyeing me suspiciously—and though I feared little from them, the last
thing I desired was to draw attention to myself, and attention I would
surely receive if I continued to hold that of the king.

"But Arell seemed particularly interested in me, and as I could not in
good grace run from him, I was forced to stand and suffer his piercing
gaze. Eventually he seemed to come to an internal decision, for he drew
back, putting his hands on his hips, and nodded to himself—causing his
beard to jut slightly.

"'Well, your eyes may be sated, lavandil, but it appears to me your
material appetite is still wanting. My cook has slaughtered a bullock this
morning, and we are having the tongue tonight. Join us, for I have a
matter I wish to discuss with you, and I would not inflict it upon you
with an empty stomach.'

"It is something I detest, Corianne, to be ordered about, but the spark
of irritation in my gut at the king's words was the first warm feeling I had
felt for a long time, and as he was my king besides, I could hardly refuse.
So I was obliged to send my boat home with a well-wishing spell, and
pushed my appearance into something less reminiscent of a vagabond
before presenting myself at the king's door ten minutes before the ap-
pointed time.

"I think it says something for the quality of man Arell was, that as his
newly arrived subjects were living in timber houses, so was he—though
his dwelling was, perforce, the largest and best-supplied. I remember I
was received with disconcerting familiarity, and shown with very little
fanfare into the main room where the king dined when receiving guests.
There a brave fire cast a glad warmth over me, and without thought I
went to it and warmed my chilled hands at its hearth.

"In time the two knights I had seen before arrived, along with a
white-haired man and—to my surprise—a small young woman with
curly dark hair and thick spectacles wired onto her face. These were
introduced as . . . oh dear, I cannot for the lives of me remember the
knights! Corein and Athelwood, I *think*. But I may have confused
their names with knights I met later. But the *man*, the man was Eutrus
Njoorüd, and the young woman his daughter Ottasca, and together they
served as the architects and chief engineers of Arell's ambitious tower.
You'll have heard of Dame Njoorüd—she went on to build a great many
interesting things in service to Arell—but this was still in the dawn of
her career, when she labored in the shadow of her aging father.

"I do not think any of them had much regard for me, though Master
Njoorüd had the good grace to be polite. His daughter, however, stared

rather, and the knights were downright cold. So it was a relief when the king arrived and I could distract myself with food.

"I do not believe I had eaten so much in a single sitting before. Though I entered the room with no great appetite—as food had lost much of its appeal—once I had a taste I found myself possessed of a great hunger, and ate as long as I was permitted. It was a curious aspect of etiquette in those days: one was not allowed to eat past the person who sat in the highest place of honor at the table. As this was almost invariably the person who was the best fed in other regards, it was the cause of some rather uncomfortable meals. In this instance, however, Arell seemed to sense my desperation, and kept calling for his, and therefore *our*, plates to be refilled. I wonder if we did not eat through the better half of that bullock by the end of the meal.

"'Now that I have you satisfied in a corporeal manner,' King Arell said when he at last called for the plates to be cleared. 'I desire your insight into a distressing matter that has recently arisen regarding the construction of my tower.'

"Regretfully I leaned back in my chair, reaching absently for a fold of my cloak—before remembering the cloth that had been supplied to me for that purpose, and used it to clean my face.

"'I am, as I swore, at your majesty's service,' I replied dutifully, though most of my being rebelled. 'As far as my powers can assist you.'

"Arell nodded, and gestured to Master Njoorüd, who in turn looked to his daughter, who drew from a satchel she carried at her side a long roll of parchment, which she spread upon the recently cleared table. It was on that parchment that I saw for the first time the completed Kingstower, impressive even as a sketch of ink upon a flat sheet. But it was to the foundation, anchored deep in the underlying bedrock, that young Njoorüd drew our attention.

"'This tower,' she explained in brief, clipped words. 'It is so high, and the winds so strong, we cannot build it as a rigid being. It would snap and break. So we look to trees, how they bend in the wind and spring back into shape. To support this, we need deep roots. Complicated. Much digging. Here is where we have problem.' She pointed with a thick, callused finger at the dark scheme comprising the bottom third of the paper.

"'The excavating team encountered a seam of rock,' Master Njoorüd took over. 'Harder and paler. Took many days to drill through, and when they had done so they discovered the space within riddled with cavities—some large enough for a man to walk through erect. At first we thought this a boon, but now it appears it came with a terrible price. Since these catacombs have been uncovered we have lost ten men—six to attacks of madness, and three to incapacitating injury, and one has disappeared completely. No sight, no sound, no sign of anything living we have found besides what we leave ourselves. We have determined it must be some demon living within the rock.'

"'I have many brave knights,' Arell said, with a glance at Corein and Athelwood. 'But none with experience hunting demons. Further, what proof have we that it is indeed a demon? I wish to know for certain, and I know I need a magician to tell me so. We would be grateful if you could lend us your expertise, so that we may see this matter reconciled.'

"'And if I find it is a demon?' I asked dryly, pulling the parchment toward me to get a closer look.

"'Then we shall have to build the tower somewhere else,' Arell said with a shrug. 'But I'll not uproot my charges without good reason. You must understand.'

"I did, too, though I did not love him for it. Despite his moderate words I knew that to refuse even such a polite request from the monarch would be tantamount to treason. Besides, if I did not go into those catacombs and flush out whatever was hiding within, the knights—not to mention Maid Njoorüd—would never forgive me. And although I did feel some small flush of curiosity, I confess my overall mood of apathy still held sway. But my king had expressed a wish, and it was my duty to grant it. So I inclined my head in acquiescence, and it was arranged I would be shown into the pit the following day.

"That day was pale, as I recall, with the sort of high, bright clouds that do nothing to dim the light of the sun. I saw little of it, however, for as soon as I had broken my fast I found Maid Njoorüd at my elbow, an unlit torch in one hand and a box of flints in the other.

"'As you requested,' she said, and I heard the misgiving in her voice.

"I took the tools and thanked her, for indeed I had asked for them. I did not like to say it was because I didn't trust my own magelight, however, and left her unspoken question hanging in the air behind me when I left.

"'Do you not wish to see the survivors?' the young woman asked me as we made the short walk through the town from the King's hall and up the knoll to the site of the tower.

"These days I would have leapt at the chance, of course, but back then I had less of a care for my work, and only wished to get the ordeal over with so that I would be left alone. I shook my head, therefore, and bade her lead me to the mouth of the tunnel where these unfortunate accidents had been occurring.

"This turned out to be many tunnels, for the foundation of the tower radiated eight passages from the main body—just a big, damp hole in the ground—and Maid Njoorüd explained how they had lost workers down all of them. I stood there, up to my ankles in mud, and tentatively pushed out a piece of my mind to probe the tunnels.

"At first they all seemed equally cold, dark, and damp, but the further I pushed the more I sensed something—so faint it was like the echo of a sound, or a taste at the tip of one's tongue. It put me in mind of something sharp and metallic, and strange beyond reckoning. Whatever was in those tunnels was like nothing I had seen before—and I had seen many things, even in those distant days.

"I took the torch and the flints and went down the tunnel where the echo seemed strongest, but I waited until I judged I was out of sight of Njoorüd's curious eyes before I summoned fire to it, with help from the flint.

"I cannot tell you how irritating it is, to one accustomed to the even, diffuse glow cast by magelight, to manage by the flaring and flickering glare of a torch. Every shadow so sharp and black it seemed to portend some evil beast, and moving with the faintest gust that disturbed the flame. It was so very irritating that I stopped, threw down the torch in disgust, and summoned up magelight for the first time in years. To my surprise, far from feeling like a thread pulling a boulder—as most magic had felt recently—it was as though the thread had been attached to a plug, and I had just uncorked it.

"One thing you must understand about magelight, Corianne, is that it is not simply *light*. It is *awareness*. To a non-magic user, that awareness is conveyed by light. But to the one doing the magic, the awareness can be cast much further, and by more subtle means.

"When I cast magelight, it radiated through the tunnels, bathing them not only in light, but also in my *awareness*. For a brilliant, glimmering moment I could see the entire network of tunnels laid out inside my mind, and what I saw astounded me.

"There were far more tunnels than shown on Njoorüd's map. There were tunnels that stretched out in directions no ordinary person could take, let alone see. From these twisted corridors breathed the stale smell of an ancient magic of a kind I had only encountered once before—in similar circumstances. It was a sobering realization that, whether by some arcane fortune or plain mad chance, King Arell had chosen as the site for his tower an ancient goblin grave.

"A thing you may not know about goblins, Corianne. They are in their way quite as magical as any elf or fairy, but at the same time perfectly unique. Their magic is the magic of stone, of darkness and of twisted space. They thrive where no other life thrives, deep beneath the surface of the earth. It is painful for them to walk under the open sky, which is why they are considered such hideous, unpleasant creatures: very few have seen them in their natural habitat. To a goblin, the surface and open air is as frightening as a deep dark pit is to us. And as we put our dead, and our prisoners, in holes in the ground, so do goblins place their dungeons and graves near the surface.

"As I stood in the dark and damp and sensed the old goblin tunnels stretching out around me, I assumed that this must be the latter, for it felt as though it had not been occupied in many a long year. Then, as I probed deeper, I noticed several odd features that set it apart from the goblin graves I'd seen in the past:

"There were no catacombs, no chambers where the dead could rest. Rather, all the passages led, by one twisting way or another, to a single chamber not far from the foundation of the tower. This chamber interested me, in that it appeared to have once been accessed by a single shaft that led down—to what I could only suppose would be the goblins' city—but that had been filled in with rock and gravel as far down as my magelight could reach.

"I was on the edge of an isolated flower of goblin architecture. Whether it had been abandoned because of its proximity to the surface or for some other reason I did not yet know.

"My natural curiosity, which had been rendered latent by my recent bout of apathy, came to the fore with a rush, and abandoning the now-useless torch, I set off down the goblin tunnels. These were both the material tunnels that Njoorüd's workers had discovered, and also the tunnels that stretched sideways, into the realm of space peculiar to goblins. From these I caught another taste of that strange, metallic magic, and with a little spiritual wriggling I was able to crawl along one of these twisted passages, feeling my way with one hand held out, forcing the magelight ahead of me.

"It was a good thing I did, for I encountered traps along the way. These were the sort clearly laid to deter intruders—but goblin intruders, for whom the darkness held no mystery. A human with a simple flaming branch had no hope of perceiving them, and judging by how many had been sprung, I guessed here was the reason for the injuries to Njoorüd's men. For although it had taken me some work to crawl into these tunnels on purpose, goblin architecture is so mercurial that it will sometimes lure humans into it rather than keep them out. I did not envy those poor people, who must have been quite lucky to escape with their lives.

"At last I came across a trap that had not been sprung, but *disabled.* This was surprising, since I doubted any ordinary human could have done such a thing. Then, upon closer examination, I discovered that the trap—which involved a nasty device like a spiked hammer—had been disabled from the *inside.* That is, from the direction of the single chamber with the filled-in shaft. To do so, someone must have come from that chamber, though how they could have reached it in the first place was a mystery.

"Edging my way around the trap, I was immediately struck by the metallic magic—this time no echo, but a full-on cacophony. It was so strong I had to pause and pull in much of my own magic that had been stretched out to feel my way ahead—as one might pull one's hand out of a bowl of hot water—and cower there until I could adjust to this new magic.

"It is a curious thing, but when you have gone off magic for a long time, when you return you are much more sensitive. Coming on so strongly, and after such a sabbatical, I was nearly overcome. I had to call upon some little-used skills to make a sort of magical bandage for myself, so I could continue down the tunnel.

"You may be surprised that I still wanted to explore: in truth I wonder at it myself now I look back. I can only imagine I was overcome with curiosity. That, and I got the distinct impression from the tone of this new magic—as it were—that whatever owned it was in great distress. And like someone hearing the cry of a wounded animal I followed it to its source."

Felpz, who had so far been relating this story from a rather uncomfortable position on the floor, paused long enough to stretch, and crawled over to his bench where he settled himself again. He idly lifted the lid of a nearby box, then let it fall closed with a sigh.

"What I found, there in the dark . . . was like nothing I had yet seen or have seen since. The size of a small dragon it was, with a tail that lay in coils, filling most of the chamber. It had no hind legs, but two powerful arms like that of a lion and a pair of feathered wings folded tight along its back. You will laugh when you hear this, but at first I thought it had no head! Then, as I approached further into the room, there was a twitch along its neck and I found a wide, feline face assessing me from the midst of a bushy mane of silver hair.

"I say feline, but it was like no ordinary cat. Not even the exotic beasts from Saffara or the Beranicas. It had a wide forehead in the center of which was set a gleaming blue stone, piercing blue eyes, and behind each ear, partly buried in its mane, was a tightly curling horn—like that of a ram. It was, from the tip of its fine whiskers to the end of its scaled tail, a brilliant, gleaming silver—shimmering with scattered reflections in my weak magelight.

"I think we stood for some time, each regarding the other with apprehension, when the silence was broken by a soft moan from the center of its coiled tail.

"This was no half-heard sound of magic, but a real noise from a very real human throat, and it galvanized me into action. Now I looked, I could see a swatch of rumpled brown hair and a thick, pink arm protruding from the coils, and as I came forward I saw it move, feebly.

"No sooner had I begun to approach, however, than the creature withdrew further, the end of its tail snaking around to come up in front of me, blocking my way. There was a further disturbance of the mane around the creature's face, and two more heads appeared. Poking out from the mass of silvery fur, they trained two more pairs of sapphire eyes upon me. I regret to say that it wasn't until I saw these two other heads that I recognized the creature for what it was: a *chimera*, one of the many species of extraordinary animals best known for the Crowan monster whose name they now bear. This chimera had the heads of an owl and a feathered snake, in addition to the horned lion, the former two being significantly smaller, and mostly hidden in the mane.

"Now all three heads were alert and staring at me, and that alone gave me pause. Then the beast spoke to me, in words audible to my ears, but strangely distorted by the fact that they came from three different mouths at once.

"'*No harm,*' said the chimera in a strange chorus. The snake hissed, the lion growled, and the owl—who was the clearest—hooted softly.

"'I assure you I mean anything but harm,' I replied at once, for aside from the creature's remarkable size, I could sense its huge, metallic magic piling up around it, and knew I would be hard pressed to overpower such a beast even at my peak condition, and in my weakened state I had no wish to offend it.

"'I come on behalf of the king above ground, whose subject you appear to hold. He wishes him returned and begs you not to torment the workers whose business it is to build his tower here.'

"'*No torment,*' replied the triple voice. '*No harm. Men come. Men go. They run from me. Sometimes they fall. Their lights fail. This one is hurt. I help him. I heal. No harm.*'

"'That is most generous of you,' I assured the chimera, daring to take another step. The tail's end—which was decorated with a small frill of stiff, mirror-like feathers—did not move to block me further, nor did it get out of my way. 'However, if you would allow me, I will take responsibility for him. He is a creature of the surface, and it will not do to keep him here. Allow me to return him to his king.'

"'*No harm,*' repeated the chimera, its coils tightening protectively around the poor man. '*So alone. So long. No one to care for. No one to comfort. No wish to be alone.*'

"'Am I to understand you are trapped here?' I asked, peering around the end of the tail. The three faces still looked at me, and in each I read clearly such a sadness that I was taken aback. This was no sinister monster but a much misunderstood creature.

"'*Not trapped. Never trapped. Imprisoned. Goblins found me. Goblins hatched me. But I grew too big. Too fierce. They built this dungeon for me, buried me next to the sky, and forgot about me.*'

"'You mean to say you have never seen the open air?' I asked in surprise, eyeing the chimera's wings.

"'*I see things in my dreams. Everything is open and blue. No walls, no stone, no darkness . . . but big white stones that do not hurt, but swallow you. They shed tears upon a faraway land.*'

"'Then you were clearly not meant to live your life underground!' I cried, horrified to think of how long the chimera must have spent in its prison, longing for a sky that was so relatively near. 'Come,' I told it. 'Follow me, and I will lead you out of this maze. For the men you see have breached your prison wall, and the way to the sky is clear for you. We may bring your foundling, as well, and you may return him to the king yourself.'

"'*I do not like kings,*' said the chimera gravely. '*Kings chain you. Kings keep you. Kings throw you in prison when they do not want you any more.*'

"'This king is different,' I said, and realized as I did so that I would be put to some serious difficulty if what I said was not true—for I knew I could not let Arell keep this beast as a pet.

"'*How do you know this? What are my reasons for trust? Who are you?*'

"I admit these questions unsettled me somewhat. I had long since given up the use of my name—it having become associated with all the most distasteful forms of my magic—and though I was becoming more comfortable using magic again, I was not yet ready to reclaim that name. So I fell back on a title that was equally my own, but which held no such connotations.

"'I am the Purple Magician,' I told the chimera. 'And I swear upon my color you will have the sky, with no king to hold you.'

"At last the chimera lowered its tail, and walking forward on its arms, it peered at me with all six of its eyes. It inhaled, deeply, and I felt a little of my magic get sucked in, turned over, and then blown back at me. It was an odd feeling; like hearing an echo of your own voice and not recognizing it right away. I was surprised at how strange and terrifying it felt, and realized why such a powerful creature would recoil from me at first sight. That, and I began to believe that the chimera did not quite understand the extent of its own powers.

"'*This is not a color I am familiar with,*' admitted the chimera. '*But you smell of wind and sky-tears and something open and . . . wet.*'

"'The sea,' I offered.

"'*The sea . . .* ' echoed the chimera. "'*It sounds like something that should be seen. Lead me, purple man. Lead me to the sea.*'

"This was, more or less, what I proceeded to do. It was something of a task getting the chimera out of the goblin tunnels—they had been built to keep it in, after all. For its part, the chimera insisted on carrying the unconscious man in its arms while it slithered behind me like a giant, gleaming snake. It was slow going, since I had to stop several times to pull the tunnels into place so we could pass through. When I found myself in the human excavation once again, it was only to lose the chimera somewhere in the dark. I had to go back in, where I found it searching for me in distress. At the last I led it out of the tunnels, one hand clamped firmly on a silver elbow. Passing into Njoorüd's corridor felt like pulling a great weight uphill, until the chimera suddenly figured out what was happening, and then it was all I could do to keep up as it surged forward, slithering easily over the uneven ground.

"We very nearly got lost all over again, in the perfectly mundane way one does in a dark pit underground, but eventually I caught sight of a pale glow that could only be daylight, and made for it with relief.

"We emerged into a crowd of expectant faces—royal knights, workers, and townsfolk alike—who gave out a collective gasp as the chimera slunk from the dark tunnel into the comparatively blinding light of day. For not only were they presented with the sight of a strange and frightening beast, but even in the weak sunlight the chimera shone and glittered, the scales on its long tail reflecting the light like countless, tiny mirrors, and its wings flashing sharply. Had it been an ordinary animal such as a dog or horse it would have been just as blinding. As it was our audience was hard put to stare as much as they wanted while at the same time shielding their eyes from the glare.

"At sight of the crowd I felt the chimera tense at my side, and I got ready to cast a stiff stasis over the lot of them should they turn hostile. When nobody so much as moved, however, I sought out Master Njoorüd and beckoned to him.

"'I have found your missing man,' I told him as he approached, with many fearful glances at the chimera—in whose arms the unconscious man still lay. 'Your demon, as it turns out, is nothing of the kind. Any misfortune that befell your men in the tunnels below was due to an unhappy misunderstanding. Now take this poor fellow and see he's properly cared for, and let your king know I have returned.'

"'There is no need for that,' came the prompt reply, and I looked up to find Arell standing on the lip of the pit, his hands resting on his hips, and surveying the scene with an unreadable expression. The crowd cleared instantly, dragging Njoorüd and the unconscious man away with them. I saw the chimera watch them go with concern, so I put a hand on its shoulder and led the way up the ramp to where the king waited.

"I shall not soon forget that sight, for the two of them—Arell with his impenetrable black face and rich robes of red and ochre, and the chimera with its gleaming silver pelt and glittering scales—made quite a contrast as they stood regarding one another. Though Arell held himself with all the regality of his office, the chimera seemed imbued with its own alien majesty, and in truth I thought they looked like two monarchs meeting for the first time—and I held my breath, knowing from personal experience how easily such meetings could turn sour.

"But then Arell laughed mightily, his white teeth flashing, and held out a hand to the chimera, which it took gingerly in one paw, and for a moment black skin and silver fur were joined in a small embrace. Then Arell was turning to me and saying:

"'There must be some good story behind this, lavandil, for never in all my years have I seen such a creature.'

"Briefly I relayed my experiences in the tunnels, my discovery of the old goblin dungeon, and the chimera within.

"'*He leads me to the sea,*' the chimera explained, when I was finished.

"To his credit Arell hardly batted an eye at hearing the chimera's triple voice, and nodded firmly. 'Though you hardly need a guide at this point, my lady. Take your wings and let them bear you north, and you shall find all the sea—why as far as you *can* see," and he laughed in that expansive, good-humored way which had already endeared him to so many.

"And the chimera—who I believe had no gender as you or I would understand it, but because of Arell's words people took to thinking of as female—shook out her blade-like wings, which when unfurled stretched clear across the pit and cast a diffuse shadow over us, and beat them experimentally against the air. She coiled her long, snakelike body beneath her, and then sprang upwards, her wings a blur, flashing in the distant sunlight.

"She made quite a sight climbing up into the sky, glinting like a mirror, and as she streaked towards the ocean a ragged cheer went up from the crowd still clumped around the pit. I saw her as a flash of silver on the grey-and-white sky, and then she was lost to my vision.

"And that, Corianne, would have made a perfect end to my little escapade, but as it turned out, it was nothing of the kind. For the chimera came back that very evening, exhausted and hungry, and Arell took one look at his panicked knights and put *me* in charge of her.

"I will not bore you with the details of feeding and tending to a large and very magical animal—she ate a great deal, which made her ill, and it wasn't until I figured out she fed on energy directly, as dragons do, that she recovered. I took her on long walks over the headlands, where she could feed on the buffeting wind, and down on the beaches where she delighted in the breaking waves. She grew stronger daily, and after about a month, she took to assisting Arell's men in placing some of the larger stones in the tower—whose construction, no longer delayed, was well underway by this time.

"Eventually, however, she tired of this, and would spend more and more of her time flying around the coast. Then one night she did not return—though we continued to see her in the distance, keeping an eye on the construction of the tower. When at last this was complete the sightings became fewer and fewer, until finally she was seen no more. I do not doubt she is still out there—chimeras like herself are not vulnerable to the ravages of time as mundane animals are—and you can find her likeness all over Kyremouth even today. Most noticeably, a coiled chimera, wings outstretched as if to take flight, rests above the main entrance to the Kingstower—though only a few locals still remember the reason for it.

"As for myself, the whole enterprise took up a year of my life and culminated with King Arell sitting me down one evening, after the chimera had vanished and the tower had been completed, and saying to me in his blunt, honest way;

"'This affair with the silver chimera, lavandil, it brings to light a shortcoming I have when it comes to the specialities of my staff. That is to say, I have no one I can trust in matters relating to magic and its peripheral troubles—the succoring of ill chimeras, for example. I therefore offer you the position of Royal Magician to the Monarchs of Kyreland for however long you deem fit to hold the title.'

"I stared back at the man in horror. I'm afraid all my propriety deserted me, and I burst out at once: 'No, my king, I beg do not ask that of me. It is everything I despise about magic, and precisely what I wished to avoid by handing my kingdom over to you.'

"'Your reluctance does you credit, lavandil,' Arell replied good-naturedly. 'It is one of the traits I find renders you most desirable as an advisor. But if you worry about being given too much nobility and power, perhaps you would consent to advising me personally on matters of magic that pertain to my dominion? You would hold no rank, no title, save that of friend to the King. Though I would ask you to choose a name by which I and others might address you.'

"This gave me some pause. I liked Arell, and that he was willing to compromise on the nature of my service spoke to how highly he regarded me. It felt mean spirited, and a bit cowardly, to refuse.

"I would not give him my name, however. I was not ready to be Bouragner d'Felpass again—in many respects I doubt I will ever be.

"'My king,' I said, 'I do not think I can improve upon the name you have yourself given me. Call me Lavandil, and let that satisfy all wants."

Felpz turned and looked at me then, and I saw a mischievous smile spreading across his face at what must have been a flabbergasted expression on my own.

"Do not tell me you didn't put the pieces together before now?" he asked.

"*You* were Lord Lavandil?" I cried, my mind finally connecting the meaning of that curious name I had so often seen linked to Arell's in my history books. To think that I had been learning about my friend as child—by reading about an historical figure I thought at the time to be long since as dead as the king he served—came as such a surprise it rendered me momentarily speechless.

"Ah yes, the *lord* bit came later," Felpz said, wrinkling his nose in distaste. "A common man with the ear of the king would not do. They made me take a title, eventually, when one was freed up by the execution of an earl. I promptly gave management of the estate over to the late man's poor daughter, and I understand her family keeps it still. There was some bother over that, as women holding titles in their own right was a new thing at the time, but it allowed me to be styled as Lord Lavandil, Magician Commander, and people were satisfied with that—if not exactly happy. Great griffins, that reminds me!"

My friend sprang from his seat at the bench and darted out the door.

Unfolding myself more slowly, I followed him, only to find he had disappeared into my bedroom of all places.

"Felpz!" I cried in protest as I entered to find him pulling aside my nightstand to look behind it. The blue demonic lamp—the result of a hair-raising adventure I had endured when still a maid—rocked precariously as Felpz threw himself to the floor and felt around under my bed. Putting a hand out to steady it I bent over the purple bulge of his back to peer at him. "Felpz, what in the heavens are you doing?"

"This room used to be my second storeroom, before I took you as my ward," Felpz explained. He had thrust one arm completely under my bed, turning his head sideways so part of his shoulder could follow. "Not everything got moved during the preparations, and I just remembered I left Lavandil's paraphernalia in a box . . . *here.*"

He removed the shoulder and arm, now brown with dust, at the end of which was clasped an old leather case. Cracked and fairly matted with dust, it was no wonder I had never noticed it before—it must have been jammed right into the far corner under my bed. It had no visible seam or lock, but after Felpz had wiped off the worst of the dust (with a handkerchief I handed him before he could use his sleeve) he blew on it, stroked his fingers along the sides, and the box sprang open.

I caught a glimpse of a fold of pale, grey-lavender cloth before that was thrown aside. There was a heavy clunk as a tarnished metal chain followed it, then a brocaded belt, and a small ornamental knife. I scooped these gently off the floor and marveled at them. They were true examples of exquisite, rich Arellian fashion. The knife's hilt was set with stones and elegantly cast in the form of a griffin, while the sheath was similarly encrusted. The brocaded belt was sorely worn, but enough pearls still clung to their threads that I could discern the delicate pattern of swoops and spirals they must have once formed. And the metal chain, upon closer inspection, turned out to be heavily tarnished silver and quite delicate—the sort of chain that was worn by Norumblanain nobles over their shoulders as signs of office.

"Felpz," I said in quiet awe. "These are your regalia . . . "

"Signs of indentured servitude," Felpz muttered, pulling out a crumbling velvet bag and dumping the contents into his palm. "Arell knew exactly what he was doing when he gave his councilors those chains. The man had a wicked sense of humor under all that—*ha!*" he broke off, having cast aside a battered signet ring (which I hastily caught up and added to the pile in front of me), and now he held, dangling by a thin chain from his fingers, a single pendant half the size of my thumb.

At first it looked like a misshapen lump of tarnished silver, but then Felpz rubbed it on his cuff, and it came back flashing and brilliant.

"There you are," Felpz said, as if greeting an old friend, and offered the little figure to me.

I found myself holding a tiny replica of the chimera Felpz had described—with a long, serpentine body, the chest and forelegs of a lion, and three heads: a maned lion with an owl and feathered snake at its sides. The chimera had been posed with its tail cast in an arc, framing its outstretched wings, the tip meeting with its torso and blending into it somewhat, from the wear. Three tiny sapphires glittered in the lion's face, but only dark holes showed where the eyes of the owl and snake had once been. Though not battered, I could tell the pendant had seen much wear, and had at one time been well loved.

"It is very beautiful," I said, handing the chimera back with reverence.

Felpz took the pendant by the chain and held it up to the light—which, since it came from my demonic blue lamp, made the silver glimmer and the sapphires shine even brighter.

"He gave this to me near the end," Felpz said, softly now, almost as if speaking to himself. "We had something of a falling out, as can happen in any relationship. He, being the better man, had the sense to let me go gracefully. He gave me this chimera as a symbol: just as he had set the chimera free, so I was free as well." Felpz got an odd look on his face then, a strange mixture of sadness, anger, and longing. It was only visible because he was holding the little pendant up to the light, and his face was raised to gaze upon it. It was such a private expression that I looked away, feeling as though I had accidentally caught a glimpse of a personal memory that I was not meant to see.

"It was an immensely handsome gesture," Felpz went on, his voice sounding more normal. "I was so touched by it that I came right back and stayed with him until the end of his life. It got a bit rough there at the end, but I am glad I stayed. It would have been selfish of me not to."

When I again chanced to look at him, my friend had lowered his hand and was now gazing around my room, as if he had forgotten where he was. He took in the curtains, the carpet beneath us, my own neatly made bed, the writing desk overflowing with journals and loose papers, and the overstuffed bookshelf. His gaze lingered a while on the eerie blue lamp, and I saw a small smile budding at the corner of his mouth.

"Time is such an odd thing," he said after a while. "There is at once too much of it, and not enough. I've heard it postulated that, to an immortal, life can become one long, dull road with no end in sight. That we become *weary* of life; worn out by it." He snorted. "It has been, to my certain knowledge, only *mortals* who say things like this. I cannot tell you, Corianne, how precious I find my continued existence. Indeed there are times when, far from being overwhelmed by the vastness of eternity, I wish to *stay*. To have a small eternity contained in a single moment. But the river of time moves ever onward, and though we may ride it for different lengths, we must all ride it just the same."

He smiled at me, and shrugged. Then he gathered up all that remained of Lord Lavandil and put it back in the box, which in turn he took into his study, and I never saw it again.

The silver chimera, however, he hung by its chain over the lamp on his desk, where it glimmered and glittered, even in the faintest light. And to my knowledge, it hangs there still.

twelve

THE HIDDEN ROAD

PEOPLE MAY DISAGREE, but I still hold that if it had not been for Tida Hammin's cat the Shatterthorn children would never have been found. For if Tida had not missed her cat, she would not have asked me to help her find it, and if we had not gone looking for it we would never have gotten lost ourselves, and Felpz would not have come looking for *us* and so been able to fix the whole mess once and for all.

But I am getting ahead of myself; allow me to begin properly.

In the spring of 2331 the city of Redling became obsessed with the mysterious disappearance of Pelim and Jora Shatterthorn. I do not know how many of my readers will remember the daily newspaper articles depicting the plight of their poor parents (who were not really so poor, as it happened, which was why the case received such extraordinary attention) and the various frauds that had surfaced claiming to have found the children. Much of this has faded with the passage of time, but I well remember how I could not walk a single block without being confronted by some glaring headline regarding the missing children.

There were in truth three children missing, but as the third was Nandy Matcher, the gardener's daughter, she was often left out of the picture. Though I am certain her parents were just as distraught over her disappearance, they had not the wealth to offer attractive rewards for her return, and this probably contributed to the lack of mention in the press. The fact was, however, that Pelim Shatterthorn, his younger sister Jora, and Nandy Matcher had all gone missing from the private garden of the Shatterthorn house in Regina Square sometime in the afternoon of

April 7th, where they had been seen playing up until midday. The siblings were missed when they didn't answer the call for tea, and Nandy shortly thereafter. A thorough search of the garden yielded no clue as to their means of escape. There was no sign that they had scaled the enormous stone wall that enclosed the place, nor that anyone had forced entry to the yard and stolen them away. Anyone who had been through Regina Square that day was caught and questioned, but no one had seen the children—nor did anyone seem suspicious. The police mages could find no trace of any malevolent magic, and there had been no sight nor sound of the children since.

It had been a fortnight, and I was beginning to despair of seeing an answer to the mystery, when I received a note from my friend Tida Hammin that put the whole matter out of my head.

Tida Hammin and I had met some years previous, on rather more uncertain ground, during events that may or may not resolve themselves into a proper story. If they ever do then be sure you will hear of it, but all that matters to *this* story is that Tida and I had been fast friends for the last five years, often exchanged notes and, since she had moved to Redling, personal visits. She lived in a modest house just below Regina Square, and so had been my main line of real information after the children vanished. This latest note, however, was about something else entirely.

> *Dearest Corianne,* [it read] *I do so regret bothering you about this, as it is such a little thing on the surface—but you have always been a good and sympathetic person so I am sure you will understand. It is about Carbuncle—you remember, my old tabby?—who has of late taken to sitting in a wild bower in the garden and will not come when called—not even at dinnertime! I have had to go in and catch him the last two nights, and it was the most unnerving experience. I know I cannot do it again, alone, and I beg that you accompany me. It sounds ridiculous when put this way, but I trust you will understand when you see things for yourself.*

This was a puzzling letter indeed, since I knew Tida to be a sensible, well-grounded woman. But she was fond of her cats—especially Carbuncle, who had accompanied her from Riddlemoor—and any time he went missing or took an ill turn she was overly distraught.

As it was almost dinner time I decided to pay my friend a visit, and after scribbling a note to Felpz telling him of my whereabouts, I set off into the sunny spring evening.

On my way it occurred to me to wonder why she didn't simply have Bilts, her man about the house, take the cat in, and I put this question to the young man when he opened the door for me.

"I do more damage than I'm worth, ma'am," he replied diffidently as he took my hat and coat and hung them in Tida's little hall. "Carbuncle and I don't get on, I'm afraid."

I didn't ask why, for I knew Carbuncle to be a shaggy, scruffy old tom the color of bright fall leaves, while Bilts was a scrupulously clean, pale young man with neat dark hair combed severely back over his head. He had the air of a much older man trapped in a young body, but there was a pretentious quality to this air that convinced me it was simply a quirk of his character, and not—as I had chance to witness firsthand in my friend Abharus—the actual case.

Tida Hammin must have heard our exchange from the other room, for she came bursting in full of her usual life and enthusiasm. She had always been a large woman, and the cramped quarters of Redling had served only to intensify her spirit—not to diminish it. In stature she was rather taller than I, with buttery yellow hair that lay in piles above her frank, open face. Fierce in pursuit of anything that caught her formidable attention, she was nonetheless a staunch and loyal friend.

"Corianne!" she greeted me. "What a relief—I had hoped you would come. I am terribly sorry to be such a bother but he does *insist* upon hiding himself out there, and when you see the bower you will understand why I wrote you. I'm sure you won't have any problems, but you'll understand why it put me off. Come, let us waste no time."

So speaking she led me through the little house and into the tiny garden that was enclosed behind it. Here the scent of roses was almost overpowering, and the dying sunlight lit the motes of the garden oak's pollen golden as they hung in the air.

The bower Tida had mentioned in her letter was immediately obvious: it took up an entire corner of the little enclosure, and consisted of thorny vines but also long grass. It looked like a sophisticated bird's nest, grown so big that a person might squeeze inside. I recalled Tida telling me excitedly of it when she first moved in, but I had never paid it much attention.

Now, in the growing twilight, I could see why my friend was reluctant to enter: the air that breathed out of the frame was sharp and cool and strangely foreign, and it was very dark within. Not so dark that I could not make out the fluffy orange shape of Carbuncle where he'd curled up in the middle of it—out of arm's reach—but dark enough that the pattern of the vines and grasses that made the bower took on sinister shapes with a little help from one's imagination.

"Come now, Tida, this is not so bad," I told my friend, but gently. "Here, you go in for him—he knows you, after all—and I shall keep your back."

"I am a great silly, I know," Tida admitted as she hiked up her skirts to enter the bower, but she ducked inside with no more prompting from me.

True to my word I followed her in, careful to avoid the stray vines she left swinging in her wake.

I heard her murmuring to the cat, and there was a plaintive meow, and then Tida cried, "Oh no, Carbuncle! Carbuncle, come back! Can you catch him, Corianne?"

Instinctively I thrust my hands down to block the cat's path, but nothing came around the bulk of Tida Hammin, and instead we only moved deeper into the bower.

I was bent double, and could still see the round, golden opening by which we had entered, when Tida turned abruptly to her right, stood up, and gasped. I came around next to her, and saw why at once.

The vines of the bower had given way to cold stone, streaked with moss. There was a dark evening sky above us, and before us, running between the two high, stone walls, was a narrow, grass-covered path. A flash of orange in the dimness indicated where Carbuncle had just disappeared around a corner.

"We must be between the houses," Tida whispered to me. "I had no idea the bower led so far . . . " and she moved off in the direction of her cat.

I followed, but I was not so confident as she. In fact, the whole turn had struck me as most unusual, and it was only glancing back through the tunnel of vines and seeing the other end, still illuminated, that gave me the assurance to go on.

We came upon Carbuncle rolling in a patch of mint that grew along the path, a few turns along. Speaking to him gently the whole time, Tida stroked his head and then scooped him up into her strong arms.

"He is almost more trouble than he's worth," she sighed, fitting him masterfully against her side as he made an attempt to escape. "Perhaps I shall have to keep him inside until we get the wall fixed. It would be a pity to lose that bower, but I simply can't have him running off like this."

I only nodded briskly and turned to leave. I was growing more and more uncomfortable on that narrow path, and the cold air that had first assaulted us when we entered the bower was becoming downright chilly.

We made our way back the way we had come, and it was with relief that I spied the tangle of vines which marked the entrance to the bower.

Relief that quickly turned cold in my stomach as I realized the vines were only growing up one side of the wall, and where there had been a tunnel, now there was solid stone.

"It must be farther on," Tida said, more hopeful than confident.

"No," I replied, and indicated the ground in front of the vines. There, two sets of footprints suddenly appeared in the soft grass, and came down the path towards us. They were our own tracks, unmistakably, and the way we had taken in would no longer lead us out.

To her credit, Tida did not say "But that is impossible!" or "How could this happen?" Our shared experiences had already introduced her to disturbing magic—were the reason she had asked for my aid in the first place.

What she did say, after a little thought, was this:

"Tis a funny thing to happen in the middle of Redling, don't you think? Seems a bit like Riddlemoor, only perhaps more like the stories

I heard about roads opening up out of nowhere and then closing again. Hidden roads, we called them, and if you knew their secrets they could take you anywhere. I wouldn't have been surprised to find one on the Riddlemoor, but I never expected to stumble upon one in the middle of the city!"

"Yes, but *are we* still in the middle of the city?" I asked, and pointed at the sky.

Something that had been bothering me about the place had finally crystallized as I realized that the sky was too blue. It was a deep, vivid, evening blue—almost violet—with a single star pinned in the middle of it. No sky like that had been seen over Redling since the invention of the coal fire, I thought, and now I got a chance to do a bit more thinking, I realized that the pervasive hum and clatter of the city was also eerily absent. Indeed the only sound—apart from that which we were making— was distant birdsong and the sigh of a gentle wind over the tops of the walls.

Tida looked around, clearly noticing the same things I had, and took a firmer grip on Carbuncle, while at the same time stroking him soothingly.

"That is most strange," she said. "Yet what can one expect from a magic path? Oh, I am such a fool! I see now why the bower frightened me so: it was because I always sensed that it was a much larger place than it seemed—and see, I was right, much good that does us. Well, what do you recommend we do now? It seems pointless to sit in one place to be rescued, as that place is no longer where we left it."

I had to admit she was right, but I was at a loss as to what we should do. *If Felpz were here,* I began to think, a trifle bitterly, and then realized that was what I always thought when problems arose that were beyond my capacity to solve. I had, in fact, been thinking it for most of my life, and in that moment it suddenly struck me as a silly thing for a woman in her seventh decade to be doing.

"Come, Tida," I said, striking off in the direction we had first gone when in search of Carbuncle. "Let us see where it leads, for it must certainly lead somewhere, and that somewhere might be a trifle more solid than this place.

Tida, now that the decision was out of her hands, fell in behind me agreeably, and together we renegotiated the twisting path between the high walls until the small path joined with a larger thoroughfare running between high, bushy hedges. This road was also green, being covered by thick, short grass and pudgy moss. A set of dark, cloven hoof prints ran down the center of it, and for lack of any better course, we followed them.

The sky above us remained the violet of evening, and the star, I noted with interest, never moved from the center of the strip visible above us. I took this as a sign that we were well and truly out of the natural world, and felt my nerves thrill anew.

Carbuncle was becoming more and more restless, and Tida grew tired of carrying him, so I took him for a spell as we made our way down the road.

Having an armful of disgruntled, fluffy cat made the journey considerably more of a trial, but I was not so desperate that I took the first opportunity to exit that presented itself. This came in the form of a wide, gravel drive that left the mossy road and ran down to the front doors of an imposing manse. These opened as we paused to inspect it, and a pale hand emerged, beckoning.

"Come in, come in, my dears," came a voice, soft and melodious. "Come in and rest your weary feet, I have a pot of cream ready for your pussycat as well."

Even if the voice had not referred to patchy, cantankerous Carbuncle as a "pussycat" I would have been thoroughly suspicious of it anyway. It was all too much like a trap out of a fairytale, and since I knew those originated from true experiences on the edges of our world, I naturally assumed the same rules must apply here.

I shook my head at Tida's hopeful expression, and she, her train of thought catching up with mine, shrugged resignedly, and we moved on.

A little ways beyond the drive to the manse we became aware, for the first time, of a new sound: that of hooves in the soft grass. I wondered for a moment if this was the owner of the tracks we had been following but was immediately distracted by Carbuncle, who at hearing the sound suddenly became possessed of a strong desire to be out of my arms, and to that end dug all of his claws into whatever part of my flesh he could reach.

I shrieked and dropped the cat, while Tida shouted in alarm and made a grab for him—but he was already dashing off down the road, back towards the manse, his tail sticking out like a bottle brush behind him and his ears flat upon his neck.

The hoofbeats took on a faster cadence, and I realized the beast—or its rider—must have heard us.

Frozen in indecision, I heard a small voice from around our feet hiss:

"Mother, mother, down *here*. You must not let him catch you!"

Looking down I found myself staring at a round, brown face with amber eyes peeking out from a patch of lamb's ears.

"How in heaven's name—" I began, and then a small, equally brown arm extended from the foliage and reached for my ankle. "*Hurry!*" said the voice, and it sounded so desperate that I was immediately convinced that I did *not* want to meet the owner of the hoofbeats.

Grabbing Tida's sleeve I led her to the side of the road and crouched down.

"How are we to follow you," I asked. "There is no possible way that we can fit!"

"Just step through the ivy," the face replied, and the hand pointed up to where, sure enough, there was a fall of ivy down the hedge. "The way will open for you."

The hoofbeats sounded just around the nearest bend now, and Tida, sensing my alarm, followed on my heel as I threw myself into the ivy.

Which, surprisingly, parted around me, and I found myself sliding down a soft earthen bank below the hedge. Looking up I saw light filtering down between the roots and branches and ivy leaves, and before me were the backs of lamb's ears and grass at eye-level.

The owner of the face turned around, and I saw it was a young girl with curly brown hair, wearing a dirty, baby-blue dress with an even more dirty apron.

"Why, aren't you—?" Tida began, but the girl pressed a finger fiercely to her lips and hushed us. "He *hears*," she whispered.

We all fell silent as a shadow crossed above us, beyond the foliage. I could hear the breath of the beast, while the heavy footfalls sent faint tremors through the earth. I held myself forcibly still and tried not to breathe too hard, until with a snort the rider moved on, and light filtered back into our hiding place.

"Now child," I said, taking a deep breath and smoothing out my rumpled skirts. "Tell us who that was and why it is so important they do not catch you."

The girl turned around and gazed at us shrewdly. On closer inspection I saw there was a smudge of dirt across one cheek, and her eyes had a wide, hunted quality about them.

"You aren't of the road, then?" she asked. "I dint think you were, but it can be difficult tell sometimes."

The question was so surreal that it took me a moment to formulate an answer. In that time, Tida drove the topic forward by announcing, in her most penetrating voice:

"Surely I know you! You are Nandy Matcher, if I'm not mistaken. What on earth are you doing here?"

"Nandy Matcher?" I repeated, taking a second glance at the girl. She was the right age, and had the look of someone who had been sleeping in thickets and not eating well.

Perplexingly, the girl seemed confused at first. Then, slowly, an understanding dawned on her little brown face.

"Nandy Matcher . . . " she said, experimentally, as if tasting the words. "Yes, yes I s'pose that's right. Good lady, I'd nearly forgotten, hadn't I? It's this place. It does that to you."

Tida and I exchanged alarmed looks, though I felt in no danger of forgetting anyone's names at the moment. In fact, two more had presented themselves in my head, demanding to be spoken.

"Nandy?" I asked. "Do you remember Pelim and Jora Shatterthorn? Whatever became of them?"

Nandy Matcher's eyes glazed over a little, and she stared off into the tangle of bushes above our heads for a moment before they cleared again. "Pelim and Jora . . . " she murmured. "Yes . . . yes, we were playing together. Jora had a secret path, and Pelim wanted to see it. I told them they would miss their tea and get into trouble, but they didn't listen. So I followed them—just to be sure they did come back. Only . . . they went down to the house, and when I went asking after them, there was something *awful* there and I ran away."

She blinked up at us. "*That's* when I began to forget things. I think the lady must have put a spell on me. I can't remember what she looked like at all."

"Sounds like a witch," Tida said, nodding sagely.

"Perhaps," I allowed. "To own the truth, I think we have come to a place where there are much stranger things. Nandy, who was that rider? And what did you mean when you said we were not 'of the road'?"

Nandy shuddered and closed her eyes. "Horny knight is of the road. Others too. Not nice people. Tried to chase me off, but I didn't know where to go."

Behind me, Tida tutted. Then she clutched my shoulder convulsively. "Oh, Corianne, what will they do if they find *Carbuncle?*"

Taking stock of the situation, I came to the decision that Tida's cat could probably handle himself better than we could, but I did not say so. I was more worried by the implication that Nandy Matcher had been living wild on the green road this whole time, and that the Shatterthorn children were trapped in that sinister house we had passed.

In the silence that descended as I tried to put these thoughts into words, once more we heard the sound of hoofbeats on the road. Nandy cowered further down into the earth, and Tida followed her lead, but I was held still, gazing out at the tips of the grass which was all I could see of the road. For with the sound of hoofbeats there had also come a smell that was both familiar and yet strange. It was a smell of fresh rain and wildflowers, and wafted over us in breaths of cool air that did not chill, like the cool of the road, but soothed us.

I caught my breath as I pushed myself further up to get a glimpse of the animal, and felt Nandy Matcher grab my arm imploringly. I might have acquiesced to her unspoken plea, had I not caught a glimpse at that moment of a hoof, pearly grey and surrounded by soft, downy feathers the color of a pink and purple sunset.

Throwing caution to the wind I heaved myself up through the branches and thrust my upper body out, bringing a good deal of hedge with me, and found myself looking up the long, powerful legs of a pale horse with two gigantic, feathery wings folded along its back. Its tail was a fall of feathers and its mane was a crest—now raised in surprise— making its gracefully arching neck look twice as thick. Its nostrils were flared, and its pale eyes glowed with a faint radiance. From the center of its forehead sprouted a jagged horn, like a piece of crudely cut glass.

Memories came back to me of a creature I had met many years before, that had been difficult to see clearly, but which had given me the strongest impression of a winged horse. It had also brought with it the smell of wet flowers, and then there was the horn. That I remembered very well.

"Yuragorn?" I asked, my voice high with nerves and excitement. "It *is* Yuragorn, is it not? The friend of Abharus? You may not remember me, but if you ask him, I am certain he would tell you I am Corianne Birch."

The beast regarded me blankly for a moment, then snorted and pointed its horn downwards, past me, to where Tida and Nandy still cowered.

"Yes, yes, I have others with me," I told the creature I was increasingly certain *was* Yuragorn, the mysterious horse who had helped us in the affair with the Royal Dragon at Crogard so many years ago. "There are others whom I would very much like to find, as well. Two children, by the names of Pelim and Jora, and also an old orange cat—his name is Carbuncle. But if you would be so kind as to take a message to Abharus and tell him where we are, I would be most grateful."

Yuragorn breathed wet, sweet-smelling breath into my face, and then raised her head and stood there expectantly. When I did nothing, she took a couple steps back and then resumed her position. Reaching one hoof forward she pawed gently at the ground. It was only then that I took her meaning and climbed out onto the road.

Like the needle on a compass her horn swung down to the hidden burrow, and her ears perked.

"Come out Tida, Nandy," I called down. "This one will not harm you."

There was some rustling, and first Tida, then Nandy's faces emerged. Tida frowned and blinked very hard at Yuragorn, but Nandy's eyes went wide as saucers as she stared up into the eerie equine face.

When we were assembled on the road Yuragorn dipped her head and snorted at us, then turned and paced down the green path, the tips of her tail feathers ghosting over the grass. She had not gone two yards before she twitched an ear, stopped, and gazed sideways at us over her back.

"Does it mean for us to follow?" Tida asked in a nervous whisper.

"I believe so," I said, offering my hand to Nandy, who was looking ready to bolt. "Come, my friends," and so speaking I led the girl down the road towards the horse, with Tida following in our wake.

Yuragorn, seeing us approach, resumed her walk, and thus led our procession at a gentle pace along the twisting path, tracking our progress with flicks of her long ears.

How long we walked that path I do not know. The sky above remained the perfect violet of evening, until the road began to widen and the walls grew lower and more overgrown. Then the sky grew lighter once more, fading to a soft blue streaked with white clouds, and eventually to a heavy grey. By this time the walls were mere tumbles of stone covered in long grass and gorse bushes, and beyond them I could see, stretching as far as sight could show, rolling misty hills. In the distance, among the thick white clouds that hid the horizon, I thought I could see the black, spiky shapes of mountains half hidden in the fog.

Then the road changed from grass-covered earth to rough stones, and the walls fell away completely. A cold wind blew down at us from the across the distant hills, blustering in our ears and pulling at our hair. Yuragorn waited patiently for us to adjust to this sudden change, and then continued down the stony path to where it dipped between two hills.

There in the cleft, out of the wind and sitting cross-legged on a wide, round stone, was a familiar, child-sized figure in a worn brown suit, with bare feet and a wild mop of glittering silver hair.

"Abharus!" I cried in relief, leaning around Yuragorn's flank.

Abharus—for it was he—looked up in astonishment, his dark eyes almost as wide as Nandy's had been, and his mouth parted in a soundless gasp.

He looked exactly as I remembered him—as he had always looked, in fact. His appearance was that of a boy, perhaps eleven or twelve years of age, with impossibly old, deep brown eyes, with the finest silver hair and strong eyebrows like brushed steel. He slid down off his rock and stood there, head barely reaching chest height of a fully grown man, but at the same time carrying the weight of decades on his small shoulders.

The peculiarities of Abharus's aging—inasmuch as he showed no signs of it in the normal way—had long since faded into the background of his person, at least to me. To Tida and Nandy it must have looked most odd to see a grown woman swoop down in throes of relief upon a boy who appeared young enough to be her grandson.

For this was, more or less, what I did.

"Abharus," I said, dropping carefully to my knees in order to embrace him. "How lucky it is to find you here. Or perhaps no luck at all—I see now Yuragorn saw it would be easier to take us to you than the other way around. I would ask after your well-being, naturally, only we find ourselves in something of a conundrum, and I am in need of your help."

"Corianne!" he replied in equal surprise and consternation. "How on earth did you get here? Wait, don't tell me, this is another of Felpz's misadventures, isn't it?"

"For once, Felpz has nothing to do with it," I replied, laughing a little in my relief. "This escapade is all my own, or nearly so. Here, you remember my friend Tida? From that affair out on Riddlemoor? And this is Nandy Matcher, also from Redling."

Abharus got down off his rock and looked at us in some perplexity. "Redling?" he repeated. "Then how—no, don't say! You did something mad like wander off down an alley you'd never noticed before, didn't you?"

"We departed from my backyard," Tida said, a little defensively. "We were only trying to catch Carbuncle."

"Her cat," I explained. "Miss Matcher here seems to have had a similar experience. Unfortunately, she has lost her two companions, and we have lost Carbuncle. If you cannot help us recover them—and I understand it is a lot to ask—could you at least guide us back to Redling?"

"Anyway, wot are *you* doing here?" Nandy Matcher asked, putting her hands on her hips.

Abharus looked up at her in open puzzlement, then shrugged and moved past her without answering. Lifting his hand to Yuragorn's soft muzzle, the two stood together, the large horse and the small boy, their heads bowed and eyes downcast.

"Who *is* he?" she asked, turning to me in frustration.

"Abharus is a very old friend of mine," I told the girl. "Yes, *old*, make no mistake; his appearance is deceptive."

"Is he some kind of elf then?" Nandy asked.

I inclined my head in allowance, though in truth I had never ascertained exactly what Abharus was. It seemed to be a sensitive point with him, and as I had no concrete evidence with which to formulate a theory, I had refrained from doing so at all.

Nandy looked dissatisfied with this response, and was gathering herself to ask more questions when Abharus's head came up and he looked at us with renewed attention.

"Yuragorn says she found you on a *hidden road*," he said.

"Is that what it was?" I asked. "It felt very magical to me."

"I should say so," Abharus said. "Hidden roads are sort of like magical conduits, linking different parts of the world together. If you're very clever, or know the right sort of people, you can walk them like you would any other road. There are some places you can *only* get to by taking a hidden road. But they don't open up and whisk people away like what Yuragorn describes happening to you. It's a little worrying. You said you had companions," he went on, turning to Nandy. "What happened to them?"

Nandy Matcher's face twisted unhappily. "It woz the knight on the road. I went and hid, but Pelim and Jora ran off, they did, down to the big house off the road. I saw the knight follow them, but I woz too airy to go after them. I stayed on the road, living under the bushes, and watching the house—but they never did come out again."

"A knight?" Abharus said, turning questioningly to me.

"The sort on horseback, I presume," I said. "We heard him too— that's how we met Nandy. We first took Yuragorn for the same, before I recognized her smell."

Abharus was frowning again, gazing vaguely down at the stones of the path and worrying at his lower lip.

"Don't forget Carbuncle," Tida added, nervously.

"Who?" Abharus said, looking up.

"Tida's old ginger cat," I said with a sigh. "You haven't seen him, have you?"

Abharus shook his head, but he seemed unconcerned. "An ordinary cat is better equipped to navigate the hidden roads than an extraordinary magician," he murmured. "I would not worry about Carbuncle. I do worry about your friends, Miss Nandy. That house sounds like it doesn't belong at all. Ordinarily I wouldn't imagine asking you to come with me, except . . . " he glanced around at the bleak and cloudy landscape. "This isn't the friendliest of places, either. So stay close to me, and don't let yourself fall behind Yuragorn. Miss Nandy, do you mind telling me more about this Pelim and Jora? Who are they? What do they look like?"

While Nandy began, haltingly, to explain, Abharus set off down the stony path, looking carefully to either side. Now and then he would glance back at Yuragorn, and the horse would nod or shake her head, and like this we progressed through the grey-green fields, until the road sank low between high, grassy banks that closed in around us. Soon afterwards the grass began coming up between the stones, and about the time the stony path became completely covered in thick grass and moss, the embankments turned to high stone walls, and the sky flushed with the familiar violet of evening.

Far sooner than I expected we came upon the break in the wall that led to the drive down to the manse, and here we clustered around Abharus's slight form, none of us eager to step down the road.

The house looked even more unappealing upon second viewing, and I noticed how its lawns were strained and yellow, and its windows were like rough holes into a dark and lonely place.

"Oh, it looks *much* worse now," Nandy said, sounding horrified.

"You can thank Yuragorn for that," Abharus said, wrinkling his nose. "She's so strongly magical herself, she tends to overpower other spells. This place, for example, has got *layers* of glamour spells all over it. You must have quite a bit of magic yourself, if you weren't caught by it."

"Corianne, didn't you say the place gave you a bad feeling?" Tida asked, touching my arm.

"Yes," I admitted. "But it looked nothing like this!"

I caught Abharus smiling at me, and raised an eyebrow at him. He only shrugged and turned back to Nandy. "And then there's people like Corianne, who have a natural sort of immunity," he said. "All right, stay close to me, if you can. If you can't, grab hold of Yuragorn."

Having spoken, he set off down the drive with purposeful strides, and we followed in an awkward gaggle. Reaching the door, he lifted the heavy ring and knocked firmly, causing a hollow *booming* sound.

No one answered, but the door swung inward with a faint creak. Abharus slid a hand carefully down to the handle and pushed it all the way open, sticking his head inside to look around before beckoning us to follow.

The hall inside was in the most complete state of ruin, in all the ways it is possible to imagine. The floor was pockmarked and dusty, mats of cobwebs dripped from the ceiling, and in the corners were piled heaps of refuse that smelled vile. Coming further into the hall to make room for the others (I did not look to see how Yuragorn managed the door, regrettably) I felt the floor pluck at the soles of my shoes, it was so rank, and shuddered to think what Abharus, with his bare feet, must have felt.

Abharus seemed unconcerned with the floor, however, and walked purposefully to the middle of the hall, put his hands on his hips, and shouted:

"I am Abharus, and I wish to speak to the owner of this house!"

His voice echoed jaggedly around the chamber, like a confused moth in a bright room, and some light debris fell from the ceiling in a cloud that made Tida sneeze. There was no answer, however, and after waiting for a minute or so, Abharus gave a little shrug and led us further into the house.

It was not a place I remember fondly: everything was dark and dim—the only light coming from the pale windows—and within the sphere of Yuragorn's influence it smelled of everything rotten. Rotten fruit and bad meat, sour milk and spoiled fish. It was enough to slay the beginnings of hunger that were stirring in my belly, and in some places it was so strong I nearly retched, and Tida complained loudly of the headache it gave her.

Nandy, for her part, walked with one hand touching Yuragorn's shoulder, fingers occasionally bunching in the soft, pale fur, as if she wished to cling to the animal, tooth and nail. I could not blame her, for the house gave off such a distinct aura of malevolence that I was certain something terrible would happen. Or had happened already.

It was this inner assurance, I think, that steeled me against what we eventually found. Up a flight of stairs from the hall we came to a corridor lined with locked doors. At the far end was a single, tiny window, which looked out onto the front drive of the house. The corridor here turned right, and we followed it, Abharus continuing to try all the doors.

Another corner, and another window—this time showing the side garden, which was dead as a dry riverbed—and around we went to the right again, only to find an identical stretch of hall with the familiar window at the end. This one, when we reached it, showed us the view from the back of the house, predictably enough, though all we could see was a rocky field disappearing into a thick, white mist. We turned right again, and there was *another* identical corridor and *another* window, and when we reached it I paused. My internal sense of direction had been put through all sorts of contortions since stepping onto the hidden road, but now it was being abused to an untenable degree.

"Abharus," I said, pressing a hand to my temple to soothe the throbbing that was beginning there. "This is our fourth right turn at a right angle."

"Yes, so?" replied Tida. "There are four corners to a square, Cori-anne."

"Yes," I said. "But this is *not* where we came in—which by rights is where we *should* be. Where are the stairs?"

Tida and Nandy looked around in alarm, finding, as I had done, that the stairs were unaccountably missing. But Abharus just shrugged and kept going, and we followed.

"Four right angles *ought* to lead us in a complete circle," I said, a little angrily. "What is going *on*?"

"Someone has been messing with the dimensions," Abharus replied tightly, and hurried forward to the next window.

This showed not the front drive of the house, but another scene entirely, and one I will not soon forget.

Beyond the ledge of the roof was a small, round block of earth that ended in a jagged cliff, and beyond that was something inconceivable: a terrible, blank, black *nothingness* that seemed to eat away into the earth, sending tendrils across the ground like grasping fingers. Yet it was not entirely void; there was *something* within that terrible dark, but whatever it was, my mind could not conceive it. If I looked too hard at the nothing I felt a sensation like my brain had been dipped in a vat of acid—not unlike the feeling of hearing a demon's true voice.

Casting my gaze aside, my eyes landed on something else—something that had already caused Abharus to stiffen and Nandy to cry out.

There was a little boy—hardly taller than Abharus—playing on the earth beside the horrible nothing. He seemed oblivious to his peril, and was running and skipping about as though he were in a spring garden.

"Master Pelim, Master Pelim!" cried Nandy, sparing a hand from Yuragorn to clutch at her hair. "What is he doing? Can't he *see*?"

"Likely not," said Abharus tensely. Then he turned to us, his face pale and lips pressed tight. "Stay *here*," he ordered, and then took a pace back from the window.

And then ... what can I say? He glared at it, and the window sprang open. A draft of icy air rushed in, dry and clean as a desert. It made us shudder, but provided a welcome relief from the stench indoors. Ab-harus took a running leap and was out the window, scrabbling across the roof and disappearing over the side. I saw Pelim Shatterthorn look up in surprise, pausing mere inches from a tendril of nothing, and found I had to look away.

Casting my gaze inside, I discovered something that Abharus had missed in his hurry to go after the boy: down the new corridor to our right one of the doors was standing open. Just audible above the gusting wind outside, was an intermittent sound like someone humming.

"Do you hear that as well, Corianne?" Tida asked, touching my elbow. "Why, it sounds like the tune of *Blue Blouse*."

It did, too, and it was the familiarity of the melody that gave me the courage to leave Tida and Nandy with Yuragorn, and to tiptoe just far enough down the corridor so I could peek into the room.

This was a disorienting experience; the farther I got from Yuragorn the more my vision seemed to blur. It was as though there were two photographs on glass being held up, one in front of the other, so I saw two versions of the corridor and the room beyond. I guessed that the fainter vision that seemed to be crowding in behind my original one was the version of the house that whoever built it wished me to see. It showed the same corridor, but where there was moldy carpet in the foreground vision, in the background there was a polished wooden floor with warm peach wallpaper. All the physical objects remained the same, however, so I was able to grasp the frame of the door to steady myself as I looked in.

What I saw was so disturbing, and so complicated—because of the double visions—that I fear I must slow down and take things one at a time in order to describe them properly.

The room was small and rectangular, with a narrow bed in one corner, a child-sized rocking chair, and an assortment of toys spread out on the floor. A young girl, no older than six, sat in the center of them, playing happily and humming the tune of *Blue Blouse*.

That was all the two visions had in common.

In the background version the room was carpeted in rich crimson and purple, with peach wallpaper like the corridor outside, and lit by a great chandelier. The bed sported a thick counterpane of satin and mountains of soft little pillows, and the rocking chair was similarly upholstered. The girl was blond, with her hair up in artful pigtails, and wore a bright blue dress with volumes of white lace petticoats underneath, and similarly bright red leather shoes. She was playing with a small herd of wooden horses, skillfully carved and painted an array of brilliant colors. It was altogether like a scene out of a child's storybook.

That vision, however, was but a distant echo behind what I took the be the true version: that the room was dark and dank with water stains on the wall, the floor was bare wood, the bed little more than a metal frame with a mildewy mattress and a tattered sheet, and the rocking chair was old and chipped. The girl's hair was mousy brown and matted, her face was stained with dirt, and her dress—which must have once been a perfectly respectable frock—was torn and ragged. Her feet were bare, and instead of toy horses, her playthings were . . . well, they looked like the desiccated remains of small animals. I recognized a magpie, several rats, and a large lizard that was missing a piece of its tail.

I swallowed a scream at the sight, as I realized this girl—doubtless Jora Shatterthorn—no doubt saw only the background vision, and thought she was in a safe, comfortable room with her dream toys. I had no idea how she would perceive *me*.

Reining in my horror, I cleared my throat politely and said, in as gentle and calm a voice as I could manage: "Excuse me, Miss Jora? You are Jora Shatterthorn, are you not?"

"No," said the girl, without looking up. "I'm Princess Mellusina." She sounded annoyed.

"That's Miss Jora!" cried Nandy from behind me.

The little girl looked up at that, her face brightening in recognition.

"Nanda!" she cried gladly, getting to her feet—still with a half-decayed rat in one hand—and ran past me into the hall, where she cast about in search of her friend. When she looked puzzled, I chanced a glance back, and saw to my horror that Yuragorn and Nandy and Tida seemed to have retreated into the distance, the length of corridor between us growing impossibly long, and they had faded a little into the background image of comfort and luxury.

This more than ever convinced me that the image of abandoned decay was indeed the true one, and I reached out and grabbed Jora Shatterthorn's free hand and pulled her back down the hall.

The little girl cried out in surprise and tried to twist out of my grip. She was very good at it, too, and might have gotten away had I not been so frightened that I clenched my hand around hers rather harder than I would have in my right mind. Then she cried out in pain, but my automatic reaction to let go was thoroughly overwhelmed by outright panic as all the doors along that corridor began to fly open.

In one version, they let out beams of welcoming golden light and soft music. In the other, they yawned onto dark rooms smelling of mold. And worse; in the corners, around the wainscoting, crept fingers of nothing that hurt to look at.

I ran, dragging the screaming child, and kept to the far side of the corridor in order to avoid the sinister fingers. Nandy was screaming too, and Tida shouted something.

Then they were a lot closer, and I felt my hair blown back in a huge gust created by the beating of Yuragorn's wings. It blew back the fingers of darkness as well, and with them the last shadows of the comforting illusion.

Disoriented, I nearly collided with Tida, who caught me, and I leaned against her, panting, while Nandy pried Jora from my grip. The girl had begun to cry in earnest then; not the piercing sound of a child in pain, but the slowly growing vibrato of a girl who was frightened and confused. Then there was an ear-splitting shriek, and the cries broke into hiccuping sobs. Looking around, I perceived that she had finally noticed what she held, and had dropped the dead rat and was now clutching at Nandy's skirts, her face buried in her friend's arms.

"Hush, *hush*," Nandy murmured, while at the same time looking at us as though she had seen a ghost. Yet she continued to speak to her young friend, soothingly, explaining what was going on as best she could.

"There, there," she said. "Everything will be all right. These are friends. They will help us get home. And look, *look*, we have a *real* magic horse with us!" She pointed at Yuragorn, who was standing crosswise in the corridor, one wing spread protectively over us.

Poor Jora Shatterthorn looked up into the huge, equine face, with its crystalline horn, feathery mane, and eyes like stars, and her sobs redoubled. Yuragorn, as far as I could judge her expressions, seemed perplexed.

"She's well into it now," Tida said resignedly. "No stopping the water once the dam has burst. Best let her have it out. Let us see how Abharus is doing."

Our little group had drifted down the hall from the window during my rescue attempt, and now we shuffled awkwardly back to it—Nandy picking up Jora so the little girl could wrap her arms around her neck and hang there.

Outside, both Abharus and Pelim Shatterthorn had vanished, and in their place the darkness had spread, eating away at the ground until only a thin strip was visible beyond the roof.

We backed away from the window almost immediately, the pain of looking at the darkness was so great. I call it darkness, and will continued to do so, because that gives the best impression of what it was. But it was *not* a living darkness in the way of the hormanders and other shadow-creatures I had met. This was darkness because there was simply nothing there that my mind could comprehend. In the instances when I could bear to look for more than a few seconds, as I did when trying to see if Abharus had become trapped in it, I got the impression of moving, wriggling things like worms or hagfish, and gaping holes like open mouths. Flashes of blue in the dark, ringed with a color like yellow only not. It reminded me of what one sees when one closes one's eyes and presses gently against their lids. It was these flashes, seen with my open eyes, that hurt the most, and I looked away quickly, feeling a dull ache spreading out from my eyes and curling deep in my ears. I heard a faint ringing sound.

"Corianne, *come!*" Tida more or less shouted in my ear. She grabbed my arm and dragged me away from the window, and I stumbled blindly after her—the interior of the building was so dark I could barely make out a thing, as though my eyes had adjusted to looking outside on a sunny day. Slowly, they refocused, and I saw that Yuragorn was ushering Nandy—still carrying Jora—back down the corridor whence we had come. The horse's feathery tail was huge, bushed out like a cross between an agitated cat and an alarmed bird's crest, and it was twitching irritably.

Shaking the ringing from my ears I hurried up and put a hand on her flank. "Lead on!" I cried, and felt the beast move under my fingers.

We did not get down the same way we got up. When we came to the next corridor Yuragorn snorted angrily, backed around so her rump was facing the outer wall, and kicked. One sharp, quick thrust of her left hind hoof, and the plaster wall shattered, collapsed into smoke, and drifted away. There were the stairs, and in every corner, fingers of darkness. They prickled on my vision like stepping barefoot into thorns.

"Oh no," said Tida, taking the words out of my mouth. "We are not going down *that.*" She had, like me, realized that it was paramount we not touch the terrible darkness, and I was grateful for her fortitude, for I still felt a little dizzy.

In answer, Yuragorn turned around and lowered her head, her ears disappearing into the frill of her mane as they laid flat upon her neck. Her eyes flashed—literally flashed—with a bright, golden light, and that light pooled in the base of her horn and began to grow, before abruptly traveling the length of the shaft and exploding down the stairs, whirling and roaring and throwing out shreds of gold light, like an angry fire spitting molten metal.

There was a sound so terrible it quickly moved beyond the scope of my ears, leaving only a persistent *keening* sound in the back of my head. I could hear nothing else, but I saw now how the stairs were clear, though a little scorched in places, and I did not need to be told to follow Yuragorn as she trotted down them.

We came clattering into the hall, where we had to pause, as Jora insisted she be put down. She had so far wrung out her sobs that she was able to ask questions, and this she did continuously as we made to exit the building.

Where was Pelim? Where were we? Where did the chandeliers go? Where was Pelim? Why did the dark hurt to look at? Yuragorn was not a proper unicorn, because her horn was not *whorled.* She was a rhinoceros. *Where was Pelim?*

The recurring question, at least, was answered when we burst out through the front door and found Abharus and the Shatterthorn boy just coming around the side of the house. Abharus was supporting Pelim, who was hopping on one leg.

"*Pelim!*" Jora screamed, and launched herself at them. She was brought up short by Nandy, who had seen what was growing behind the two boys, and wisely kept her head pointed away as she wrestled the smaller girl into a firm hold.

Eating into the landscape like a terrible night, the darkness rose up behind Abharus and Pelim, just as the former put on a burst of speed at seeing Yuragorn and flung himself—and Pelim—into our path.

"Can you carry him, Cor?" Abharus asked, breathless. "You need to get out of here—it's the strongest *and* strangest demon I've ever seen. Go on ahead, Yuragorn and I will hold it off!"

But we had no sooner turned, myself holding a sudden armful of quivering, shaking boy, when a shadow fell across the entrance of the drive.

"Not the thorny knight *now . . .* " Nandy wailed.

I cannot tell you how my heart sank at the sight of our escape firmly blocked by a coal-black stag with a rider mounted on its back. This then must have been the owner of the first set of hoofbeats that had driven us into hiding with Nandy. Then I blinked, and saw that it was not someone riding a stag, as I had first thought, but a single animal. It had the body of a huge, black elk, but where its neck should have been there was a human torso, similarly colored, on whose shoulders sat the head of a stag with branching antlers. It carried a long staff in its ebony hands, which was gently curved and crowned with a sprig of green leaves. And even as I felt despair begin to grow on me, at the same time I thought: *This seems like an entirely different entity than the monster in the house . . .*

Then a complete reversal of emotions overcame me as the stag-man stepped nimbly aside and made a beckoning gesture with one hand, and who should answer but Bouragner Felpz! He stepped into view, tall and dark-headed and immaculately clad in a vivid purple coat, carrying a fluffy orange cat in his arms.

"Felpz!" I cried, relief and joy so overcoming me that I began to weep just like Jora, only not as loudly.

At the same time Tida shouted, "*Carbuncle!*" and Felpz, whose eyes had widened at the sight behind us, said: "What the *blazes* are you doing? Get *out* of there!"

We did not need telling twice, and I hurried towards him, bouncing Pelim in my arms. Nandy and Jora and Tida came on either side, with Abharus and Yuragorn behind us.

We crowded out through the break in the hedges and onto the road, where the coal-black elk-man had retreated to give us room. I set Pelim down on the soft moss and turned to Felpz, in time to see an arm of darkness, its end branched like claws, snap closed behind us—and I realized how narrow our escape had been.

Behind me I heard the children crying. Abharus was trying to explain things to Felpz, Tida was asking for Carbuncle, and Nandy was shouting to Jora and Pelim to get away from the elk-man, all at the same time.

"*Here,*" Felpz said, unloading the cat into Tida's arms. "Now get back, all of you. Abharus, see to that boy's foot—Wendin will help you. Will you please be *quiet* young lady!" he shouted at Nandy, who closed her mouth with a wet clap, but continued pointing at the elk-man with a trembling finger.

"But he's . . . he's *of the road!*" she gasped.

"Of *course* Wendin is of the road," Felpz snapped. "He is one of its wards. Now will you kindly allow him to help you—I would myself, normally, but at the moment there is something that requires my full attention. Corianne, good to see you!" he said, grasping my arm and smiling for the first time. "Not too shaken up, I hope? It would do me good to have you at my side for this next part, if you feel up for it."

"Gladly," I said, as gamely as I could.

"And Yuragorn," Felpz said, raising a hand to the horse, who bobbed her head and snorted. "You have done well, I see. I must request your assistance one more time."

"*Felpz*, what is going on here?" I hissed as the commotion among the group died down. I did not look to see, but it sounded as though the elk-man — Wendin — had carried young Pelim down the mossy road a ways, and now Abharus was speaking to the boy soothingly. By muffled sobs and Tida's placating voice I guessed the woman had followed him.

This left only Felpz, Yuragorn and myself standing before the breach in the hedge, beyond which the landscape was entirely eaten up by the horrible darkness that I was careful *not* to look directly at.

"What *is* that?" I asked, pointing at it without turning my head.

Felpz did look, and seemed only a little inconvenienced in doing so — more like a man looking up at the sky on a bright, sunny day. He squinted and wrinkled his nose at the foul stench that rose out of the blackness.

"I fear I cannot say for certain," he replied, softly. "I have seen demons like it, but none so alien. What on earth *possessed* you to go near it?"

"The children," I began, but Felpz cut me off with a wave of his hand.

"Never mind," said he. "There will be time enough for explanations after. Now, however, we must deal with this — and quickly. Stay close if you can, but if you feel yourself succumbing to its power, do not hesitate to run."

His words struck a chord of nerves within me, and I retreated to a corner of the hedge where I could keep Felpz in sight but not look directly at the darkness. Yuragorn stood behind him, her wings half open, forbidding the darkness to come any closer. Tendrils of it still licked at the grass beneath Felpz's feet, but to my relief it did not hurt so to look at them. The road itself, it seemed, dampened their power.

"Greetings," said Felpz, to one of the little fingers. Or perhaps the entire darkness. I was not sure. "I do not know if you were being intentionally malicious, or merely misunderstanding, so I will ask you with all due respect to leave. This is not your world, and you do it grave harm by your presence. Kindly take yourself elsewhere — I will show you the exit, if necessary."

He spoke in a respectful, magnanimous tone, but I saw the tension in his whole body, outlined in the arch of his back and neck and the rigid way he held his hands. He looked like a man preparing to do battle.

It was a look about him which stirred uncomfortable memories. Decades old memories of Felpz, bleached and tired, walking into that horrible sinking land, whence he had disappeared for so many years. I might have feared that a similar thing was about to happen, except then the darkness spoke, and rational thought was driven completely from my mind.

The voice was not like the voice of the demon I had heard so many years ago. It was deeper, darker, and altogether more unsettling. Where the demon had been like acid on my mind, this voice began as an ominous ache in all my extremities, like the forerunners of the most dire kind of pain. It shot through me, taking with it my capacity for independent thinking. I became, for a little while, like an empty glass, and the words of the terrible blackness passed through me like beams of light.

What it said, in words I did not recognize and yet which forced their meaning upon me, was this:

You cannot command me, you bite of flesh. This world is mine, for I have made it so—yes, I have made it mine in ways beyond your flimsy comprehension. I am the culmination of all you do not understand. I am the dark behind the dark, the night behind the night. I am the form in the void which bends your little plane to my own end. Such fragile words as those your head holds cannot describe me—for I am beyond all description, and all understanding.

Felpz sniffed a little, and seemed unimpressed. I would have feared for him, but all emotion had been pressed out of me, like water out of a cloth, and I was flattened and dried beneath the presence of the thing in the dark.

Then I heard his voice, and I felt myself expand a little, drawing strength from the sound.

"I understand you well enough," said Felpz dryly. "I have met your kind before. In a thousand years of travel across a multitude of worlds I have been stretched, scattered, and in my darkest hours I have known you, I have walked in you, I have *been* you. It is not something I wish to repeat, but it allows me to state with some confidence that you, whom we do not fully understand, likewise do not fully understand *us*."

Then Felpz took a step off the road and into the void, where he hung suspended in the blackness, his arms outstretched.

"I would that we had met differently," he said quietly, and brought his hands together.

Behind him Yuragorn reared up onto her hind legs and beat her enormous wings, sending a gale of fresh, damp air rushing past me. And those wings, which had once driven back the breath of a dragon, now drove the grass and stone and moss of the road out into the void. Form and reason spread into the chaos, taking root and shooting up stems and flowers, reaching, feeding off the night, crafting it into familiar, physical shapes.

The creature—if creature it could even be called—let out a scream like an electric shock. It was far, far worse than anything I had ever experienced; there was one horrible instant where all the nerves in my body felt aflame, and then the pain whited out my vision and I fell into another kind of void.

I remember a blank sort of whiteness, and then a shadow, and a soft touch upon something it took me a moment to remember was my *face*, and then all the knowledge that comprised my waking mind came pouring back, and I became aware of Felpz's voice speaking urgently above me.

"Corianne, Corianne, my dear, come back to me. Come back, or I will never forgive myself! I swear . . . "

The voice trailed off as I blinked my eyes open, and found myself gazing up into the concerned face of Bouragner Felpz, who looked more upset than I had ever seen him. His brow was a mess of worried lines, and his eyes glittered with something that might have been tears, while his hair had been shaken loose and now trailed off one side of his face.

I believe we stared at one another for a mere instant, and then he pulled me into an embrace so fast I lost my breath for a moment. It was one of the few times in our long relationship that he ever showed me direct physical affection, and the surprise of the thing rendered me motionless even without the added numbness that had infected my limbs.

"I am an *utter fool*, Corianne, never forget that," he murmured in my ear. "If you had come to grief because of my own childish weakness — I should have cast *myself* into the void. I really would have."

"My dear friend," I said, feeling a little overwhelmed at this outpouring of emotion. "That would have been a terrible waste. But never fear, here I am!" And, having regained some feeling in my arms, I raised one and gave him a comforting pat on his wide, tense back.

Releasing me, Felpz held me at arms length and stared at me as though astonished at the sight. It made me feel a little embarrassed, so I tried to distract him.

"Perhaps now you could explain what that thing was? And, how did you come to be on the road in the first place?"

Felpz rolled his head back and gazed at the sky for a moment, and then he dropped his gaze and smiled at me blazingly. "Corianne, you never cease to amaze me. A thousand wonders could not replace you, truly. Yes, a full explanation you shall have. As full as you please. But allow me to help you up, so that we may rejoin the others. Abharus, I am sure, is even more anxious for an explanation."

I was a little unsteady on my feet, but with Felpz's assistance I was able to walk down the road — which now ran straight and true between high, overgrown stone walls, with no breaks or branches, and no sign of the painful darkness. Soft shadows lay across the road, but they were filled with the vibrant green of the moss and grass, and above, the sky was deep violet, the cream curve of the moon just peeking out above the wall.

Our companions were huddled in a group a few yards down the road, overshadowed by Wendin's coal-black figure. He was leaning on his staff and peering down at his feet curiously, where Abharus crouched over the form of Pelim Shatterthorn. Nandy and Jora sat hunched to one side, and Tida was standing opposite Wendin, looking perplexed. Carbuncle, it seemed, had disappeared again.

"Corianne, are you all right?" she asked upon our arrival. "I am so sorry . . . I don't know how it happened . . . one instant Carbuncle was in my arms, and the next—I don't know."

"Do not fear for your cat, Mrs Hammin," Felpz said. "He is almost as much of a walker as Wendin here and knows these roads well."

"Where in the world did you find him in the first place?" Tida asked.

"One thing at a time, please," said Felpz. "Our first concern should be this boy, who appears to be the misplaced Master Shatterthorn. How is he, Abharus?"

Abharus straightened up, gave me a piercing look, and then turned to Felpz. "I've managed to save his foot," he said gravely. "But he can't walk on it."

"I can manage!" Pelim Shatterthorn protested in a high, quavering voice.

"No, you can't," Abharus told him firmly. "That stuff was like concentrated evil, and you stepped right in it."

"I couldn't see—" Pelim protested, even as Felpz shook his head.

"I am not certain it was evil," he said mildly.

"You didn't see the inside of that house," Abharus retorted. "You," he said, addressing Wendin. "You can make yourself useful now. Help me get Pelim up onto your back."

Wendin looked a little offended at this, his nostrils flaring ominously, but he caught the look Felpz was giving him, and silently lent one strong arm to help hoist Pelim up onto his back. Then at last I saw the boy's bare foot, which was the angry purple of an old bruise and slightly swollen, and I realized all over again how lucky we had been.

I was jolted out these dark musings by young Jora who, upon seeing her brother riding astride the elk-man, insisted that she wanted to ride too. Wendin looked momentarily panicked at this, until Yuragorn was convinced to lend a hand—or, in this case, her back—and as soon as Jora was nestled between those powerful wings we began our journey home.

We walked slowly, for which I was grateful, as I still suffered bouts of dizziness—though these decreased in number and intensity the longer we traveled. The road was peaceful and unchanging, and with Felpz on one side and Abharus on the other and the looming form of Wendin in front, I did not worry about our destination.

"Now," said Felpz, when he seemed confident I was sufficiently recovered. "Clearly our adventures have run in somewhat different channels. I would appreciate it if you filled me in as to your doings, and then I can tell my side."

Abharus and Tida took charge of telling Felpz our story, for which I was grateful. I was a little flattered at Tida's depiction of me, but Felpz seemed to take it as a matter of course.

"No, no, you behaved perfectly sensibly," he said. "Admirably, in fact. Corianne is the best person to have at your side during a frightening experience, I find. And a good thing you got little Jora out of that house when you did. I am sorry," he added, turning to Nandy, "if Wendin frightened you. He is not used to humans on his roads, you see, and was only trying to shoo you back home—as I imagine any of us might do upon encountering a stray dog."

"Speaking of Wendin," I said, with a glance at the elk-man, who had thus far remained mute. "How do you come to know each other? And how *did* you come by so fortuitously?"

"Ah, as to that," said Felpz with a sigh, "I happened by simply because I was looking for *you,* dear Corianne. The note you left was quite clear as to your whereabouts, so you can imagine my distress when, upon casting my mind out to confirm this, I found that, not only were you *not* where you said you would be, but that you were *nowhere* to be found *in this world.* Since your note said nothing about traveling in other dimensions I assumed something unexpected had befallen you, and so I paid a visit to Mrs Hammin. At least, I intended to. When I arrived at her house I found only a flustered servant, who informed me that you and Tida had disappeared into a bower in the back garden. Upon inspection, this proved to be a capricious entrance to the hidden road which crosses Kyreland by way of a piece of Faerie and the Thin Land. It had closed off by the time I approached it, and so I was obliged to get on in a different place.

"The first person I encountered was none other than Carbuncle, who seems to have absorbed some of the magic of the road. He told me you and Tida were likely in trouble, but was unable to give me directions. It was fortunate, therefore, that Wendin found us not long after, and requested my help with what he thought was a demon who had set up a nest beside the road and was trapping children to eat. Since this seemed to be in the same general direction as Carbuncle felt you were, we made haste to follow Wendin—which is how I came upon you, fleeing from the very jaws of . . . well. What it was appears open to debate."

I reflected on this, remembering that terrible blackness with a shudder.

"It did not feel like the demon we met before," I said at length. "You remember, the blue one you put in my lamp?"

Felpz inclined his head. "No two demons are exactly alike," he allowed. "But I rather think this was something different."

"It had a very strong misdirection spell all over its nest," Abharus said. "It was weakened by Yuragorn's presence, and it spoke like a demon."

There was a deep rumbling noise, and looking around I realized it came from Wendin.

"Wendin says it did not come from the demonic realm," Felpz translated with a frown. Then he shrugged. "Well well, the world is made of legions. I, for one, am satisfied to believe it came from a place whose rules are sufficiently different from ours to make us functionally incompatible. So different, in fact, that I could not say for certain whether it was truly evil. Perhaps it intentionally lured Pelim and Jora away with some sinister intent . . . but for all I know it was merely curious, and playing with them—albeit rather cruelly. But no more cruel than the ignorance of a child who pokes at a worm with a stick just to see it writhe. Nevertheless, I am glad we were able to cut off its access to *this* realm, for I can only imagine it would have caused pain and destruction had it lingered."

Wendin grumbled a heavy, relieved noise, causing Pelim to jump.

"Are we almost home yet?" Jora asked, from amongst Yuragorn's feathery back. Nandy shushed her, but Felpz smiled.

"Home is relative on the hidden roads," Felpz said. "But in the grand scheme of things, yes. We are almost home."

As it turned out, this was one of the few times my friend was utterly wrong. We spent what felt like hours on that road, though it was hard to tell with the unchanging sky. My feet began to ache, and Jora fell asleep nestled between Yuragorn's wings.

Then at last the road turned, the sky faded to a gentle blue-grey, and Tida let out a glad cry.

Up ahead the walls ended, framing the road as it turned from moss and grass to packed dirt, with low, flowering hedges on either side. Beyond them was the gentle swell of a hill, split by more hedges and dotted with sheep, and beyond that was a clear, blue, earthly sky.

And in the middle of the road, right where the stone walls ended and the hedges began, sat the fluffy, smug form of Carbuncle, his bushy tail wrapped tight around his legs, staring at us expectantly. Then he got up, and tail held high, he led us off the road and back into the world.

Epilogue

WENDIN LEFT US AT THE EDGE OF THE ROAD, handing Pelim down to Felpz, and Nandy took Jora off Yuragorn's back. I think the horse accompanied us off the road, but as soon as we left that magical dimension she became practically invisible—hardly more than a shimmer in the air and the suggestion of wings. It was this change more than anything else, that convinced me we were finally home.

Only we were *not* home. As we soon discovered, the road had let us out some fifty miles from Redling, in a little village called Stanton Leaning. Tired and hungry, the seven of us descended upon the largest inn and ordered refreshments while Felpz contacted the Shatterthorns and Tida arranged for a wicker basket to house Carbuncle for the journey back—which took the form of a train ride that was blissfully uneventful. Abharus and Yuragorn accompanied us as far as the station, and from there took themselves away by means even more mysterious than that of the hidden roads.

It pleases me to say that the Shatterthorn children suffered no lasting harm from their misadventure, though I understand Pelim's foot never

regained its proper color. They remain firm friends with Nandy Matcher, and the three of them share a close bond that is incomprehensible to their parents.

Tida, Felpz and I returned home, but ever after it was impossible to keep track of Carbuncle—the cat seemed able to walk through locked doors and get into any pantry. It drove Tida nearly to distraction, but I think she was secretly proud of him.

For my part, I had found Stanton Leaning to be such a pleasant little town that I arranged many visits over the course of the following summer, and some years later, when I had the opportunity to move into quarters of my own, it was to Stanton Leaning that I chose to relocate. This move marked a sharp decline in the adventures I had with Bouragner Felpz—since we were no longer living under the same roof, I was no longer swept up in the spontaneity of the moment—and though they did continue, they were of altogether a more deliberate nature. So it was that our adventure on the hidden road was the last we undertook as living companions, and it is here I have chosen to close this collection. Though some readers may mourn the fact that this means there will be no more, they may take heart in the knowledge that living on my own has finally afforded me the peace and quiet needed to get these stories written down at last.

Felpz visits frequently, though he has so far resisted my attempts to persuade him to join me in the country. It is just as well, though, for I do not think the quiet, sleepy life of a small village would suit him. For myself, however, I find that I am satisfied in this time and place, and though—as Felpz himself has observed—it is impossible to stop time from moving entirely, I am determined to stay here for as long as I can.

I have my demonic lamp, which seems positively tame compared to the monster on the road, and I have my books and my writing. I also have a cat of my own who, though not as magical as Carbuncle, serves to fill the corners of my day with all the excitement I could ever want.

Felpz still keeps the house in Redling. I hear he has taken on a new apprentice, which seems to have reinvigorated him, and if any of my readers ever find themselves beset by magical conundrums, I would not hesitate to recommend they pay a visit to the house marked oooo that lies between Kings Street and Bridgeton Way, in the great city of Redling, Kyreland.

ABOUT THE CHARACTERS

Corianne Harper Birch

Born February 18, 2267 to Mr Alford Miller Hallgreave (solicitor) and Mrs Wenda Hallgreave Birch (antiquarian), Corianne Birch is a Kyrish writer best known for her biographic tales of her lifelong friend, the famed magician Bouragner Felpz. She is the mother of Dr Milain Clifford Birch, the dracologist.

Born in Greywall, she lived with her parents until the age of 14, when they died in an accident aboard the steamship *Candiza*. She then moved to Redling, entering into the care of her godfather, Bouragner Felpz. The connection between Felpz and her parents is somewhat vague, although it is widely believed that Felpz had performed an important service for Alford Hallgreave, and Hallgreave made him godfather of his daughter as a sign of respect.

It was during her teenage years under the care of Felpz that Corianne Birch began accompanying him on his adventures, which served as the inspirations for the tales in *A Study of Magic*.

After the disappearance of Felpz in 2287, she married Willem Harper. They had one daughter together (Milain, born in 2288), and divorced in 2302 — Willem Harper having abandoned them for a mistress in Delpheon. Corianne worked as a typist to support herself and her daughter, at which time she began formally setting into prose the adventures of her youth. She was present for the return of Bouragner Felpz in 2307, and returned to live with him in 2311, in order to concentrate on her writing. From 2313 onwards she began publishing her accounts of their adventures, which soon became popular.

Although best known for her first-hand accounts of Felpz's adventures, she is also an acclaimed children's writer: her first novel, *The Bird from Clarkwell* (Putenham Bros., 2318), won the Redling Literary Circle Award for Notable Book for Young Readers. Since the 2330's she has focused almost exclusively on her original fiction, despite the soaring success of the *Bouragner Felpz Adventures,* producing such works as *The Manticore Laughs, Next to Nothing,* and *Twelve Tales of Tobius,* a collection of modernized retellings of the classic Tobius Leander fables.

Mrs Birch lives in Stanton Leaning, but often makes trips down to Redling to visit her friend, and vice versa.

Bouragner Felpz

A foremost expert on magic, Bouragner Felpz is the modern name used by the ancient Kyrish magician Bouragner d'Felpass. Born in Torland sometime in 1480, he has appeared throughout Antellonian history and in many folktales. Appearing and disappearing seemingly at random, he is possibly best known for his rivalry with the half-dragon Machalion in the late 1700's. He served as King Arell's High Magician from 1880 to 1900, after which he disappeared. He reappeared briefly in Enwall in the 1980's going under the name Bouragner Falpath. He was then absent from Kyreland for almost two hundred years, until 2190 when he first appeared under the name Bouragner Felpz. In 2240 he opened a practice in Redling as a consulting magician which continued until his most recent disappearance in 2287.

Called the Purple Magician because of his strange affinity for that color, Bouragner Felpz is considered by many to be the greatest (if at times the most elusive) magician in Antellonia. Many details of his life, such as where he learned his magic and how he has lived so long, remain a mystery. The most accurate account of his character and life can be found in the biographical tales by his former ward and close friend, Corianne Harper Birch.

Since his return to Redling in 2307 Bouragner Felpz has resumed his consulting practice, and still accepts new clients — provided, of course, that they can find him.

ABOUT THE AUTHOR

Goldeen Ogawa is a self-taught writer, illustrator and cartoonist. She is notable for having been raised outside the standard educational system, never attending grade school, high school, or college. Instead she has worked as a stable hand and a white-water raft guide, shown horses and raced mountain bikes. She is a lifelong fan of science and all things fantastic, and has a deep and abiding love for telling of stories. In addition to her fiction she has produced three webcomics and provides the illustrations for all her books.

Born in 1987 and raised in California, she now lives in Bend, Oregon. Her official website is goldeenogawa.com

TEXT AND DESIGN

The body of this book was typeset using LaTeX in Stempel Garamond.

Cover art, interior illustrations and book design by the author.